PRAISE FOR THE NOVELS OF

JOHN SANDFORD

"SANDFORD WRITES GREAT, UNAPOLOGETIC GUY FICTION."
—Stephen King, *Entertainment Weekly*

"SANDFORD WRITES ENTERTAINMENT THAT'S NOT TO BE MISSED."
—*The Cleveland Plain Dealer*

"A MASTER OF THE THRILLER."
—*Richmond Times-Dispatch*

"IF YOU LIKED LUCAS, YOU'LL LOVE VIRGIL."
—*The Tampa Tribune*

"FLOWERS IS A WELCOME ADDITION TO [SANDFORD'S] BODY OF WORK."
—*Chicago Sun-Times*

One fall Thursday in southern Minnesota, a farmer delivers a load of soybeans to a grain elevator. There, a young man beats him to death with a baseball bat, drops him into the grain bin, and then calls the sheriff to report the "accident."

The sheriff breaks the boy down. The next day the kid is found hanging in his cell. Remorse? Virgil Flowers isn't entirely convinced. Then he uncovers a multigenerational, multifamily conspiracy of crimes so extreme, so unconscionably evil, even he has difficulty in comprehending it, or in figuring out where to turn next. Now he wonders just how deep into a private hell this case is going to take him.

Praise for

BAD BLOOD

"Flowers is a fun character, smart and honest with a healthy supply of cynicism and snark . . . a thoroughly engaging, suspenseful, satisfying story." —*The Washington Examiner*

"John Sandford is the master of his craft."
—*Dayton Daily News*

"Sandford's exciting fourth thriller to feature Minnesota Bureau of Criminal Apprehension agent Virgil Flowers. [His] biggest . . . case to date." —*Publishers Weekly*

"A Pandora's box of multiple murders, criminal behavior . . . and revelations of deviancy that go back generations. As usual, Sandford delivers a great mystery with action, suspense, humor, and, yes, sex. Virgil always gets his man, but he also gets the girl. Good reading." —*Booklist*

continued . . .

ROUGH COUNTRY

"Rich, satisfying, and frequently hilarious."
—Stephen King, *Entertainment Weekly*

"[Sandford] succeeds brilliantly here . . . Not to be missed."
—*The Cleveland Plain Dealer*

"Fast-paced [and] action-packed."
—*Minneapolis Star Tribune*

"An entertaining . . . and completely engrossing page-turner."
—*The Post and Courier*

HEAT LIGHTNING

"Sandford . . . at the top of his game."
—*Richmond Times-Dispatch*

"Enthralling." —*The Post and Courier*

"The very last surprise . . . is a honey." —*Kirkus Reviews*

DARK OF THE MOON

"A great ride." —*The Post and Courier*

"Sandford keeps the reader guessing and the pages turning."
—*Publishers Weekly*

"An adrenaline rush." —*Booklist*

DEAD WATCH

"*Dead Watch* is anything but politics as usual."
—*San Antonio Express-News*

"Goes straight to the heart in page-turning fashion."
—*Richmond Times-Dispatch*

"A new hero [and a] breakneck pace."
—*Minneapolis Star Tribune*

"A compelling read . . . There is no doubt that Sandford scores again." —*Orlando Sentinel*

Praise for

JOHN SANDFORD'S PREY NOVELS

"Relentlessly swift . . . genuinely suspenseful . . . excellent."
—*Los Angeles Times*

"Sandford is a writer in control of his craft."
—*Chicago Sun-Times*

"Excellent . . . compelling . . . everything works."
—*USA Today*

"Grip-you-by-the-throat thrills . . . a hell of a ride."
—*Houston Chronicle*

"Crackling, page-turning tension . . . great scary fun."
—*New York Daily News*

"Enough pulse-pounding, page-turning excitement to keep you up way past bedtime." —*Minneapolis Star Tribune*

continued . . .

"One of the most engaging characters in contemporary fiction." —*The Detroit News*

"Positively chilling." —*St. Petersburg Times*

"Just right for fans of *The Silence of the Lambs.*" —*Booklist*

"One of the most horrible villains this side of Hannibal." —*Richmond Times-Dispatch*

"Ice-pick chills . . . excruciatingly tense . . . a double-pumped roundhouse of a thriller." —*Kirkus Reviews*

TITLES BY JOHN SANDFORD

Rules of Prey

Shadow Prey

Eyes of Prey

Silent Prey

Winter Prey

Night Prey

Mind Prey

Sudden Prey

Secret Prey

Certain Prey

Easy Prey

Chosen Prey

Mortal Prey

Naked Prey

Hidden Prey

Broken Prey

Invisible Prey

Phantom Prey

Wicked Prey

Storm Prey

The Night Crew

Dead Watch

KIDD NOVELS

The Fool's Run

The Empress File

The Devil's Code

The Hanged Man's Song

VIRGIL FLOWERS NOVELS

Dark of the Moon

Heat Lightning

Rough Country

Bad Blood

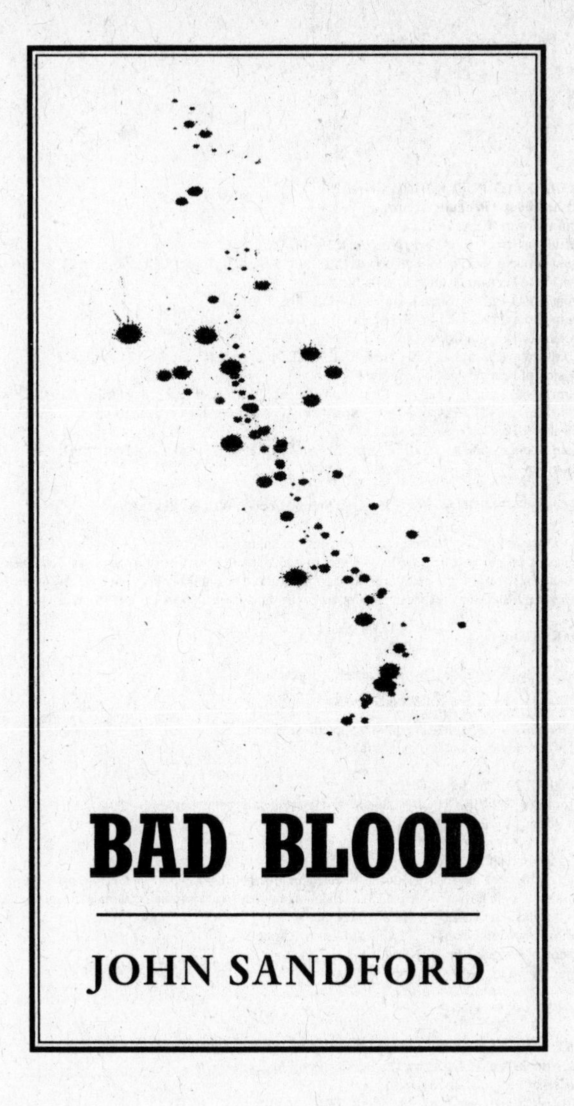

BAD BLOOD

JOHN SANDFORD

BERKLEY BOOKS

New York

THE BERKLEY PUBLISHING GROUP
Published by the Penguin Group
Penguin Group (USA) Inc.
375 Hudson Street, New York, New York 10014, USA
Penguin Group (Canada), 90 Eglinton Avenue East, Suite 700, Toronto, Ontario M4P 2Y3, Canada
(a division of Pearson Penguin Canada Inc.)
Penguin Books Ltd., 80 Strand, London WC2R 0RL, England
Penguin Group Ireland, 25 St. Stephen's Green, Dublin 2, Ireland
(a division of Penguin Books Ltd.)
Penguin Group (Australia), 250 Camberwell Road, Camberwell, Victoria 3124, Australia
(a division of Pearson Australia Group Pty. Ltd.)
Penguin Books India Pvt. Ltd., 11 Community Centre, Panchsheel Park, New Delhi—110 017, India
Penguin Group (NZ), 67 Apollo Drive, Rosedale, Auckland 0632, New Zealand
(a division of Pearson New Zealand Ltd.)
Penguin Books (South Africa) (Pty.) Ltd., 24 Sturdee Avenue, Rosebank, Johannesburg 2196,
South Africa

Penguin Books Ltd., Registered Offices: 80 Strand, London WC2R 0RL, England

BAD BLOOD

A Berkley Book / published by arrangement with the author

PRINTING HISTORY
G. P. Putnam's Sons hardcover edition / September 2010
Berkley premium edition / October 2011

ISBN: 978-0-425-24393-0

BERKLEY®
Berkley Books are published by The Berkley Publishing Group,
a division of Penguin Group (USA) Inc.,
375 Hudson Street, New York, New York 10014.
BERKLEY® is a registered trademark of Penguin Group (USA) Inc.
The "B" design is a trademark of Penguin Group (USA) Inc.

PRINTED IN THE UNITED STATES OF AMERICA

10 9 8 7 6 5 4 3 2 1

I wrote this novel in cooperation with Mike Sweeney, a fine reporter and longtime leader of the Twin Cities Newspaper Guild. We've been friends for thirty years and more, and Sweeney's the one who led me on a long, wild canoe trip down the St. Croix River, only to be ultimately defeated by raccoons. But, like, they were big, *vicious* raccoons. And *really* big.

—JOHN SANDFORD

1

One of those days: late fall, bare black tree branches scratching at a churning gray sky, days cold, nights colder. The harvest was very late—record late—and moving fast. The soybean crop had been delayed because of a cold summer, and then in the middle of October, with half the crop in, rain began to fall, a couple of inches a week, and didn't quit for a month. Now it was dry again, but a landslide of bad weather hovered over the western horizon, and the combines were working twenty hours a day, bringing in the last of the beans and corn.

Bob Tripp leaned against the highway-side wall at the Battenberg Farmer's Co-op grain elevator, knowing that Jacob Flood was on his way.

You could not only see the harvest—the working lights in the fields at night, the tractors and wagons on the roads—but you could hear it, and smell it, and even taste it in the air. Tasted like grain, and a little like dust, Tripp thought. His favorite time of year for the outdoors: regular deer season just over, muzzleloader coming up, snowmobiles ready to go.

Flood had called from his field in the early afternoon: "I need to get in and out fast. You open?"

"I got two wagons being weighed right now," Tripp had said. "John McGuire's coming in probably twenty minutes, nothing after that. If you can get here in an hour or so, we should be open. People have been calling to check, nobody's called about coming in after John."

"Put me down for three," Flood said. "And goldarnit, I gotta get in and out."

"Help you the best we can," Tripp said.

Tripp was nineteen, a high school jock who should have been playing freshman football at a state college. An automobile accident in June, which had broken his left leg, had put that off for a year. The leg had mostly healed by September, and he'd taken the temporary clerk's job at the co-op, where the leg hadn't been too important. He was getting along well, doing rehab exercises every night. The doc said he'd be as good as ever by spring.

Maybe he would be, he thought. Maybe not.

He looked at his watch. Five minutes to three. Nobody coming in. He walked back to the small elevator office, worked the combination on his locker, and popped it open. He wore coveralls on the job, kept his civilian clothes in the locker. He pushed them aside, took out the aluminum T-ball bat he'd hidden there.

He'd had the bat since he was five years old, even then a budding star. He swung it a few times, getting reacquainted with its weight, and thought about what he was going to do. He might get caught, but he'd do it anyway. He looked at himself the way athletes do, spotted the fear, the trepidation, and the anger, and let them percolate through his muscles, jacking himself up for the battle.

RUNNING LATE AND barely able to keep his eyes open, Jacob Flood leaned on the truck's horn as he nudged the old Chevy up to the edge of the scales. He'd been working since early Wednesday morning, with four hours of sleep in the middle of it. He was beat, and not done yet.

The clerk came out in gray coveralls and a feed cap worn backward, over long hair. The kid knew his business: weighed the truck, helped guide it as Flood backed it through the elevator's twenty-foot-high receiving doors. The fit was tight, with just enough room for a man to pass on either side. Flood watched in his rearview mirror until the kid waved at him to stop.

The kid moved onto the dump grate to open the hatches in the middle and at the bottom of the truck's larger dump doors. The hatches needed to be opened first, to start the grain flow and ease the pressure on the main doors. Once that was done, Flood would engage the hydraulics and tilt the bed for the dump, overloaded to about thirty tons of soybeans.

Flood heard the dump start, and then the kid yelled something and waved, and he engaged the hydraulics. When the truck bed stopped rising, he leaned back in the seat and closed his eyes. If he could get just an hour . . .

He'd take an hour when he got home, he decided. But if that incoming storm turned to bad snow, he'd leave a few tens of thousands of dollars' worth of beans out in the fields. He'd hire another combine in, but everybody from the Missouri line to central Minnesota was going hell for leather, and there was no reliable equipment to be had.

But—he'd get it in, if the weather held. If he could stay awake.

FLOOD HAD ALMOST fallen asleep when there was a sharp rap on the glass next to his face, and he jumped. "What?"

"I can't get the main door open," the kid said. "The handle's stuck. Gimme a hand?"

Flood climbed down from the truck. He wasn't a big man, but he had the hard muscles of a forty-year-old who'd spent his life doing heavy labor. He was wearing OshKosh overalls and a hat with a front label that read "John 3:16."

He walked around the back of the truck and stepped onto the grate. Beans trickled from the larger door's open hatch. The farmer leaned in and grabbed the handle and pushed up hard, expecting resistance. There was none, and the bar slipped out of its slot and the doors swung open. Beans flowed out in a wide, fast stream.

Surprised, Flood hopped back a few feet to the edge of the grate, and turned to where the kid had been. "What the hell . . ."

The kid wasn't there. He was behind Flood, with the

T-ball bat, light and fast in his athletic hands. Flood never saw it coming.

THE BAT CRACKED into the back of the farmer's head and Flood went down like a sack of dry cement. "Fuck you," Tripp said. He spat on the body. "You sick fuckin' prick . . ."

Then the fear lanced through him, and he looked up, guilty, expecting to see somebody watching: nobody there. He walked around to the edge of the building, peered down the highway. Nobody coming. A pigeon flew out of the rafters up above, and he jumped, stepped back, and looked down the road again.

"Nobody there, man, nobody there. Don't be a pussy," Tripp said aloud, to himself, for the simple reassurance of his own voice.

He went back to the body, watched the flow of grain coming out of the truck. Already half of it was gone: He stirred himself, said, "Move, you dumbass."

He bent over the older man, lifted his head and slammed the back of it against the grate, hard as he could, as though trying to crack open a coconut, and at the same time, trying to hit at the precise point where the bat had. He'd thought about this, had lain in bed and planned it out, visualized it, the way he would a pass pattern. He was right on schedule.

With Flood profoundly unconscious, or maybe already dead, Tripp lifted the man and pushed him into the grain flow, face up, reached out, and pulled his mouth open. Soybeans were spilling from the truck like water from a pitcher, flowing around the unconscious farmer, filling his mouth, nose, ears. They gathered in his eye sockets, and in his shirt pockets, and in the John 3:16 hat. They squirted down into his overalls, slipping through the folds of his boxer shorts, hard and round, looking for a resting place in a navel or a fold of skin.

Tripp watched for a minute, then hurried back to the side of the elevator to make sure there were no more trucks coming, then went inside, washed the bat, stuck it under the mat in the trunk of his car. Back inside, he filled out the paperwork on Flood's visit. Five minutes passed.

Had to be dead, Tripp thought. He went outside and looked at the man on the grate. His eyes were open, but there was nothing going on. Tripp leaned forward and put his hand over Flood's mouth, and pinched his nose with the other hand. No reaction. Held them for a minute. Nothing. He was dead. He hadn't seen many dead bodies that he could remember: his grandfather, but he'd been in a coffin and looked more waxed than dead. He'd gone to a couple more funerals when he was a kid, but he could hardly remember them.

But this guy was dead.

Tripp stood, caught sight of the hat, said out loud, "Three:sixteen, my ass." He knew what it meant—"For God so loved the world, that He gave His only begotten Son, that whosoever believeth in Him would not perish, but have everlasting life."

He knew what it meant, but it didn't apply to Flood. Tripp bent over, grabbed the farmer by the feet, and dragged him off the grate. Watched him for another moment, thought, *Shit, if he's not dead, he's Lazarus.*

He called 911 from the old Western Electric dial phone in the office. He'd been frightened by the killing, by even the thought of the killing, and he'd known that he would be, and he'd known there'd be a use for his fear and anguish: He let it spill out when the cop answered.

"Man, man, this is Bob Tripp, there's been a bad accident at the Battenberg elevator," he shouted into the phone. "We need somebody here, we need an ambulance, man, I think he's dead. . . ."

THE NEXT SATURDAY. End of the golf season.

Lee Coakley collected twelve dollars, her biggest score of the year, and almost enough to get her even. She had a last Sprite, and looked at the gray wall of clouds in the western sky, and said to the others, "I'll see you girls on April Fools' Day, if I've spent all this money by then. It's such a bunch, I probably won't."

"Stay out of Victoria's Secret," one of them said.

"Right. I'll remember that." Walking with a grin through an indelicate stream of scornful comments, she carried her golf bag out to her car and threw it in the trunk, with only a mild pang of regret. She'd been golfed-out for a month, and though she'd be right back at it in the spring, the winter break was always a relief. When she took her two weeks in Florida, the clubs would stay at home.

In the driver's seat, she opened the center console and

checked her cell phone: two calls, one from Darrell Martin, her private attorney, who was, she thought, looking to assuage her grief over the divorce—probably at the Holiday Inn in Rochester, far enough away that his wife wouldn't hear about it—and one from Ike Patras, the medical examiner in Mankato. The call had come in forty minutes earlier, about when she'd been standing on the eighteenth green, waiting to putt out.

Coakley thought, *Huh. Working on a Saturday.*

She punched redial, and a woman answered, and she said, "This is Lee Coakley down in Warren County. I'm returning a call from Ike."

"Yeah, just a minute, Lee," the woman said. She added, "This is Martha, Ike's in the back. I'm gonna put the phone down—"

"What're you doing working on a Saturday? Something happen?"

"I think so," Martha said. "Let me get Ike."

And Coakley thought, *Uh-oh.*

PATRAS CAME UP a minute later and said, "There's something fishy in Battenberg, and it ain't the lutefisk."

"What happened?" Coakley asked.

"I looked at Flood. The back of his head had two deep cuts and impact impressions like you'd expect from a grate. Same pattern as the grate. But there was another blow, before those two. Hit him right in the back of the head, and it came before his head hit the grate."

"Like something from the truck hit him?"

"Well, something hit him, but I don't think it was the truck," Patras said.

"What was it?" Coakley asked, with a bad feeling about the question.

"I think the boy there might have hit him. I don't know with what. A big pipe, a baseball bat, something on that order. The boy says he was the only other one there . . . and I think somebody hit Flood on the head."

"He's a pretty good kid, Ike," Coakley said. "Bobby Tripp, I know him and his folks."

"Well, something happened, good kid or not," Patras said. "Let me give you a couple items. I did some dissection around the wound. The grate cut sliced through a small artery in his scalp. It bled some, but not nearly enough."

"So his heart wasn't pumping."

"That's right. He was already dead when his head hit the grate. If he'd been hit by a truck, and if he'd fallen straight down and landed on the grate, his heart would have kept pumping for a minute or two, even with a fatal brain injury. Sometimes, the heart keeps going for a long time after a fatal brain trauma, depending on what it is. But even if it was the kind of thing that would cause almost instant death, there was hardly any way it could stop that quick. There should have been a lot of blood. There wasn't. That suggests to me that the grate wound came at least a minute or two after the original wound. Also, the original wound was cup-shaped, and the grid of the grate doesn't show in the middle of the cup, which means that the cup-shaped wound came first."

Coakley closed her eyes and rubbed her forehead. "Okay. What else?"

"The guy was full of soybeans. The goddamn things are like ball bearings, Lee. He had them up his nose, he had them in his ears, he had them in his throat, he had them in his navel, he had a few where the sun don't shine. But he didn't breathe any in. I should have found some in his lungs, like water in a drowning man, but I didn't. When the beans hit him, he wasn't breathing."

"Ah, shoot," she said. "No chance that some of the other damage got done when Bobby hauled him out of the bean pile?"

"No. The sequence is clear. A heavy hit, followed some time later—minutes later—by impact on the grate, a very heavy, deliberate impact, on exactly the same site as the original impact. To me, that suggests intention. And then the beans. The very least the kid did was fake the accident. It didn't happen the way he says it did."

"He says he didn't witness the actual accident—"

"Lee, I'm telling you. It's not right. I believe Flood was murdered, with maybe a one percent chance of an accident of some weird kind."

"All right. I hear you, Ike," Coakley said. "I'll get my guys together, we'll work it over. Damnit, he really is a good kid."

2

Virgil Flowers was winterizing on his boat: time to get it done, since there was almost a foot of snow in the yard. Despite the cold, he worked with the garage door open, for the light. He added stabilizer to the remaining gas, checked the grease levels in the Bearing Buddys, yanked all three batteries, hauled them into the house, into the mudroom, and stuck them on the auto-conditioners.

He was back in the garage, removing the bow and stern lines—best to buy disposables in the fall, when the sales were on, than in the spring—when a white SUV pulled into the driveway. A tall woman with red hair got out of the driver's side; she was thin, with a bony face and nose, and the nose looked like it had been broken sometime in the past. She wore her hair pulled back in a short ponytail, and plain gold-rimmed glasses, a hip-length canvas car coat, black gloves, and cowboy boots that pushed her total height to six feet.

She had a wintry look: A few unhidden strands of gray

showed in her hair. Her face was a bit weathered around her pale eyes. She walked up the driveway and took off her gloves and asked, "Are you Virgil Flowers?"

"Yes, ma'am," he said.

She said, "You don't look much like a law enforcement officer."

"Just because you're a cop, doesn't mean you can't be good-looking," Virgil said.

She cracked a thin smile, then stuck out her hand and said, "I'm Lee Coakley, from Warren County."

"Oh, hey, Sheriff, pleased to meet you," Virgil said. He wiped his right hand on his pants and shook. "I've been meaning to get down there to talk to you, but I've been busier'n heck."

"I've come over to ask for your help. Or to find out who I talk to, to get your help," she said. She had a dry, crisp voice, something you'd expect from a green apple, if green apples could talk.

"I'm the guy you talk to," Virgil said. "Come on in. I'll get you a cup of coffee or a Diet Coke. I'm about done here."

"Pushing the season a little," Coakley said, looking at the boat.

"I was," Virgil agreed. "I'd be back out there tomorrow, if it wasn't fifteen degrees out."

"Tomorrow's a workday," Coakley said.

"Well, except for that," Virgil said. He thought she might have been joking, but her tone was flat, and he wasn't sure. "Come on in."

SHE TOOK COFFEE, and instant microwave was fine, she said, but she could use an extra shot of coffee crystals: "I'm so tired I can't see straight."

Virgil got her the coffee and dug a Diet Coke out of the refrigerator. He was a tall man himself, tall enough that he could still look a bit down at her eyes, cowboy boots and all. He had unruly blond hair that hung down over his ears, and was slender enough that, except for her red hair, people might mistake them for brother and sister.

"So what's up?" he asked.

She'd been sleepily checking out the house—bachelor neat, not fussy, furnished for comfort. She sighed, brushed a vagrant lobe of hair from her eyes, turned back to him and said, "I've been in office for less than a month and I have the biggest problem our office has ever run into," she said. "At least, if Ike Patras is right. Ike's the one who told me how to get to your house."

"Ike doesn't make many mistakes," Virgil said. He knew Patras well. "You had a kid hang himself in the jail. I heard about that."

"That's part of it," she said. "But there's more."

THE TROUBLE STARTED, she said, with an apparent accident at a grain elevator in Battenberg the previous Thursday. A kid named Robert Tripp, called Bob or B.J. by his friends, had phoned 911 to say that a farmer named

Flood had apparently fallen on a grate and knocked himself out, and then drowned in the beans that poured on him.

"We shipped the victim's body up to Ike, and Ike decided it was no accident. He said it was about ninety-nine percent that it was a murder, that Flood was dead before he ever hit the grate. Probably killed by a blow to the head with something like a pipe, or a baseball bat. The Tripp boy already said there'd been no one else there but he and the farmer, so . . ."

"He had to be the one," Virgil said.

She nodded. "You could think of other scenarios, but it was pretty thin. So Ike called it a murder, and another deputy and I went over to interview the boy. Read him his rights, pushed on him, he started crying. He didn't actually confess, but it was close. This is a kid I've known since he was born. Know his parents. Really nice people, really nice kid," she said.

"Anyway, he said enough that we thought we had to hold him. Took him down to the jail, processed him in, went back to his house with a search warrant, looked in his room, looked around the house. Out in the garage, among a bunch of really dusty, unused stuff, we found a clean aluminum T-ball bat. Cleaner than it should have been—you could smell the gasoline on it. Looked in the trash, found some paper towels that smelled of gas, had a few hairs on them . . ."

"So you had him," Virgil said.

"Oh, yeah. He did it. Wouldn't say why," Coakley said. "He said he would talk, but only to one guy—a newspaper reporter. A gay newspaper reporter. I'm not sure if the gay part is important, but Bobby was a big jock, got a full ride over at Marshall starting next fall, could have slept with half the girls in town, but you didn't hear about that. Maybe he was discreet, maybe he was shy."

"Maybe he was gay."

"Don't know," Coakley said. "But it was an odd request. His father said Bobby didn't have any particular relationship with the reporter, except that he'd been interviewed for newspaper stories a few times. But he must have had some kind of relationship—Bobby told me, when I talked to him, that the reporter was the only person in town he would trust, outside of his family, and he wouldn't talk to his folks about it."

"Odd. Interesting," Virgil said.

"So, I was going to set it up," Coakley said. "But early the next morning, I got a call from the jail. He'd hanged himself. He was dead."

"Nobody checking during the night?" Virgil asked.

"Oh, yeah. The overnight deputy. Jim Crocker. *Jimmy* Crocker. He said Bobby was fine at five A.M., dead at six o'clock." She set her coffee cup down and looked away from him. "Just . . . appalling. I couldn't believe it. But there he was. I went down and looked at him—Crocker didn't touch him, because it was obvious that he was long dead when Crocker found him."

"It happens," Virgil said. He turned the Diet Coke can in his hands, rolling it between them. "I could come up with a bunch of theories about what could have happened, especially if the kid was gay. Gay people can have a pretty hard time when their situation starts becoming undeniable. Especially small-town kids. Especially small-town jocks. Willie Nelson even has a song about it."

"'Cowboys Frequently Secretly,'" she said. "I've heard it. Makes me laugh."

"So are you looking for an outside opinion?" Virgil asked.

"No, I'm not. I'm looking for a hard-nosed investigation. See, we sent B.J.'s body up here to Ike and . . ." She stopped talking, looking for the thread of her story, and then said, "First, let me say that Jim Crocker used to be the chief deputy. When Harlan announced he was going to retire, Jim thought he'd automatically get elected to be the new sheriff. Well, he didn't. I did."

"You were a town cop in Homestead. . . ."

"Yes. I was the lead investigator for the city. Anyway, I got elected, Crocker didn't. He said some things both before and after the election that made it impossible to keep him on as chief deputy. It wasn't legal to fire him, and he'd always been a bureaucrat, more than a street cop or an investigator, so I moved him into a staff job. Anyway, he was working the overnight.

"We sent Bobby's body up here for the autopsy, and that goddamn Patras—excuse my French—that goddamn Patras called me back and said it all looked like a suicide."

She paused, and Virgil said, "Except . . ."

"Except for two things. Maybe three." She scratched her eyebrow. "First: There was a bruise in the middle of Bobby's back. A round bruise, almost like he'd been hit by a baseball. Maybe a little bigger than that. A softball. Hadn't had time to develop much before the blood stopped, but it was there. Almost had to be incurred while he was in the cell. We took him in at four o'clock in the afternoon. Ike says if the impact that caused the bruise had happened before that, it would have been much more developed. The thing is, we couldn't find anything in the cell that would make a bruise like that. You could almost say it looked like he had a knee in his back."

"Okay. That's one thing," Virgil said.

"Two. He hanged himself with a strip of cloth he'd ripped off the end of a blanket. An acrylon blanket. Looped it around his neck."

"His penis out of his pants?"

"No. Wasn't sexual. Anyway, it looked all the world like he'd hanged himself, and Ike agrees. But Bobby had a broken fingernail, like he'd clawed at the cloth."

"Changed his mind," Virgil said. She shook her head, and he added, "Except . . ."

"Except that when they looked at the fibers under his nails, they were wool. Not acrylon. In fact, they were green wool. Our uniform pants are green wool. Ike says Bobby was scratching at green wool. And he says the way the blood from his nails mixed with the wool, there's no doubt. He was alive when he was scratching at it."

"What's the third thing?"

"It's not evidence, but . . . Bobby's parents say he'd never commit suicide. Never would. They're so sure, I give it some weight," she said.

They sat at the table, looking at each other for a moment, and then Virgil said, "Crocker."

"But why?" she asked. "When we brought them in, they acted like they didn't even know each other. I mean, Crocker lives all the way out in the west end of the county. He's closer to Jackson than he is to Homestead, so maybe they *didn't* know each other."

"So there's no motive, that you know of."

"Maybe a thin one. I've heard, but I don't know, that Crocker and Jacob Flood, the man Tripp killed, were childhood friends. But I know Crocker, and that seems so unlikely—for one thing, he's way too much of a chicken to do that."

"Did they have any contact when Crocker processed him in? I mean, if they did the body cavity search . . . Tripp might have thrashed around some."

"No. He was handcuffed during the search, and Ike says his nail was broken at the time of death. He's sure about that."

"Huh."

"You see my problem?" Coakley asked. "The guy who ran against me, who I demoted, I'm now going to investigate for murder, in what everybody, including most of the people in the department, think was a suicide," she said.

"I do see your problem," Virgil said. "Let me make a phone call."

SHE MADE HERSELF another cup of coffee, and Virgil got on the phone to his boss, Lucas Davenport. He outlined the situation, and Davenport said, "Go on down there. We bail her out of this, we'll own her."

"Not only that, but we'll solve a vicious crime," Virgil said.

"That, too. I mean, we can't lose, huh? I'll clear you out up here," Davenport said.

VIRGIL PUT the phone down. "We're good to go. If you want to head out, I'll be a half hour or so behind."

"Why do they call you 'that fuckin' Flowers'?" she asked, leaning back against his kitchen counter and crossing her ankles. He noticed her cowboy boots had handsome turquoise details of the type called pigeon guts. "You seem reasonably straightforward to me."

"Cop alliteration, mostly," Virgil said. "I didn't mind at first. Then it started to piss me off. Now I've given up, and don't mind again."

She cocked her head. "So it didn't have anything to do with romantic activity . . . on your part."

"Good God no," Virgil said. He gave her his third-best innocent-cowboy grin. "I'm a lonesome guy. I don't understand it, but . . ."

He noticed then that her pale eyes weren't the same color: One was blue, and one was green. She closed the green one, squinting at him. "I'm a trained investigator. I sense a certain level of bullshit here."

"Hey . . ." Virgil said. And, serious again, "If Crocker killed the kid, it's possible he doesn't know about the pants. That the pants might have the kid's blood on them. If they're wool, he'd probably dry-clean them, so maybe we could still get them—but we gotta move fast.

When you get down there, could you pull me a search warrant? I'll pick it up coming through town. Maybe send a couple of deputies along with me? You personally ought to stay clear."

"I will," she said. She turned to rinse her cup at the kitchen sink. "I've got a judge who can keep his mouth shut, too."

Virgil said, "That's always an asset." He watched as she fumbled the cup, and said, "If you're seriously sleepy, I mean, the roads aren't that good. If you want to bag out on my couch for an hour or two, you're welcome to it."

She stretched and yawned and said, "Thanks, but I've got to keep going. I'll see you in Homestead. Quick as you can make it."

3

Deep snow, with barely a nose stuck into December.

Sometimes it happened that way, and then Minnesotans would be running around warning each other that they were about to get payback for all those warm winters. Exactly what warm winters weren't specified, but it was that one back a couple of years ago when there was a forty-degree reading in January. Or maybe that was five years ago, and actually, they'd been freezing their asses off ever since.

In any case, it was cold, with snow.

VIRGIL BELIEVED THAT he might be in Homestead for a while, so he packed up his winter travel kit, which he kept in a plastic bin, and put it in the back of the truck, along with a duffel bag of winter clothes. The National Weather Service said it wasn't going to get any warmer, which usually meant it was going to get colder.

He wore a fleece pullover and jeans, with Thinsulate-lined hiking boots, and threw a parka and downhill-ski gloves on the passenger seat. A shotgun and a box of four-ought shells went in the back, and a 9mm Glock, with two extra magazines, in the center console. Only two extra, because he figured if he needed more than forty-two shots, he'd be better off running away.

He turned the house heat down to sixty-four and hooked up his new answering gadget. When you called, and pressed "9," the machine would answer and tell you the inside temperature. That way, if the furnace went out while you were gone, you had a chance to catch it before the pipes froze, burst, and flooded the place.

He went next door and told Mrs. Wilson that he'd be out of town for a few days. "See anybody in my house, go ahead and shoot 'em."

"I'll do that," she said. She was about a hundred years old, but reliable. "You take care, Virgil. And don't go fuckin' around with them country women."

HE ROLLED OUT of the driveway at noon, got Outlaw Country on the satellite radio—the Del McCoury Band with "1952 Vincent Black Lightning"—and was on his way, down Highway 60 to Highway 15, and down 15 to I-90 to Fairmont, and west from there to Homestead. Eighty-plus-plus miles, snowplow banks on both sides of the highways, but bare concrete under the wheels.

The countryside was nothing but farms: corn and beans and corn and beans and corn and beans, and over there some wild man had apparently planted wheat or oats, judging from the stubble; the countryside all black trees and brush and white snow and houses and red barns, with a little tan where the wind had scoured the snow down, squared off acreages rolling away to the horizon, with lines of smoke climbing out of chimneys into the sky.

And over there, a yellow house, like a finger in the eye.

He didn't worry much about the fact that his target was a cop. Virgil wasn't a brother-cop believer; he was not disposed to either like or dislike other cops before he met them, because he'd known too many of them. To Virgil, cops were just people, and people with more than their fair share of stress and temptation. Most resisted the temptations. Some didn't. Fact of life.

He did wind up liking most of them, though, simply because of shared backgrounds, and the fact that Virgil was a social guy. So social, he'd been married three times over a short space of years, until he finally gave it up. He didn't plan to resume until he'd grown old enough to distinguish love from infatuation. He felt he was making progress, but he'd thought that the other three times, too.

He considered Lee Coakley, and thought, *Huh.* She had a glint in her eye, and he knew for a fact that she was recently divorced. And she carried a gun. He liked that in a woman, because it sometimes meant that he didn't have to.

HE CUT I-90 at Fairmont, stopped to stretch and get a Diet Coke, and headed west. The sun was already low and deep into the southwest, and the sky was going gray.

Homestead was an old country town of fourteen thousand people or so, the Warren County seat, founded in the 1850s on rolling land along a chain of lakes. Warren was in the first tier of counties north of the Iowa line, west of Martin County, east of Jackson. Most of the downtown buildings, and many of the homes, were put up in the first half of the twentieth century. Interstate 90 passed just to the north of town, and Virgil stopped as he went by and reserved a room at the Holiday Inn. That done, he drove on into town, to the sheriff's office. Her office was in an eighties-era yellow brick building built behind an older, mid-century courthouse. The office included working space for the worn deputies, a comm center, and a jail.

COAKLEY WAS WAITING, with two deputies, big men in their thirties, both weathered, square-jawed Germans, one in civilian clothes, the other in a sheriff's uniform.

"Agent Flowers," Coakley said, "I've got your warrant. These men are Gene Schickel and Greg Dunn, they'll be going out with you."

He shook hands with the two, and Virgil said to Dunn, "I remember you from the Larson accident." Dunn nodded and said, "That was a mess," and added, "I gotta tell you, I don't like this."

"Nobody ever does," Virgil said. "Me coming in, it's like internal affairs. When I was a cop up in St. Paul, I shaded away from those guys as much as anybody. No reason to, but I know what you're talking about."

Dunn said, "Just a feeling that maybe we should clean up our own messes."

Virgil nodded. "But you've got a lifetime job, if you don't screw up. Sheriff Coakley has to get elected, and you've gotta see the political problem in all this."

Dunn nodded. "Yeah, I do. I just don't like it."

Virgil looked at Schickel, the one in uniform. "What about you? Or are you the strong and silent type?"

Schickel's lips barely moved: "We got to look at Crocker. I'd do it, even if nobody else wanted to."

"Then let's go," Virgil said.

•

SCHICKEL RODE with Virgil, to fill him in on Crocker, while Dunn took a sheriff's truck and led the way. Crocker lived seventeen miles out, most of it down I-90. Schickel said, "Greg wasn't trying to give you a hard time. He says what he thinks."

Virgil nodded. "I appreciate that. He didn't cut Larson any slack, either."

Larson had been a state senator who'd gotten drunk, but not very, had run a rural stop sign and T-boned another car on his way home from the bar. The driver of the other car was killed. The question had been whether it was purely an accident, or vehicular homicide. Virgil had helped with the investigation, and though Larson had been indicted on the homicide charge, he'd been acquitted.

"Greg's a good guy, but he doesn't cut anybody a lot of slack," Schickel said. Then, loosening up a little, "Including his wife. He's halfway through a divorce."

"Been there," Virgil said. "So what's with Crocker? Good guy? Bad guy? You think he knew Tripp? Any rumors around?"

"Jimmy's not a good guy," Schickel said. "I'm not talking behind his back. He knows what I think, and I've told him to his face."

"What's his problem?"

"He's got some bully in him, for one thing. Not physical—that's one thing I'm not sure about in this Tripp thing. The Tripp boy was a hell of an athlete. Jim Crocker is a big guy and strong as a bull, but I don't know if he'd have the guts to take on Bobby Tripp."

"So when you say Crocker's a bully . . ."

"He's political, always sucking around for something," Schickel said. "He was Harlan's messenger boy, when somebody had to give out the bad news. You know, if somebody was gonna get fired, or laid off, or disciplined. He was like the assistant principal, if you know what I mean."

"Yeah. Exactly."

"And he enjoyed doing it. But he was also one for dodging serious work. When he went for the sheriff's job, practically the whole department was out there talking up Lee. I would've quit, if he'd won."

"But not crooked . . . not on the take, or anything."

"Not like payoffs, like protection. But he'd do a favor for somebody," Schickel said. "One time, two or three years back, a doctor's kid got caught driving drunk, one-point-one blood alcohol. No accident or anything, pretty good kid, otherwise, but drunk. His old man came in to talk to the sheriff. Said they had a family cabin up in Canada, and the Canadians wouldn't let the kid into the country with the conviction. He wanted a *little consideration.*"

"And the sheriff said . . ."

"Basically, that it was too late. Everybody in town knew about the situation. Best to hire a good lawyer. Anyway, when they went to send the file over to the county attorney, the key evidence was missing. The original ticket with the blow-tube numbers on it," Schickel said. "So the prosecutor refused to prosecute, because of tainted evidence and mishandled paperwork. She was happy to do it, because she didn't want to hang up the doctor's family anyway. And she had an out: She blamed our office. Hell of an embarrassment. The eventual . . . conclusion . . . was that Crocker lifted the file."

"But no proof."

"No proof, but I'm on board with the conclusion," Schickel said. "Crocker . . . you can have a beer with the guy, and he can tell a story, but basically, not a good guy."

THEY FOLLOWED DUNN off I-90 at Highway 7, turned south through the town of Battenberg. Schickel pointed out a grain elevator: "That's where Tripp killed Jake Flood."

"Oh, yeah? Was Crocker in on that? The investigation?" Virgil asked.

"No, he had nothing to do with that. That all happened in the daytime, and Crocker's been working nights," Schickel said.

"Did he work last night?"

"Nope. Yesterday and the day before was his weekend. He's on tonight."

They passed the high school and went on down Main Street to the intersection of a county highway, turned back east for a couple miles, jogged south.

"He's really out here," Virgil said. "He got a family?"

"No. Wife took off a few years ago. She's married to a guy over in Jackson, now. Or was. This house belongs to his uncle: He gets it free, as I understand it. Otherwise, it'd probably be abandoned. His folks have a farm further on south."

THE FARMHOUSE SAT on the south side of a tangled woodlot of cottonwoods and box elders, beside a shallow drainage creek that crossed the roadway south of the house. The house was typical old Minnesota: a narrow two-story clapboard place in need of paint and new shingles, and probably new wiring. A thin stream of heated air was coming from a chimney, visible as a shimmer against the sky.

A machine shed, showing fresh tracks going in, but not out, with a new garage door, sat to the left of the driveway, with a ten-foot-long propane tank to one side.

The front porch was covered by untracked snow; entry was apparently through the side door, next to the driveway. A satellite dish was bolted to one of the porch pillars, aimed to the southwest.

Dunn led the way in, and Virgil parked behind him, and they got out and stretched and stomped their feet in the snow-covered drive, and Dunn said to Virgil, "Well, time to do your thing."

Virgil nodded and said, "You know what?" He went back to the truck and got the Glock out of the center console and put it in his pocket.

Schickel's eyebrows went up: "You don't carry?"

"I'm more of an intellectual," Virgil said.

Dunn actually smiled. "I've heard that."

VIRGIL CLIMBED the stoop and knocked on the door. No answer. No sound, except the faint hiss of the chimney. Knocked again, louder. Called, "Crocker? Jim Crocker?"

Silence.

Virgil stepped back from the stoop, asked the deputies, "There's no chance that anybody called him? That he's running for it?"

Dunn shook his head. "I know for a fact that the sheriff didn't tell anybody but me and Gene, and Judge O'Hare, who's about as tight-lipped as a guy could get."

"O'Hare didn't tell anybody," Schickel said. He climbed the stoop and banged on the door again, yelled, "Jimmy?"

Dunn said, "Let me look in the shed. Maybe he's over

in Jackson or something." He walked across the driveway to the shed, peered in a window, came back. "His Jeep's there," he said.

The three men looked at each other, and Virgil said, "I'm going in, on the warrant."

Dunn nodded and said, "Probably best to take out a pane of glass, instead of breaking the door. Be hell to get somebody out here to fix the door."

Virgil used the barrel of the Glock to knock out a pane of glass in the door, reached in, and turned the lock. He pushed the door open, then stepped back.

"Somebody dead in here," he said.

Dunn, suddenly pale-faced, said, "What?"

"I can smell him," Virgil said. "Not much stink, but somebody's dead in here."

"A mouse?"

"Not a mouse . . . You guys step careful, here. If he's dead, we don't want to screw up the scene."

They found him on the living room couch, staring with blank eyes at a rerun of *Married . . . with Children.*

"Ah, Jesus, Mary, and Joseph," Schickel said, crossing himself. "He ate his gun. He must've killed Bobby."

A pistol, a matte-black Glock like Virgil's, except in .45 caliber, lay on the floor next to the couch.

"Did he carry a .45 Glock?" Virgil asked, looking at the big black hole at the end of the barrel.

"Yeah, he did," Dunn said.

Crocker was on his back, an entry wound under his chin, a massive exit wound at the back of his skull. The arm of the couch, covered with a plush green material, was soaked with blood, hair, and what might have been pieces of bone; a couple of small holes in the wall beside the couch looked like they might have been made by fragments of the exiting slug.

"Maybe he knew he was gonna get caught," Dunn said.

"Didn't kill himself," Virgil said. "He was probably murdered. Let's clear the house, just to make sure there's nobody hurt, somewhere. We don't want to dig around, just clear it. Two minutes."

The three of them moved through the place, but found it empty. Crocker had lived only on the first floor; the second floor was closed down, the door at the top of the stairs sealed with 3M insulating tape. They pushed through, and found a bunch of old dusty furniture sitting in cold, dry, dusty rooms.

When they were sure there was nobody else in the place, Virgil said, "Let's call the sheriff. This is really gonna make her day."

They stepped carefully past the body and back outside. Dunn made the call, and Schickel asked Virgil, "Why'd you think it's murder?"

"When Lee was telling me about B. J. Tripp, she mentioned him being hanged from the bunk. I asked her if his dick was hanging out—you know, strangled himself while masturbating."

"Heard of that, but never seen it," Schickel said.

"Yeah, well, it wasn't. Hanging out. But if you go up there and look, you'll see that Crocker's fly is down, and you can see his dick sticking out. I never, ever, heard of anyone who was yanking his crank and stopped to kill himself. Or anyone who took his dick out, and left it out, and killed himself. It's not dignified. When people kill themselves, they tend to think about how they'll be found—they imagine it. They imagine how sad everybody'll be. They're going to *show* them . . . but they don't stick their dick out."

"I didn't pick up on that," Schickel said. "His dick."

Dunn came back. "The sheriff's on the way. What about his dick? Whose dick?"

LEE COAKLEY LOOKED in on Crocker's body. Her mouth was a thin line, with a twist at the end, as though she'd been sucking on a lemon. "He could be a jerk, but I'd never have wished this on him," she said.

"I called our crime-scene people up in the Cities. I thought you might want to go that way, given the situation, instead of using your own man," Virgil said. "You say yes, I'll get them on the way."

She nodded. "Yeah. Get them started. I'll get Gene to set up in the driveway, keep people out. I better go down and tell Jim's folks."

"You okay with that?"

She nodded again. "Yes. My job, and I won't dodge it. I'd feel better if I could spit, but I don't think I can."

"Got a preacher you can take along?"

"We do, but his folks belong to some kind of private religion. I think it'd be best not to try to sneak a Lutheran in the door. I'll just have Greg ride along."

They went outside, and she told Schickel and two other deputies to shut the scene down and wait for the crime-scene crew from the Cities. "I don't want anybody in or out. *Anybody.*"

"They'll be three hours," Virgil said. "They're loading up."

"What're you gonna do?" Coakley asked.

"Not much to do until the crime-scene guys have a look," Virgil said. "I think I might go get a bite to eat."

He walked along with Coakley to her truck, and said, "I'd like to look at the files on this whole chain of events—the Flood killing, Tripp's death, the personnel file on Crocker."

"I'll call in. You'll want to talk to a deputy named John Kraus. I'll have John put you in the conference room. I'll be back in a couple hours, at the latest. I'd like to read through them again myself."

VIRGIL STOPPED at the Yellow Dog Café in downtown Homestead, got a California burger and home fries, with a Diet Coke, and thought about the three killings. Had to be tied. He didn't know how often Warren County had a murder, but he'd guess one about every ten years or so, if that often. To have three, in a week, all cryptically linked, was pressing coincidence.

They had no reason for Tripp's murder of Flood; no reason for Crocker's murder of Tripp; no reason for an unknown killer to murder Crocker, especially when Crocker was lying on a couch with his penis sticking out.

Crocker hadn't been surprised; everything in his old house rattled, so he must've known that he wasn't alone in the house, must've known the person who killed him. And he hadn't feared that person; probably had some sexual relationship with her. Or him.

Hmm. Or him. A few months earlier, Virgil had worked a case in the North Woods in which a bunch of lesbians had been involved. Didn't seem likely that he'd go right on to another case involving homosexuals.

On the other hand, Tripp may have been gay, active or inactive. He had wanted to talk to a newspaper reporter about the Flood killing, and the only fact known to Virgil about the reporter was that he was gay.

On the third hand, he *did* only know one fact about the reporter, and taken with all the facts he didn't know about him, his sexual orientation was probably irrelevant.

Maybe.

He took out his cell phone and called Coakley. She answered on the third ring, and he asked, "Are you at Crocker's folks'?"

"Yes."

She didn't say anything else, and Virgil realized that she was sitting there with them, and they were listening. "Is there any possibility that Crocker had homosexual inclinations?"

"Very, very unlikely. But nothing's impossible, as I'm sure you know," she said.

"You gonna come with me when I talk to this newspaper reporter?"

"Absolutely. I'll see you in an hour."

Virgil hung up, toyed with his home fries. Unless the crime-scene crew came up with something that definitely pointed at a particular person as the killer, or somebody came forward with information, it would be tough to get into the Crocker killing . . . though it would be interesting to learn more about friends and relatives of Tripp, to see if they blamed Crocker for the death.

And with Crocker dead, it'd be tough to get into the Tripp killing, as well. Had to be some private motive. Some motive that involved Tripp and Crocker and almost certainly Flood.

Tripp had wanted to talk to somebody about Flood, so that killing can't have been on impulse. Tripp planned it. Took the T-ball bat with him. Could be an entry there . . .

HE WAS ABOUT to leave the café when a man in a dark suit and close-cut silver hair came through the door, followed by a pretty, dark-haired woman carrying a briefcase and dressed in a gray lawyer suit. He looked familiar, and the man did a double take when he saw Virgil.

"Virgil Flowers," he said, and, introducing himself, "Tom Parker—I cross-examined you in the Larson case." He said it with a friendly smile and Virgil remembered him. Good attorney, he thought, though he'd been on the other side.

"Oh, sure," Virgil said. "Nice to see you again."

They shook hands, and Parker said, "This is my associate, Laurie . . . and I bet you're not here on a social visit. There's a hot rumor going around the courthouse that Jimmy Crocker's been murdered. That true?"

Virgil said, "I can't really talk to you about it in detail. But, yeah. I'm just in from his place. The sheriff's out telling his folks."

"Better her than me," Parker said.

Laurie asked, "You know who did it?"

"No idea, yet."

"When you find out, let me know," Parker said. "I want to rush out there with my card."

"Maybe not. That didn't work for me the last time," Virgil said. They chatted for a couple more minutes, Parker and the woman probing for more facts, Virgil telling them only that it superficially looked like a suicide, by gun, but that he thought it was probably a murder. Other than that, he didn't know anything.

"Three murders, though, I figure they should be connected," he said, aware that everybody in the café was listening to the conversation. "If you have any ideas, I'd listen to them. I'm fresh out of my own."

"I'll give you a ring," Parker said.

But Laurie said, "In a way, it's four murders."

Virgil: "Four?"

"About a year ago, a girl was murdered out there . . . not murdered here in Warren County, but across the line in Iowa, north of Estherville. But she came from a farm by Blakely."

"That's right," Parker said. "Kelly . . ."

"Baker," Laurie said.

Virgil snapped his fingers. "I remember something

about that. Found her in a cemetery, right? The Iowa guys covered it, out of Des Moines. Did she go to school here in Homestead?"

Laurie said, "Maybe, but her house would be out in the Northwest High area. . . . I mean, some people transfer around depending on where their parents work. So, I don't know where she went."

"Had she graduated, or was she working?" Virgil asked.

Laurie said, "I don't know, really. . . ."

A man two booths down from them cleared his throat and said, "She was homeschooled. She had a summer job here in Homestead, at the Dairy Queen. My daughter knew her."

"You know how old she was?" Virgil asked, turning in the booth.

"About the same as my daughter—my daughter was a junior when the girl was killed, so, sixteen, seventeen."

Virgil said, "Huh. Another mystery. I wonder if I could clear it all out, with another order of home fries?"

"You'd clear something out, but I don't think it'd be the murder case," the man in the booth said.

A waitress said, "Hey. No pie for you, Earl."

4

Virgil left the café pleased with himself. He'd learned something, and it had made the case more intricate and therefore more interesting, and also more breakable. The more ways in, the better. He drove over to the sheriff's office and found John Kraus, a tall, portly bald man who wore the department uniform, and looked like a cook, or a potential department-store Santa.

"Got your files right down the hall," Kraus said. "We got them either on computer, or on paper, but I got you the paper ones. Easier to shuffle things around."

"That's terrific. Just the way I like it," Virgil said.

Kraus said, "I'll leave you to it. We got some coffee going down the hall, to the right. Can's around the corner."

Virgil started by calling Bell Wood, an agent with the Iowa Division of Criminal Investigation. "Tell him his personal hero is calling from Minnesota," Virgil told the woman who answered the phone.

Wood came up: "That fuckin' Flowers. Everything

was going so well, too. Just a minute ago, I told Janice, everything's going too well—something's wrong."

"I heard the fools who run the National Guard made you into a major," Virgil said.

"That is indeed the case. People now call me Major Wood."

"That wouldn't be any women you know," Virgil said, "or have known, or will ever know."

"Au contraire, my ignorant Minnewegan friend. My standing is well known in the female community. So, is this a social call?"

"Nope. Something's wrong," Virgil said.

"Ah, crap," Wood said. Wood was the number two guy in the major crimes section. "Let's hear it."

"You know the murder of a young Minnesota girl named Kelly Baker?" Virgil asked. "Down by Estherville, a year or so ago?"

"That would be 'up by Estherville,' if you were correctly oriented. Yeah, I do know about it. Ugly. Ugly case, Virgil. October eleventh. Fourteen months ago. Our sex kitten. We got nothing."

"You got sex kitten," Virgil said.

"We do. Are you at your office? I'll send you the file."

"Actually, I'm in Homestead. . . ." He filled in Wood on the three murders, beginning with Flood. Wood listened, then said, "I heard about the jail hanging, but I didn't know it was murder."

"Just found it out today," Virgil said. "This morning. Listen, that file on Baker, shoot it down to me. Up to me."

"Sure. You want e-mail?"

"I don't know if they're running wireless," Virgil said. "Hang on, let me walk down the hall and find my guy."

Kraus said they did not have a wireless hookup. He got on the line with Wood, agreed that they could take and print a color PDF document, gave Wood the address, and handed the phone back to Virgil.

"It's on the way," Wood said. "It's big, three hundred pages, in color. Let me look at this, for a minute, I'm looking at the computer. You probably want to read the whole thing, to see who we interviewed, and what they said, but right off, go to page thirty-four. That's the beginning of the autopsy report."

"That's a big deal?" Virgil asked.

"Yeah. That's *the* big deal, so far," Wood said. "Virgil, if you can nail the guys who did this, man, I'll get you tracks in the Iowa Guard. That's the same as a Minnesota general."

"I've had tracks," Virgil said; he'd gotten out of the army as a captain. "When you say 'guys,' plural . . ."

"Read the report," Wood said.

"You got DNA on these guys?"

"Read the report. And listen, keep me informed."

VIRGIL DECIDED that he wanted to read about the murders in the order that they happened, and so went down and got a cup of coffee, then waited, watching, as the file came out of Kraus's laser printer.

The autopsy report, including findings and conclusions, was fifteen pages long. When the last of it came out, Virgil said to Kraus, "Holler when it's done. I'm going to start with this."

The first few pages of the report laid out the reasons for Iowa DCI involvement: The department was asked in by Emmet County authorities after Baker's body was found in the Lutheran cemetery north of Estherville. The body was nude, and half-hidden behind a tombstone in an older section of the cemetery, where it was found by chance by an elderly woman who'd come out to put the year's last blooming wildflowers on her husband's grave.

The Emmet County sheriff's office had put out inquiries, and had been informed by the Warren County sheriff's office that Leonard Baker, of Blakely, Minnesota, had reported that his daughter had not come home the night before, after an afternoon's visit with an aunt, uncle, and cousins on a farm near Estherville.

The description fit, and the parents had later identified the body as Kelly Baker, seventeen. Her mother's car, a 2004 Toyota Corolla, was found in downtown Estherville. Witnesses said it had been there overnight, and after nailing down the times, by interviewing owners of local businesses, and Baker's uncle, DCI investigators determined that Baker must have left it there shortly after leaving her aunt and uncle's farm.

That made it an Iowa murder, and explained why Virgil hadn't heard more about it.

As Wood had suggested, the autopsy made interesting reading. The autopsy had been done in Des Moines, and the pathologist reported that Baker had died from strangulation, her windpipe crimped by some kind of collar with a sharp edge, either metal or stiff leather. The collar had been pulled straight back, as if it had been attached to a rope or chain, like a heavy leather collar on a pit bull.

Exact time of death was uncertain, because nighttime temperatures had gone down into the upper twenties, and the body had been heavily cooled. The contents of her stomach had been fully digested, and her uncle said the last thing she'd eaten was an ice cream sundae at about two o'clock in the afternoon. She'd left shortly before supper.

Baker's buttocks and breasts were lightly striped, as though she'd been beaten with a narrow leather or flexible wood whip, or switch. There were indentations on her wrists, consistent with metal handcuffs. She had been sexually used, according to the pathologist, orally, vaginally, and anally, almost certainly by more than one man, and perhaps as many as four or five, judging from bruising around her anus and vagina. There was evidence that she had been simultaneously entered anally and vaginally.

There were faint marks, not quite scars, on her buttocks and breasts, indicating that she had been beaten before, with a whip similar to the one that had marked her this time.

There was no indication of resistance, which, along with the earlier whip marks, suggested that her involvement may have been voluntary. Virgil didn't think the conclusion followed from the evidence: She could have also been too afraid to resist, although the earlier whip marks were hard to explain, unless she'd been thoroughly brainwashed.

There was no DNA evidence. Lubricants were found deep in her anus and vagina, of a kind used on a national brand of condoms, suggesting that the men had worn condoms. Whether they had worn them as protection against sexual diseases or pregnancy, or as a way to eliminate the possibility of DNA, was unknown.

If the former was the case, the pathologist noted, then the death may have been accidental, in the course of extreme sex play; and may have indicated that the perpetrators didn't know Baker very well—that it may have been prostitution. If the latter, it would suggest that the men involved were protecting themselves against criminal prosecution. If Baker died in the course of criminal activity, the death could be classified as a murder, depending on the exact nature of the criminal activity.

She had abrasions around her mouth, indicating that she had been orally penetrated, but no semen was found in her trachea or stomach. That might have meant that the oral sex had taken place well before her death, and the semen digested; that the man had withdrawn before ejaculation, which seemed unlikely in this kind of abusive sex play; or that he or they had worn condoms.

The latter case would again suggest protection against DNA evidence, which could lead to a finding of murder.

Even more disturbing was the lack of any kind of DNA evidence at all on the body: no sweat, no stains. There was no lubricant on the outer parts of her vagina or anus. She was wearing no deodorant. The pathologist suggested that the body may have been washed after death, and thoroughly. The care with which it had been done suggested cool deliberation, not panic.

Virgil leaned back and closed his eyes. A prostitute? The age was right. Probably half the prostitutes in Minnesota were seventeen or younger. Why was the body left in the cemetery? Was there some effort to do right by her, as ludicrous as the effort seemed? Could it have been done by panicked high school boys? But the level of sexual deviation suggested older men, with longer-standing sexual tastes. Would her parents know the older men? Could it have been teachers, or familial abuse?

The care with which the DNA had been obliterated again suggested older men, and perhaps men experienced in removing DNA. Had they killed before?

HE WAS THINKING about it when Kraus appeared with a thick stack of paper and handed it to him. "That's it. We have some paper of our own on the case; we did interviews with friends and schoolmates of hers, but most of that's in the Iowa reports. Ours might have a little more detail, but probably nothing too significant."

"What I'd really like is a list of names of everybody you interviewed," Virgil said. "Not what they said, just a list."

"I could put that together. I'll do it now," Kraus said. "You think this is really tied to Flood and Bobby Tripp and Jim?"

"Well, Flood was killed in Battenberg, and came from two miles northwest of there. Crocker lived on a farm a couple miles southeast of Battenberg, and Baker here came from a farm five or six miles south. So you could probably put all their places in a twenty-five- or thirty-square-mile area. How big is the county? Seven hundred square miles? With maybe a murder every decade or so? And you have three killings, in little more than a year, with all the victims from that little square, who knew each other? Or another way—they all lived within a mile or so of Highway 7. . . ."

"I'll get busy," Kraus said.

VIRGIL DID a quick scan of the Iowa file, looking for names, especially Bob Tripp's. It wasn't there.

Going back through the paper, he found photos of Baker when she was alive, as well as crime-scene shots and several autopsy photos. The autopsy photos didn't do anything but gross him out, and he put them aside. She had been a reasonably pretty girl, blond, busty. When she'd fully filled out, she would probably have been stocky, with broad shoulders and hips, and overlarge breasts.

In the early flush of womanhood, though, she looked good. *Salable*, Virgil thought, with a little thrum of guilt. The Iowa investigators had dug hard into the possibility that she'd been involved in prostitution, and had found nothing.

Virgil got back on the phone to Wood. "Solved it yet?" Wood asked.

"About halfway there," Virgil said. "I've been reading the file, and want to know what you thought about the prostitution angle. Your guys asked a lot of questions. . . ."

"Let me run down the hall and grab a guy," Wood said.

He was back in a minute, and another phone was picked up. Wood said, "I've got Mitch Ingle on the phone; he worked that the hardest."

"I've got all the paper here," Virgil told the Iowans. "What I want is some opinions. Was she hooking?"

Ingle said, "It's easy to think so, looking at the whole package. But I don't believe it. In a community that size, the word would get around. You got a school full of horny high school boys in a small community, where everybody knows everything, and we couldn't turn up a hint of that. What I started to believe was that she may have been picked up by a couple of older guys who were working on turning her out, and killed her before that got done. That would also explain the other prostitution problem—there was no sign that she had any money. And she had no birth control pills, she had no condoms. She had no *hooker* stuff."

"Estherville can't be that big. . . ."

"Checked every apartment and every loose male, anyplace she might have gone for sex. We concluded that she might not have actually . . . performed whatever it was . . . in Estherville. She might have been dumped there from somewhere else."

"Her car was found there."

"Yes, but we don't know that she drove it there. Nobody saw who parked it. It was alongside a convenience store and coin-op laundry, off to the side, people coming and going. Could have been her, but maybe not. The thing is, we're assuming that she was not kidnapped. She went with these guys, maybe not because she wanted to, but she didn't fight them. She met them. She left her uncle's place, and drove somewhere and met them. Judging from those earlier marks on her breasts and legs, she'd met them before."

"I haven't been through all the paper, and I'm not sure you put every name in, but do you remember if the names Jacob Flood, Bob Tripp, or Jim Crocker show up anyplace along the way?"

After a moment's silence, Wood said, "Doesn't ring a bell with me," and Ingle said, "Me neither. I can run a search on my computer."

"If you could," Virgil said.

He and Ingle exchanged phone numbers, and Ingle said, "Minor Wood has filled me in on your investigation there, and if there's anything I can do, I'll come up. If you need help down on the Iowa side . . ."

"Don't know where it's going yet," Virgil said. "But I appreciate it."

HE WAS BACK in the paper when he heard cowboy boots coming down the hall, and Coakley stuck her head in the door. "You got the file. John said you're pulling the Kelly Baker case into it."

"I haven't found any direct connection, but it's a pretty interesting coincidence," Virgil said.

She came in and sat down at the side of the table, leaned toward him, and said, "I got to Baker about halfway back from Crocker's folks' house. I would have gotten to it quicker, if I hadn't been so run over by the murder. The Baker case is no coincidence, Virgil. You remember I told you that Crocker belonged to a private religion? Flood was a member of the same group—and so was Baker."

"Okay—that's good," Virgil said. "What about Tripp? Was his family—"

"No. Lutherans. But still, there has to be a connection."

"I think you've made up the same story I have," Virgil ventured.

She said, "Crocker and Flood somehow get on to Baker's availability, maybe because of their church activities. Who knows how? They begin some kind of complicated sexual relationship, probably a four-way, between Crocker, Flood, Baker, and the other woman. Baker's in on it, voluntarily. Maybe Bobby and Baker have a secret relationship of some kind. She tells him what Flood is doing to her . . . maybe doesn't tell him about Crocker . . . and he reacts by killing Flood. We bring him in. Crocker realizes that Bobby could spill the beans about their sex ring, and also realizes that Bobby doesn't know who he is. But he's a danger, so Crocker sneaks into Bobby's cell while he's asleep, and kills him."

"The other woman?" Virgil asked.

"The woman who was doing oral sex on Crocker when she killed him."

"You think?"

"I think. It's plausible." Her mismatched eyes narrowed as she ran through it. "His penis is sticking out of his pants, he's lying way back on the couch, with his legs spread, one foot on the floor, and he gets shot under the jaw. If it's murder, and I think it is, that means that he let somebody get close enough to him to put that gun right under his jawline, and doesn't react. That's because he's reacting to something else."

"Why would she do it?"

"Because she was in on the Baker murder," Coakley said. "She was in on a statutory rape, which meant that Baker's death was murder."

"Like she had some legal knowledge. She knew she'd been contaminated by the death of Baker. And she knew Jimmy and knew how to handle his gun," Virgil said, with a faint smile.

She leaned back, picking up the implication. "I didn't do it, you jerk. If I had a choice between giving that moron a blow job and going to the chair, I'd take the chair."

"We don't have the death penalty—"

"You get the point," she said. "Jeez, I'm starting to understand 'that fuckin' Flowers' thing."

"Don't get in a huff," he said. "I was filling out your line of reasoning. And maybe teasing you a little."

"Fill it some other way," she said.

"Any other female deputies, or cops, who might have known what Crocker had done? Who he might have confided in?"

"Two, but they didn't do it. I know them well enough to say that. Though I guess we have to talk to them."

"You knew Crocker pretty well, too," Virgil pointed out. "Was he attractive to the other women in the department? Did he hang around with any of them? Where was his social life? In the department, or outside?"

She shook her head. "Not an attractive man, no. The other deputies . . . no."

"Of course, even if Crocker was getting oral sex, we don't know it was a woman."

"You think . . . ?"

"What I think is, the sex with Baker was so crazy that they probably do a little of everything. Just for the excitement."

"That's a point," she said. And, "You know what? We need to talk to Bob Tripp's folks, like right now."

"And a newspaper reporter," Virgil added. "And Flood's wife."

SHE WENT to make phone calls, and Virgil kicked back and thought about Bob Tripp. And he thought, *Why did he wait this long?*

If Baker had told Tripp that she was being sexually abused, and he killed Flood out of a misplaced sense of justice, why did he wait more than a year? One possibility was that Tripp had been afraid to do it, and that suddenly having access to Flood at the grain elevator had triggered him. Maybe that was why he wanted to talk to the reporter—he'd confided in the reporter, in an effort to get something done, and the reporter hadn't been able to help.

Virgil preferred a second possibility: that Tripp had only recently learned something that triggered the murder of Flood. If that was true, then there was a way into the case, a source of information, if he could find it. If Tripp had learned something, then Virgil could find it.

Coakley came back and said, "We're in luck. Everybody's around. We'll do the Tripps first, and then run over to the *Dispatch.* The reporter's name is Pat Sullivan. Sully. I hate to say it, but he's usually pretty accurate. Flood's wife works in Jackson, but her father says she's due home at six o'clock."

THE TRIPPS, George and Irma, lived in a fifties ranch-style single-story house, yellow, with a two-car garage at one end, arborvitae poking out of the snow along the driveway and under the picture window. George Tripp was standing behind the picture window, with his hands in his pockets, when they pulled into the driveway.

"The big issue here," Coakley said on the way over, "is that we haven't released Bobby's body yet, and they are getting pretty upset about it. They want to have a funeral, get him in the ground."

"When are you going to release him?" Virgil asked.

"Ike Patras says he doesn't think he can get anything

more off the body, so I'm going to okay the release tomorrow morning. I'll tell George as soon as we're in the house. Maybe that'll loosen them up a little."

"You said you guys were friends."

"Friendly. Not friends," Coakley said. "We didn't see each other socially or anything, but we'd stop to talk on the sidewalk. They've been pretty unhappy with me since Bobby's arrest, and then his death—like I betrayed them."

GEORGE TRIPP WAITED until they were halfway up the walk before he left the window and opened the front door. He said, "Sheriff," with a nod, and a cold chill in his voice; he backed away from the door, his hands back in his pockets. Not going to shake with the law. Irma Tripp came out of the kitchen, wiping her hands on a dish towel. The house was neatly kept, with family photos in frames, and wildlife art on the walls; it smelled of chili and wood cleaner. Virgil thought the Tripps were probably in their middle forties, Irma a bit younger than her husband.

Coakley said, "We have some news for you, George, Irma. We'll release Bobby tomorrow morning, so you can get on with a service."

"'Bout time," George Tripp said. He was looking at Virgil. "Who would this be?"

"Virgil Flowers, he's an agent with the state Bureau of Criminal Apprehension," Coakley said. "He works the southern part of the state."

Irma said, "I thought we were all done with investigation."

Virgil shook his head. "No, no. We do have some more news for you. Could we sit down? We really do need to talk."

They sat in a conversation group, a couch on one side of a wood-and-glass coffee table, two overstuffed chairs on the other side. Virgil leaned forward and said, "I really want to express my sympathy over the death of your son. It's an awful thing."

"How would you know?" Irma asked.

"Because I see a lot of awful things, and I'm pretty much like you folks. I grew up in Marshall, and my father is a minister. When a kid died, half the time the service would be in our church, and I'd know him. Know the family. I've been through it a lot."

Irma nodded. "He was the best thing we had. He was our only child."

Virgil glanced at Coakley, who nodded at him, and Virgil turned back to the Tripps. "We need to tell you that we no longer think that your son committed suicide. We've developed evidence that he may have been murdered by Jim Crocker, the sheriff's deputy who was on duty that night."

George Tripp lurched off the couch, to his feet, and said, "I knew it. I knew it," and Irma began to weep. George Tripp said, "Where is he? Crocker?"

Coakley said, "He's dead, George. We went to his house with a search warrant, and found him dead. He also looks like a suicide, but Agent Flowers and I both believe that he was also murdered."

"What the hell is going on?" George Tripp demanded. His wife was twisting the dish towel into a rope; but Virgil's statement had stopped the weeping.

"We don't know yet, George, but . . . uh . . ."

"Things are getting very strange, and very complicated," Virgil said. "We need to ask you something: Do you know whether or not Bobby was acquainted with, or dating, a young woman, a girl from the west end of the county, named Kelly Baker?"

Irma: "Baker? Wasn't that the girl who was murdered?"

"Yes. Last year, down by Estherville," Coakley said.

"You can't think that Bobby had anything to do with that," George Tripp said, anger threading back into his voice.

"No, no, we don't," Virgil said. "But we're wondering if Jacob Flood might have."

The Tripps stared at him for a moment, then Irma Tripp rocked back on the couch and said, "Ohhh. Oh, no. You think Bobby found out about . . . Ohhh."

"Did they know each other?"

The two looked at each other, and then George Tripp said, "Our son, you know, never really had much to do with girls, yet. He was shy. But there was something going on a year ago. We don't know with who, because he wouldn't talk about it."

"He didn't take anybody to the junior prom," Irma Tripp said. "We kept trying to get him to take Nancy

Anderson, she's really a nice girl, and we'd hoped . . . Do you think he was seeing this other girl? Kelly?"

"She lived out in the countryside," Virgil said.

"He was always borrowing the car, soon as he got his license," George Tripp said. "That wouldn't have been a problem."

"She worked at the Dairy Queen here in Homestead, during the summers," Coakley said.

"There you go," George Tripp said. "The Dairy Queen's a regular meeting place for the kids. He would have been down there most every day, at one time or another."

"So there's a possibility he could have known her, but you don't know that specifically," Virgil said.

Irma's head bobbed. "That would be it. But now that you bring it up, I think he must have known her. He was so strange last fall. He grew up a cheerful, outgoing kid . . ."

"Got a football scholarship, over in your hometown," George Tripp said to Virgil.

"I heard that," Virgil said.

". . . but last fall, he was so gloomy," Irma continued. "We thought maybe the football team, it didn't do as well as people hoped. We thought he was down about that. But if . . ."

"We would like to look through his private things . . . anything would help," Coakley said.

"What would you look for?" Irma asked.

"Any indication that he had prior contact with Flood, with Baker, with Crocker, any notes or letters . . ."

"Oh, I don't know," she said, turning to her husband.

"Probably the best thing would be to have Agent Flowers look," George Tripp said. He said to Coakley, "I know you were doing your duty, Lee, but I gotta say . . . if you hadn't taken him . . . if your men were up to standard . . . he'd still be alive. I think I'd prefer it if you didn't come back here. Not unless you have to."

Coakley bobbed her head and said, "I know what you're saying, George, and I'm so sorry. But Virgil would do a fine job, as good as anybody in the state. He's one of their top men."

"So let's do that," George Tripp said. "Not right now. Irma and I have to . . . do things. If we get our boy back tomorrow . . ."

"There's a time problem," Virgil said. "How about if I give you my cell number, and you call me when you're okay with it. Tonight or tomorrow. There is the time thing. We've got at least one murderer running loose, and probably more."

George Tripp nodded. "We can do that."

5

Pat Sullivan, the newspaper reporter, covered cops and everything else in town, and had been calling the sheriff's office on a fifteen-minute schedule since the rumors of Crocker's death began to leak out. Coakley called him back, with Virgil sitting next to her desk.

She said, "Pat? Lee Coakley. You called?" She listened for a minute, then said, "Why don't you walk over? We've got a state investigator here and we can fill you in." A few more words from the reporter, and she said, "See you then," and hung up.

To Virgil: "He's on his way."

"Good guy?" Virgil asked.

"Yeah, for a reporter," she said. "He's accurate, usually, but he's ambitious. The editor tells me his friend—his relationship, his guy—lives up in the Cities. He'd like to get up there with the *Pioneer Press* or the *Star Tribune*."

"Fat chance," Virgil said. "Those places are bleeding to death. Bet there are a hundred good reporters looking for jobs."

"You know them?"

"A few," Virgil said. "And they talk about it."

"You think they'll be down here? For these murders?"

"May get some TV," Virgil said. "The newspapers, you're more likely to get a call. I mean, they could have a staff meeting in a phone booth."

They sat for a minute, looking past each other, then Coakley asked, "You at the Holiday?"

"Yeah."

They looked past each other some more, until Virgil asked, "You didn't mention to Sullivan that we wanted to talk to him about Tripp."

"I thought I'd leave that to you. Best to ask him first, before we get to Crocker. That way, we're holding the Crocker information over his head. Or, you are. I'm just a humble county sheriff, who has to defer to the state agent, if he decides to screw over the local media." She leaned back in her chair, turned, put her boots up on top of a wastebasket, put her hands behind her head, and stared at the ceiling. She did it in a comfortably coordinated way, which made Virgil think it was her regular thinking posture. "I have two possibilities."

"Only two?"

"No, there are several more, but two I'm thinking about. One: Flood and Crocker were friends, which we know, and that Crocker killed Bobby out of simple revenge. Two: Crocker killed Bobby because he was afraid that when Bobby told us why he killed Flood, that it'd come back on Crocker."

They considered that for a moment, then Virgil said, "Crocker didn't kill Tripp until early morning, almost time for a shift change. I wonder why he waited? I wonder if he needed to talk to somebody about it? Like your other woman. We oughta check the phones here, see if he called anyone during the overnight. And check his cell."

"We can do that," she said. Another moment, and she asked, "You cook? Or you eat out?"

"I'm not much interested in food," Virgil said. "I mostly eat microwave. Healthy Choice, like that. Cereal. Milk. Scrambled eggs."

"My husband used to cook, a lot, when I was married," Coakley said. "I used to work some odd hours. Now, I get home in time to cook, most nights, but can't get it going again. The boys are happy with pizza and burgers and fries, but I feel guilty about it."

"How many kids you got?" Virgil asked.

"Three. Sixteen, fourteen, and twelve," she said. "The twelve was supposed to be a girl. So was the fourteen, for that matter. All I got is a bunch of big lugs. Though I love them to death."

"Sounds like you kept busy for a while. Three kids in four years."

"Yeah, well. Going to Mankato State, got married halfway through my senior year. I was knocked up by Memorial Day," she said.

"What'd your husband do?"

"He's the new car sales manager over at Gable Ford," she said.

"Still see him?" Virgil asked.

"Oh, no. The new wife wouldn't like it, for one thing," Coakley said.

"Oh-oh."

"What can I tell you? He got married three weeks after our divorce was final," she said. "I guess it had been going on for a while. Never saw it coming."

"She have really big breasts?" Virgil asked.

The thin smile again. "Ample. Or ample-and-a-half."

"Give her any speeding tickets?"

"Hadn't thought of it, but now that you mention it, I'll keep it in mind," she said. Her phone rang, and she picked it up, listened, and said, "Send him in."

PAT SULLIVAN was a short, thin man, of the sort that Virgil thought of as "weedy." He had brown hair, a prominent nose, a brush mustache, and square Teddy Roosevelt teeth. He wore brown boots with studded soles, was carrying a parka and a reporter's notebook.

"Virgil Flowers," he said, when Coakley introduced him. "I've followed your adventures. That shoot-out up in International Falls, with the Vietnamese dragon lady. The one out by Bluestem, with the federal guys."

"They're like bad dreams slowly fading away," Virgil said. He pointed at a chair. "Sit down. We gotta talk. There's more going on than a story."

Sullivan sat down, a skeptical look on his face. "Like what?"

"We have to go off the record for a bit," Virgil said. "That good with you?"

"Depends. We can start that way. If I can't keep it off, I'll tell you," Sullivan said.

"When Bob Tripp was arrested, he wouldn't talk to the sheriff until he talked to you first," Virgil said.

Sullivan's eyebrows went up. "Me?"

"Yes. Are we off the record?"

"Okay. For now."

"We wondered if you knew what he might have wanted to talk about," Virgil said.

"So you didn't ask me to come in as a reporter, but as a possible witness."

Virgil shrugged: "I don't care if you're both. Not a problem for me."

Sullivan said, "I'll have to think about it . . . but if Bobby wanted to talk, why would he have committed suicide?"

Virgil said, "He didn't. He was murdered. Probably by Jim Crocker."

"Whoa." Sullivan went pale, leaned forward. "This has got to be on the record. Not about Bobby wanting to talk to me, but about Bobby and Crocker."

"We'll come back to it, give you a formal interview, on the record. Let's stay off for now."

Sullivan paused, then nodded.

"Crocker isn't a sure thing, for Bobby's murder," Virgil said. "I can think of scenarios where he didn't do it—but we think he probably did. We may have more definitive answers after the investigation."

Coakley jumped in, pressing the question, "Do you have any idea why Bobby might have wanted to talk to you?"

Sullivan leaned back, looked at Coakley, then Virgil, then back at Coakley. "Lee, I assume you know that I'm gay."

"I knew that," she said, nodding.

"I cover a lot of sports. People around town had heard I was gay, and some of the high school kids knew about it. Maybe most of them. Anyway, I interviewed Bobby a few times, he was a star. Then, one time, he asked me if he could stop by my apartment and chat. I said, 'Sure,'" Sullivan said. "By that time, I had an idea of what was coming. Anyway, he came over, and beat around the bush for a while, then said that he'd heard that I was gay, and that he was worried that he might be, and he just wanted to talk about it."

"Was he?" Coakley asked.

"Oh, sure. As far as I know, he hadn't been sexually involved with anybody—including me, we never were—but he had already gone through most of the self-recognition stuff," Sullivan said. "You know, feeling this strong attraction toward some of his teammates, and he'd fantasize about them, instead of the girls in his class, and all the rest—checking out the scene on the Internet, maybe checking some gay porn."

"Did he ever mention Jacob Flood to you?" Virgil asked.

Sullivan shook his head. "No. When I heard that

Bobby was dead, and that he'd been arrested in the Flood case, I was amazed. We talked quite a bit, and he never mentioned Flood's name."

Virgil: "And nothing about Crocker."

"Not a thing. Not even during the election."

"Do you know if Flood or Crocker were active in the local Homestead gay culture? There must be a few more gay people here."

Sullivan nodded. "Quite a few," he said. "Maybe a hundred, or more? But not all of them are active around here, and I've never heard of those two. That doesn't mean much, though—it's not like we all hook up. I know maybe . . . a dozen gay people here? Something like that."

"Did Bobby ever mention a girl named Kelly Baker?"

Sullivan, who'd been slumping in the chair, straightened, and tipped an index finger at Virgil. "Now *her*, we did talk about. Is she involved in this deal?"

"Wait," Virgil said. "You say you talked about her. Did he know her?"

"Oh, yeah. He met her at the Dairy Queen. He used to give her a ride home, sometimes. I think he was hoping that he might, you know, get involved with her, find out that he really wasn't gay. It didn't work out that way. I think . . . I *think*—he didn't actually tell me—that she picked up on the fact that he was gay. Didn't bother her, and they became friends."

"The Iowa people didn't talk to him? The cops?"

"Not as far as I know. I mean, Bobby and Kelly were a summertime thing, when the Dairy Queen was open.

After school started, she was gone, and then, you know, she was killed. He didn't know anything, and they never really had a relationship, so . . . it just went away, I guess."

"Doesn't help much," Virgil said.

"Let *me* ask a question," Sullivan said. "Have you actually checked on Flood's sexual orientation?"

"Not yet, but it's on the list," Coakley said. "We know he was married, but we also know that whoever killed Kelly Baker was into some extreme sexual behavior. Homosexuality might fit in there."

"Doesn't seem all that extreme to me," Sullivan said. "Homosexuality."

"You don't know the details," Virgil said. "But here's the thing that hangs me up. Bobby wanted to talk to *you*. Not his father, or one of his pals. So, I have the feeling that you would already know something about what he wanted to talk about, and that most likely would have to do with sex. You say it's not Crocker, not Flood, so it has to be Kelly Baker. But why would he want to talk to you about Baker?"

"I don't know," Sullivan said. "Maybe because I knew about the situation between them."

"He never said anything to you about Baker being involved in . . . extreme sexual situations?"

Sullivan let a grin show. "That's the second time you guys have used the phrase. . . . I'm starting to get interested. But no. He never mentioned anything like that."

"Damnit. I was hoping for magic," Virgil said.

"Let's go back on the record, so I can get a few questions in," Sullivan said, flipping open his notebook.

"Talk to Lee," Virgil said. "I've got to make some phone calls before it gets too late."

"I'm going to say that you were called in to work the case," Sullivan said.

"That's fine. Refer to me as the affable, good-looking, outdoorsy blond guy," Virgil said.

"With a serious line of bullshit," Coakley added.

VIRGIL CALLED Jacob Flood's home number, got a woman who said she was his daughter, and who said, "Mother's out. She'll be back at supper time."

"Does she have a cell phone?"

"No. I can give her a message."

Virgil identified himself and said that he'd like to come over after supper. He left his cell phone number and asked for a call-back if Alma Flood wouldn't be there.

He called the duty officer in St. Paul, learned that Beatrice Sawyer and Don Baldwin had the crime-scene van and should be at Crocker's place. He called Sawyer, a cheerful middle-aged woman, who, Virgil thought, was sometimes a little too interested in death.

"Got here half an hour ago and had a look, eyeballin' it," Sawyer said. "It's murder, all right. Tell you something else—the sun went down, and it's dark as the inside of a horse's ass out here."

"You're sure?"

"Well, I've never actually been inside a horse's ass."

"About the murder?" Virgil asked.

"We feel that after the slug penetrated his lower jaw,

tongue, roof of his mouth, sinus passages, eye socket, brain, and skull, he probably wouldn't have had time to wipe the gun, or any interest in doing so," Sawyer said. "But the gun was wiped. With a cotton blouse, we think. A couple threads got caught in the action. Ergo . . ."

"All right. So he wasn't alone," Virgil said. "You saw his penis? Exposed?"

"Yes. We believe he was involved in heterosexual activity immediately prior to his demise. Whether he actually ejaculated we won't know until the autopsy is done, but we have no signs of semen on his clothing or the couch."

"There was a suggestion here, by the sheriff, that he may have been involved in oral sex," Virgil said.

"That would be accurate," she said.

Virgil was surprised that she was so positive. "Really?"

"Yes. Because that explains the lipstick on his penis," she said. "That's also why we think it was heterosexual, and a blouse was involved in the gun-wiping. We could be wrong, but we rarely are."

"Bea . . . you're my huckleberry."

"Yeah, you say that to everybody," she said. "If it was oral sex, we have the possibility of getting some DNA. I won't go into the details of how we plan to collect it."

"Thank you."

"But we will be doing that. I'll tell you, Virgil, there might not be much more. This shag carpet, this fuzzy couch, there was a blanket . . . it's an old house, and there's a lot of dirt around. The furnace has been blowing dust on everything. It's going to be a chemical mess. Our best hope is the DNA on his penis, and we'll check the fly of his pants."

"We're also looking for a pair of uniform pants, green wool, with blood on them," Virgil said. "Could be a very small amount, but you've got to find them. Check every pair of green wool uniform pants you can find. The blood comes from a ripped fingernail, so there might not be much. We'll need DNA on that, too."

"If it's there, we'll get it," she said.

"Bea . . ."

"Don't say it," she said. "The huckleberry thing. Once was annoying enough."

ON HIS WAY back down the hall to Coakley's office, Virgil got a local call, from a number he didn't recognize. He answered, and found Bob Tripp's father on the other end. "I've talked to my wife, and we're going over to the funeral home tonight at seven-thirty. If you wanted to get here at seven twenty-five, we could put you up in Bob's room by yourself. We'd just as soon not be here when you go through it."

"I'll see you then," Virgil said. "Thank you."

Coakley was alone when Virgil got to her office. She had her boots back on the wastebasket, and was staring out her office window. When Virgil stuck his head in, she pointed at a visitor's chair.

"Look a little bummed," Virgil said.

"I am."

"We'll get this cleared up, you'll be the town heroine," Virgil said.

"Three murders," she said. "And probably four. You know the last thing I did before I got elected sheriff? My last investigation? I was looking for some kid who was going around keying trucks."

"Catch him?"

"No, but I know who did it," she said. "I got myself close to the little asshole's father, down at the diner, in the next booth. I was having lunch with the chief, and I said, 'There's gonna be trouble when I catch this kid. He's done fifty thousand dollars' worth of damage, and the insurance companies will be after him or his parents with a chain saw.' That stopped it, you betcha."

"Well, that's good," Virgil said.

"But you never did car-keying investigations," she said. "And I can tell you, you can flat get whiplash from the change in speed, from car-keying to quadruple murder."

"Never did a car-keying investigation, but I once investigated the theft of toddlers' pants," Virgil said. He told her about it, and they exchanged a few more stories, and Virgil told her about the phone calls, and finally she sighed and said, "It's supper time. You should get out to Flood's, and I'm going home to cook some . . . crap. Macaroni and cheese. I can't stand to think about it."

"So take some time, cook something good. Think about the case while you're doing it. Call me when you think of something."

She poked a finger at him. "And you call me. Tonight.

I want to hear about Flood, and about Bob Tripp's room. Tonight."

They walked out to the parking lot together, and then Coakley said, a frown on her face, "By the way, when we were talking to Pat, you said you could think of a few scenarios where Crocker didn't kill Bobby. So what're the scenarios?"

Virgil shrugged. "Crocker is having an affair with a female deputy, who came in to shut up Bobby. She kills him, while Crocker is off someplace, doing something. Gets her pants scratched. But she's worried that Crocker is going to tell somebody that she was there—use her for an alibi, if somebody finds out Bobby was murdered. And maybe she knows enough about autopsies to know that we might find out. So she goes over to Crocker's and kills him to shut him up, before he can tell anyone that she was at the jail."

"Well, goddamnit, Virgil, you're coming back on me again," she said.

"No, I'm not," Virgil said. "I was just thinking of scenarios. Besides . . ."

"Besides, what?"

"Bobby was a star athlete," Virgil said. "I don't think you're strong enough to keep him pinned long enough to strangle him."

"Ahh . . . Go away."

"You gonna think about it?" Virgil asked. "The scenario?"

"I'll think about it, but it's bullshit," she said, and Virgil went away.

VIRGIL GOT to the Flood house well past dark, but could tell the house was a big one, a cube, white clapboard around the first floor, dark brown shingles around the second floor and the attic level. It sat squarely facing the county highway, on a low rise a hundred yards back, with a shelterbelt of fir trees to the northwest and west, dark against the Milky Way. Five snowmobiles were rolling down the ditch to Virgil's left as he came to the Floods' driveway, and they went bucketing on past into the night.

The yard was illuminated by three lights—one over a side door to the house, a yard light on a pole by the corner of the house, and another on a pole by the barn. The barn and a couple of lower outbuildings, a garage and a machine shed, sat off to the right of the drive, with the glint of a silvery propane tank off to the left. No cars were visible in the yard lights: Everything was buttoned up, and dark.

Virgil could see no tracks going to the front porch as he came up the drive; not unusual. The side door would be the main entry. He climbed out of the truck, took a second to look around, and to feel the cold night air on his face, and to look at the stars, then walked to the side door and rang the bell.

He could hear a thumping inside, somebody running. A moment later, the door popped open. Two teenage girls stood looking at him, in the dim light of a small overhead bulb, and he nodded and said, "I'm Virgil Flowers," and one said, "Yes, we were waiting," and the other, "Come in. Wipe your boots."

"I could take the boots off."

"No need. Nobody else does."

The girls appeared to be about twelve and fourteen, junior high school age. They were dressed almost identically, in dark blue jumpers with white blouses and black tights, with black lace-up shoes. They were sallow with winter, with deep shadows under their eyes: Their father had been murdered.

Virgil asked, "So, what are your names?"

"I'm Edna," said the older one, and the younger one said, "Helen."

He followed them up four stairs into a kitchen and around a corner and through another door into a living room. One of the girls called ahead, "Mother, Mr. Flowers is here."

Alma Flood was sitting on a couch in a book-lined living room, a reading lamp over her shoulder, a Bible on the arm of her chair. A man, older, big, farm-weathered with a white beard, a big red nose, and small black eyes, sat facing her on a recliner chair. A glassed-in bookcase, built under the stairs going up to the second floor, was full of what looked like fifty-year-old novels, the kind you'd find in a used-book store or an aging North Woods resort.

Alma Flood was square in the body, as the girls would be, with her hair pulled into a bun; she wore a dark brown dress. There was a resemblance between her and the older man, and Virgil thought he might be Alma Flood's father. She said, "Mr. Flowers. You have news?"

"Maybe," Virgil said, smiling. The man gestured at the second recliner in the group of furniture, and Virgil sat down. A comfortable chair, and the house looked prosperous; but no sign of a television set. Virgil said, "You know the sheriff arrested Bob Tripp for Mr. Flood's murder. Bob Tripp was then killed in jail—"

"I thought he committed suicide," the older man said.

Virgil said, in his polite voice, "I'm sorry, who are you?"

"Emmett Einstadt. I'm Alma's father."

"Okay. . . . An autopsy was done on Tripp, and the medical examiner believes that he was murdered."

"That's nonsense," Einstadt snapped. "We were told by the sheriff herself that there was nobody there but Jim Crocker."

Virgil nodded. "That's correct. The autopsy turned up indications that Tripp may have been killed by Crocker."

"Oh, no, that's not possible. Jim Crocker is a righteous man," Alma Flood said.

"When we went to talk to Deputy Crocker this afternoon, we found him dead at his house. He'd also been murdered."

They were astonished. Not faking it at all, as far as Virgil could tell. Alma's hands went to the sides of her head: "Jim Crocker is dead?"

"Somebody shot him," Virgil said. "There are indications that it may have been a woman."

VIRGIL GOT ALONG okay with animals—dogs, horses, chickens—but his relationships with them were nothing special. Cats were different. For some reason, which he didn't entirely understand, cats liked him.

He'd come from a cat family, of course, and that might have had something to do with it. They'd supported numerous cats over the years, ranging from the conservative red tabby Luther to the radical black Savonarola, with a dozen in between, all named for religious figures by Virgil's minister father. Now a cat walked into the Floods' living room and sniffed at him, and Virgil reached out a hand.

Alma Flood and Einstadt exchanged exclamations about Crocker—"Can you believe that? How could that happen? What's going on?"—and then Edna Flood said to Virgil, about the cat, "Don't try to pet her. She'll bite your fingers off."

Virgil nodded and pulled his hand back, and he gave them a short summary of the findings at Crocker's place, then asked, "Do you know any reason Jim Crocker would want to . . . take revenge on Tripp, because of what happened to Mr. Flood?"

"Well, they were friends all their lives," Einstadt said. "If they weren't hanging around here when they were kids, they were hanging around the Crocker place.

Started rabbit hunting together when they were ten, when we gave them their first .22s."

"So there might be something," Virgil suggested.

"There might be, but I can't see Jim killing because of that. He'd let the law take its course," Einstadt said. "If justice didn't get done, then he might . . . well, as a matter of fact, I doubt he'd do anything. He wasn't that kind."

The cat sniffed Virgil's pant leg, then hopped up on the arm of the chair, sniffed his ear, and then crawled up on his shoulders and settled down behind his neck. He could hear her purring.

"That's the darnedest thing I've seen in years," Helen Flood said, as though she were forty.

Virgil reached back and scratched the cat under the ear, and asked, "Did any of you know, or did Mr. Flood know, a girl named Kelly Baker, who was killed a year or so ago down by Estherville? She came from down south of here, a few miles . . ."

Flood and Einstadt looked at each other, and then both shook their heads. "We know them," Einstadt said. "They belong to the same church we do. But we don't know them well. We're not close. We know about what happened to Kelly Baker, of course. Everybody was talking about it."

Alma Flood asked, "Do you think they are connected? Kelly Baker and what happened to Jacob? That the Tripp boy did it?"

Virgil had been considering the possibility, but hadn't worked through it until Alma's question clocked a new scenario into place: What if Tripp and some other kids had been using Baker, and Flood found out? What if Tripp had confessed to Crocker, and Crocker had killed him because of some relationship between himself and the Baker family? And that the other person involved in the murder of Baker had killed Crocker . . .

But that didn't work well: Crocker had been involved with a woman. Could there have been some kind of teenage sex ring, that included females, and something went wrong with Kelly Baker? But why wouldn't Crocker simply have alerted the sheriff, rather than murdering Tripp?

There was no logic to it—though that didn't always mean much. But Virgil shook his head at Alma Flood and said, "No, we can't make that work. Although Tripp did know Kelly Baker."

"Then you've got one boy you know for sure is a cold-blooded killer, who killed Jake. And he knew another girl who was killed, somehow. I won't tell you how to do your business, but that looks like a solid connection to me," Einstadt said. "How many murderers do we got in this county, anyway? Looks to me like the Tripp boy and one of his friends might have been up to something here."

Another scenario flashed: Suppose Kelly Baker had been gay, and they had a three- or four-way thing going, involving the other woman? Too far-fetched . . .

"Well, we'll sure look into it," Virgil said. "Like I said, we think Crocker was murdered. We'll know for sure soon enough, and we'll probably get some DNA from the killer." The cat made a snogging sound behind his ear, and he reached back and scratched her again.

They talked for a while longer, but on the central issue—what Jacob Flood might have known, or said, that triggered his murder—they came up empty. "I'd never heard of this Tripp boy before we were told that they arrested him," Alma Flood said.

When they were done, Virgil stood up and said, "I may come back, if I find more questions. I'm not familiar with this corner of the county. But if you talk to your acquaintances around here, you might ask if anybody knows of a connection between Deputy Crocker and Kelly Baker. Or Crocker and Tripp, for that matter."

"We'll do it," Einstadt said. "We're just buckling down for winter, so we'll be coming and going—we'll see a few folks."

Virgil gave them a business card, carefully removed the cat from his shoulders, scratched her head, and put her back on the floor. "I appreciate all your help," he said.

WHEN HE WAS GONE, Einstadt looked at Alma Flood and said, "You know who killed Crocker?"

"I was thinking Kathleen."

"I was thinking the same thing," he said. "I'll get Morgan and we'll go have a talk with her."

He stood up and said, "Rooney will be over tomorrow."

Alma Flood whined, "We can get along all right. We don't need Rooney."

"Rooney's a good man and you'll knock some edges

off him. The thing about it is, you leave a bunch of women alone in a house like this, you can't tell what they'll get up to. Rooney'll handle that, and take care of the farm, too."

"He's rougher'n a cob," Alma Flood said.

"Like I said: You'll knock some edges off him."

"Be happy if he took a bath," Alma Flood muttered.

"I'll tell him that," Einstadt said. He looked at the two girls, standing in a corner. "You girls get your asses upstairs. I'll be up in a minute."

One of them said, "Yes, Grandpa," the other one said nothing, and they both headed for the stairs.

Einstadt said to his daughter, "When Rooney gets here tomorrow, I want you to make him welcome. I don't want any trouble about this. But—don't tell anyone that he's moving in. That's private business."

He turned away and followed the girls toward the stairs. He hadn't had any sex for two days, and he needed it, and the last time he'd bent Alma over the kitchen table, she'd been dry as a stick.

The girls, though . . .

He left Alma sitting in her chair, with her Bible, and hurried up the stairs, the hunger upon him.

6

The Floods were unusual, Virgil thought, as he drove away. Reticent. The daughters looked morose, as might be expected, but had never mentioned their father. Neither had Alma Flood or Emmett Einstadt, except in direct discussion. There was no hand-wringing or remembrance or tears: They spoke of him almost as though he were a distant acquaintance.

Einstadt looked like an Old Testament image of Abraham, as he was about to stick the knife in Isaac's neck. And the way they dressed, all brown, black, and blue—he didn't know if this was a religious thing, similar to the plain dress of the Amish, or personal preference.

Back at Homestead, Virgil took the exit, looked at his watch: coming up on seven o'clock, not enough time to eat before he had to be at the Tripps'. He stopped at a convenience store, got a bottle of orange juice, a pack of pink Hostess Sno Balls, and a couple of hunting magazines to take back to the motel.

One of the problems with working in a small town

was that whenever you went somewhere, you were already *there*—it was only six or eight or ten minutes from one end to the other, so if you were running early, you stayed early, and if you were running late, there was no way to make it up by speeding or taking shortcuts.

He stopped a block from the Tripps', parked, ate the Sno Balls and drank the juice, and watched a man walking along the dark street with two Labrador retrievers. The dogs were looking for a comfortable snowbank in which to take a dump; the product of their efforts would sink into the snow and freeze, and in March, when the snow went away, there it'd be. Sometimes, if your yard was on a popular corner, whole piles of newly thawed dog poop ushered in the spring.

Virgil thought about the unfairness of it, and checked his watch. Still early, but not too; he stuffed the juice bottle and Sno Ball packaging in a trash bag hung from the back of the passenger seat, and went on down the block.

THE TRIPPS HAD GOTTEN dressed up for their visit to the funeral home. George Tripp was wearing a church suit, black wool with a white shirt and black-and-blue tie, and Irma was wearing a black dress with black boots with low heels. They looked simply, ineffably, sad.

George Tripp was standing in front of the picture window again, waiting for him, and opened the door when he came up the walk. "Come in, please," he said.

Irma Tripp came into the living room, carrying a long

coat. She said, "We haven't gone into his room except once, to make his bed. It's just . . . too much."

"Did you figure anything out?" George Tripp asked.

"We did learn one thing—your son did know Kelly Baker," Virgil said. "We know that for sure. They hung around together the summer before last, but probably stopped seeing each other when the summer ended. We don't think they were intimate, but, of course, we really don't know, one way or the other."

"Crocker killed them both," George Tripp said. "Or Flood killed the Baker girl, maybe with Crocker. Is that what you think?"

"It's a possibility," Virgil said. "But I just talked to Flood's wife, and they turn it around from that—they think your son killed Baker, and Flood found out something, so Bobby killed him." They both objected, and Virgil held up his hands: "I'm just sayin'. I will tell you that I'm not buying any theories, yet. But we know that we have at least one killer running around loose, and that's the thread we've got to pull on."

"You don't have any idea who he is?" Irma Tripp asked.

"Well, we're pretty sure it's not a *he*. We think it's a woman," Virgil said. "Somebody who was intimate with Deputy Crocker. We're pushing that aspect of it."

"If you look hard enough, you'll find out that Bobby comes out okay," George Tripp said.

"That's why I want to look at his room," Virgil said. "Maybe there's something. Maybe he left a letter or a note or something that would explain this to us."

Bob Tripp's bedroom was at the far end of the house, in the front corner. The bed was neatly made—Irma went in and made it after he was killed, as though it were a final favor—but the rest of the room was about as messy as any teenage boy's might be. Books and papers were scattered over a desk, where a MacBook sat in front of an old-fashioned wooden office chair. A backpack lay at the foot of the bed, and a sports trophy, with a tennis player on top, stood on a chest of drawers. There were none of the expected jocko pennants on the wall, but there were posters for the Minnesota Vikings and New Orleans Saints, a couple dozen postcards, mostly of nude women, stuck on the wall with pushpins. The place smelled faintly of sweat socks and male deodorant.

Irma said, "Those postcards aren't anything—those dumb boys would find them and mail them to their friends with, you know, messages, on the back. Trying to embarrass each other. They were all doing it."

"We'll just leave you," George Tripp said. "We don't want to see any of this, to be honest. And we have our appointment, you know, we have to pick out . . ." He trailed off, and Virgil mentally filled it in: a coffin.

"Take off," Virgil said. "I'll wait until you get back."

They left him, but then Virgil stepped into the hallway and asked, "Did he have a cell phone?"

"Yes, it's on his desk."

"Okay. You don't know if he had a password on his computer, do you?"

Irma smiled for the first time, an almost shy smile, and she said, "Yes, he did, and he wouldn't tell us what it was. He said it was his private business. You know, I think with what boys look at on the Internet . . . We have wireless."

"Okay. I may want to take the computer with me," Virgil said. "We have some people in St. Paul who can work around the password."

George Tripp said, "I don't know how valuable it might be. . . ."

"I'll get it back to you," Virgil said. "I'll give you a receipt. You go on—we'll work it out later."

HE WENT to the computer first, and the first thing it did was ask for a password. He tried "Tripp" and "BJ" and "Bobby" and "RJ," "Irma," and "George," and, from a school poster taped to the wall, "Cardinals" and "Vikings," "wide receiver" and "receiver." Nothing worked.

He checked the phone and came up with a list of names and phone numbers. He recognized "Sullivan," the reporter, but the rest meant nothing to him. No Baker, Flood, or Crocker.

The phone would have to be run. He set it aside and turned to the room, starting with the chest of drawers. He pulled each drawer three-quarters of the way out, felt through the underwear and summer clothing, then pulled each drawer completely free to look under it.

Under the bottom drawer he found a plastic baggie containing a couple of joints and a package of rolling papers. He thought about it for a moment, then put the dope and the papers in his pocket.

Going to the closet, he shook down all the clothing, looking for paper, found a few gasoline receipts. Nothing in the shoes.

On impulse, he went back to the computer and typed in "gay" and "homosexual" and "homo" and the computer shook him off. He lifted the mattress off the box springs, found nothing. He went through the desk drawer, found it stuffed with receipts, ticket stubs, photographs. Nothing that set off a buzz.

He started sifting through papers and books, looking for anything that might be personal. Not much—no notes from anyone, just old schoolwork. The backpack contained workout clothes and two twenty-pound weights, probably to work his quads, and a printed-out calendar with a workout schedule on it, over the background image of a running horse, its tail flaring out behind it.

And a much-folded piece of copy paper, with a line drawing of the Statue of Liberty on it. No words, just the drawing. There was a long oval drawn from the base of the statue right up to its face, which might have been the number "eight" but, if so, heavily distorted, with the upper loop nearly round, the lower loop a very long oval. The distortion seemed to mean something, Virgil thought, but he couldn't think what—but it looked as though the paper had been something that Tripp had looked at over and over, and carried with him on his daily workouts.

Virgil looked at the statue drawing, then the calendar with the horse, went back to the computer, typed "Mustangs"—the Southwest Minnesota State Mustangs, where Tripp would have gone to college—and the computer bit: He was in.

"Excellent," he said to himself, as the Mac started to load.

He found 776 incoming e-mail messages and 538 outgoing. He clicked on the "From" queue to alphabetize the incoming messages, and found twenty-two from KBaker.

Nothing from a Crocker or a Flood.

With the sense that he was on to something, he began paging through the KBaker mail, noting the dates. The e-mail began in June of the summer before last, and rather than ending at the end of the summer, continued through the autumn, with the final KBaker note coming two days before Baker was killed.

As he went through the mail, his sense of anticipation dwindled: The exchanges were letters between teenagers, about when Baker would be in town, about who was dating whom, about summer jobs, about football. Baker was apparently religious: She mentioned a couple of times that she couldn't come to town because she had to go to church that night—the nights included Tuesday and Friday.

Three interesting notes from Baker.

The first: "Definite stud muffin."

The second: "I wish I could go with you. If I was in high school, it'd almost be like I was normal. You're about the only outside person that I know, who knows how lonely this can be."

The third: "Can't: Got Liberty."

The third note was the last e-mail from Baker, the one just before she was killed. He looked for antecedents to the two notes, either from Baker or Tripp, and found nothing. They were like remnants of oral conversations.

The e-mail, as a whole, had a curious flatness to it: no flirtation, nothing in the least controversial. Something, he thought, was missing—and he suspected that Tripp had cleaned it up. The "definite stud muffin" message struck Virgil as a reply to something—and possibly a hint that Baker knew that Tripp was gay, and was commenting on some previous e-mail about somebody Tripp was attracted to.

"Can't: Got Liberty." There was that paper in the backpack with the Statue of Liberty drawing on it. A connection? But to what? Or who? Was the capitalized word "Liberty" a proper noun, a specific person or place?

Could the computer guys recover the deleted mail? Have to try.

He looked through all the rest of the mail, scanning quickly, and most of it was the same as the mail to and from Kelly: Meet me there, let's do this or that, going up to the MOA with my folks. MOA was Mall of America, in the Twin Cities.

Huh.

He went to Safari, the browser, and clicked on "History," and came up empty—not a single entry. He checked the settings and found that Tripp had set the browser to erase his website visits on a daily basis.

He went to the "Security" icon, clicked on it, and found that the computer was set to accept cookies from the sites Tripp visited. He clicked on "Show Cookies" and came up with a list that ran into the hundreds of items. Scanning down the list, he found a lot of what appeared to be sports sites and, from the names, what appeared to be gay porno sites.

All right, he knew that.

A thought popped into his head. What if Flood had somehow discovered that Tripp was gay, had ridiculed him, or challenged him—or even solicited him—and Tripp had lashed out purely in anger, with no other connection to anything?

No: Tripp had taken the T-ball bat from home. He'd gone to work prepared to kill Flood.

Besides, there were too many dead people for something that simple.

And where in the hell did a woman fit in, a killer?

Virgil continued working the room, no longer expecting to find much: Tripp had been covering himself.

THE TRIPPS WERE back in a little under an hour, and Virgil was done with the room, sitting on the bed, looking around, wondering what he'd missed. He heard them come in, sighed, stood up, picked up the cell phone and the computer, and walked down the hall to meet them.

"Find anything?" George Tripp asked.

"I don't know—I *will* have to take the computer. Your son was e-mailing back and forth with Kelly Baker, right up until the time she was killed. They were pretty friendly. . . ."

"You figured out the password?"

"Mustangs," Virgil said, and George Tripp showed the tiniest of smiles.

"How friendly were they?" Irma asked. She asked in a way, Virgil thought, that solicited a response that Bobby Tripp and Kelly Baker were in bed together. Because, Virgil realized, Irma knew or suspected that her son was gay.

"Friendly. I can't say more than that, but there's no feel of . . . violence in it," Virgil said. "Of potential violence. At this point, I really don't believe your son was involved in hurting her."

"Of course he wasn't," George Tripp said. "It was that goddamn Flood, or Crocker, or both of them."

"I'm going to look into that," Virgil said.

He asked them to go through the contact list on Tripp's phone; standing together, they did that, and identified each of the people on the list, including Sullivan, who, they said, had interviewed their son a half dozen times.

"Everybody knew Bobby was going to be a college star. He could've gone to the Gophers, but they wanted to make a cornerback out of him and he didn't want that," George said. Wistful, now, with a glint of tears in his eyes: "He was going to be something."

On his way to the motel, Virgil threw the joints out the window—they were biodegradable—and crumbled the Ziploc bag into the trash. No need for Tripp's parents to know about that.

He called Coakley from the motel, told her about the search, about the relationship with Baker, and about the "Liberty" note.

"Good, sounds like you're getting somewhere," she said. "I set up meetings with both of the female deputies for tomorrow morning. You're not invited. I've been thinking about them since I left the office, and I already know they're not involved. I'll push them anyway, which means my popularity is going to take a hit, but I'll do it."

"You've got four years—I think pushing them now will be pretty small potatoes when you break these murders," Virgil said.

"When I get done, to show that I trust them, I'm sending all of them out to the countryside around Battenberg, to talk to folks," Coakley said. "The community out there is so sparse that somebody must know who Crocker was sleeping with—people know each other's cars, and even if it was just seeing a car parked in his driveway, somebody knows."

"Okay. I want to talk to Kelly Baker's parents. There's something going on there."

"See you tomorrow," she said.

HE MADE a late check with Bea Sawyer: "We got the pants," she said. "We can see a snag and what could be blood, and from what you said, I believe it is. So does Don. There's enough blood for a DNA check, so we'll be able to nail that down for you."

"Excellent. When will you be done?" Virgil asked.

"We've already shipped the body up to Ike in Mankato," Sawyer said. "We're going through the house now, but we're about to quit. We'll be back tomorrow."

"You at the Holiday?"

"Nah, we're staying at a little ma-and-pa place in Battenberg. Pretty handy," she said.

"All right. I'll see you out there tomorrow. Try not to destroy any evidence."

He called Coakley back. "Got a piece of information for you: The crime-scene guys have a pair of uniform pants at Crocker's, with a snag and a smear of blood. Probably Tripp's, I expect."

"Good. That really does take my other people out of it," she said.

"Pretty much," Virgil agreed.

Two inches of snow fell overnight, kicked out of an Alberta Clipper that swung down through the state and just as quickly departed. Virgil could hear the winds coming up as he went to bed, and then the muffling effect of the snow.

He thought about God for a while, and the early and traumatic end of expectations: Bobby Tripp "would have been something," his father said, and those expectations were now gone and might never have existed.

And he thought about the commonality of comfort, stretching back over the centuries and millennia, a guy lying alone in a warm space, listening to a clipper just outside the cave, igloo, hut, teepee, motel, whatever, a long thread reaching all the way back to the apes.

Then he went to sleep.

IN THE MORNING, he'd just gotten out of the shower when his cell phone rang, and Coakley said, "Why don't we hook up at the Yellow Dog? Get some pancakes."

"Half an hour," Virgil said.

He got dressed, checked e-mail, packed up his computer, and put on his parka. The clipper had slipped away, and the day would be sunny but cold: He brushed the light, fluffy snow off the truck and, by the time he was done, could feel the sharp near-zero temps on his cheekbones.

He pulled into the café just as Coakley did, and she asked, as she got out of her truck, "Any more ideas?"

"I think you had the best one—go out to Battenberg and stir around, see what happens."

They went inside, got a booth, peeled off their parkas. Coakley was wearing a plaid wool shirt over a black turtleneck, with just a hint of lipstick. They discovered a common interest in blueberry pancakes and link sausages, and after they ordered, she said, "Kelly Baker—it has to be local. I mean, local-local. Here, not Estherville, not Iowa."

"Close to here," Virgil agreed. "The killers weren't travelers."

The pancakes arrived with the café owner, who introduced himself as Bill Jacoby, and asked if there was anything new in the case. "Maybe," Virgil said. "We think whoever killed Deputy Crocker was a woman, and we're looking around for whoever may have had an ongoing sexual relationship with him."

"He was killed by somebody he was sleeping with?"

"We think so," Virgil said. There were a couple of dozen people in the café, and the nearby tables had gone quiet. "We're kind of looking around for someone who knows who that might be."

"Well, I don't," Jacoby said. "Be an interesting thing to know, though."

"And something else," Virgil said. "You know that Kelly Baker girl who was killed down by Estherville a year ago? We think that murder is tied into the new ones."

"Really," Jacoby said. "Man, that's freaky. That's a lot of dead people."

"Sure is. We're looking for all the connections we can find," Virgil said.

A grizzled, rancher-looking guy in the booth behind Coakley said, "You know, you should talk to Son Wood. He used to hang around with Crocker, some, and they go back a ways. He might know who Crocker was going with."

Virgil leaned sideways so he could see the guy past Coakley: "Son Wood. S-O-N? Where's he at?"

"He's got Son Wood's Surface Sealers out on 15 South," the rancher-guy said.

Coakley said, with a little razor in her voice, "Virgil, eat your pancakes. They're getting cold."

Virgil said, "Hey. I'm just trying to be a friendly guy."

"Come in anytime for a cup of coffee," Jacoby said. "We don't have doughnuts, but we got twelve kinds of pie."

"I'll do that," Virgil said.

WHEN JACOBY HAD GONE, Coakley leaned into the table and said, "What? You're a talk-show host?"

He said, "What good does it do to keep the information private? The killers know everything we do. Why shouldn't the taxpayers know it?"

She said, "Well." Thought about it, then said, "It doesn't seem law enforcement–like."

"That's a problem for law enforcement," Virgil said. "You can get a lot more done if you ask around, and spread the joy."

"I'm still a little annoyed," she said. "Sitting here in a café, blabbing to every Tom, Dick, and Harry."

"Your eyes sparkle when you're annoyed," he said, giving her his second-best cowboy grin. His first-best grin was so powerful that he reserved it for places where the woman had her back against something, for support; like a mattress.

"For God's sakes, Virgil, try to keep your mind on what you're doing. . . ."

"Slender, yet firm body," Virgil said, wiggling his eyebrows at her.

She showed some teeth. "I'm gonna stick this pancake up your nose, in about one minute."

"All right. All right," he said, holding up his hands, palms out. "I'll suppress my feelings, if you say so. You're the sheriff."

"I'm going to talk to the girls, then send them out to Battenberg. I'll go with them. I've got John Kraus talking to that list of kids on Bobby's phone. What are you doing?"

"Well, I developed one solid lead since last night," Virgil said.

"Really?" Her eyebrows popped up.

"Yes. There's a guy named Son Wood on Highway 15 South who hung out with Crocker, and who might know what women he was hanging with. I'm gonna talk to him."

"Virgil . . ."

"Then, I'm going to go talk to Kelly Baker's parents."

"Good. That's a plan. Maybe I'll meet you there—I've never talked to them, myself."

THEY FINISHED their pancakes under the eyes of the café patrons, Virgil telling her about the strangeness of the Floods, and about this and that. Coakley looked at her watch and took a last hit of her coffee and said, "Call me."

She left, and Virgil watched her go. Slender, yet firm body. And she gave him a hard time, but she sort of liked it. It was, Virgil thought, drifting toward the philosophical, a truism that no woman was really upset when somebody suggested she was attractive.

Jacoby came over with a carafe: "More coffee?"

"Thanks, Bill—maybe a half cup."

"Anything more that Lee didn't want us to know?" Jacoby asked as he poured.

"Well, not really, not much that wasn't in the paper this morning. We know the Tripp boy killed Flood, and now we know that Deputy Crocker killed Tripp. We've got that nailed down with DNA, and I expect we'll get some DNA off Crocker's body, from the woman, so if we can find her, we'll nail that down, too."

"DNA from the woman—what, like a hair? Blood?"

"Saliva traces," Virgil said.

Jacoby leaned forward and dropped his voice. "Saliva? How'd you know where to look?"

"Crocker was . . . his dick was sticking out," Virgil said, pitching his voice down below Jacoby's.

"You mean . . . ?"

"I do."

"Oh, jeez. Maybe I ought to try to find her before you do," Jacoby said.

"Think about it, Bill. What happened to Crocker."

Jacoby scratched once, in the general area of his groin, and muttered, "Might be worth it. I'm so goddamn horny the crack of dawn ain't safe."

7

Virgil hadn't known exactly what a surface sealer did, but when he found the small dealership and showroom, he discovered that Son Wood used a variety of paintlike substances to seal concrete or wood floors from whatever might get poured on them—like cow or pig urine, gasoline or oil, or grease.

An auburn-haired woman was sitting behind the reception counter, typing into a computer screen and, when Virgil walked in, took off her reading glasses and asked, "Are you Harvey?"

"Nope. I'm Virgil. Flowers. I'm an agent for the state Bureau of Criminal Apprehension, looking into your murders. Is Mr. Wood around?"

"Well, yes, he's in the back, talking to Roger. Can I tell him what it's about? Specifically?"

"He was a friend of Jim Crocker's, and we're talking to all of Crocker's friends."

"That was just *terrible*," she said. "Let me get him."

WOOD CAME OUT a moment later, followed by the woman. He was a tall man, thin, weathered, with flinty blue eyes and a three-day beard. He was wearing a red flannel shirt and pipe-stem jeans, and cowboy boots. He and Virgil shook hands and Virgil said, "We've been interviewing people around town, and a couple have mentioned that you knew Deputy Crocker. We know that he'd been intimate with a woman shortly before he died, and we'd really like to talk to her. Do you have any ideas?"

"Well, you know, I don't," Wood said. "As a matter of fact, I can tell you right out front that I'm surprised there was a woman with him, because he never seemed that much interested."

"In women?"

"Well, not so much women . . . as any particular woman." Wood scratched his head, just above his left ear, and said, "I don't know how to put it. He was interested in women, okay? He was married for a while, but I never knew him to *date*. You see what I'm saying? He didn't seem interested in particular women. He didn't go out with anyone."

"Would there have been any takers?" Virgil asked. "If he started looking?"

"Oh, yeah. There's not a big surplus of women around here, but he had a good job. You know how it is."

Virgil nodded. "So you guys hung out, had a few beers. . . ."

"That was pretty much it. We'd go fishing a couple times a year," Wood said. "We weren't all that close. I'm married and he's single . . . but, yeah, we go back a way."

"Can you think of anything . . . ?"

"Well, you know he was tight with Jake Flood. They knew each other since they were kids. There must be something in there . . . something in that whole mess. Jake getting killed, then Jim."

Virgil said, "That's what we think, too. We're looking for the connection."

"Maybe you ought to talk to his ex-wife," Wood suggested. "She's over in Jackson, her name's Kathleen Spooner. Kate. Changed her name back to her maiden name after they broke up."

"Bitter breakup?"

"Well—no. He told me he didn't know what the hell happened. He came home one day, and she said she was moving on, that she'd filed for divorce that day at the courthouse, and did he want pork chops for dinner, or meat loaf?"

The woman chipped in: "I talked to her for a minute, downtown, and she said she just got tired of his act. She said she didn't much want to marry him in the first place, and she'd been right."

"So she just went on down the road," Wood said.

"You know if he went for the meat loaf?" Virgil asked.

"More of a pork chop man," Wood said.

They talked for a few more minutes, but nothing else came up—Wood didn't know Kelly Baker or any of her family. "I know where they're at, but they ran a pretty small grain operation, and that doesn't need my product so much."

"Do you know anything about the religion he belonged to?" Virgil asked.

"Just that it was a little unusual," Wood said. "He didn't talk about it that much, and he didn't go to services much. But some."

"I thought they stayed pretty much to themselves."

"Some of them do, some of them don't so much," Wood said. "I never exactly figured them out, because, to tell the truth, I wasn't much interested. But they're not like the Amish. I've been in some of their houses, and they have TVs and stereos and computers and so on. They're not so much for fancy cars—Fords and Chevys, mostly. But they do buy the Star Wars farm equipment. They got money."

VIRGIL GAVE HIM a card, and walked out to the truck. He'd just gotten in and started it when Wood came out of the front of the showroom, jogging toward the truck, his shoulders up against the cold. He pointed at the passenger seat, and Virgil popped the door and Wood climbed in.

"I didn't want to say a couple things in front of Delores, because she's a good bookkeeper, but the woman does tend to run her mouth. This all might be nothing, and I don't want to get good people in trouble, because of a bunch of rumors."

"They won't be in trouble, if they didn't do anything," Virgil said.

Wood shook his head and said, "Okay: Every few years I'm out at the Flood place. They run a hundred head of Charolais up there, grass-fed stuff for the specialty stores, and they've got some winter feeding platforms that I coat. . . . Anyway, I was up there a couple of years ago, and I made some comment to Jim about how religious the Floods were. He was a little loaded and he said, "Yeah, really religious, but that don't keep them from fuckin' like a bunch of goats.""

Wood paused, put his hands over the warm air registers on the dashboard, then said, "The thing is, he said it in a way like there was something weird about it. Then he shut up. When I asked him about it the next time I saw him, he said he couldn't remember saying anything like that, but I could see he did. Like he was keeping a secret. He really seemed to want to walk away from what he said."

"So what was weird?"

"Just his . . . voice. And then his attitude. Not scared, exactly, but like there was some dark secret. About the religion, I think. So—for what it's worth."

"But you really don't know about the religion."

"No, I don't. There are a lot of little different ones scattered around here, mostly, you know, Bible-thumpers of one sort or another. There's quite a few Muslims around now, immigrants, and there's even a rabbi or two over at the slaughterhouse—that's what I understand, anyway." He shook his head again, and added, "Anyway,

I thought I should mention it, because it seems odd, and because both Jim and Jake Flood have been murdered."

"Glad you did. If anything else pops into your head, give me a ring. Whoever did all this is dangerous, and we need to get him off the road."

Wood nodded and said, "The other thing that I didn't want Delores to hear is that Jim was seeing his ex every once in a while. He didn't even want me to know that, I think, but it came out a couple times. They weren't talking about getting back together, but they were . . . you know, whatever the kids call it: hooking up."

Virgil said, "Thanks for that, too. Stay in touch."

"I'll do that," Wood said, and he popped the door and ran back through the cold to his shop.

VIRGIL MADE a note to talk to Crocker's ex-wife as soon as he could, and eased out onto the highway. As soon as he got going, he called Coakley; she had finished talking to the women, was sending them out to Battenberg to knock on doors.

"I'm going out to the Bakers' place. You want to go out in your truck, or you want to ride along with me?" he asked.

"Huh. Why don't I meet you there? I might need my truck later on."

"Tell me how to get there. . . ."

She gave him some simple directions, said, "That's not the shortest way, but it's the easiest, you won't get lost—and it'll let me catch up to you."

"See you there. Before you come out, run Jacob Flood through the NCIC, see if you get a hit."

"Already did that—no hits."

"See you at Bakers'."

The trip out took half an hour, the countryside not quite flat, but rather a series of broken planes, now a frozen wash of gentle blues and grays with the new snow. Virgil had read once that Grandma Moses was a primitive painter because she thought snow was white. The writer said if you really looked at it, snow was hardly ever white. It mostly was a gentler version of the color of the sky—blue, gray, orange in the evenings and mornings, often with purple shadows. When he looked, sure enough, the guy was right, and Grandma Moses had her head up her ass.

On the way over, he called a researcher named Sandy at the BCA and asked her to find Kathleen Spooner, called Kate, formerly called Kathleen Crocker.

"If she's still in Minnesota, I'll get it in a minute or two," she said.

"Text it to me so I'll have a record."

LIKE MOST of the farmhouses around, the Baker place sat facing a county highway, a hundred yards back, perched on a rise with a windbreak of box elders and cottonwoods to the northwest. Virgil slowed to check the name on the mailbox and saw Coakley's truck coming up from behind. He waited on the side of the road, and she slowed, and pointed, and he followed her up the freshly plowed driveway to the house. On the way up the drive, his cell phone burped: a text message. He looked at the screen and found an address and a phone number for Kathleen Spooner.

Out of the truck, Coakley said, "I called ahead. They're both here, and waiting. They've got a boy, he's off studying wind power at Minnesota West in Canby."

"Would he be Bobby Tripp's age?"

Her eyes narrowed. "I think . . . he might be three or four years older. We can ask."

They were walking up to the side door of the farmhouse, and Virgil filled her in on the conversation with Son Wood, and added, "I'll try to find Crocker's ex-wife this afternoon."

"Worth a try," she said. "She's been gone for a while, though. Five or six years, I guess."

"But Wood thinks they may have been back sleeping together," Virgil said. "That's interesting. A familiar female."

"We could use some DNA. . . ."

THE BAKERS WERE as different as grapes and gravel; Leonard Baker had yellowish-red hair that flopped over one side of his head, so that if it had been black, it would have looked like Hitler's haircut. He had a pointed chin and a pointed nose, and freckles all over his face and hands.

When he nodded and smiled at them, a formal smile, as they followed him through the door, Virgil saw that he was missing one of his upper eyeteeth; and a moment later, picked up a periodic whistle that came through the empty space when Leonard said a word that began with a "W."

Louise Baker was raven-haired and black-eyed; not pretty, but noticeable. She wore a formless dress, with a tiny red-dotted floral design, that fell to her ankles, and she was not, Virgil thought, wearing anything beneath it. Like, nothing—but what was under there was definitely of an interesting quality.

Leonard Baker said, "If I understand this right, Miz Coakley thinks that our daughter's death might be mixed up with this murder at the elevator? Then we heard that Jim Crocker got killed, and that maybe a woman did it?"

"That's what we think," Virgil agreed.

"But whoever killed my daughter, they were men," Baker said. "That's what the Iowa folks said."

"That's probably right," Virgil said. "But we've discovered that a boy named Bobby Tripp murdered Jacob Flood, and then that Tripp was murdered by Deputy Crocker. And that Bobby Tripp was a friend of your daughter's. A good friend."

Louise was silent but Leonard Baker said, "Well, that's not right. I would have known about something like that."

Coakley said, "Not intimate friends . . . they didn't have a personal relationship. They were friends. They talked to each other, e-mailed each other."

"I keep a pretty sharp eye on that computer," Baker

said. Then, "But I suppose once they learn how to use it . . . we're not here all the time."

"And there are computers everywhere," Coakley said. "Libraries, schools . . ."

"We homeschooled," Louise Baker said. Her voice was crinkly, like when a sheet of vellum is crumpled in a hand. "Leonard taught her mathematics and German, and I taught her English and literature, and we both taught her religion."

Virgil caught what seemed to be an irritated look pass from Leonard to his wife when she mentioned religion, and he jumped on it.

"If you don't mind my asking, what religion? I'm a preacher's son," Virgil said.

"We have a personal and private religion," Leonard Baker said. "We really don't talk about it to nonmembers."

"Okay," Virgil said, and then quickly, following up, "Bible-based? Or . . ."

Leonard Baker nodded. "Yes. We're followers . . . well, yes. The Bible."

Virgil said, "I haven't had a chance to review all the investigation from Iowa, but I know the outlines of your daughter's case. The Iowa people say that you had no idea of what had happened with Kelly. Have you had any thoughts since that time? Has anything come up?"

The couple looked at each other, then simultaneously shook their heads. "We are mystified. The police said . . . well, that Kelly was sexually active."

"That was ridiculous," Louise Baker said. "When could she be?"

Coakley: "You let young girls work in town, things happen. They grow up so fast now."

"We didn't even know that she had male friends her own age, like this boy you're talking about," Leonard Baker said. "That she was not a virgin when she was killed—that doesn't seem possible to us. The time factor . . . when could she have gotten out? She did work, summers, but she was a quiet girl."

"It's a mystery," Louise Baker said, her voice crackling with what might have been stress.

"Do you know somebody named Liberty?" Virgil asked.

The two looked at each other again, and Virgil had a sudden intuition: They knew, and they'd lie about it. They turned back to Virgil and both shook their heads. "No. Nobody named Liberty."

They said they knew who the Floods were, but weren't really acquainted, and they did know Crocker. "He was a righteous man," Louise Baker said. "He patrolled out here, before he was assigned in town, so everybody knew him. I suppose . . . no offense, Sheriff . . . I suppose most people out here voted for him."

Leonard Baker nodded. "If he killed the Tripp boy, it was for a reason. The Tripp boy must belong to a gang. If he knew Kelly, then I think you've taken a big step in finding out who killed her."

"Do you think your son might have known Tripp?" Virgil asked.

Leonard Baker shook his head. "I don't think so. He never worked in town. He was homeschooled, too, both of them were. When he graduated, two years ago, he got a job in Blue Earth, so he never was around Homestead. And then he went off to study wind power."

They talked for a while longer, and Louise Baker asked if they should be afraid for their own lives: "There're killers out there, and they've already taken Kelly from us. What if they're crazy people?"

"If you don't know what's going on, then I think you're safe," Virgil answered. "There's a thread that links all this together, and if you're not pulling on the thread, then you should be okay."

Louise shivered. "I'm still scared."

"At times like this, you need to be strong and courageous. Don't be afraid or terrified; we're with you," Virgil said.

They nodded, and Leonard Baker said, "Just . . . mystified. Mystified."

BACK OUTSIDE, Coakley said, "That wasn't a lot of help. But they're also pointing us back to Tripp. Maybe there's something—"

"They were lying through their fuckin' teeth," Virgil said. "The Bakers know something and they're scared. That probably means they know something about their daughter's death, and they're hiding it."

"What'd they lie about?" Coakley asked. "I missed it."

"Louise said Crocker was a righteous man. Mrs. Flood said the same thing, the same words, but they deny that they know each other. Bullshit. They know each other and they've been talking. And this Bible thing, the righteousness thing. Mrs. Flood had a Bible, and now the Bakers say they belong to a Bible-based religion, and they're pretty serious about telling you that."

"So?"

"So I threw a little Deuteronomy thirty-one:six at them, one of the most famous verses in the Bible. They had no idea," Virgil said. "'Be strong and courageous. Do not be afraid or terrified because of them, for the Lord your God goes with you; he will never leave you nor forsake you.'"

"Well—just because they're Bible-based, doesn't mean they know every word," Coakley said.

"They should know those words," Virgil said. "There's something going on here, out in the countryside, and we don't know what it is, do we, Mrs. Jones?"

"My: From the Holy Bible to Bob Dylan. I'm impressed," she said. "Did you notice that Louise was a little spare on the clothing?"

"I noticed," Virgil said.

"I noticed you noticing," Coakley said.

"She didn't look prim, she didn't look controlled, like a fundamentalist usually does. She looked a little out there, in a morose kind of way," Virgil said. He smiled at Coakley. "There's something going on, and that makes me happy. Second day on the case and we've got something. We need to think about the Bakers and the Floods. About their religion. Something's going on, Lee."

"What's next?"

Virgil looked at his watch: He had time. "I've got

Kathleen Spooner's address over in Jackson. I'm going to run over and talk to her," he said. "If I have the time, I might check with Junior Baker up in Canby . . . though that might have to wait. That's a ride."

"I'm going to check back with my girls up in Battenberg," Coakley said. "Stay in touch."

8

Kathleen Spooner had her back to the wall—the front room wall—facing off the three men who'd shown up unannounced as she took her lunch break. Emmett Einstadt, flanked by two younger men, all three farmers, dressed rough in work coats and pants and boots, tracking dirty snow across her floor.

She said, keeping her voice low, controlled, "I don't know what you're talking about, Emmett. I heard Jim was killed, and I felt bad about it for one minute, but I had nothing to do with it."

"You two were going at it, the last pool," Einstadt said. "They says it was a woman who done it, and he wasn't going with nobody else."

"Old times' sake," Spooner said. She was an average-sized woman, a little heavy, but not too, with dark hair and eyes. She wore a University of Minnesota fleece, dark slacks, and a touch of red lipstick. "Besides, everybody else was taken up."

"But we thought about who else it might be, and we

can't think of nobody," said Wally Rooney. "The thing we know is, that nobody else knows, is that you're crazier than a bucket of frogs. It didn't bother you one little bit to put a bullet through his head."

"And you got the guns," said Ted Morgan.

"Killed with his own gun, is what I heard. It could have been suicide," Spooner said.

Einstadt glanced at the other two, then said, "You know what? I keep my ear to the ground, and I haven't heard it was his own gun. Nobody told me that. Anybody tell you boys that?"

The other two men shook their heads, and Morgan said, "Nobody told me."

"What I want to know, more than whether you did it, 'cause I know you did, is *why* you did it. If you tell me that, I'll give you a piece of good advice."

"Not even your advice is free, huh, Emmett?" she asked. And, "You tight sonofabitch."

Einstadt shook a finger at her, but before he could speak, she said, "That Tripp kid found out that Jake was one of the boys who was there when Kelly died. He told Jim that Jake came in with his shirt off, and he saw that Liberty head above his belt buckle, and that Kelly had told him that she was fuckin' some rough guy they called Liberty because of the tattoo. He was going to spill the beans to some newspaper guy. So Jim killed him. But by the time he got home, he was scared to death. He knew all about this crime-scene stuff, and he thought they'd figure it out."

Emmett's face had gone still, and he said, "So . . . he did right by us. Why'd you kill him?"

"He said if they got him, he wasn't going to prison. He said he knew what happened to cops in prison. He got a little drunk, and he started to cry, and that's what he said. What he meant was, he'd make a deal. He started out right, but then . . . he would of took us down."

"A deal."

"That's right. I mean, Emmett, I know you've got your theories and all, but the state's got *its* theories, and if they knew about your little religion, they'd put you *under* the jail. All of you. All of *us*. And I think there'd be some who'd talk. Look to Alma: I hear she's got the Bible real bad."

"The Bible is the core. . . ." Einstadt said.

"This is Kate Spooner you're talking to," Spooner said. "You've been talking Bible to me since I was five years old, and your dad before you, and his dad before him, and all you ever hear is Lot and his daughters and Tamar and Judah and Jacob and Leah and Rachel and you don't hear about anything else. I'll tell you what, Emmet, reading the Bible for the fuckin' parts is not really reading the Bible. That's okay with me; but now Alma is reading the *other* parts."

"I'll take care of Alma," Rooney said.

"Rooney, excuse me, but you couldn't take care of a fuckin' rock," Spooner said. They heard the sound of a car in the parking lot, and Einstadt stepped to the window and looked out. Pizza delivery truck.

"You got a pizza coming?" he asked.

"No," she said, and she took the moment to step up beside him and away from the two other men, to look out the window, and then step quickly past them so she could sit on the far end of the couch. That was a comfort, because her .45 fell under her hand, nestled in the pocket off the end of the couch.

She asked, "So what advice have you got, Emmett?"

Einstadt stared at her, his mouth turned down in a sour line, and he said, "They know a woman did it. They're probably going to get some of this DNA stuff off Jim's body—that's the word in town. They say you were sucking his cock, and they can get the DNA from dried spit. So if it was you, you best stay away from the cops. And after you've kept your head down for a while, you might think of moving someplace else. Like Alaska, or somewhere."

She said, "I'll think about that, Emmett. Now, I've got to eat my lunch, or I'll be no good the rest of the day. So you go along. And you remember, I put my ass on the line for all of us."

"Bullshit. You done it because you wanted to. If it had to be done, there'd be better ways to do it," Einstadt said. "Coulda had him out to the house, taken him out back, and buried the body in the field. Never would have found it in a thousand years."

"That's water down the drain," she said. "I had to do something, and I did it."

Morgan took a step toward her, but spoke to the others: "We oughta get her airtight one more time, then wring her neck."

She lifted her hand from over the arm of the couch, with the .45 in her grip, and laid the hand and gun across her lap. "Time to leave," she said.

A quick relay of glances, and Rooney took a step back. She *was* crazier than a bucket of frogs.

WHEN THEY'D GONE, Spooner put the .45 back in the couch sleeve, looked out to the parking lot, saw them talking and looking up at her apartment window. Cold out: steam coming out of their mouths as they talked, mostly Morgan and Einstadt. Rooney's opinions were given to him by Einstadt, especially since he'd given Rooney Alma and the girls.

Maybe, Spooner thought, she ought to give a gun to Alma. Or the girls. Surprise that old sonofabitch someday. She waited until the men got in their trucks and rolled out of the parking lot, then went and put a Lean Cuisine chicken carbonara in the microwave. While she waited for it to ding, she thought about Morgan and his threat, went and got the small 9mm Taurus pistol from her purse, and put it in the pocket of her fleece.

The microwave dinged, and she took out the plastic tray, ate standing up at the kitchen counter, thought about DNA, thought she should know more about it, and had just tossed the tray into the trash when the doorbell rang.

The doorbell hadn't rung unexpectedly more than three or four times since she'd been in the apartment. She went to the door and looked through the peephole, and saw a tall, blond man, hatless, waiting in the hall. Didn't know him. Wary, she left the chain on the door, opened it, and peeked out.

"Yes?"

Virgil said, "Miz Spooner? I'm Virgil Flowers, with the state Bureau of Criminal Apprehension. I'm investigating the death of your ex-husband, and some related problems. I'd like to talk to you a minute."

"Oh . . ." A chill ran up her spine. They were already *here.* "I've got to get back to work," she said. "I'm due back in ten minutes."

"I could talk to your boss. I'm sure he'd be cooperative. . . ."

She looked at him for another two seconds, then said, "Let me get the chain." She took the chain off, opened the door, and said, "Come in. I really haven't seen Jim in a long time. I heard about it, him being killed, but I just . . . I mean, I felt a little sad, I guess, we were married for five years, but that's all back then."

And Virgil thought, *Interesting. She's lying already.*

Virgil stepped inside, looked around. Compact kitchen off to the left, with the smell of pasta still in the air; a small living room straight ahead, down a hall, with another door to the left, presumably to a bedroom. Neat, not expensive. "Okay, well, if we could sit down for five minutes . . ."

They sat in the living room, Virgil taking the couch as it faced the television, and started with a thirty-second summary of what he thought: that Tripp had killed Flood for reasons unknown, that Crocker had killed Tripp to hide something that Tripp had known—something linked to the killing—and that both killings were somehow linked to the murder of Kelly Baker.

"Do you know if Jim knew any of those people? The Floods, the Bakers, the Tripp family . . . any of those?"

"He and Jake Flood were old friends since they were kids," she said. "We all came from the same place. And we knew the Bakers, 'cause we were all from the same part of the county, and the same business. Went to church services together."

"You're from the same area? Over around Battenberg?"

"Oh, yeah—my folks have a farm a mile down the road from the Floods. They all go back like to the nineteen hundreds, the families. Came from Germany. So we all know each other." As she was talking, she was trying in her mind to stay out front of the conversation: What he could find out easily, she'd tell him, so she couldn't be caught in a lie.

"When Iowa investigated, I guess they talked to all the folks in the church to see if anybody knew or heard anything?" Virgil asked.

She shook her head. "I don't think the church ever came into it. It's not really a church, you know. There's no *church.* We'd have services at different people's houses, usually in the barn, unless it's too cold. Sometimes, there'll be a couple different services going on, so we don't all go to the same one. We talk about the Bible, and all of that."

"Huh. Okay." Virgil scratched his head. "I thought Iowa had been all over everything—that they'd have talked to all of the Bakers' friends and neighbors. Anyway, when Kelly Baker was killed, did you have any feeling of what she might have been involved in? Who she might have been hanging with? Was she still going to the religious services, or had she dropped away?"

"I really couldn't tell you. I mean, she was there, but the Bakers are down at the far south end of the county, so we didn't see them every day," Spooner said. "I really don't know. I mean, I guess . . . they say, the word is, she was sexually active. I was surprised, but I wasn't really close enough to her to have any . . . *instinct* . . . about that. Maybe she was working in town, maybe she got loose somehow. I don't know."

"Were you homeschooled?"

"Oh, yes," she said. "Reading, writing, arithmetic, German. Every year, for thirteen years, five days a week."

"Is that part of the, uh, religion?"

"That's one of the main parts—to keep the kids away from the influences in schools," she said. She glanced at her watch. "I've really got to go."

Virgil asked, "Jim—was he violent with you?"

She shook her head. "No. Jim was boring. That's why I left. He'd get up, eat eggs, go to work, come home, eat dinner, sit on the couch and drink beer, go to bed. Every day. I couldn't see living my whole life like that. This idea that he could have killed the Tripp boy . . . I mean, that's very strange. I couldn't believe it."

"Do you know if he was dating anyone?"

"I don't know. Really. I haven't seen him in years. . . . All I know is history." She looked at her watch again and said, "Now I've got two minutes to walk two blocks."

"Come on," Virgil said, "I'll give you a ride. Where do you work?"

"At the CVS. I'm the assistant manager, I take care of the non-pharmacy items."

On the way down the hall, zipping their parkas, he said, "I'm interested in the relationship between Jacob Flood and the Bakers. Flood and Baker both being murdered. Were they close?"

"Everybody in the church is fairly close—that's mostly eighty or a hundred families, I guess. But I don't know that the Floods were any closer to the Bakers than anybody else—they're at the other end of the county from each other."

Virgil said, "I chatted with Emmett Einstadt about Jacob Flood, and their relationships with the Bakers, Kelly Baker. He seemed to have about the same feeling as you did—close, but not every day. He was pretty upset about Kelly, you know, in a German way. If you know what I mean. . . . My mother is pure German."

She smiled. "I do know," she said. "Emmett never shows much, but because there aren't so many church members, compared to the big churches, when somebody dies, you feel it. He gave a nice talk at her funeral."

Virgil nodded and said, "That's good. That's good."

They were outside, and he pointed her at the truck, and they climbed inside.

"How long has the church been around? Is this a longtime thing, or did you all get converted?"

"Been around since the families came over from the Old Country," Spooner said. "My great-grandfather was in it."

"Most people marry into the church?"

"Oh, yeah. Because we know each other all our lives, and we have all these background things—don't go to regular schools, so we don't have any regular school friends. I always thought I might marry an outsider, if I fell in love, but when it came time to get married, I wound up with Jim. Somebody I'd known all my life."

They pulled into the pharmacy, and Virgil said, "I might come back and talk to you again. I'm puzzled about Jim's part in all of this. Why he might kill somebody like Tripp, and why he'd be so quickly killed in return."

"I don't have the faintest idea," she said. "But if the Tripp boy knew both Kelly and Jacob, and you know he killed one of them . . ."

"But then why did Jim kill him?"

"That's the mystery," she said. "The only thing I can think of is that he went a little crazy if the boy told him about killing Jake. Maybe he made a joke out of it, or something. Jim and Jake grew up together—they used to hunt and trap together, when they were kids, wander around the countryside. That's all I can think of."

"But then who'd kill Jim? And why?"

She shrugged. "Don't know. Have you investigated the Tripps?"

"Well, we think the killer was a woman."

"Oh. Well, it wasn't me," she said. "Mrs. Tripp is a woman. . . ."

"You're right. You're right. I'll think about that," Virgil said. He put out his hand and they shook, and she popped the door and climbed out, wiggled her fingers at him as she went through the door.

Virgil sat staring at the door for a minute, running it all through his head.

Einstadt had lied about not knowing the Bakers; he knew them quite well. That seemed critical, somehow. With Crocker being close to Flood, and married to Spooner, the church seemed more and more central to the whole situation. The only person not involved with it was Bobby Tripp.

And he wondered who'd been in Spooner's apartment, not very long before himself, who'd left behind the damp footprints on the carpet, big bootlike footprints. And whether those footprints had anything to do with the fact that the hausfrau-looking Kathleen Spooner had a pistol in her pocket.

And he wondered about the color of the lipstick found on Crocker's penis. Most Minnesota working women didn't use lipstick, during the day, anyway. It was like a Minnesota *thing*. But Spooner wore it. Could the crime-scene people get enough of it off Crocker to match it to lipstick in Spooner's bathroom or dressing table?

Stuff to think about: And while he was thinking

about it, he carefully peeled off his parka and pulled back the sleeve of his shirt. He had a two-inch piece of double-sided carpet tape on his wrist. The sticky side was covered with fuzz, with a few dark hairs, from Kathleen Spooner's couch.

Should be enough for DNA, he thought, if the lab guys would just give him the time. He peeled the tape off his wrist and stuck it in a Ziploc bag. Might not be an entirely legal search, but he was invited in . . . and once he *knew*, he could always come back.

Or not.

9

Virgil headed south to Iowa, and called Bell Wood, the agent with the Iowa Division of Criminal Investigation: "I'm going down to Estherville," he said, when Wood came up. "There're interesting things going on, and I need to talk to John Baker and his family."

"You won't get much. They were pretty much mystified—Kelly backed out of their driveway and went on down the road," Wood said. "We took a look at them, and nothing came up. We interviewed them all separately—John and . . . I can't remember the wife's name. . . ."

"Luanne."

"Yeah. John and Luanne, and their kids, and they all had the same story. Not rehearsed, just . . . the same."

"All right. But I want to ask them about these new killings, see if they knew any of the people involved. . . . Did you guys look into their religion?"

"Not really. I remember they were churchy. Very dark dressers, kids homeschooled, and all that."

"Huh. Okay—listen, would it be possible to get a

highway patrol guy, or maybe an Estherville cop, whichever is better, to ride along with me? Somebody with an Iowa badge?"

"Let me make a call," Wood said. "I'll get back to you before you're there."

"Thanks."

"Virgil . . . you're getting somewhere?"

"Somewhere. But it's murky. I'll stay in touch."

•

THE HIGHWAY PATROLMAN'S name was Bill Clinton, "but not that Bill Clinton," he said, as he shook Virgil's hand. He was a thick-set, shaved-head man of perhaps thirty-five; he had three fleshy wrinkles that rolled down the back of his neck like stair steps. They'd hooked up at a café across the street from the Emmet County Courthouse.

"Hope you're a Democrat, anyway," Virgil said. Virgil got a cup of coffee while Clinton finished his lunch.

Clinton shook his head. "Lifelong Republican. My old man is the Republican county chairman down in Sac County. But I didn't mind—it was kinda fun. I was in the army back then."

Virgil gave him a quick outline of the investigation, and Clinton whistled and said, "Man, that's a hell of thing."

"You heard anything about Kelly Baker since last year?"

"Oh, sure, all kinds of stuff. But it's all bullshit," Clinton said. "There was a cop from Des Moines who came up here on his own and was poking around, looking for Satanists. One of the churches here, pretty fundamental, he got the pastor all churned up, but it didn't come to anything. Nobody believed it."

"Neither do I," Virgil said. "I've met a couple Satanists. They're about what you expect—people who never got over Halloween."

Clinton nodded. "Exactly right. People here are pretty commonsensical. The thing nobody could get around was what actually happened to her. The state ran the investigation, but technically, the Emmet County sheriff was in charge, so they got all the reports. When the autopsy came in, word about it got out in a couple of hours. Whips and multiple partners. People here look at the Internet, just like anybody, but they don't believe that stuff happens here. Not with little farm girls."

VIRGIL HAD CALLED ahead to the Bakers' and had gotten directions on how to get there. Clinton left his patrol car in Estherville, and they rode together out to the Baker place. The Bakers' house was a low, pale yellow rambler, with a miniature windmill in the front yard and an attached garage. The usual collection of farm sheds and buildings stood behind it, along with an early-twentieth-century brick silo, with no roof. A collection of rusted farm machinery was parked behind the old silo.

As they went up the drive, Virgil asked, "You know anything about these folks?"

"Not a thing. I looked them up after Bell Wood called, and law enforcement doesn't even know they exist. Not even a traffic ticket."

JOHN BAKER was Kelly Baker's uncle. He was a tall, thin man with hollowed cheeks, long, lank black hair and a beard going gray; he wore oversized steel-framed glasses, like aviators, dark trousers, and a dark wool shirt. His wife was more of the same, without the beard, and with smaller glasses, and an ankle-length skirt that looked homemade.

A brilliant crazy quilt, made of postage-stamp-sized snips of cloth, hung from pegs on the front-room wall; Virgil liked quilts, and this was a good one. He took a minute to look at it, as they were sitting down, and realized that in its natural craziness, it concealed a spring landscape.

The house smelled of vegetable soup—very good vegetable soup—and something else, some kind of herb, perhaps.

"Terrific quilt," he said to Luanne Baker.

She nodded, and then, almost reluctantly, "My mom made it." She had a dry, tinny voice, and Virgil realized that she was frightened.

Virgil smiled and asked, "Do you quilt yourself?"

"Yes, I do," she said, and nothing more.

John Baker asked, "Is this about Kelly? It must be."

Virgil said, "Yes, it is. . . ." He looked around, tipping his head, and asked, "I understand you have kids?"

"They're over at a neighbor's," John Baker said. "We got them out of the way of this—they're scared enough."

"All right," Virgil said. "What we've got going up north . . . you may have heard some of it—"

"You have a killer running around loose," John Baker said.

"Yes. And we think the killer knows something about what happened to Kelly. We're linking up the cases. For one thing, Kelly, and two other victims, Jim Crocker and Jacob Flood, are members of your church. That doesn't necessarily mean anything—there are a lot of church members out in the same area—"

"A lot of people don't like us. They say we're standoffish," Luanne Baker blurted. "Kelly was wearing her bonnet when she left, and I think some perverts spotted her and they took her right off the street. This boy who killed Jacob, he must've been one of them."

Virgil shook his head. "That really doesn't fit with the facts, Mrs. Baker. It appears that Kelly had been with these men more than once."

"I don't believe it," she said. "She was a good, cheerful girl. I would have spotted something like that. We all would have. There's something rotten in the state of Iowa, and I think that medical examiner is part of it. You know, he's a Muslim?"

"I don't see—"

"Then you should look harder," John Baker said. "A good Christian girl gets kidnapped off the city streets and who examines the body? A Muslim. And what happens? People start saying stuff about our church. Start tearing it down."

THEY ALL SAT looking at one another for a moment, the Bakers rigid in their chairs, Bill Clinton staring at them with his mouth open, not quite in amusement, and Virgil finally said, "Why don't we just talk about what happened that day? When Kelly was here. Did she leave in a rush? Was she in a hurry? Did she seem like she had an appointment?"

John Baker: "No. You know why she came down?"

"I don't—"

"She was going down to the locker in Estherville. My brother and I go in together on a couple of stocker calves every spring; we got a piece of pasture down by the crick. We take 'em to the locker in the fall, and she drove down to pick up some beef. She stopped here on the way."

"There was no beef in her car when it was found," Virgil said.

"No. She never got there. There were two women and a man working at the locker place, and they said they never saw her. The police believed them, and so do I. I know them, a bit, and they're okay, in my opinion."

Virgil said, "So she left here, in daylight, and went to Estherville, and something happened there. She met somebody or was picked up, probably in daylight, if she was on her way to the locker—"

"That's not the way I see it," Baker said. "I think somebody probably stopped her on the road, flagged her down, asking for directions or something, or acted like they was having car problems, and they took her. And the accomplice drove the car to Estherville. There's parking right at the locker, and the car was found four or five blocks from there."

"Maybe she decided to stop and do some shopping—"

"That's not the way I see it," Baker said. "For one thing, it was later in the afternoon by that time, and she was picking up beef for dinner. Len likes his dinner at five o'clock sharp, so she would have gone straight to the locker, and then home."

"But you said she wasn't in a hurry when she left," Bill Clinton said.

"She wasn't. She had time, but she had to move along."

"Maybe she was in a little bit of a hurry," Luanne Baker said. "But she wasn't in a *rush* or anything."

"LET ME ASK you about the church," Virgil began.

John Baker interrupted: "What religion are you?"

Virgil evaded a direct answer: "My father's a Lutheran minister. Over in Marshall." He paused, then asked, "Is it possible that Kelly was meeting, or was flagged down by, members of the church? Why would she stop for strangers, or go with strangers?"

"Because we do that around here," John Baker said. "If somebody has a problem, we don't expect them to be crazy killers. We stop and help out."

"That's nice," Bill Clinton said. He fished a piece of Dentyne gum from his shirt pocket, unwrapped it with one hand, and popped it in his mouth. "But I thought you were standoffish."

"That's what people *say*, but we help as much as anybody," John Baker said. "We're just private in our beliefs. This whole country is dying from a lack of good morals and proper behavior, and we don't want no part of it. We keep ourselves out of it, and we keep our children out of it, and we tend our farms."

"You don't know any church members who might have run off the tracks, or had a reputation for being a little wild . . . ?"

"*It's not the church*," John Baker said. "It's not. You're barking up the wrong tree. You know who killed Jake Flood. That boy is the one who did it—he's the devil. He's the devil in this. I heard that you think Jim Crocker killed him, and maybe he did, but if he did, it was because that boy attacked him. I think Jake found out something, and the boy killed him, and then maybe Jim asked him something, and he went after Jim—"

"Then Jim was murdered—" Virgil said.

"By the accomplices," John Baker said. "It's as plain as the nose on your face."

Virgil pushed them on the church, but got nowhere. A bit of history: The church members had been a branch of a fundamentalist movement in Germany that began in the 1830s, and had immigrated en masse to the U.S. in the 1880s. After arriving here, the group split up. Most of the various branches had eventually merged with other churches and movements around the Midwest and, finally, except for the Minnesota branch, had disappeared.

"We're the last of them," John Baker said. "The last who know the old ways."

They talked for a while longer, but got no useful information—Kelly Baker had arrived, had sat in the kitchen and chatted, had looked at a Christian computer game with the children, and had left, moving quickly but not rushed, to go to the locker. That was all.

BACK IN THE CAR, they rolled out the driveway, and Virgil asked Bill Clinton, "What do you think?"

"Not much," he said. "That thing about the Muslim medical examiner . . ."

"You see that a bit out here. People have ideas about Muslims and Jews," Virgil said.

"Yeah, but . . . not like that. Not like some giant conspiracy," Clinton said. "Then there was that whole thing about morals and good behavior. I'm not sure exactly . . . I'd like to know what their definition of 'moral' is. I mean, you smell that place?"

"You mean the soup? It smelled pretty good."

"I mean the smoke. The dope. The spliff, the ganj. As these good Germans would say, the dank."

Virgil put a hand to his forehead and rubbed. "That's what it was. I was thinking it was some kind of herb in the soup."

"It is some kind of herb, but I don't think it was in the soup," Clinton said. "I think it was in the curtains and the couch and the rugs. I think she was cooking up that soup to cover the odor. Those people are Christian fundamentalist stoners. I was sitting there grinning the whole time, listening to them. They were totally full of shit . . . depending on how you define 'moral.'"

"What is it with these guys?" Virgil asked. "These church people . . . I talked to one today who was carrying a gun in her pocket. I think some of them know a lot more about Kelly Baker than they're saying. I think—"

"I'll tell you what it is," Bill Clinton said. "What it is, is, something is seriously fucked. I wish you luck in detecting what it is."

10

Virgil called Coakley, who suggested that they meet at the Holiday Inn restaurant, away from the office and "not at the café, where half the town is, waiting for you to show up."

"Works for me," Virgil said. "I'll see you in twenty."

MOST SHERIFFS in Minnesota wore uniforms; a few didn't. Virgil hadn't seen Coakley in a uniform until she showed up at the Holiday Inn. When she took her parka off, she was wearing a star and had a pistol on her hip.

Virgil had gotten to the restaurant a couple of minutes earlier, and already had a booth. When she came up, he said, "You look like a cop."

"Feels weird, wearing a uniform," she said. "I wore one for five years before I became an investigator, and never did like it. But since I was working with the girls today . . ."

"Show some solidarity," Virgil said. "They come up with anything?"

"Nothing that we didn't know. Crocker and Jacob Flood were close. They all belong to a fundamentalist church that goes back to the Old Country, meaning Germany. They homeschool their kids, church services move around from one home to another."

"Services are held in barns," Virgil said.

"Nobody seems to know much about the religion, except that it's conservative," Coakley said. "They're all farmers, or come from farm families. Some people say they're standoffish, but other people say they know members of the church who work in town and are like anyone else. Which sounds like Crocker."

A waiter came up, and they ordered hamburgers and fries, and Coakley got coffee and Virgil got a Diet Coke, and when the waiter went away, Coakley asked, "Did Spooner have anything to contribute?"

"Not much," Virgil said. "She kept trying to get around the questions. But I expect she's the one who killed Crocker."

Coakley's eyebrows went up. *"What?"*

"She let me sit on her couch, and using a special BCA investigatory technique, I got some of her hair," he said. "I need to get it up to our lab. Then I'm going to use unfair tactics to get the lab to do some rush processing on it, so we ought to know for sure by day after tomorrow."

"Virgil, how . . . ?"

Virgil told her about it: about the gun in Spooner's pocket, about the lipstick, how nobody knew of anyone

Crocker was seeing. "On that basis alone—somebody familiar enough with him to get involved with oral sex—she'd be a suspect. The gun thing is big. She's a member of the church, born to it. I've got a feeling that the church could be involved here. Or maybe there's just something going on with this tight little knot of people, coming down through the generations. Most of them are related to each other, if I understood Spooner right. Lot of intermarriage."

"If she's the one, that'd be a pretty amazing clearance," Coakley said. "It's like you plucked her out of the air."

"Nah. All you do is, you look around," Virgil said. "Everybody says Crocker didn't have much to do with women, and the woman we know that he had something to do with, happens to carry a gun in her pocket. So she knows how to use one, and is maybe prepared to do it. Plus, she wears lipstick, which most women out here don't, except on special occasions. It's just . . . obvious."

"What if she killed him for some personal reason that has nothing to do with Flood or Tripp?" Coakley asked.

Virgil was already shaking his head. "Too big a coincidence. I'll tell you something else. I led Spooner on a bit . . ."

"How unlike you . . ." But she said it with a smile.

". . . and she told me that Einstadt gave a nice talk at Kelly Baker's funeral. Einstadt and the Floods and the Bakers know each other *very* well, and they're lying about it. Why would they do that?"

"They . . ."

"They're covering something up. Maybe Kelly Baker's death," Virgil said.

She looked at him for a long time, then said, "Maybe. But it's a jump."

THE FOOD CAME, and Virgil asked if she could send one of her deputies up to the BCA, in St. Paul, with Spooner's hair samples. She nodded. "Most of them would be happy for the chance, on the county's dime. Do some shopping."

"I'll give you the sample when we leave," he said.

SHE WAS PICKING at her food without much interest, and then she said, "I was talking to a friend up at the BCA. She said you've been married so often that the judge gives you a discount."

Virgil nearly spat out his hamburger. "What? Who told you that?"

"A friend. She's anonymous," Coakley said. "She said she thought you've been married and divorced four times."

"That's slander; I'd arrest her if I knew who it was," Virgil said.

"So how many times, then?"

"Three," Virgil admitted. "But it's not as bad as it sounds."

"Tell me the truth," Coakley said. "How bad did it hurt? When you got divorced?"

"It hurt," Virgil said. "I'm human."

"But she said all of this, all three marriages and divorces, were like in five years. And you have another girlfriend about every fifteen minutes. And that you've supposedly slept with witnesses. I don't know. I was kind of shocked."

"Hey . . ."

"Because when I got divorced, I mean, I was lying there for months, at night, trying to figure out what went wrong—and whose fault it was. I still do it," she said. "You know. I could no more have gotten married again in six months . . . I was still a basket case in six months."

"Well, I didn't have so much of that," Virgil said. "It was pretty clear, pretty quick, that me and my wives weren't going to make it. One of them, it was about a week and a half, you know, that we had the talk."

"That's absurd," Coakley said.

"Yeah," Virgil said. "I know. I did like the first one. But she had lots of plans. I didn't have much input into them, and I wasn't doing what she planned. Then, one day, I just wasn't in the plans anymore. She'd decided to outsource her expectations."

"How about sex? Did she outsource the sex?"

"Not that I know of—that wasn't the problem," Virgil said. "The problem was more . . . business-related. She'd decided I couldn't really be monetized."

"Hmph," Coakley said.

"That was a denigrating hmph."

"Well. Might as well get it out there," she said. She glanced around the room. "The thing is, when Larry stopped having sex with me, I thought maybe he was . . .

just losing interest in sex. I'd never gotten that much out of it. I'm not especially orgasmic, and so, I just let it go. But then, he dumps me off, for this other . . . person . . . with big . . . and I start to wonder, maybe I'm just a complete screwup as a woman."

Virgil held up his hands, didn't want to hear it. "Whoa, whoa, this is a lot of information—"

She said, "Shut up, Virgil—I'm talking. Anyway, I'm wondering, am I a complete screwup? The major relationship in my life is a disaster—"

"Hey, you've got three kids," Virgil said. "Is that a disaster?"

"Shut up. Anyway, I know I'm not all that attractive—"

"You're very attractive," Virgil said. "Jesus, Lee, get your head out of your ass."

"Well, see, nobody ever told me that—and you might be lying," she said. "I suspect somebody who got married and divorced three times in five years probably lies a lot."

"Well . . ."

"So, you can see where this is going," she said.

"I can?"

"Of course you can. I'm the sheriff of Warren County. There are twenty-two thousand people here, and all twenty-two thousand know who I am. I can't go flitting around, finding out about myself. If I pick out a man, that's pretty much it. But how can I pick out a man if maybe I'm a total screwup as a woman? I mean, maybe I should be gay. I kind of dress like a guy."

"Do you feel gay?"

"No, I don't. What I feel like, Virgil, is a little experimentation, something quick and shallow, somebody with experience," she said. "I can't experiment with the locals, without a lot of talk. So I need to pick somebody out and get the job done."

She peered at him with the blue eye and the green eye, waiting, and Virgil said, finally, "Well, you've got my attention."

WHEN VIRGIL LEFT the Holiday Inn, he drove over to the café, thinking about Coakley on the way—the proposition seemed pretty bald—parked, went inside, and ordered a piece of cherry pie and a Diet Coke. Jacoby, the owner, sidled over with the pie and asked, "Hey, Virg. Any more news?"

The close-by people stopped eating, and one man who'd been at the end of the bar picked up his coffee and moved to a closer stool.

Virgil asked, "Have you ever heard of a man, or a place, called Liberty? Some man around here, or some place around here?"

"Liberty?" Jacoby moved his lips as though he were sampling the word. Then, "No, I never did. Is it important?"

"Could help us out with the Kelly Baker murder," Virgil said.

"There's a 'New Liberty,' but it's way down in Iowa, way down past Cedar Rapids," said a guy in the booth behind Virgil. "That wouldn't be it."

"I got a feeling it's something around here," Virgil

said. "And maybe a person. Huh. I guess I'll just have to keep asking around."

"Well, if we hear anything, we'll let you know," Jacoby said. He watched as Virgil took a bite of the pie. "How is it?"

"I've had worse," Virgil said.

"He just can't remember when," said the guy on the stool.

HAVING DONE his data dump at the café, Virgil was headed out to his truck, followed by one of the customers, a thin man with thin hair, wearing a sheepskin-lined jean jacket and leather gloves: a cowboy-looking guy, except for his big round plastic-rimmed glasses, and not ungrizzled.

He said, "Uh, Virgil. I need to chat for a minute. About the Tripp boy."

"Sure," Virgil said. "Back in the café, here, somewhere? Or we could take a ride in my truck."

"Not here. How about the truck?"

The man's name was Dick Street, he said, and he had a farm out toward Battenberg, though he lived in Homestead. "I use the elevator at Battenberg, and met the Tripp kid. You know he was a football player?"

"Yeah. Hurt himself this year, was going out to Marshall next year," Virgil said, as he backed out of the parking place and started around the block.

"Yup. Anyway, I mentioned to my daughter that he seemed to be a pretty nice kid. Hard worker, good-looking. She was the same grade as him. She said, 'Yes, but I think he's gay.'"

"Your daughter said that?"

"Yeah. I almost fell off my chair," Street said. "I said, 'Why do you think that?' and she said, 'I don't know, I just think so.' Turns out, some of her girlfriends thought the same thing, that he might be a homosexual."

"Did everybody think that? His schoolmates?" Virgil asked.

"I don't know. But it wasn't exactly nobody. *Some* people suspected. So anyway, if he was a homosexual, I guess that's neither here nor there, when it comes to killing somebody. But. This sort of came to be a hot topic around the dinner table, because my daughter also thought that he might've been . . . doing something . . . with somebody."

"Does she have any idea who?" Virgil asked.

"I was gonna say, you oughta talk to her," Street said. "She works at the Christmas Barn. Anyway, I can tell you that a lot of the farmers around here don't care too much for homosexuals. I was thinking, maybe Flood found out and said something, like he was going to tell everybody. And Bob Tripp hit him to stop that from happening. I mean, if he's gay, maybe he'd lose his football scholarship or something?"

"I hadn't thought of that," Virgil said, though he had.

"Or, maybe he had something going with Jake Flood, and it was like a lovers' thing."

"Jake Flood was married," Virgil said.

"Yeah. But just between you, me, and the fence post,

there was something not quite right about him," Street said. "He had a strange way of looking at people. There was a sex thing in it. You know how some guys will look a woman up and down, seeing what she got? You got the feeling that Jake did that with everybody. Men, women. Whatever. Well, not dogs or anything. Maybe a heifer, if it was a good-looking one." He shot a quick glance at Virgil, and hastily added, "That was a joke, Virgil."

"I'm laughing myself sick, inside," Virgil said, but he said it with a grin. "Back to Jake Flood . . ."

"He was a weird one. I would not have wanted one of my daughters to be around him," Street said. "I just wonder if that weirdness might have set something off with Bobby?"

"Huh. Something to think about." They were almost back at the café. "I'll stop and talk to your daughter. What's her name?"

"Maicy. She'll talk to you. She's a talkative girl."

They turned the corner and Street said, "You can let me out by that Tundra up there, the gray one. Don't tell anybody what I said about this—the fact is, we don't know if Bobby was a homosexual, and it's not right to bad-mouth the dead. But since more people were getting killed, I thought I should mention this."

"Glad you did, Dick. Thank you."

"The Christmas Barn is four blocks straight ahead, on your right. They also sell some of the best saltwater taffy on the face of the earth."

"Okay. How do you like that Tundra?"

"It's all right. It's my first Jap truck," Street said. "They had a recall for the floor mats, and then for the gas pedal, but I haven't had any trouble. Probably go back to Chevy, though. I don't know why I ever jumped the fence. You have any trouble with your 4Runner?"

"Not yet," Virgil said. "I asked you about the Tundra because the 4Runner is based on it. . . ."

They chatted about trucks for a few minutes, especially the tow package, then Street looked at his watch and said, "Got to get back. See you at the café, maybe."

"Thanks again," Virgil said, and he rolled on down the avenue.

MAICY *WAS* a talkative girl: "A lot of us thought Bobby might be a little, you know, gay. We'd be sitting around talking, and he wouldn't be checking you out," she said. "He'd be checking out the guys. Not real obviously, he wasn't drooling over them or anything, but you could kind of feel it."

Virgil: "You don't know if he was actually actively involved with somebody?"

"I don't know, but I could tell you who might. He had a friend named Jay Wenner. Jay's kind of a geek—totally straight, though. He's up at the university in Minneapolis, at the Institute of Technology. You should call him."

"I'll do that," Virgil said.

He called the BCA researcher, Sandy, from the car,

and asked her to find Wenner's phone number. She said, "Hold on." A minute later, she was back with a cell phone number.

"How do you do that?" Virgil asked.

"It's technical," she said. "You'd have to take a couple of years of computer science to understand the explanation."

"So you look it up on a computer," Virgil said.

"Virgil . . . Yes. That's what I do. I look it up on a computer. Any fool could do it."

And she was gone. Sandy had been prickly for a while, but Virgil thought she might be mellowing out. Then again, maybe not.

Virgil caught Wenner between classes, identified himself, and Wenner asked, "How do I know you're not spoofing me?"

"I don't know what that means," Virgil said. "I'm a cop."

"How'd you get this phone number?" Wenner asked. "It's unlisted."

"A BCA researcher looked it up on a computer," Virgil said.

"You have to excuse me, but that doesn't sound likely," Wenner said.

Virgil said, "Look. I'm sitting here in my truck in Homestead, and I could go over to your parents' house, and show them my ID, and have them call you. Or, you could call the BCA and ask for the duty officer, and get my phone number. But, one way or the other, I need to talk to you."

"Huh. You make the offer, you're probably okay. I've been reading about Bobby on the net. I'm like totally freaked. So: What do you want to know?"

"Do you think Bobby was gay?" Virgil asked.

A moment of silence, then, "Who are you going to tell about this?"

"Nobody who doesn't need to know," Virgil said. "The question is, did some kind of homosexual involvement lead to his murder? Or his murder of Jacob Flood?"

"Huh. I couldn't tell you about that. But he was gay," Wenner said. "Only a couple of us knew. He'd had some contact with . . . somebody. I don't know who that was."

"You mean sexual contact? We haven't heard that, though we know he was talking to a gay man in a more . . . what would you call it? More of a mentoring thing."

"Pat Sullivan. Not him, I think there was somebody else," Wenner said. "Do you know about that Kelly Baker girl, who got killed a year or so ago?"

"Yes, and we know that she and Bobby had some kind of relationship."

"They did. I think she might have known somebody else who was gay, and put Bob in touch."

"Was Baker a hooker?" Virgil asked.

"Interesting question," Wenner said. "I have no idea. I only saw her a few times, and she looked like a regular girl except . . . she looked kind of beat up, too. You know?"

"Not exactly," Virgil said.

"Well, sometimes you see girls who look like they've been around a little too much," Wenner said. "They start to look tired when they're still young. She looked like that."

"Good description . . . I know what you mean. Did her relationship with Bobby extend to sex?"

"No—but they talked about sex all the time," Wenner said. "Bob once told me that she told him about doing some really freaky things, but he thought maybe she was lying, because he couldn't believe she'd do that stuff. But then, a friend of ours from Northwest said the Iowa cops came around and were asking about whether she might have been a prostitute. Or something like that—that was the idea."

"But she didn't go to Northwest."

"No, but she knew kids who did. So they were checking out the guys."

Wenner didn't have much more—said he'd be back to Homestead for the funeral, that he'd be a pallbearer. "I knew that guy since first grade. I didn't care if he was gay, he was a good guy."

"You didn't see the violence in him?"

"I didn't, except on the football field," Wenner said. "The Flood thing is hard to believe. Maybe he was framed, or something. You think?"

"Not really," Virgil said. "It's pretty clear he killed Flood. Listen, if you think of anything else, call me. You can get me through the BCA, or I may see you at the funeral."

"One more thing," Wenner said. "Pat Sullivan and Bob were talking quite a bit, and we were all talking at the Dairy Queen a few times, and Kelly was there. If Sullivan ever saw who Kelly was hanging with, another guy . . . that might be the one. If she was really involved in some heavy sex things, maybe she gathered up gay guys to be her friends. You know, people she could trust."

"Good thought, Jay. Thank you."

He called Pat Sullivan. He was told the reporter was in Mankato for a regional flood-preparation meeting and wouldn't be back until late.

Virgil met Coakley back at her office, where she'd been talking with a couple of deputies. She looked up when he stuck his head in, and she said, "You got something."

"Maybe. I need all that paper from Iowa, again, and a place to read it."

She looked at him for a long moment, considering him, and not in a collegial way, Virgil thought, and then she nodded.

And Virgil thought: If what Wenner said was true, and Baker had set Tripp up with a homosexual contact, then there was at least one person out there who might know as much as Baker did—and exactly what kind of activities Baker had been into. But tracking that person down would be a problem, especially if he had to do it without broadcasting the fact that Tripp had been gay.

He would do that—broadcast, sit in the café and tell the patrons about it—if it became necessary, but he hoped it wouldn't.

Coakley got him the Iowa paper, a spot in an interview room, and a Diet Coke, and he started wading through the paper again, looking for anything that might pinpoint a possible lover.

Two hours: He found nothing.

COAKLEY WAS STARING at a computer, and he asked, "Are you online?"

"Yes. What's up?" she asked.

"Could we go out to Google Earth and spot the Baker place?" Virgil asked.

"We can." She hit a few keys, enlarged the screen a couple of times, found the house, lost it, found it again, and enlarged to the maximum. "What do you need?"

"I want to know who lives in the houses closest to them." Virgil got her to change the scale up and down, to get a map of a couple dozen farmhouses within a couple miles of the Baker place. "Print that," he said. And, "I wonder who runs the rural route out there?"

"We can find that out," Coakley said, looking at her watch. "Should still be some carriers around."

She got on the phone, called the post office, talked to somebody, hung up, and said, "Clare Kreuger's your girl. She's not there at the moment, but she's due back in anytime."

"Good—now, where's the post office?"

"Are you going back out there? To the Bakers'?" Coakley asked.

"Yeah. Gonna whisper in the ears of the neighbors . . . after I talk to Clare."

KREUGER WAS SKEPTICAL: "What you're saying is, you want to turn their friends against them."

"No, no. I don't want friends. I want people who already don't like them," Virgil said.

"That just seems rotten," the carrier said. She was a dusty-looking woman, who looked like she'd spent too much time in the wind. She wore a nylon parka, nylon wind pants, and galoshes. They were standing at the post office loading dock, where Clare had parked.

"It is a little rotten," Virgil said. "But we have four dead people, and a killer still on the loose. I wouldn't do it otherwise."

Kreuger said, "Neither would I. But you got me. Too many dead people. I know there's bad blood between the Bakers and Brian Craig, because of a drainage problem off the Bakers' land that they've never been able to work out. There's another guy, Peter Van Mann, and I don't think they get along, either. I don't know what the problem is, something about a dog. That's before my time on the route. Let's go inside, and I'll spot them on the map. . . ."

THE SUN WAS SLIDING hard to the southwest when Virgil pulled into the Craig place. Craig, said his wife, was out in the barn trying to fix the front frame of a hay wagon, which had bent while they were pulling in the last cut of hay in late summer. They had lived with it then, but once winter shut down the field work, it was time to do repairs.

Virgil found Craig struggling to get the left side of the frame up on a jack, under a couple of work lights. He saw Virgil come through the door, stopped struggling, and asked, "Who are you?"

"A cop. State Bureau of Criminal Apprehension," Virgil said. "I need to talk to you for a bit."

"About what?"

"About Kelly Baker, and the Bakers in general," Virgil said.

"I don't know much about Kelly. . . ."

His wife pushed through the door behind them. She'd pulled on a letter jacket and run over to listen in.

"I'll tell you the truth," Virgil said. "We've got a hell of a problem here and . . ." He hesitated, then asked, "What's the deal with your frame?"

"I cut out the bent part, and when I jack up one side, there's enough torque to twist the frame when I'm jacking up the other."

"Let me give you a hand with that."

Craig didn't say no, and they spent five minutes getting both sides of the front frame up on jacks and lined up to each other. Craig fit a piece of steel across the gap and clamped it in place, put on welding glasses, and said, "Don't look at the spot." He made a number of quick welds to hold it square, and the barn was suffused with the odor of burning iron. When it cooled, he used a spare piece of L-bar to check the squareness, and took the clamps off.

"Thanks," he said.

"You want to come in for coffee?" his wife asked. "It's pretty cold out here."

Virgil shrugged, and Craig said, "Might as well. I can do the final weld anytime, now."

They sat at the kitchen table, and Virgil said, "I understand that you and the Bakers haven't always gotten along. One thing cops do is, we talk to people who don't like other people, because they're usually less reluctant to talk. It sounds mean, but that's the way it is."

"Does sound mean," Craig's wife said, and Virgil said, "You didn't mention your first name."

"Judy," she said.

"It *is* mean," Virgil said. "But we're talking some nasty murders here. I've spoken to the Bakers, and what they tell me isn't as consistent with the evidence as it should be."

"For example?" Craig asked.

"For example, Jacob Flood and members of the Flood family say they don't know the Bakers that well, and the Bakers agree with that, but we've talked to other people who have suggested that they're actually quite close. And that they're all involved in a fundamentalist religion that's really pretty tight."

Craig and his wife glanced at each other, and then Judy Craig asked, "What do you know about their so-called religion?"

"Nothing," Virgil said. "It seems to be pretty private, but you do see some of that around."

Brian Craig leaned forward and tapped his finger on the table. "Our kids both go to public schools, and I'll tell you what: I do not encourage them to hang around with anybody from this church. I just don't want those people around them."

"Tell me why you feel like that," Virgil said. "I'm not talking about formal testimony, here. Nobody's going to write anything down. Anything helps . . ."

The couple glanced at each other again, and then Judy Craig said, "You see people every day out here, and even if you don't talk much, you *know* them. Know when they have babies, for example, and about how old their kids are. Even when they don't go to school. You know what I mean?"

"Sure. I'm a small-town kid," Virgil said.

"Okay. If you keep track of what's happening around the countryside, it doesn't take too many years to realize that all the people from this church are intermarrying with each other, and some of them, the girls especially, at a pretty early age. And to some pretty odd guys. You see a lot of eighteen-year-olds getting married to guys who are thirty or forty, and you wonder, how'd they get to know each other that well? When they are that young? Then Kelly gets murdered, and the Iowa police came around and asked if we knew who she dated, and we said, 'No,' because we didn't. We had no idea she was dating *anybody*. But every once in a while, you'd see her riding around with some older guy, somebody old enough to be her father, somebody who's already married. All members of the religion."

"Do you think, uh, these young girls are being abused?" Virgil asked.

"Haven't ever seen any proof—but I wouldn't want my kids around them," Brian Craig said, unknowingly echoing the verdict of the man who'd known that Bobby Tripp was gay.

"They meet on Sunday? I understand they meet in people's barns and so on."

"Yes. Not everybody's barns, just a few of them. The Floods, the Bochers, the Steinfelds. The biggest barns, all sealed up, with some heat. They meet Wednesday nights, too. Sundays in the mornings, Wednesdays after dark. Sometimes they've got something going on Fridays."

They talked about that for a while, and then Virgil moved on to the Tripp angle: "Had you ever seen Kelly Baker around with a boy who you thought might be gay?"

Craig frowned. "Don't have many gays out here."

"There must be some," Virgil said. "There usually are."

"I just wouldn't know that," Craig said.

"Do you know Peter Van Mann?"

"Sure, we know Pete," Craig said. "He's not gay. What'd he do?"

"I was told he's another guy who might not care for the Bakers."

"That's true," Judy Craig said. "He once had a German shepherd who bit Louise Baker pretty bad. He paid for the doctor and everything, but then the Bakers sued him for pain and suffering, and they won. He had to sell off some land to pay up."

"She wasn't disfigured or anything, was she? I didn't notice anything," Virgil said.

"No, not much of that. I think it was just pain and suffering," Craig said. "They saw their chance, and they took it."

Craig, on his way back to the barn, walked Virgil to his truck and said, "If you really need to find out what's going on in that church, it's gonna be tough. I don't know anybody around here who really walked away from it. It's all the same families, and they stick to it."

VIRGIL WENT DOWN the road to the Van Mann place, and saw a lonely figure walking up a snow-packed drive, followed by a black Labrador retriever. Virgil turned in, and he and the man got to the farmyard at the same time. Virgil hopped out of his truck, introduced himself, and Van Mann said, "Come on in. Come on, Jack."

They settled at the kitchen table, with Jack lying by Virgil's feet, where he could smell Virgil's pants.

Peter Van Mann was a widower farmer, a tall, thin bald man with gold-rimmed glasses and a way of looking at Virgil from the corner of his green eyes. From their chairs, they could look out through a bay window, at a tree with a tire swing. His kids had all gone out to California, Van Mann said, one after another, looking for jobs in computers. “They won’t be coming back, except to sell off the property when I croak,” he said.

“Gets dark here in the winter,” Virgil said.

“And quiet and cold,” Van Mann said. “I think it was the quiet that pushed them out. I’ve always liked it, the quiet and cold both.”

His wife, he said, had died of cancer, which he suspected was brought on by farm chemicals used when she was a girl, after World War II. “I can remember when the mosquito sprayers used to come, and blast everything with DDT. We’d walk around in a cloud of it, sometimes. Now I think we’re paying for it.”

He didn’t have much to say about the Bakers, except that their lawsuit against him had been a fraud. “The thing is, there’s a lot of asparagus that grows in the ditches, and Louise Baker was out cutting a mess of it. Old Pat, that was my dog back then, went after her. I don’t know why, he’d never bit anybody before. I suspect she threw a rock at him or hit him with a stick or something, though she says he just came at her. Anyway, she got bit, no doubt about that. Mabel Gentry, she was the rural route carrier out here then—this was years ago, maybe twenty years now, all the kids were still here—carried her down to her house, and then her old man took her to the doc. I paid for that, a couple hundred bucks, she had stitches and pills and so on. Then they sued. This was back when farming times was pretty bad. When they won, I had to sell forty acres to pay them off. Land prices was nowhere at the time. That same land is worth five or six times as much now. Pains me every time I see somebody on it."

"So why was it a fraud?"

"Well, it wasn't exactly, but you know what I mean," Van Mann said. "Things happen when you're farming. She was bit, and it hurt, but it was nothing anybody else would have thought was serious. No farmers, anyway. And sure as hell not fifty thousand dollars' worth."

"No insurance?"

"Let it slip—the liability. Like I said, things were really tough back then," Van Mann said. "This was back before gasohol."

They talked about bad times for a couple of minutes, and Van Mann said that he didn't know much about the church, but that his father had said that it was "bad business" and wouldn't talk about it. "They keep to themselves, and always have. They're very tight. Don't socialize with their neighbors, don't get involved in politics, never run for anything."

"Is there a sex thing going on in the church?"

Van Mann leaned back and crossed his legs, a defensive move, but then said, "The thought has occurred to me. But I don't have any direct information."

"You ever know anybody to take off? Leave the church?"

Van Mann's eyes narrowed as he thought about it, and he said, "There was some talk about a woman who ran away to somewhere. Her name was Birdy, that's what I remember about it. Must have been ten or twelve years ago. Birdy Olms. I can't remember what the situation was, or even how I know about it, but it seems to me that she was going to a doc, and left the office, and when her husband came to pick her up, she was gone. They went looking for her, and it turns out she'd gotten on a bus and that was it."

"Never came back?"

"Not that I know of. She was an outsider. From up north, somewhere. I don't know where Roland Olms picked her up."

"Birdy Olms."

"Yup."

Virgil asked the gay question, and Van Mann shook his head. "The thing about those people is that they're standoffish. If Kelly Baker knew a gay boy, he was probably a member of the church. Or maybe a relative."

"She worked at a Dairy Queen in the summer."

"Yeah, you see some of them working around," Van Mann said. "I think maybe the Bakers needed the money. For somebody who's been doing it as long as he has, Baker is one horseshit farmer."

By the time Virgil left Van Mann's place, it was dark. He tried calling the newspaper again, and was told that Sullivan had already filed his copy from Mankato, and might be heading north to the Cities to spend the night.

He called Coakley as he turned onto I-90 and said, "Holiday Inn, twenty minutes?"

"The restaurant. See you there."

He thought about that as he drove into the gathering

darkness: They could have met at the restaurant, or they could have met in his room. He'd known and carefully observed a reasonably large number of women in his life, and the choice of the restaurant was significant, he thought, and in a good way.

COAKLEY WAS BACK in civilian clothes, tan canvas jeans, a black blouse and deep green sweater, and her cowboy boots. Virgil had found a booth well away from the three that were already occupied, and she slid in across from him and said, "I can't do it."

"Really."

She leaned toward him and said, "I want to, but I just can't jump into bed with somebody, cold. I've been thinking about it all afternoon."

"So have I," Virgil said.

"And what do you think?"

Virgil leaned back and closed his eyes and said, "You know what? It's been a while since I've been in bed with a woman, and I miss it. I'm just . . . needy enough . . . that I would have gone for it, and tried to patch the holes later. You are a seriously attractive woman. But this is better. We need to talk a lot more. Then jump in bed."

"Deal," she said, and she smiled, and the smile lit up the booth—and Virgil's heart as well. But then, his heart wasn't all that hard to light up. "God, you made that easy. Is it because you're generous, or because you're slick?"

"Hey, I'm from Marshall. There aren't any slick guys from Marshall."

"I once knew a slick guy from there," she said.

"Now you're lying," Virgil said. "There are no slick guys from Marshall."

"No, no, really—his name was Richard Reedy—"

"Richard," Virgil said, laughing. "I know Richard. He was two years ahead of me. My God, you're right. He used to wax his hair, so he had this little pointy thing that stuck up from his forehead, like the crest on a cardinal. He used to wear sport coats to school when he didn't have to."

"I saw him up in the Cities a couple of years ago," she said. "He wears these plutonium suits and his hair is still waxed and he's got one of those little telephone clip things on his ear, like he's expecting a call from his agent," she said. "Like his movie is being made."

They both had a nice laugh, and then Virgil said, "All right. Now. Whoops, here comes a waiter. Shoo him away."

She did and Virgil went on: "I'm getting more and more of a feeling that there's something seriously wrong with this church. And that it might involve underage sex on a pretty wide scale. How underage, I don't know."

"Farm girls, not all of them, but some of them, can grow up pretty early. Sex is no big mystery if you grow up on a farm with animals," Coakley said. "And when you're out in the country, you spend quite a bit of time on your own, if you want. It's easy to sneak off with a boyfriend."

Virgil nodded. "Get a blanket out in a cornfield and you're good."

"Except you get corn cuts all over your butt, and itch like crazy," she said.

They looked at each other and laughed again, and then she said, "If it's under age seventeen, I think people would look past it. If it's under age thirteen, we could get a lynch mob going."

"Think about the fact that Kelly Baker was pretty badly abused, in a hard-core way, a porno-movie way," Virgil said. "Whips. Multiple partners, possibly simultaneously, according to the Iowa ME. And that she'd been previously abused in the same way, and that nobody can find any sign that she was hooking, or any partners."

"Virgil, that's really ugly, what you're thinking," Coakley said, dead sober.

"Yes. It is."

He told her about trying to call Sullivan, based on the interview with Tripp's friend Jay Wenner, that she already knew about. "These farm guys, Craig and Van Mann, kept coming back to the fact that these church people are really tight with each other, and don't much socialize with outsiders. If this gay kid was a friend of Kelly Baker, then he's probably a church kid, and he probably knows everything she did. About everything. We need to find him. We need to talk to Sullivan, soon as we can."

"He's probably with his friend up there. You think we should try to track him down?"

"Ah, they told me he's working tomorrow, so we can

probably get him early tomorrow. Can't do much more tonight, anyway," Virgil said.

"Have you thought about the possibility of spying on one of these church meetings?"

He smiled. "Yes."

"I'm up for that."

"It'd have to be one of your guys you absolutely trust," Virgil said. "It's possible that Crocker was actually planted on the department by the church. . . . If you're involved in some kind of mass child abuse thing, even if it's religion-based, you're going to be curious about what the local law enforcement agency is up to."

She said, "It'll be someone we can trust. Me."

He nodded. "Okay. We'll be like ninjas, black ghosts slipping unseen across the Minnesota countryside."

"Probably get eaten by hogs," she said.

"Minnesota ninjas fear no hogs," Virgil said.

"And what else?"

"We need to track down a woman named Birdy Olms," Virgil said. He explained. "With a name like that, I think we've got a chance."

"I'll get on that. And your DNA sample is at your lab. Jeanette took it up, and said they whined at her."

"Yeah, well, I got my boss to jack them up," Virgil said. "The problem is, everybody wants DNA. DNA for everything. We're jumping the line, which pisses everybody off."

"We've got four dead," she said.

"But if the DNA pans out, we'll have a hammerlock

on Spooner. She grew up in the church, but she's already stepped away from them. If we can get her with a murder charge, we might be able to open her up."

She thought about that, and then said, "They've been out there for a long time, this church. I wonder what they'd do if they thought it was about to come down on them?"

11

Patrick Sullivan, the reporter, woke Virgil at seven o'clock in the morning: "Hope I didn't wake you up. I just found your message."

"I need to talk to you," Virgil said. "Are you at home?"

"Right now, I am. I need to get cleaned up and head into work by eight," Sullivan said.

"I'll be there in half an hour," Virgil said.

He got cleaned up in a rush, stood for an extra minute in a hot shower, storing up some warmth, dressed, and headed out. The predawn was bitterly cold, the dry air like a knife against his face; and dark, as the season rolled downhill to the winter solstice, and the days were hardly long enough to remember. Sullivan had given him simple directions, and Virgil was at the curb outside his house twenty-nine minutes after he'd gotten out of bed, streetlights twinkling down the way.

Sullivan lived on the second floor of a stately white-and-teal Victorian on Landward Avenue. When Virgil arrived, the reporter was in the driveway, chipping frost off the windshield of a three-year-old Jeep Cherokee.

"When did you get in?" Virgil asked, as they headed up the walk to his apartment. If he'd driven down from the Cities, he wouldn't have been chipping frost.

"I came back late last night. I was afraid if I stayed over, I'd get jammed up in traffic. What's up?"

"A couple more questions about Tripp," Virgil said. Sullivan led the way through the front door and up an old wooden staircase with a polished mahogany railing curling around a halfway landing.

"Not bad," Virgil said.

"The price is right," Sullivan said. He unlocked the door of his apartment. "Up in the Cities, this place would cost me fifteen hundred more'n I'm paying here." He had three rooms—living room, bedroom, and kitchen, with a bath off the bedroom. "Microwave some coffee?"

"Fine," Virgil said. He took a chair at the kitchen table, and when Sullivan brought the cups over, took one, and Sullivan sat opposite. "So."

"There's a lot going on out there," Virgil said. "Kelly Baker, these other killings, they're all hooked together, I think. We've been talking to people, and one guy who should know tells us that Kelly hooked up Tripp with another gay guy. Probably somebody she knew from this church she belonged to."

"And you want to know if I know who he is," Sullivan said.

"In a nutshell."

"I don't," Sullivan said. "I'd be a little surprised if Bob was sexually active."

"What if he kept it from you? I mean, this would be something he might not even want to admit to himself, much less to somebody outside the relationship," Virgil said. "Since whoever he is was a friend of Kelly's, we wonder if you ever saw a guy hanging around with her, who might've given you a look. . . ."

Sullivan stared down into his coffee for a minute, then said, "There's something. . . ."

Virgil took a sip of coffee, waiting.

"I didn't hang around with Bob in public. He wasn't ready for people to know. But I ran into him once at the Dairy Queen, and he and Baker were with another man. The other guy gave off this vibration. . . . I didn't remember until you asked."

"You know him?"

"No. He was a real tall guy," Sullivan said. "I mean, six-seven or six-eight. Not real good-looking, but interesting-looking, like somebody had chipped him out of wood. Abe Lincoln."

"How old?"

Sullivan fingered the rim of his ear, thinking, then said, "I can't say for sure, but I'd say, older than Bobby. Twenties. Probably not thirty. Dark hair, wore it long. Not hippie-long—farmer-long."

"Huh," Virgil said. "Thank you."

THAT WAS WHAT Sullivan had, and Virgil stood up to leave. "Give me one thing for my story," Sullivan said. He reached over to the kitchen counter and picked up a narrow, half-used reporter's notebook and a ballpoint. "Anything good."

Virgil considered, then said, "We think we've linked the Baker killing to the murders of Jacob Flood and Bob Tripp. I can't tell you more than that. I will say that we've collected a variety of evidence, which is now being processed by the BCA lab, and we could get a break in a day or two. Chemistry takes time. But—I would like you to attribute this to an unnamed source, if you can. If not . . . I could take some heat."

"I can do that." Sullivan scribbled in the notebook. "What about the evidence involving Bob in a homosexual affair?"

"We don't know that there was one," Virgil said. "I guess you can't libel a dead man, but what's the point in saying that, until it leads somewhere?"

Sullivan nodded and closed the notebook. "So—why are you looking into it? If it doesn't matter?"

"The sex in itself doesn't matter, though it might technically be a crime, if there's a disparity of ages, and depending on when Bob's birthday was."

"Oh, horseshit . . ."

"I'm just sayin'," Virgil said. "But the main thing is, if this other guy was tight with Baker, he might know what happened to her, and who might have done it. You've given me enough information that I think I can find him. And if he is older, and if he was involved with

Tripp when he was a minor, then we might have a handy little sex-crime tool kit for getting him to talk."

"But you're not going to mess with him just because he's gay."

"Look—I really don't care what people do with each other, as long as everybody consents. And they're old enough to consent," Virgil said. "I've got more important things to think about. Like what to have for lunch."

"I knew you were a secret liberal," Sullivan said.

Out in his truck Virgil called Van Mann, the farmer whose dog had bitten Louise Baker. "I've got a question for you, which I'd appreciate it if you could keep it under your hat."

"I can do that," Van Mann said.

"I'm looking for a guy who may be a member of the church. . . ." He relayed Sullivan's description.

"That's probably Harvey Loewe," Van Mann said. "He lives a couple of miles down south of me. He's got an old farmhouse more or less across the road from his folks' place. His folks are Joe and Marsha Loewe. Harvey's probably twenty-six or twenty-seven. He would have been God's gift to the Northwest High basketball team, if he'd gone to public school."

"Is Harvey married?"

"No, I don't believe so. Never really seen him with a woman," Vann Mann said.

"Thank you. And listen, keep it—"

"Under my hat. I'll do that."

Virgil called Coakley: "You up?"

"Not entirely," she said. "I still got the boys to get out of here, and I've got to figure out my word for the day. Hang on—okay, it's 'porcine,' which means related to pigs, or piglike. I have to use it five times, in context."

"I'm going to go interview the homosexual guy who had the affair with Bobby Tripp. I need to spot his place, and—"

"Is he porcine?"

"Not as far as I know. But if you could look him up . . ."

"All right. And I'm coming," she said. "Give me forty-five minutes."

"I thought you might be," Virgil said. "Bring a gun with you."

"You think there might be trouble?" she asked.

"No, but we're cops, and I think somebody should have a gun."

Virgil went by the Yellow Dog for some pancakes. Jacoby came over with a cup of coffee and asked if there was anything new. "Not at the moment," Virgil said. "But we're pushing ahead."

"Let me know," Jacoby said. He dropped the cup of coffee on the table and went to get the pancakes.

Ten seconds later, a short, thin man with a waxed mustache stood up from the booth where he'd been reading the *Star Tribune*, folded it, looked around, and walked down and slipped into the booth opposite Virgil.

"I'm Rich," he said.

Virgil nodded. "Good for you. Hard to get that way, with all the high taxes."

The man half smiled, showing brown teeth. He leaned forward on his elbows and said, "I know something that might be of interest in your investigation."

"I'm listening," Virgil said.

"Is there any kind of reward?"

Virgil nodded again. "The knowledge that you've helped your fellow man."

"I was afraid of that," the man said. His furtiveness seemed to be a built-in part of his personality, Virgil decided. "Anyhow. People are talking. They're saying you're looking at all these church people, out there in the sticks. And they might have been doing dirty by this Kelly Baker girl. That got me to thinking."

Virgil said, "We'd be very interested in anything about Kelly Baker."

"Not exactly about her. But I work down at the Wal-Mart. You know where that is?"

"I do."

"So. I'm the photo technician. I used to run the print-making machine and so on, back when we developed film, and I got to know who was who in the local photography community. One of these church people out there, his name is Karl Rouse, this is back in the film days, he used to buy a *load* of Polaroid film. I mean, a *load*. You know what I mean?"

"A lot," Virgil said. He took a sip of coffee.

"A load. And when people bought that much Polaroid, unless they were a real estate agent or something, I'd get ideas of what they were taking pictures of. You know?"

"Okay," Virgil said. "You ever see any evidence of that?"

"No, not exactly. But I can tell you, it's a heck of a lot cheaper to shoot with a film camera and have us develop it. And he did that, too. He was a regular shutterbug, taking church pictures and so on. So I'm asking myself, 'How come we're only getting half of his business? The non-Polaroid part?'"

"But no real indication . . ."

"No. I can tell you, when digital came in, he was first in line to buy a photo printer, and he still buys a lot of paper from us. Keeps really busy. Anyhow, I thought you'd like to know that."

"Well, I'll keep it in mind," Virgil said. "But I'll tell you, there's no Rouse in this investigation so far."

Rich was disappointed, but said, "Well, you oughta take a look. I got an instinct for these things, and I think something was going on there."

Jacoby came back and said, "Hey, Rich. You find a clue?"

"Maybe," Rich said. He slid out of the booth. "I gotta get going, I'm due at work. But: think about that. I believe it could be important."

"What was that?" Jacoby asked, when Rich was out the door.

"Nothing much, I'm afraid," Virgil said. "Another guy trying to help out."

Jacoby dropped his voice: "Not so much a guy, as the village idiot."

VIRGIL PICKED COAKLEY up at her house, a pleasant wood-and-brick sixties rambler. She met him at the door, invited him in, led him through a kitchen that smelled like toast and peanut butter and jam, to a tiny office. "I've got Harvey Loewe's house spotted on Google," she said. She touched the mouse, and a satellite shot popped up on the screen. "He's on Twentieth Street, way down here in the southwest. Right . . ." She reached out and pushed the scale on the map, then tapped the screen with a fingertip. "Here."

The picture had been taken in the summer, in a raking, early-morning light, and Loewe's house, which was white, stood out clearly in the green fields that ran right up to it.

"No yard," Virgil said. "Not even a front yard. No outbuildings."

"It's like with Crocker. It's an old vacant farmhouse," she said. "Some of them get burned by the fire department, but some of them aren't so bad. You can live in them, with a little work, if you're handy. Most farm kids are."

"His folks are right around there someplace," Virgil said. There was nothing exactly across the road, but there were single houses both east and west of Loewe's, and both were across the road, and appeared to be inhabited. "I'd rather not have them know we're talking to their kid, you know?"

On the way out, Virgil detailed his talk with Sullivan.

"Do you trust him?" Coakley asked.

"No, not entirely," Virgil said. "He seems like a good enough guy, but he is a reporter, and they are weasels, just by their nature. Though I don't know what he'd be hiding from us."

"Maybe had a sexual relationship with Tripp that he'd rather not talk about," Coakley suggested. "Talking about it could cause him some trouble. You know, with his boyfriend."

"That's possible. But I still don't see where it'd take us. I think Tripp was the end of a string of information, and Sullivan would be even further out. We need to follow the string into the source, not further out."

THEY FOUND Loewe taping 3M window-sealing plastic over his kitchen windows. He saw them coming, met them at the door. They told him what they were doing, and a transient little muscle spasm seemed to pass over his face, and the corners of his mouth turned down, but he was polite: "I don't know how I can help, but come in."

He was a tall man, who did look a bit like Lincoln, thin but hard, with knobby shoulders and hands, and big, square, slightly yellow teeth. His hair was as long as Virgil's, and he was wearing low-rise jeans, a purple cotton shirt, and loafers. "Putting this plastic up—the house has got no insulation in the walls whatsoever. I put in sixteen inches of fiberglass in the attic, and when I get the windows sealed, I can at least keep the place warm without going broke."

"You own it, or gonna buy it?" Coakley asked.

"Nah, probably not," he said. "I'm thinking of moving up to the Cities, after next fall, go back to school."

"Good idea," Coakley said. "What'd you be taking?"

"Studio art, at the U," he said. "I'm a painter, when it isn't too cold. So: How can I help, and why me?"

Coakley said, "We're looking at these murders—Flood, Tripp, Crocker. And Kelly Baker."

His eyebrows went up. "They're connected?"

"That's what we're trying to find out," Virgil said. "We've heard—we're keeping our sources pretty close to our chest, and we'll do the same with you—but we heard that you were friends with Baker and with Bobby Tripp."

Loewe sort of leaned back, the way people do when they've heard something they don't like. He didn't answer for a minute, then said, "Yeah, I was. I talked to the Iowa police a couple of times. Nothing ever came of it."

"We're coming at it from a different angle," Virgil said. "Because we also know about the relationship between Tripp and Kelly. We're wondering if Kelly ever told you about that relationship, or if Tripp did. If there was something in there that could cause Tripp to kill Flood. Did Flood have some sort of abusive relationship with Kelly?"

"I wouldn't know about that," Loewe said. "Jake

could be a jerk, that's for sure. I just wonder if there wasn't a fight between him and Bobby, and it got a little too serious?"

Virgil shook his head. "If there'd been a fight, it would have shown up on Tripp—he would have been bruised or cut up or something. Flood was a big guy, and solid. We think Tripp snuck up on him, hit him with a ball bat."

"Mmm, boy, I don't see him doing that. He was a pretty tough guy, football player and all, but he wasn't mean," Loewe said.

"Do you think he was gay?" Coakley asked. She asked it with a motherly, understanding undertone that gave her thought away.

Loewe flinched. "Gay? Doesn't seem likely. He was a big football guy."

"It's been suggested that you may have had a relationship with him," Virgil said.

Loewe took a step back, but didn't say anything for a moment, then, instead of saying, "No," he asked, "Who said that?"

"Look, we're keeping all of this very close. And we don't even need to know whether or not you did, because that's private, and I don't see how it could affect the case. But: We need to know what Kelly did, what caused her to be murdered, and why Tripp would murder somebody in return, and then be murdered himself . . . and on down the line. Do not forget that there's still a murderer running loose."

"You don't think I'm involved . . ."

"I don't know," Virgil said. "Are you?"

Loewe turned, walked away from them, picked up a roll of the plastic window sheeting. "I'm not going to talk to you anymore. This is crazy—I don't know what happened to anybody." His voice was climbing in pitch: He was scared, and Virgil decided to push it.

"Do you think the killings might have anything to do with your church? We've noticed a lot of connections there—you know. Kelly Baker, Flood, even Crocker."

"The church? What connection could it have to the church?" he asked. "I think there might be some connection because everything happened in the same place . . . but not the church. Look, I really don't want to talk about this anymore. But I'll tell you: I have nothing to do with this. Any of it. I was freaked when Kelly Baker died, and I was freaked when Jake Flood got killed, and even more freaked when B.J. was killed."

"Did you ever know a woman named Birdy Olms?" Virgil asked.

"Birdy? What does she have to do with it? She took off years ago. Back when I was a kid."

"Any idea where she went?" Coakley asked.

"Nobody does," Loewe said. "I guess that's how she planned it. She's gone."

Virgil looked at him for a couple of beats, and then asked, "You don't have any idea why Kelly Baker was killed? Your friend Kelly."

"I'm not even sure she was murdered—the Iowa cops didn't seem all that sure of it. Maybe . . . it was an accident."

"She'd been pretty severely abused," Virgil said. "So that almost certainly makes it murder. If they were older than she was, the killers, that makes it statutory rape, a crime. If she died in the course of a crime, then it's murder. Everybody involved, and everybody involved with hiding the killers, is going to prison for thirty years, no parole. No art school, nothing."

"Okay, that's it. I'm done," Loewe said, but his voice didn't seem to Virgil to contain as much anger as it did fear. "I didn't have anything to do with Kelly. We knew each other: That's all. Now, please leave. Please."

Virgil said, "Wait a minute, Harvey. We're investigating three murders, for Christ's sakes. We're not trying to inconvenience you—we're trying to find a killer. And there's still a killer out there, trying to shut people up. You wanna be on that list?"

And Coakley said, "Harvey—we know about you and Bobby. We really don't want to embarrass you. And we're not embarrassed about gay people; one of the people who's helping us on this case is gay."

"Who'd that be?" Loewe asked.

"Well, we can't say."

"So you're making it up," Loewe said.

"I'll tell you, as a police officer, that I'm not," Coakley said. "What we need to know is, if you were close to Bobby—we won't even ask you about sex—but if you were close to him . . . do you have any idea of why he'd go off on Jake Flood?"

"We think it's something he learned not long ago,"

Virgil said, "because if he'd known it all along, he would have done something sooner."

Loewe looked down at the floor, as if trying to make up his mind.

Virgil prodded him: "Bobby was murdered, not out of revenge, but because he knew something. Jim Crocker was killed because he knew something. We need to know what that was."

Loewe backed up and sat down in a chair and said, "You can't tell anybody."

"We won't, unless we absolutely have to—if we're required to in court," Coakley said. "I tell you that last part so I won't be lying to you. It could come out that way, but that's the only way. And we'll do everything we can to avoid that."

"Ah, God, it'll come out," Loewe said. And, "I've got to get out of here anyway."

"Tell us, Harvey," Virgil said.

LOEWE SAID, "I really felt close to Bobby. And I want to tell you that our relationship didn't start until he was eighteen, almost nineteen. He was a good guy, and I don't say that because of our relationship. He was a good guy with everybody."

"I buy that. He *was* a good guy," Virgil said.

Loewe said, "When Kelly got killed, nobody knew anything. But, she was in the church, and the word got around pretty fast, about the sex and all. Bobby had been around with her quite a bit, and they'd gotten pretty close. They used to talk a lot, about everything. Ah, jeez . . . we were together once, and I told him about the sex. But he already knew."

"He already knew what? That she had a sexual relationship with somebody?"

"Yeah. She told him. She told him that things got rough, sometimes, and that she kinda liked it, I guess. She didn't tell him everything, though. I told him . . . the rest of it. From the autopsy report—that got around the church pretty fast. About how a bunch of guys were on her. About how somebody had whipped her and all of that. Everybody in the church knew about it, I think from her parents, or maybe her uncle. He was really freaked out."

"Had Bobby had a sexual relationship with her?" Coakley asked.

"Oh, no. Kelly knew he was gay. She actually introduced us. . . . Kelly and I knew each other for a long time, and she knew I was that way. But I think they both felt a little bit like sex freaks, him being a gay football guy, and she because of the sexual things she did."

"So he freaked out," Virgil said. "But how did that get him to Jacob Flood?"

"I did that, too, I guess," Loewe said. He looked everywhere but at Coakley and Virgil. "The last time I saw him, he asked me if Jake Flood knew Kelly. I said, 'Well, yeah. They're in the church.' He asked if Jake ever hung around Kelly. I don't know why I said it, but I said, 'They know each other, for sure.' Then he said that Jake had come into the elevator, with his shirt off, and he had a Statue of Liberty tattoo on his stomach. I said, 'Yeah, he does. It goes right down to his . . ." He glanced at Coakley. ". . . You know, down there."

Virgil: "And he said?"

"He said Kelly used to . . . have rough sex with somebody named Liberty. And I said, 'Maybe it was him. People who know him call him Liberty sometimes.' You know, I was joking."

"Did people really call him that?" Virgil asked.

"A few," Loewe said.

Virgil said to Coakley, "On the drawing of the statue, the one I got from Tripp's backpack, there was a long oval, drawn in pencil. You remember that?"

"Yes," she said.

"It was an erect penis," Virgil said. He turned back to Loewe: "Did he say anything about taking the information to the police?"

Loewe shook his head. "No, he never said anything about that. I think, you know, he thought that if he told anybody about all that, about him and Kelly, that it'd all come out. About him being gay, and all. About me being gay. So . . . I didn't think he'd do anything. It never really . . . occurred to me."

"I want you to tell me the truth, here, Harvey," Virgil said. "Does this sex thing have anything to do with the church? I mean, okay, you're gay, so you're out of it. But a lot of church guys are hooking up with young women. Real young women. Is there some sort of thing where the church says the marriage age, in the eyes of God, is younger than, you know, the regular age?"

"No, no, nothing like that," Loewe said. "The people in the church are close, so they all know each other, and I guess guys are looking for girls who share . . . church stuff. I don't share it so much anymore. I'm thinking about getting out. But, the church is the church."

"So you know Emmett Einstadt?"

"Everybody knows Emmett. He's like . . . the pope of our church."

"And there's no kind of organized sex."

"It's a *church*," Loewe said.

They talked about it a bit more, and Virgil said, "You're going to have to come in and make a formal statement, Harvey. This is important stuff."

"Ah, God."

"Doesn't have to be right this minute. But we're going to need it, sooner or later."

"You said it wouldn't have to come out."

"That was before we knew how important it is. Maybe the information won't get us anywhere, and you won't have to. But if it breaks this case, then you will." Virgil slipped a business card out of his pocket, dropped it on the kitchen counter. "If you think of anything, call me. Don't talk to anyone else about it. We were serious about there being a killer out there."

LOEWE FOLLOWED THEM to the door, said, "Please help me out. Don't tell anybody."

They left him standing in the doorway, and when he shut the door behind them, Coakley said, pulling on her gloves, "I feel a little bad about Harvey."

"He should have talked to the Iowa cops a long time ago," Virgil said. "It might have taken them to Flood. Then there'd be three guys still alive."

"Not if he didn't know that Kelly was having sex with Liberty when he was talking to the Iowa people," she said.

"All right. Maybe he didn't," Virgil conceded. "But maybe he did. I think he was lying to us, a little bit."

"I just hope he doesn't do anything awful," Coakley said. They looked back at the house and saw a sheet of plastic move in the window.

"What do we do from here?" Coakley asked. She'd been wearing a Fargo-style watch cap, and now she took it off, tossed it in the backseat, and shook her hair out.

"Surveillance. They'll be having church services tonight. We watch Flood's place, and we watch Baker's, and we follow them to wherever the service is."

"That'd be tough out here," she said. They both looked across the flat, snow-covered fields; you could see a car a mile away. With lights at night, maybe three or four miles.

"I'll make some calls—see if I can get a highway patrol plane to park over the Floods' place, track them from a distance," Virgil said. "They can call us on the ground. We could wait in Battenberg or wherever."

"You think you can get it?"

"I think so. I'd have to talk to my boss, but the dimensions of this thing are getting to be interesting," Virgil said. "He'll go for it."

"It *is* interesting," Coakley said, "but I doubt that it'll do me much good in the next election."

"You can live with it," Virgil said. "If what I think is going on, is going on . . ."

"I can live with it," she said.

HE STARTED the truck and eased out of Loewe's driveway, turned left, back toward town. "The thing is," Virgil said, as they drove along, "if we get the DNA back from the lab tomorrow, we may be close to finished—if we can show that Spooner killed Crocker, and that closes the chain of murders."

"But we're not done," Coakley protested. "Flood is dead, but there were more people involved with Kelly Baker—"

"That's an Iowa case," Virgil said. "We send them a file with what we think."

"Oh, come on, Virgil," she said. And apparently without thinking about it—or maybe she did, he thought later, because he sometimes tended toward cynicism, or at least the study of human calculation—she reached over with her inboard hand and put it on his thigh. "This is our case now. Iowa's going nowhere with it."

She pulled her hand back, leaving behind a hand-sized warm spot; and she still seemed unaware of the casual intimacy. Virgil tended to think that women were hardly ever unaware of even the *most* casual intimacy; they had intimacy detectors more powerful than a rat's cheese detector, although, he decided, the analogy might not be precise.

"So we agree on that," he said. "In fact, I was planning to kill most of the rest of the day hanging out, waiting for the DNA to come in. But now I'm thinking I'll go talk to Alma Flood. I'd like to catch her without her father around."

She patted him on the thigh again. "Do that. Check the plane first. And call the lab about the DNA, see where they're at. I'm going to get some of the boys who know about the church, get a list of names, and run every one of them through the feds. Maybe something will pop up."

They came up to a stop sign and Virgil said, "I hate this truck for this. The guy who invented consoles must've been some kind of über-nerd."

"What?"

He put the truck in park, reached an arm around her shoulder, pulled her as close as the console would allow, and kissed her. She saw it coming and went with it, and when they ran out of air, he backed off a few inches, then kissed her again, and when she sank into him, he twisted a bit more so he could cup her far breast in his left hand. She went with that, too, though only for a few seconds, before rolling away from him, and she said, "Mmmm."

"Well, hell, it's a start," he said, putting the truck back in gear. "I've never kissed a sheriff before."

"Probably never felt one up, either," she said, patting her hair back into place. "Not that I didn't like it."

He thought about a wisecrack, but instantly suppressed it, going instead for a sincere-sounding, and possibly shy-sounding, "I wouldn't have . . . characterized it like that."

She squinted at him, one eye blue, one eye green, and then, he thought, bought it. If you can sell sincerity to a woman, you're halfway home. Not to be cynical about it.

VIRGIL CALLED the BCA office as soon as he got a cell phone signal, talked to Davenport. "You fly around in that plane more than any six other guys," Davenport said.

"I don't want to fly in it," Virgil said. "I'll be on the ground. We'll send along one of Lee's deputies to watch one of the houses, maybe the Floods, or this Einstadt guy, see where the meeting is."

"I sense an emotional resonance in the way you said 'Lee,'" Davenport said. "I heard she's a looker."

"That's correct," Virgil said. "I plan to further explore those aspects of the case."

"Yeah, yeah, I don't want to hear it," Davenport said. "Well, actually I do, but some other time."

"Wouldn't be good right now," Virgil said.

"She's sitting right next to you, right?"

Virgil nodded at his phone. "Yup."

"You know, if the DNA comes through, we could just let the rest of it slide."

"Lucas, there are girls in this church who are much younger than your daughter," Virgil said.

"Ah, man," Davenport said. "Where do you want the plane?"

THEY SETTLED THAT, and he got Davenport to switch him up to the DNA lab, where he talked to a tech. The lab was still processing the DNA from the hair taken from Spooner's couch, but, the tech said, she'd have something to tell Virgil by noon the next day.

Virgil got off and said to Coakley, "Noon tomorrow. I do believe we'll have Miz Spooner in jail by two o'clock."

"That could crack it," Coakley said. She patted him on the thigh again.

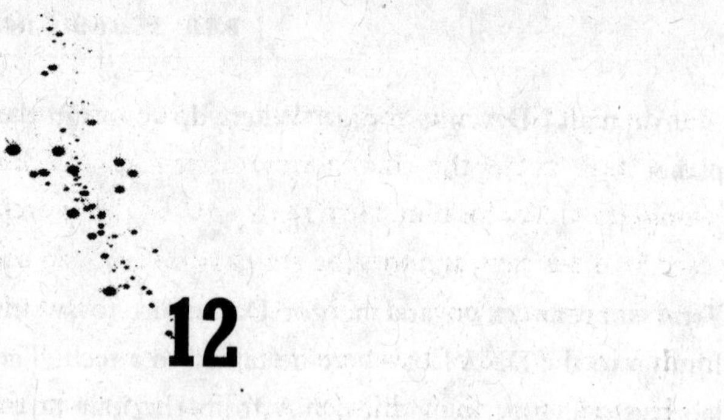

12

Loewe watched the two cops go out to their truck and pull away, and he stepped away from the window and grabbed the roll of window plastic and began unrolling it, quickly, then frantically, his hands shaking. He cut a sheet and carried it to a window and began trying to tape it up, but he was so frantic now, shaking so badly, that he finally let it crumple to the floor, and dropped into his only easy chair and covered his face with his hands.

He should have left. He should have left right after Kelly was killed, should have gotten everything together and gone out to San Francisco. He was a good carpenter, had taken cabinetry classes, knew enough electric and plumbing to get along. He'd been told he could make a fortune out in San Francisco. He could find jobs in the underground economy, paid with cash, and live quietly and invisibly and mostly legally, until he found out how everything shook out.

Now, they were looking right at him. He had nothing to do with Kelly Baker, but he *knew* about it, and that was enough. That was their message. They were floating a deal, but if the church were blown up, no deal would stick. Not for him. He'd been a boy in the church, used by older men, and then he got to be a man, and had used the younger boys as he had been used . . . and nobody in the World of Law would forgive that.

He had more than thirteen hundred dollars in the bank, and a good paid-off F250, only six years old. He could still run to San Francisco, sell the truck, move down to a little-used Tacoma, license it in a fake company name, put together a Mexican crew from the Wal-Mart slave markets, live underground. . . .

He put the first knuckle of his right fist into his mouth and bit until it hurt. What to do?

Twenty minutes after the cops left, he'd cooled down, and he called Emmett Einstadt. "I need to see you. The sooner the better. I think . . . at the Blue Earth rest stop."

"Blue Earth? What are you talking about, Harvey?"

"Because we need to see who comes in after us. That's why. I need to talk to you, and we need to see who comes in after us. Be there. One hour from now, exactly. Don't get there one minute early, or one minute late. If you aren't there, you won't be seeing me again. Ever."

There was a long silence as Einstadt took that in. He started, "Harvey—"

"I'm not fooling around here, Emmett, and I'm not going to talk about it on any phone or cell phone or any other way, or in any building," Loewe said, and the panic was bleeding into the phone. "You be there."

Loewe hung up and watched the phone: When it didn't ring, he figured Einstadt would be there.

AND HE WAS.

He followed Einstadt's Silverado into the highway rest stop, parked next to him. The Silverado had a crew cab, and he climbed out of his Ford and into the back of the Chevy. Einstadt turned half-sideways in the driver's seat to take him in. "What in the heck was so blamed urgent—"

"The cops came this morning. The sheriff and the state guy, whatever his name is. Flowers. They've hooked up Jake Flood and Kelly Baker, they've got information coming from someplace, I don't know where. But they *know*, Emmett, or they're about to find out. They were hinting around that I could deal with them. . . ."

"What'd you say?"

"I said I didn't know what the heck they were talking about. What did you want me to say? That I fucked Jacky Shoen last week?"

"Watch your language, Harvey," Einstadt said. "You're talking to the Senior."

"I'll tell you what, Senior, if they crack the church, you're going to spend your senior days in the state penitentiary. The only lucky thing for you is, you're too old to last long. They told me: thirty years. Thirty years for *knowing* about Kelly. You think somebody won't crack, looking at thirty years?"

"What else?"

Loewe had the old man's attention now: His green eyes were half-shut, focused.

"Oh, heck, they wanted to know if I'd had a relationship with Bob Tripp, they wanted to know about my relationship with Kelly Baker. They wanted to know if she had a sexual relationship with Jake—they're that far down the road, Emmett. They asked about Birdy Olms—"

"What about Birdy?"

"I don't know. They asked where she went. I said I didn't know . . . 'cause I don't."

Einstadt was peering at him.

Loewe asked, "Do you know?"

Einstadt turned away, then said, almost pensively, into the windshield, "Flowers was down at the Main Street, asked about Liberty."

Loewe bobbed his head and said, "Well, there you go, Emmett. There's only one way to know about Liberty—somebody told him."

"All right," Einstadt said. "I'm going to talk to some of the others. We'll figure this out. You sit tight—you don't know anything about anything. We'll ride it out. We had a problem like this thirty years back, rode it out."

"Emmett—"

His voice harsh, a prophet's voice, Einstadt said, "Keep down, keep your mouth shut. Like you said, if you talk about anything, you're gone. It's not only Jacky Shoen you fucked. If the whole thing comes out, there won't be no deal strong enough for you."

They looked at each other for a minute, then Loewe

said, his voice calmer, "I believe you can take care of it, Emmett. That's why I called. But you need to know how serious this is. I'm going home. I'll keep my mouth shut. I'll even pray. But you gotta do something."

Einstadt nodded and said, "Take off."

LOEWE GOT OUT of the Silverado, back into his Ford. Watched, slumped in his seat, as Einstadt wheeled out.

Thought, *San Francisco.*

His folks didn't need him, with the crops in for the year. His old man could handle the winter work on his own.

Loewe looked at his watch: He could go home, load up, and be in Omaha by dark. Thought about it a little more. Maybe not, he thought. If something happened, they could put out an alert to the highway patrols between here and there, and pick him up.

He needed to sell the truck in Minnesota. Up in the Cities. List it on the Internet, Craigslist, with a low enough price, and it'd be gone in a day. Get a bank draft for it, put it in the bank, then yank the money out in cash. Take off. Three days. That way, if something broke, they couldn't track him across the country. . . .

EINSTADT PULLED OUT of the rest stop thinking about *those damn women.* He didn't worry about Liberty, because Liberty was dead, and there wasn't anything anybody could do about that, including the World of Law. He didn't worry much—maybe a little—about Loewe, because Loewe had a taste for the boys, and he was right: If the World of Law found out about it, they'd call him a predator and put him in jail forever. So he *would* keep his mouth shut.

But those damn women: Kathleen Spooner and Birdy Olms. Spooner had gone and shot Crocker and should never have done that. Never. Crocker was a cop, and the other cops would never let go, now that they knew he'd been murdered.

And Flowers, blabbing all over the place, had hinted that there was some DNA involved. DNA was the latest curse from the World of Law. If they had DNA on her, they could use her as a wedge to open up everything.

Then there was Birdy. Birdy wouldn't listen to anybody about anything. Even after her initiation, she'd continued to fight them. Finally, she'd run away. In some ways, it was a relief; in other ways, a threat. She was still out there, somewhere. They'd never heard a peep from her, but she'd cleaned out her husband's cash and tax account before she left, and had enough cash to hide pretty thoroughly.

Now, maybe, they should take another stab at finding her.

First, something had to be done about Spooner. He thought about that for a long time, to the first exit, across the bridge, back onto I-90, and finally called his oldest son, Leonard, and told him they needed to meet. "Tell Junior to be there. . . . We've got a problem."

LEONARD AND JUNIOR were hard men in their forties, both farmers, dark hair, dark eyes, perpetual five o'clock shadows across the saturnine faces they'd inherited from their mother. They met at Emmett Einstadt's house on the hill, climbing up the driveway past the line of bare apple trees, Concord grape arbors, and snow-covered garden flats.

Einstadt told them what he thought: that as desperate an act as it was, Spooner had to be eliminated. They listened wordlessly, then Leonard looked at Emmett, and at Junior, and asked, "What do you think?"

"Makes me sour just thinking about it, but Father's right," Junior said. "If they're really testing for her DNA, I don't know how long that takes, but it can't be too long. So we'll have to do it soon."

All three of them had grown and butchered animals, so death was not an abstract concept to them. They could do it; the question was, How?

Einstadt said, "She's always liked you, Leonard. You could send Mary and the kids on the way, tonight, get her there after they're gone. Get it done, take her over to Junior's, get her in the ground. Out in the woodlot, we've been in there working. It's supposed to snow again tomorrow night. Once it snows—"

"Give me the creeps, knowing she's there," Junior said.

"You can live with it," his father said, and Junior nodded.

"What about her car?" Leonard asked.

"Put it in Junior's barn, stack hay around it. Soon as

we've got a little space, the two of you put it on a trailer, drive it to Detroit, leave it in the street with the keys inside, drive back."

"That's a risk," Leonard said.

"We've got to take some risks," Einstadt said. "If Kathleen hadn't killed Crocker . . ."

"But she's right about Crocker. He might've talked."

"If she'd come and talked to us, we could have handled that. She didn't, and so now she's got to pay," Einstadt said.

"We all ought to sell out, go up to Alberta and start another colony up there," Junior said.

"Maybe someday," Einstadt said, "but we can't right now. Right now, we've got to do something about Kathleen. And I've been thinking: Here's how we do it, keeping in mind that gun of hers."

THEY WORKED IT OUT in detail, right down to the rope they'd use, and then Leonard went to his home phone to call her, with the other two listening in on handsets in the living room and the upstairs bedroom. They called on her cell phone, and she answered on the second ring.

Leonard said, "We need to talk, seriously, Kathleen. The police are looking for Birdy. We know where she is—she's down in Dallas—and somebody's got to go down there and . . . settle her. We thought of you."

After a silence, she said, "Where in Dallas?"

"Dad's got the exact address, I don't know it myself. But they're going for her. What we want to do is, meet here at my place tonight, while the others are headed off to church, figure out exactly what we want to do, and then get it done. We need to set it up so you can get down there, do it, and get back before anybody notices. We're thinking next weekend, so there'll be two days. Junior will drive down with you. Go down in one shot, twelve hours straight through, trade driving, one of you sleeping in the back of the truck. Do the whole thing in twenty-six hours."

"I'll call you back in two minutes. I'm going to take a cigarette break outside," she said.

The three of them looked at their phones until she called back, and when she did, she said, "Don't ever think I'm as much as a dumbass as you Einstadts are," she said. "The chances of my meeting with you, in your farmhouse, at night, are zero. You get me in there, wring my neck, and you're just goddamn dumb enough to think that would solve your problems. But it wouldn't, it'd just get you in deeper. This Flowers guy, from what I hear, is about to tear the ass off the World of Spirit. You got one chance, and I'm it. And I'm going to give you the chance. Are you listening to this, Emmett?"

Emmett, embarrassed, didn't say anything for a few seconds, then, grudgingly, "Yeah."

She said, "You come down to my house, you and Leonard. No guns, but I'll have mine, and I'll tell you what we're going to do. Then I'm going to let you talk me out of it. By the way, I've been figuring, one thing and another, and I figure the church can raise two hundred thousand dollars without breaking much of a sweat.

Hell, Emmett, you could raise it by yourself, probably. I'm gonna need that money, and soon."

Emmett said, "I don't think—"

"Don't bullshit me, Emmett. I've been living out here all my life, and I know who's got what. And when I tell you the plan, I don't think you'll worry too much about the money. So: one hour, at my place. No guns."

She hung up, and the Einstadts looked at each other for a few seconds, and then Junior asked, "Are we going?"

Emmett Einstadt nodded and said, "Not much choice. She's in deeper than we are—she's a cop killer—so it couldn't really be a trap."

Leonard asked, "I wonder how she knew we were going to wring her neck?"

"Let's you and me find out," Emmett said.

LEONARD HAD SENT his wife, Mary, and the three kids off to the supermarket, to keep the meeting with his father close to the vest. He and Emmett left for Jackson, and Junior sat in the living room, looking out the window, until Mary's Ford Explorer turned up the drive.

She met him with a smile in the driveway—she always liked him—and he helped carry the groceries in. The three kids were still too small to have received the Spirit, and they put them in the front room to watch television and went up the stairs.

Mary, a jolly blonde, said, "You always had a hard time waiting, on meeting nights, didn't ya?" and Junior helped her unbutton her blouse and she helped him undo his pants and she fell back on the bed, all white as marble—Junior loved the blondes, he told his pals, because you could see so much more—and she said, "How do you want this, brother? You want it quick, or you want something you can watch?"

IN JACKSON, the night was just coming on when the Einstadts left the truck in the street and crunched up the packed snow on the driveway to Spooner's place. Spooner had been looking for them. She opened the side door, waved them upstairs, then backed away into the living room, where she'd set a chair against the wall. She dropped down into the chair with a pistol in each hand. She did like the feel of them.

The Einstadts came in, checked the guns, and she pointed the men at the couch. When they were sitting, she asked, "Whose harebrained idea was it to bring up Birdy?"

Emmett Einstadt said, "Not harebrained. They've got her name and they're looking for her. If she's still living under it, they could find her. She could be a real danger."

"But you don't know that she lives in Dallas," Spooner said.

"No."

Leonard said, "What's this big idea you've got that's gonna save us all?"

She said, "I want you to talk me out of it. If you can't, I'm gonna go ahead."

"What is it?" Emmett asked.

"I'm gonna confess."

The Einstadts looked at each other as though they might have heard wrong, and Emmett asked, "What the heck are you talking about?"

"I'm going to confess that I was there when Jim killed himself," Spooner said. "I'm going to confess that I was sucking his cock, and I'm going to confess that he might have been scared because they were afraid they'd find his DNA on the Tripp boy, and then on Kelly Baker. And they're looking for Liberty, so I'm going to give them Liberty. What do you think?"

Emmett said, "You should have your mouth washed out with soap. If you can't control your language—"

"Give me a fuckin' break, Emmett," Spooner said. "You been in my face as often as any—if I wasn't sucking your cock, what was I doing? Felt like suckin' to me."

"Sexual contact—"

"Hold the bullshit, Emmett. Okay? Just this once?"

Emmett said, "You don't have to give them Liberty. They've already got Liberty." He recounted Loewe's story of his interview with Flowers and Coakley.

"All the better," Spooner said. "They don't know that I know about that—so when I give them Liberty, I won't be giving them anything new, and at the same time, it'll make it seem like I'm telling the truth."

Leonard cut to the heart of it: "Your idea can't be as goofy as it sounds. I'm still listening."

So she told them about it, in detail.

13

A battered Ford F350 dually sat next to the barn when Virgil turned up the Floods' driveway, and as he got to the top of the rise, a short, square man came out of the barn with a dead chicken in his hands. He'd been plucking it, Virgil realized when he got out of the truck: He could smell the hot, wet feathers.

The man said, "Who're you?"

"Virgil Flowers, Bureau of Criminal Apprehension," Virgil said. "I'm here to talk to Mrs. Flood. Is she in?"

"This is not a good time," the man said. He lifted the chicken: "I'm tied up."

"Who're you?"

"Wally Rooney . . . I'm helping Alma with her chores," the man said.

"Nice of you," Virgil said. "But my interview with Mrs. Flood will be confidential, anyway, so—"

"She's got the right to a lawyer, don't she?" Rooney asked.

"Well, yeah," Virgil said. "Though to tell you the truth, I didn't know she needed one. If we have to go through all that, we'd have to take her down to the sheriff's office. . . . I just thought it'd be easier to have a chat."

Rooney gestured with the chicken again, and Virgil took that as assent. "If she doesn't want to talk to me, I'll certainly be happy to arrange for a lawyer to sit with her while I do," he said. "Because I *am* going to talk to her."

HELEN MET VIRGIL at the door, said, "You again," but she said it with a smile, and then a wink, and the wink actually startled him, coming from a twelve-year-old. Maybe she'd picked it up from an old-timey movie, he thought, and in an old-timey movie, it would have been called a come-on.

Interesting.

He followed her into the house, and Helen called ahead, "Mr. Flowers is here again," and she used his name with a familiarity that suggested that he'd been talked about.

Alma Flood was sitting on a platform rocker, as morose as she'd been during the first visit, with the Bible still at her arm. She said, "My father isn't here—"

"I actually wanted to talk to you," he said. He looked at the girl. "Privately."

Flood said to her daughter, "Go on and watch TV with your sister."

The girl nodded and headed up the stairs and out of sight, and Virgil said, "I hope the Bible's providing you with some comfort. It certainly does provide me with some, in hard times."

"You're a Bible reader?" A rime of skepticism curled through her question.

"All my life," Virgil said. "My father's a Lutheran minister over in Marshall. But, when there's trouble, you've got to pick your chapters. Stick with Psalms, stay away from Ecclesiastes. Probably stay away from the Prophets, too."

She nodded. "I have read the twenty-third Psalm a hundred times over, and I have to say, it doesn't really bring me that much comfort."

"The problem with that one is, it's been attached to too many funerals, so it makes you feel a little sad, just hearing it," Virgil said.

"Maybe," she said, but she picked up the Bible and leaned sideways and put it on the floor next to her chair. "You're not here to talk about the Bible, minister's son or not."

"No, I'm not. I have to ask you something, and I'm happy that the girls aren't around. I'm wondering if you have any knowledge . . . Is it possible that your late husband had some kind of relationship with Kelly Baker? We're getting some pretty substantial hints in that direction."

She didn't jump in to say, "No," or cut him off, or sputter in disbelief, or any of the other things that she might have done. She sat stock-still for a moment, then said, lawyer-like, "I really have no knowledge of anything like that."

"When she died, he didn't seem distraught or anything? He didn't talk about her?"

"I don't believe he ever mentioned her name, in my hearing," she said.

"Could you tell me, does your church introduce young men and women to each other . . . ?"

She was shaking her head. "We don't have to. We grow up in the church, in the World of Spirit, and the children know each other from the time they are babies."

"And the adults know the children," Virgil said.

"Of course. The Bakers are not our close friends, but we knew Kelly Baker. My father may have left you with the impression that we really didn't, but he was just trying to . . . avoid involvement in this dirty case."

"Ah. So to put it another way, it's possible that your husband knew Kelly Baker quite well, and that you wouldn't know about it."

She surprised Virgil by saying, "Possible," which sounded almost like an affirmation.

"We talked to a fellow who is familiar with your church, and he noticed that there were quite a few older men marrying girls right after they turn eighteen, and the question arises, is there some kind of religiously based, or church-sanctioned, contact between these older men and the younger women?" Virgil asked.

Another improbable pause, and then she said, a light growing in her eyes, "We have no specific rules regarding that. Specific rules come from the World of Law; and you can look around the world, and see what the World of Law has done to you, with your wars and crime and corruption. Two Peter two:nineteen—'They promise them freedom, but they themselves are the slaves of corruption.'"

"But like it or not, you also live in the World of Law," Virgil said. "And look at the next sentence in Two Peter: 'For whatever overcomes a person, to that he is enslaved.' Are any of these church members enslaved to that which overcomes them?"

She sighed and shook her head.

Virgil said, "'For the one who sows to his own flesh will from the flesh reap corruption, but the one who sows to the Spirit will from the Spirit reap eternal life.' Are you having a little trouble with that, Alma?"

"I can't talk to you," she said. "My husband has just passed, I can't—"

Virgil said, "Miz Flood—"

"I can't talk," she repeated. Then: "I've been reading the Book hard and long. It's all I do when I'm not cooking or making beds. I'm thinking about it. Maybe we could talk again . . . someday."

VIRGIL LEFT IT at that. There were more questions to be asked, but he'd gotten some answers, even if they weren't stated aloud. Wally Rooney, plucked chicken in hand, stepped out of the barn to watch him leave. At the bottom of the hill, he turned toward I-90 and got on the phone to Davenport.

"We got the plane?" he asked.

"You got it. He'll fly into Blue Earth, they've got a little strip down south of town, off 169," Davenport said.

"Lee Coakley suggested that would keep curious people from wondering where the deputy was going."

"Good. Now listen, Lucas, I'm serious here: We may have the biggest goddamn child abuse problem that we've ever seen," Virgil said. "It might have gone on for a hundred years. I mean, really, a hundred years. It's one of those weird cults, and they raise their children in the cult and I have the feeling that they go at them when they're pretty young. I'm talking twelve. That's with the girls; I don't know about the boys."

"When you say big—"

"The cult—they call themselves the World of Spirit—looks to have maybe a hundred families or more, including a lot of kids," Virgil said. "I asked one of the women, Flood's wife—the first guy killed—if the older guys ever hooked up with the younger women. Girls. She wouldn't talk about it, but the answer was 'Yes.'"

"Oh, boy. Work it as hard as you can, Virgil, but put Coakley out front," Davenport said. "These kinds of things generate a terrific smell. If you're out front, you could spend the next two years of your life doing depositions, and I don't want to lose you for that long."

"All right. Push those DNA guys for me. I need to know, soon as they get it."

"I've been doing that—and they say, noon tomorrow," Davenport said. "No sooner, maybe a little later. I'll be standing there, and I'll call as soon as they tell me."

"Thank you."

"One more thing, Virgil. I'm going to brief Rose Marie on this, and I suspect she'll want to have a quiet word with the governor. You know, so that if it really blows up, they'll know what's coming, and they'll have had a chance to talk through the response."

"Okay, but you gotta keep it close," Virgil said. "These people don't see us coming yet, and I don't need them burning evidence."

VIRGIL RANG OFF, took out his notebook, looked at it, then called Coakley: "I need the address of Greta and Karl Rouse, R-O-U-S-E. They live west of Battenberg somewhere."

"Give me ten minutes. I'll check their fire number."

Virgil drove toward Battenberg, taking his time, thinking over his options. Coakley called back and said, "Okay, I've got them spotted. Starting at North Main in Battenberg, you go out on Highway 7 until County 26 splits off. . . ."

Virgil crossed 94 into Battenberg, trundled through town, took the turn west with Highway 7. It was ten minutes, more or less, out to the Rouse place, following the web of small roads through the countryside.

The Rouse farmhouse, like the Floods', sat on a low rise, with a woodlot behind and a thick L-shaped wall of evergreens on the north and west. A little slough, frozen over, came down to the road, with brown broken cattails sticking out of the crusty snow. A mailbox at the end of the driveway read, "Rouse," and Virgil went on by. Couldn't see a kennel.

What to do? He could go hassle Loewe some more—he'd been nervous, and might be cracked—or the Bakers, or he could go socialize with Coakley. But what he really needed was the DNA report on Spooner.

He thought about it, yawned, turned back to I-94, went on down the highway to the Holiday Inn at Homestead, and took a two-hour nap.

UP AT FIVE, when Coakley called on his cell phone. "Where are you?"

"Just got back to the Holiday," he said. "I'm colder'n hell. I want to stand in the shower for a while."

"We're all set here," Coakley said. She was excited. "Gene Schickel's on his way over to Blue Earth to get the plane. He should be off the ground in fifteen minutes. The Wednesday meetings are after supper, starting usually around six-thirty."

"Okay. I'll be over at your office in half an hour," Virgil said.

"Better come to my house. I'm trying to keep this as hushed as we can."

"See you there."

AFTER SHOWERING, Virgil got his super-duty winter gear out of the duffel in the back of the truck and tossed it on the backseat—heavy, hooded, insulated camo coveralls of the kind sold to late-season deer hunters and musky fishermen, a pair of insulated high-top hunting boots, a full-face ski mask, and insulated downhill ski gloves. He got to Coakley's in a half hour and found her stacking similar gear in the front hallway, along with a couple of sleeping bags.

Her three boys, in annual sizes from high school down, all with long, honey-colored hair and round faces, were watching with heavy-lidded teenage curiosity, and nodded politely to Virgil and said, "Hi," when she introduced them.

She gave them last-minute instructions involving pizzas and a girl named Sue who probably should stay home and study that night, and went out the door, carrying her gear. They'd agreed earlier to go in separate trucks with one of the trucks ditched a mile or so from the worship service, as a backup.

"I got sleeping bags from the guys in case we have to lay out there awhile, and binoculars, flashlights, some granola bars to chew on," she said, as she loaded it into her truck. She handed him a radio handset. "It's all set to a command channel. Just key it and talk. Gene's on the same channel up in the plane."

Virgil nodded and said, "Okay. You lead, you know the maps better."

"I printed out satellite and terrain maps of that whole area of the county. I'll call you on the radio when we're close. Might not be any cell service, depending on where they go." She put the radio to her face, keyed it, and said, "Gene?"

"I'm here." Schickel's voice was clear as glass: Virgil realized he was probably very close by, but straight up. He looked for the plane's wing lights, but didn't see them.

"We're heading out," Coakley said. "Let me know . . ."

"Gotcha covered," Schickel said. "Boy, it's pretty up here, all the lights out on the lake."

AN HOUR LATER, Virgil and Coakley were sitting inside Virgil's truck seven or eight miles east of Battenberg—the meeting was apparently later than they'd thought—when Schickel called. "I've got the Platts moving out. More than one, but I couldn't see how many. I think it could be all of them, but the truck's parked outside the barn light."

"Stay with them," Coakley said.

"They're heading south on 28. . . ."

"Got that." Coakley bent over the map, marking the Platts' movement with a highlighter pen. Schickel came back. "Okay, I got Floods. More than one, but I can't see how many . . . in their truck . . . okay, they're moving, they're heading south. . . ."

After following the two vehicles on the map for five minutes, Coakley said, "They're going to the Steinfelds'."

She leaned across to show Virgil, said, "We'll leave your truck . . . here. Or right around there. It's a back road, no traffic, but it's plowed."

"I'll follow you," Virgil said. "Let's go."

They went, Virgil following Coakley's taillights through the winter night's gloom. The temperatures were in the teens, not too bad, but there was no traffic at all. They rolled along, alone, for nine minutes. Schickel called to confirm that the Platts and the Floods had gone to the Steinfelds' farm.

They dropped Virgil's truck on a narrow loop road away from the major routes into the Steinfelds', and Virgil loaded his gear into Coakley's truck. In another two minutes, they were down another small lane across a half-mile-wide cornfield, looking south, at the back of the Steinfelds' barn, barely visible through a heavy woodlot.

They unloaded without speaking, got into the winter gear, picked up the sleeping bags and a pack with the binoculars, flashlights, and granola bars. Coakley was breathing hard, excited; Virgil said, quietly—the night was so silent he could hear his heart beating—"The one thing that could go really big wrong is if somebody's sitting in that woodlot with a starlight scope. If we should take some fire, stay on the ground and scream for Schickel to start calling them. Don't try to run unless we're still way out."

She stopped her preparation for a moment and asked, "What are the chances of that?"

"Small, and very small, but not zero. But I doubt they'd actually shoot somebody down without knowing who they are."

THEY CROSSED a ditch and then a fence, crunching though the snow; hardly any wind, but deep, deep darkness, broken only by the lights around the farmstead.

Schickel said that there were at least thirty cars around the barnyard and driveway.

Crossing the field took almost fifteen minutes. They were walking with the furrows, rather than across them, which made life easier, but not easy. At the edge of the woodlot, they paused to listen and heard, very faintly, somebody singing.

Coakley whispered, "It's like a choir song."

"'Lift High the Cross,'" Virgil whispered back. "Let's get in the woods."

The woodlot was a tangled mess, and after pushing twenty or thirty feet in, they gave up and sat down.

Watched the barn, heard more hymns. Watched the barn. Heard somebody speaking, but couldn't make out the words. The rhythm of the speech, though, sounded like that of a sermon. They sat for a half hour, and then Virgil put his face close to Coakley's and said, "It's a bust. Let's go."

"What?"

"We're not going to see anything—I'm feeling sort of dumb. Let's go."

"Just like that?"

"Lee, we're not getting anywhere. Come on."

She didn't argue. They couldn't see anything, couldn't hear specific words, couldn't get closer. They walked back out of the woodlot, running into stumps and downed limbs, then trudged back across the field, following their incoming tracks as best they could. They hadn't even had a chance to eat a granola bar, or use the binoculars, Virgil thought. At Coakley's truck, they pulled off the heavy gear and climbed inside, and Coakley fired it up and they headed back to Virgil's truck.

"What a waste. Got the airplane and everything." She got on the radio and told Schickel that they could head back to Blue Earth. He said okay, and she clicked off and grumbled, "I oughta dock my own pay."

"Wasn't your idea," Virgil said.

"Ah, well."

Virgil asked, "When you were a cop, were you pretty law-abiding?"

She thought about that for a full fifteen seconds, then said, "As much as possible." Then, "What do you have in mind?"

"Karl Rouse is an amateur photographer. A guy in town told me he used to buy a ton of Polaroid film, and as soon as digital came in, he began buying a lot of digital paper. In other words, he wanted to make photos that nobody else would see. He has a young daughter, probably a year younger than Kelly Baker. They may have been friends."

"And . . ."

"If you were to drop me off at their place, I'd make sure they aren't home, and then take an unofficial look around."

"You mean . . . inside the house?" she asked.

"If I can get in," Virgil said.

"Oh, jeez, Virgil, I don't know. What if they come back . . . what if they have a dog?"

"I don't think they have a kennel, and if you were down the road with a radio, I could get out," he said.

"But people lock their doors now," Coakley said. "They don't leave them open."

"If they've got good locks, I couldn't get in," Virgil said. "I don't know how to pick locks or anything. I'd just have to go up and try the door. . . . I mean, I'd knock first."

"Just drive right up the driveway—"

"And knock, and leave me there if nobody answers, like you were looking for them, and then you left, in case anybody's watching," Virgil said. "And if somebody answers, we ask for the Rouse girl. Kristy. We ask her about Kelly."

"What about a dog?"

"If there's a dog, we leave," Virgil said. "I don't do dogs."

"Ah, jeez, Virgil. I don't know." She looked at him anxiously. "If we get caught . . ."

"That would be a problem, but . . . I think it's worth the risk. If what we think is happening, is happening."

THERE WERE no dogs. There were two or three lights on in the house, but no answer to repeated, loud knocking. Virgil went back to the truck and said, "Take off."

"You think you can get in?" she asked. She wanted him to say no.

"The door is loose. I think I can," Virgil said. "I need my camera and my butter knife."

"You carry a butter knife?"

"The Holiday Inn does. . . ."

He got his camera from the backseat, slung it over his neck, and she turned around, white-faced in the headlights reflected off the farmhouse, and took off. Virgil went to the door, rattled it a couple more times, then went to work with the butter knife. He needed a long, smooth curve in the blade, so he wouldn't damage the wood around the old lock. He bent and re-bent the knife, finally got it right, felt it push back the bolt, and he was in.

He shouted, "Mr. Rouse? Mr. Rouse?" No answer. He whistled for the dog; no barking. He carefully wiped his feet, went up a short flight of steps, found himself in the kitchen, with a single fluorescent light over the stove. "Mr. Rouse?"

Up the stairs, into the Rouses' bedroom. Stuck the flashlight in his mouth, began swiftly going through the bedroom drawers. Found a sex toy, a vibrator, a group of transparent negligees, but nothing else. Went quickly down the hall, more and more nervous, to another bedroom, the girl's bedroom, checked her bureau, found more negligees. Negligees that were too old for her, negligees that might be worn by a woman in her forties.

Nothing else. Went back down the stairs, did a quick scan of the first floor, found a small office with a computer and two printers, one a small Canon photo printer along with a box full of blank 4x6 photo paper. Opened a closet and found a jumble of old photo equipment, including small 35mm film cameras and no fewer than three Polaroids, and a slide projector, but no slides. Pulled the drawers on four file cabinets.

No photos, no cameras.

Had to be photos somewhere, because he had that printer. Thought about it, hurried back up to the main bedroom, looked under the bed. Nothing there. Looked at the bedroom closets. One closet was fairly large, and jammed with clothes. The other was not much bigger than the door itself. Something wrong about that.

Virgil looked at the side wall, found a seam halfway up, hidden by the jackets in the closet. He pushed on it, and a hatch popped open. He lifted it: and inside, saw a stack of boxes, boxes jammed with photographs.

He lifted off the top one, an old boot box, and carried it to the bed. Photos. A hundred of them, maybe two hundred, or more, all about sex, a man with one or two women, two men with two or three women, two or three men with a woman.

Women and children.

With the flashlight in his mouth, he took a dozen of them, lined them up on the bed to rephotograph them.

The radio beeped, Coakley's voice, harsh: "Somebody's coming. They're still a mile out."

Virgil said, "Shit," scooped up the photos, put the lid on the box, and, moving more slowly than he might have hoped, carefully put the box back in place. He had to struggle with the hatch, getting the pins matched up with snaps, and then he was down the stairs, through the kitchen, through the mudroom, and out, pulling the door shut behind him. He ran across the barnyard to the side of the barn, put the radio up, and said, "Where are they?"

"Still coming. Are you out?"

"I'm jogging down the driveway," he said. "I see them now."

The car was five or six hundred yards out, coming on at forty or fifty miles an hour, slow because of the snow. When he couldn't risk running any farther down the drive, he went sideways into the ditch, behind one of a line of arborvitae.

Tried not to think of the car: He believed that if you thought of somebody, they could pick up the vibration, and they would see you. The idea was nuts, of course, but he'd seen its effects on any number of surveillances.

Held his breath, tried not to think of the car . . . and the car went on by, down the road. Not the Rouses, but there was no way he'd go back in the house.

"Ah, Jesus," he said to the radio.

Coakley said, "I'm coming."

WHEN HE WAS BACK in the truck, she said, "This was awful. We were crazy to even try this."

Virgil nodded. "You're right."

"Nothing, right?"

"Wrong. Just about everything, maybe." He dug in his pocket, pulled out the photos. "Let's get someplace where we can look at these."

On the way back to Virgil's truck, her cheekbones seeming to stand out with the stress, she said, "That fuckin' Flowers. That's what they said. I paid no attention. This . . . I mean, I dunno. I dunno. I mean, I really don't know."

"I know what you mean," Virgil said.

"Maybe I should turn us in," she said. "That'd be the right thing to do. I'd inform the court, then resign—"

"Ah, for Christ's sakes, don't be a child," Virgil said.

She was quiet for a while, then asked about how he'd found the photos. He explained about the printer, and about finding them in the closet. About the vibrator and the negligees. "Nothing illegal about a vibrator," she said. "Or a negligee."

"Shut up," Virgil said.

They came up to his truck, and she followed him back to the Holiday Inn. In Virgil's room, they spread the photos out on the desk and pulled a desk lamp over them.

Twosomes, threesomes, foursomes, two-on-one, three-on-one. "I went on an Internet porn site, once," she said. "My oldest boy was looking at it; I found it in his history. This is like those pictures."

"What'd you do about your kid?" Virgil asked.

"Nothing. I was too embarrassed. And I suppose the curiosity is normal enough . . . as long as it doesn't get out of control. He's a good kid."

"This is Rouse, I think," Virgil said, tapping one of the photos. "He's in almost half of the pictures." He tapped a woman in another of the photos. "I wouldn't be surprised if this is Mrs. Rouse, because she's all over the place, and that's the style of the negligees in the chest of drawers. That kind of black lacy *Playboy* look from the sixties. And I would not be surprised if this is Kristy Rouse, because she looks like a combination of the other two. Look at her face. And the negligee."

"But she's . . ."

"Having sex with her father and another man," Virgil said. "This is the kind of sex that Kelly Baker was involved in."

"This girl, if this is Kristy, she can't be fourteen in this picture," Coakley said. "She looks more like eleven or twelve. If the FBI came through the door right now, they could arrest us for child porn."

"So now we know," Virgil said, sitting back. He pulled the photos together in a pile, tired of looking at them. "That's all I wanted. We burn these pictures, we never tell another soul about them, as long as we live. If anyone found out what we've done, it'd break the case. The evidence would be thrown out."

She nodded. "And you say there are more where these come from?"

"A few hundred in the one box. I didn't have much time, but I tried to take a representative sample. I doubt they'll be missed. Even if they are, who are they going to complain to?"

They burned the photos in the shower, washed the ash down the drain, turned on the ceiling fan to get rid of the odor.

"So we know," Coakley said. "Now what?"

"Now we wait until tomorrow. If we can get Spooner, I think we can break the whole thing out. I'd trade the whole murder charge for a full story of the World of Spirit—call it self-defense or whatever she wants, if she talks to us. She talks, we get a pile of search warrants, call in a whole bunch of BCA guys from the Cities, and hit them all at once. The Rouses alone will hang them. . . ."

"All right," she said. "All right. Tomorrow."

THEY WERE STANDING next to the bed, still with a little stink of photo smoke in the room, and Coakley said, "This afternoon, I had this . . . vision, kind of. We'd be lying out there in the sleeping bags, you know, not much going on, and we'd start to neck a little. Then nothing would happen, and we'd go back to the truck, and fool around a little more, then we'd come back here. You know?"

Virgil shrugged.

"But those pictures," she said. "How could you have any kind of decent sexual experience with those pictures still in your head?"

He shrugged again. "They were . . . out there."

"So maybe . . . maybe I could stop by again? Like tomorrow night?"

"Sure. Don't do anything you don't want to, Lee," Virgil said. "I mean, you know. Do what you want."

She stepped away and said, "Tomorrow."

"Okay."

Then she stepped back, grabbed his shirt, shoved him back on the bed, following him down, and said, "Oh, screw it. Right now."

14

Well, Virgil thought, when he woke up the next morning, *that was different.*

Whatever sexual frustrations Coakley had developed over the ten declining years of her marriage had been fully resolved, he thought. He groaned when he tried to sit up, reaching for his back. He'd pulled one of the hinge muscles between his back and butt. He'd felt it go at the time—it was a recurring injury from his baseball days—and then had forgotten about it. Overnight, it had tightened up, and now felt like a steel clamp.

He dropped back on the pillow. On most nights, before he went to sleep, he spent some time thinking about God, a leftover from the first eighteen years of his life when he'd gotten down on his knees each night to say his evening prayers. Virgil was neither a complete believer nor an unbeliever, though he was skeptical about God's interest in such things as divorce, debt, or dancing cheek to cheek, or much of anything that human beings got up to, short of murder, rape, or driving a Chrysler product.

Last night, he hadn't been thinking about God.

Last night, he'd been trying to stay alive in the face—and also the chest, hips, and legs—of unchained femininity. Coakley was in extremely good shape, and nearly as large as Virgil; when he was astride her, spurring her down to the quarter pole, he realized that he was looking at her nose and mouth, rather than her forehead, or even the top of her head, as had been the case with the other women he'd known.

And she just . . . manhandled him. Woman-handled him.

Then there was the whole question of her whatchamacallit. Actually, there were two questions.

The first was, "My God, what'd you do down here?"

As a blonde, when she blushed, she got pink from head to toe. "Some girlfriends talked me into it. We got lasered."

"Really?" Virgil couldn't think of what to say, but he liked it, so he said, "Cool. Interesting. It's kind of like a little landing strip."

The second question was one of nomenclature. If you're going to talk about the whole lasering concept, the ins and outs, so to speak, it seemed like there should be some word for it. *Vagina* was too specific and simply wrong, as were all the other Latinate words for specific parts. While examining the situation, Virgil suggested that only *pussy* was expressive of the area.

"I *really* hate that word," she said.

"Well, it's warm and fuzzy—"

"Virgil, do you want to get your hair ripped out?"

"There's a radio guy up in the Cities who refers to it as the 'swimsuit area,' but he uses that for both male and female, I think."

"That's so romantic," Coakley said. "'I love your swimsuit area, darling.'"

Virgil looked up at her and said, "I'm trying to fill a linguistic void here, and you're not helping. There is no noun for what we're talking about. Except—"

"Don't say it."

"And if we can't say that one, we should feel obligated to come up with another. One that's harmless, non-offensive, et cetera."

"Like . . . apple?"

"An Apple's a computer," Virgil said. "And I'm not sure that adapting either fruits or vegetables would really be appropriate."

"Or minerals. I'd rule out minerals."

They hadn't resolved the question, but Virgil determined to work on it in his spare time, if he ever had any.

HE LOOKED at the clock. Ah, man: 9:22. Had to get up. The DNA report would be coming in.

Anyhoo . . .

He yawned, scratched, trotted into the bathroom for a shower. All the towels had been used, and all but a sliver of the free soap—"Oh, yeah"—but he stood in the hot water for ten minutes, until he heard his cell phone ringing. He used the least-damp towel to pat himself dry, then went to see who'd called.

Coakley.

And at that moment, a text message arrived, also from Coakley.

"My office, IMMEDIATELY."

"Fifteen minutes," he tapped out, and went to shave.

Something had happened, and when you hadn't made it happen, that was usually bad.

HE WAS TWENTY-FIVE MINUTES, tired, dragging his aching ass into Coakley's office. There were two cops standing in the doorway, with an attitude on them: Something had happened. They stepped back when Virgil came up, and he found Coakley, trim, businesslike, looking across her desk at Kathleen Spooner.

And Virgil thought, *Oh, shit*, while he smiled and said, "Miz Spooner. Nice to see you."

Coakley said, in a voice as crisp as a green apple, "Miss Spooner says she has something to tell us. She wanted you to be here."

"It's a statement," Spooner said to Virgil, and Virgil took a chair. The two deputies were still leaning in the door. "I did something really bad. Then I ran away, but I felt so guilty. I can't afford a lawyer."

"We can get you a lawyer," Virgil said. "If you're going to tell us something you think might be criminal, I should remind you of your rights. . . ."

She listened quietly as he recited the Miranda warning, then said, "I don't want a lawyer now. I just want to get it off my chest. But maybe I'll want one later."

"That's just fine," Coakley said. "The minute you feel you need a lawyer, you tell us."

Virgil said, "So . . ."

Spooner looked down at her hands. "I was . . . there . . . with Jim, when he killed himself."

Virgil thought again, *Oh, shit.* He said, aloud, "He killed himself."

"Yes . . . I lied to you. Jim and I had started talking about getting back together. He called me up, and said something terrible had happened at the jail, and could I come over. I went over, and he was freaked. He said a guy in the jail had hanged himself, while he was on duty."

Coakley: "He said Tripp hanged himself?"

"That's what he said . . . at first. Then, he got kind of shaky, and I got a really bad feeling about it, like he wasn't telling me what really happened. He was *crying*. I've known him for a long time, and I'd never seen him cry, and here he was, bawling like a baby. Anyway, I didn't know what to do. I wanted to make him feel better. . . ."

"You had sex?"

"On the couch. He always liked it . . . that way."

Virgil said, "Miz Spooner, we're police officers, and we . . . know just about everything people get up to. When you say, 'that way,' what do you mean?"

Her eyes clicked away from him, but he suddenly had the sense that she was enjoying herself. "I, um, performed oral sex on him."

Virgil nodded. "Then what?"

"Well, I went into the bathroom after he was finished . . . you know, to gargle. . . ." Again, the sense that she was enjoying herself, a kind of exhibitionism.

Coakley said, "There's nothing criminal about oral sex."

Virgil thought, *Thank God*, but he said, to Spooner, "You were in the bathroom. . . ."

"When I heard the shot. It was so loud. *So loud*. The shot in that little house. I knew what it was. . . . I ran back in there, and he was dead. There wasn't any doubt about it, he was gone, and I was . . . freaked. I was so *scared*."

"He was wearing his gun while you were having sex?" Virgil asked.

"No, no . . . it was on his hip, and when we, uh, opened his fly and pulled down his underpants, he took it out and I took it from him and put it on the floor."

Coakley: "You took it."

"Yes," she said. "There was no end table, and he was kind of sideways on the couch, and I said, 'Give me that damn thing,' and I put it on the floor. I should have thrown it out the window. I think, you know, he'd always get a little sad after sex, and he'd already been a wreck . . . and I think he just grabbed it and did it. Just did it."

"And there'd been no sign that he was suicidal before that . . . shot?" Coakley asked.

"Well, he was really upset."

"Did you touch the pistol when you came out of the bathroom?" Virgil asked.

She nodded, looking straight at him. "I knew he was

dead, and I knew he was into something really bad, and I was afraid that I would get tangled up in it. So I picked it up and tried to wipe my fingerprints off with my shirt. Then I put it back by his hand . . . and left. Way out in the country like that, nobody saw me. My car had been behind the house. . . ."

"How did you know he was into something bad?" Coakley asked. "We must've skipped over something here."

Spooner didn't answer for a moment, but her lips moved, silently, as though she were looking for the right words. Then, "When we were talking, when I first got over there, he told me that Bob Tripp had found out something really bad about Jake Flood. Something about Jake Flood and that girl, Kelly Baker. I mean, Jim didn't exactly say what it was, but I formed my own conclusions."

Coakley: "Which were?"

"Jake Flood must've had something to do with Kelly Baker's death. And, everybody knew, that involved a lot of sex. I got the feeling . . . he didn't say anything . . . that Jim might've been involved. He kept talking about DNA."

Coakley and Virgil sat and looked at her, and she squirmed, and eventually asked, "What?"

"You suspected this, but you didn't come to us. . . ."

"What was I supposed to do?" she said, her voice rising into a whine. "Here they might have been involved in something awful with this girl, and if I came in, I'd be *involved*. I needed time to *think*. I mean, they were dead, anyway. I didn't have any proof. So . . . but here I am."

There was more talking to do, but when they'd wrung her out, Coakley said to Greg Dunn, one of the deputies in the door, "Take Miss Spooner down to the interview room and do this over, for a formal statement. When that's done, walk her over to Harris's office. I'll call him right now and tell him what's up."

To Spooner, she said, "Greg will take your statement from you—this is purely routine—and then we'll have you talk to Harris about whether or not you'll need a public defender. I couldn't really say one way or the other."

"Okay . . . Do you think I could get out early enough to make it to work?"

"I kind of doubt it," Coakley said. "But talk to Harris. Maybe."

WHEN SPOONER was gone, Coakley got on her phone, dialed a number, and said to Virgil, "Harris Toms is the county attorney."

"I knew that," he said.

She got Toms, explained the situation, hung up, and said, "Push that door shut."

He reached over and pushed the office door shut, and said, "We're fucked. She was lying through her teeth—she was enjoying the whole performance—but she covered all the bases. Every piece of evidence we have against her, she explained. And she came to us. Voluntarily. She just did a number on us."

"But we know what's going on, with the church," Coakley said.

"Yeah, but the case itself is pretty much gone," Virgil said. "It's solved. Flood and Crocker were taking little Kelly Baker out and banging her brains loose. Then something happened. They accidentally killed her or she died . . . whatever. Everything is cool until Flood takes his shirt off, and Tripp figures out that he was the one with Kelly."

Coakley picked it up: "Flood finds out that Bob was 'friends' with Kelly, and he assumes that Bob was having a sexual relationship with her, not knowing that the boy was gay. Could just be one of those man-to-man things, 'Pretty great piece of ass, huh? I could tell you stories. . . .'"

Virgil: "You get Bob to the jail, everything is fine. But during the night, he tells Crocker the whole story, the one he was saving for Sullivan. Crocker thinks, *Holy shit, they know I'm Flood's best friend. If they got any DNA out of Baker, it'll be in the database, and they'll ask me for a sample. . . .*"

"So he kills Bob to keep him from talking. Then he freaks out because of what he did—"

Virgil: "Or because he thinks that we'll figure it out, and do DNA on him in the jail death. In fact . . . I wonder if he might have called up to the ME, as a sheriff's deputy, and somehow got the murder verdict?"

"Whatever reason, he's cooked, if he's in the database."

Virgil picked it up again. "Now, one of two things happened. He really did commit suicide, which I don't believe, because people say he was too much of a chicken, and because I could see in her eyes that Spooner was lying like a motherfucker; or, he told Spooner about it, and she realized that he'd bring down the whole World of Spirit, trade them in, to keep himself out of jail. Or if not that, to get special handling and a shorter sentence. And she killed him."

Coakley: "You think it's the second one. That she killed him."

"I do. But I don't see how we can get her," Virgil said. "She's got the perfect alternate story. We've got ours, she's got hers, and there's no way a jury will find her guilty beyond a reasonable doubt. A nice middle-class drugstore worker killing a man she hoped to get back with? No. Not without something else that would show animus on her part."

THEY THOUGHT about that for a minute, then Coakley said, "I could do you again right now."

Virgil slipped a little lower in his chair and said, "Well, the spirit is willing, but the flesh might be a little weak after last night. That was . . . something else."

"Did you enjoy yourself?" she asked.

"Does a chicken have lips?"

She frowned. "What does that mean?"

"I don't know. I think it means, 'Yes.' 'Cause I did. My God, woman, you were a prodigy."

She stretched, smiled back, yawned, and said, "I felt so good until the moment I walked in the door, and there she was. Goddamnit." She jabbed a finger at Virgil: "But we know what's going on out there, and we're going to trash those fuckers. We're gonna trash them."

"Maybe I'll take a nap first," Virgil said.

COAKLEY DIDN'T REALLY believe that he was going back to take a nap, but he did. A nap, of sorts. He put his keys, cash, coins, and cell phone on the motel desk, took off his boots, and lay on the bed, closed his eyes, and slept for fifteen minutes. When he woke, he lay still, and began to plot.

The case, as such, was over—and if he hadn't gone into the Rouses' place and found the photos, it'd be finished for sure. But now that he knew about the Rouses, he couldn't let it go, and neither could Coakley.

One problem: They couldn't tell anyone *why* they wouldn't let go.

SOLUTIONS:

- Find a legitimate reason to hit the Rouses' place with a search crew. Even if the photos were destroyed before they got there—unlikely, now that the World of Spirit people most likely thought they were safe again—they'd been printed on a computer printer, which meant that the pictures might still live somewhere on a hard drive. If they could get the Rouses on charges of child abuse, pedophilia, and incest, they might, in exchange for some other consideration, crack and unload on the World of Spirit.

- Crack Loewe. Loewe was gay, which might mean that he hadn't had sex with any of the younger girls—or might be able to credibly claim that he hadn't. There might be a deal there, Virgil thought, as long as the WOS didn't permit homosexuality. If he'd had relationships with any little boys . . . no flexibility there.
- Go after Alma Flood. There was something cookin' behind Alma Flood's forehead, and the pressure was building up. If incest was a regular feature of the WOS, then she may have been forced to have sex with Einstadt, and her daughters with Jake Flood or other members of the church.
- Pressure Spooner. Spooner had murdered Crocker—Virgil had no doubt about that. If he confronted her, told her that he was going to put her in jail for murder, one way or another, if she didn't talk about WOS, would she call his bluff? Or would she talk? At this point, she'd probably call his bluff. He needed something else.
- Go after the Bakers. Did they know that Crocker and Flood had gang-raped their daughter? And then there was that whole thing about Kelly Baker visiting relatives before she disappeared for the night. Had that actually happened, or had there been a party, with more than Flood and Crocker involved? Perhaps the Bakers themselves?

Other possibilities occurred to him. A small fire at the Rouses' place, while they were gone . . . a fireman discovering the box in the closet. But that was fantasy, that would involve a conspiracy too big to sustain.

Still: had to get into that house, legitimately. If he could extract those photos, they would identify other members of the WOS and pull down the whole structure, leaping from one family to the next in a chain reaction.

As soon as it became apparent that the whole church was involved, they'd be able to get search warrants for all members, would be able to get all the children talking privately with Social Services investigators.

Huh. Had to find a way to get the chain reaction started.

He called Coakley, said, "Let's go someplace—not here—and talk. Bring a couple of deputies that you're sure about. Who won't talk. The county attorney—"

"His wife is the biggest gossip in Warren County," she said. "Not a good idea."

"All right. But let's meet."

"My house," she said. "Noon. The kids will be at school. I'd like to bring in Dennis Brown, too; he used to be my boss—"

"I've met him," Virgil said. Brown was the Homestead chief of police. "You're sure he's okay? He wouldn't be under your thumb?"

"He's one of the best people in Homestead, and he knows everybody in the county, I swear to God. And I'm thinking Schickel. He's a tough old boy, and he'd go after these people with a chain saw, if he knew about this."

"We can't talk about the photos," Virgil said. "Let me

handle the briefing. You just arrange the meeting, and I'll be briefing you, along with the others. Ask questions. We've got to get into the Rouses' place, but we've got to forget about the photos."

"Got it."

"See you in an hour," he said.

He brushed his teeth, loaded up, and headed into the café, which was in its mid-morning customer slump, no more than eight or ten people scattered around the booths and stools, reading newspapers, talking two by two.

Virgil took a booth, and Jacoby came right over. "Pie?"

"Diet Coke, hamburger with no mayonnaise, or any of that other sauce you put on there."

"You don't like Thousand Island?"

Virgil shuddered. "Not on my hamburgers, no. Also, French fries with no salt, and . . . blueberry."

The guy in the next booth asked, "Anything new?"

"Woman came in this morning and said she was there when Jim Crocker shot himself," Virgil said.

Jacoby sat down across from him, Virgil's order forgotten for the moment. "Would I know her?"

"Crocker's ex-wife, Kathleen Spooner. Said he was all morose about Tripp, and he shot himself."

"Whoa." Jacoby scratched his nose, said, "I know her. Dark-haired gal. I think she was one of those religious people out there."

"Yeah, she was. Or is," Virgil said. "Her story's a little shaky, but I don't see any way to break it."

A couple more people moved in, on stools, and in the booth behind Jacoby. One of them said, "You said you thought Jim Crocker was murdered."

"Still possible," Virgil said. "The same set of facts that say he was murdered can, if they're turned around just right, say it could be a suicide."

"But you don't believe it," Jacoby said. "I can tell by your voice."

Virgil nodded. "You're right. I don't believe it. I think it was murder."

"You think you can get her?" Jacoby asked.

"I don't know. Haven't even arrested her, for what she did, unless Coakley did it after I left," Virgil said.

Jacoby got up and walked down the café and clipped Virgil's order to the cook's order rack, then came back, sat down, and said, "Damnedest thing. She might've done it, and she might walk away."

"No way to tell, for sure, unless there was a third person there," Virgil said. "I don't think that's likely."

The guy behind him said, "But if she murdered him, why did she do it?"

"Cover something up," Virgil said. "She told us that Crocker might have been scared because he thought we might take DNA evidence from him, because of the jailhouse suicide when he was on duty. And that he might have had something to do with the death of that Kelly Baker girl last year. Him and Jake Flood. And they might have left some DNA behind."

"Holy shit," the man in the back booth said.

The one on the other side, behind Jacoby, said,

"They're all those religious people. Spooner, Flood, the Bakers . . ."

Virgil nodded.

The guy behind him said, "If you ask me, you need to know more about that church."

Virgil said, "They don't talk much to outsiders. . . ."

HIS FOOD CAME, and he sat munching through it, as the panel discussion continued, then confessed, "I'm pretty much stuck if I don't get more information coming in. But, you know—win a few, lose a few."

"That ain't right, Virg," somebody said.

Virgil shrugged and said, "We're talking about law enforcement, not television. Nothing's perfect. Without the information . . ."

"I'd hate to see you quit and leave town," Jacoby said. "You're better than TV. Business is up ten percent since you started coming in."

"Happy to do it, Bill. Just wish this could come to a better end."

The waitress appeared and slid a saucer with a slice of blueberry pie across the table.

Virgil picked up the fork and cut into it, became aware of the silence around him. He looked around and said, "What?"

The guy in the booth behind Jacoby asked, seemingly fascinated, "You really gonna eat that?"

Jacoby twisted, said, "Hey!" Back to Virgil. "That's perfectly good . . . pie."

THE CONSENSUS in the café was that Virgil should keep pushing, and find a way around Spooner's confession; the patrons voted unanimously that she was lying, that Crocker's death was murder.

"Maybe we should get up a lynch mob," Jacoby joked. He added, "That was a joke."

"I'll hang around a day or two to see what happens," Virgil said. He ran the tip of his tongue around his gums. "I'm really gonna miss the . . . pie."

WHEN HE CAME out of the café, with a feeling that he had purple sticky stuff lodged between all of his teeth, he still had some time to kill. He looked up and down the street, spotted the redbrick tower of a church, and ambled down that way. The sign out front said, "Good Shepherd Lutheran Church," and Virgil climbed the granite steps, pulled at one of the big wood doors, and walked in. A woman was pushing a dust mop down an aisle between pews, looked around at him, said, "Can I help you?"

"Is the pastor around?"

"He's in the office. Do you have an appointment?"

"No. I'm an agent with the state Bureau of Criminal Apprehension. I'd like a few minutes of his time, if he's got it."

"Well, c'mon back. He's not doing anything but reading the paper, anyway."

Actually, he was polishing his shoes, with his feet on

the paper he'd apparently finished reading. He was a soft, middle-fiftyish man, with white curly hair, blue eyes, and gold-rimmed glasses that sat on a wide German nose. He was listening to soft rock on a Wave radio.

Virgil introduced himself and the minister half stood and put the polish rag in his left hand and stuck out his right. "John Baumhauer," he said. "I've heard about you, Virgil. Down at the café."

"I do my best thinking there," Virgil said. And, "I guess Joshua was right: The house of God still has its hewers of wood and drawers of water."

Baumhauer brightened, ticked a finger at Virgil, and said, "Not many people pick that up, Baumhauer being a chopper of wood. And you know your Old Testament."

"My dad's got a church over in Marshall."

"Flowers? Oh, heck yes. He's your dad? We're old pals, we overlapped in grad school, he was a year ahead of me. How's your mom? She was a looker, let me tell you; still was, I saw them a year ago at a conference up in St. Paul. . . ."

They spent a minute or two connecting, then Virgil said, "John, I've got a problem. We're starting to turn up some answers on this string of murders, and also the murder last year of Kelly Baker, down across the Iowa line."

"I remember that. That was a mystery."

"It was, but now . . . Look, I've got to ask you first. I want to keep this talk private," Virgil said. "At least for a while. Even if it turns out you don't know anything, or don't want to talk about it."

Baumhauer was interested, intent with a small smile. "Sure. As long as it's not, you know, illegal."

Virgil nodded. "But you might not want to talk about it when you hear the question."

"The question is . . . ?"

"I've only been here a couple days, but we've made some progress—but everywhere I turn, in this thing, I stumble over the World of Spirit."

"Those guys," Baumhauer said.

"Yeah. Have you heard anything that would suggest there's something wrong with that group? Something not right?"

"You do make me feel a little like a rat," the minister said. "But . . . yes, a bunch of us church people in town have thought about them. We had a Catholic priest here for a few years, Danny McCoy—he's up at the archdiocese now, doing something important. We used to play poker with a couple of other guys. He was no good at it, he couldn't bluff worth a darn. He won't tell you anything, because I think it came in a confession, but he apparently heard from somebody that there was no good going on there. He was conflicted. He mentioned it to me privately; I'm sure he wouldn't talk to you. I don't know if it went any further than me, or if he took it up with his superiors—he took the bonds of confession seriously. He was never explicit, but I got the feeling, though, that there was something sexual going on."

"Have you ever felt that?"

Baumhauer took a deep breath, looked away for a moment, then said, "Yes. I can't say where or how, because

I can't remember—it's just rumors and implications and comments over the years, about marrying them off young over there, and things like that."

"Mmm. You never mentioned it to anyone?"

"Well, I suspect you'd find a lot of older people around here, especially churchgoers, who have heard something. But it's all vague," Baumhauer said. "The other thing is, when I was a kid, I was working in an area in Indiana with a lot of Amish. I got to know some of them, and they're good folks. Solid. They have some of the same characteristics as the World of Spirit—they keep themselves separate, they homeschool, they intermarry. And they're good people. So you get the feeling, you can't pick on a whole church. If you even hint at it, people are going to go off in all directions. That's just not right, either. Tainting a whole church, with no real knowledge at all."

Virgil sighed and said, "Yeah."

"But, that said, they're not the Amish," Baumhauer said. "The Amish are separate, but not secretive. They're not paranoid. And you can see why they believe what they do—they're staying away from the modern world, and it carries right through from the way they dress, to the vehicles they drive, to the way they furnish their houses. No TV and so on. The World of Spirit, you don't see that—they've got TV and nice cars and big tractors, and back during Vietnam, their boys would get drafted and go off to fight. The only thing they're different about is what happens with their church, what it's all about, and they're secret about that. Paranoid."

"As you say, you don't have anything specific."

"No, no, I don't. But . . . did you ever hear of Birdy Olms?"

"I have. She supposedly ran away from them."

"I've heard that, too. Quite a few years back. The story in the church circles here was that the local Jehovah's Witnesses took to witnessing on her porch when her husband wasn't around, and she began to doubt the church and got into some kind of trouble with the church and ran away. If you can find her, she'd be worth talking to, I think."

VIRGIL WAS RUNNING behind when he left the church, and was five minutes late to Coakley's house. Coakley, along with Schickel and Dennis Brown, was waiting in her living room. Brown was a tall, fat man, with a round, red face and white hair. He did not look jolly, and would have been a rotten Santa Claus; he carried a sad, deep-eyed brooding look, and perpetually pursed lips. When he and Virgil shook hands, Virgil was surprised to find his hand hard, dried, and callused, like a sailor's.

Coakley said, "Okay, Virgil. You called the meeting."

Virgil dragged an easy chair around so he could face Brown and Coakley on the couch, and Schickel on another easy chair. Schickel had a laptop and a legal pad, used the laptop as a lap desk as he doodled on the yellow pad.

Virgil asked, "Everybody know about Spooner, and her story?"

They all did, and Schickel said, "I think she killed him. I've known Jim Crocker for a long time, no goddamn way he ate his own gun. He would have wiggled and squirmed and cried and hired lawyers and done everything he could to get out of it. If he *was* going to commit suicide, he would have taken pills."

"I'll second that," Brown drawled.

Virgil nodded. "My boss is going to call me anytime now and tell me if we got DNA on Spooner. If we had it, we were going to charge her, and then use the charge to see if we deal with her on issues like the Kelly Baker murder, and what I believe is a cult-operated child abuse ring. That's all out the window. No way we're going to get a conviction on what we've got—and she's signaling that she's going to trial, if we decide to take her. She ain't gonna talk. So now, we need to figure out what we're going to do. We got nothin'. But we've got to do something about those kids."

"How sure are you about the kids?" Brown asked. "I've lived here all my life, and I've never heard a hint of that."

"There've been some hints, Dennis," Coakley said. "We just didn't hear them. Or see them. Virgil's talked to a couple of people out west, and they both said they wouldn't want their kids around church people. And those names I called you about, when I was collecting the names of church families. I took the names over to the courthouse this morning, while Virgil was probably down at the Yellow Dog eating pie. . . ."

Virgil nodded and said, "Man's gotta eat."

She brushed him off. "I went through vital records, marriage licenses, over the past fifty years or so, hooking up as many families as I could. I found fifty-four cases where one of the church families, out there, married off an eighteen-year-old girl to a man more than thirty. There have been as many as eighty families involved in the marriages. And there are more of these families over in Jackson County and down across the line in Iowa. Right now, I've got one hundred and eight family names, all still on the tax rolls."

AFTER A MOMENT, Schickel said, "Girls grow up fast in the country."

Coakley said, "Yes, they do, Gene, and so do the boys. And when I was looking at marriage certificates, I went and looked at people who were not part of this church, from other farm areas, and what you find is a lot of kids getting married young—both people are young. I mean, the boys may be a couple years older, or three or four, but hardly ever over thirty. My feeling is, this is systematic, and it's part of this cult."

Brown came back: "The law makes it illegal to have sexual contact with a younger woman, but you know, Lee, that a lot of seventeen-year-old girls out here are women. They've been working all their lives, and they're grown up."

"How about twelve-year-olds? Eleven-year-olds? How

about repeated extreme sex with a seventeen-year-old, involving a forty-three-year-old deputy sheriff and a forty-five-year-old farmer?" Virgil asked.

"Then we kill them," Schickel said.

"Yeah, we do," said Brown.

Virgil told them about the Flood girls, and their odd behavior, about the comments from non-cult farmers who'd seen a lot of too-young girls with older men from the WOS.

Brown jabbed a finger at him. "You want strategy, why're you sitting on your thumb while Spooner is over talking to Harris Toms?"

Virgil leaned back, wondering how smart the guy could be, and said, "Because she's taken herself out of it—"

"Bullshit," Brown said. "*You* think she committed murder, and the facts say that she might have. But you're buying her story. Or, you're buying the idea that you can't convict her. You're getting out in front of yourself."

Coakley said, "Dennis, what's the point?"

"The point is, you don't *have* to buy her story. You've got a perfectly good and legitimate reason to tear her house apart—her own testimony that she was there, at what you suspect might have been a murder. Go look at every piece of paper and letter and e-mail and picture she's got in her house. Go do it. Maybe you can find something that'll unravel the whole thing for you."

They sat for a moment, then Virgil grinned and said to Coakley, "You told me he was smart."

Coakley growled to Virgil, "Where'd we leave our

brains?" She walked out to the kitchen, got on the phone, and started dictating the terms of a search warrant to whoever was on the other end.

Virgil asked Brown, "What else you got? I liked the first thing."

Brown said, "It's apparent, if you're right about this whole thing, that the only way you're going to tear them down is to find a weak spot. A family or a kid or somebody who wants to get out—"

"That's right. If we can do that, we could get a chain reaction," Virgil said. "The problem is, nobody knows these people. They stay to themselves, they homeschool the kids, everything is really tight. So who do we go after?"

"Somebody with kids in the target range—where the sex is too young to be excused," Brown said. "If you get some Lolita farm girl with big tits, who's been watching heifers and sows getting bred all her life, the jury's going to look at her and say, 'Hell, I would have done it, too.' So forget those. We have to figure out which families have the eleven- and twelve-year-olds. Get those folks on any excuse, so we can put the kids with Social Services. We get them with the right shrinks, and the kids will talk."

Virgil nodded. "Maybe the Flood girls . . ."

Coakley came back: "We'll have the warrant in fifteen minutes. Spooner is still in the courthouse. We really gotta run on this thing."

Schickel said, "We need a list of everybody in the church. Lee, you've got a bunch of names. . . ."

She nodded. "Dennis gave me some of them."

"I might have a couple more, that I thought of later," Brown said. "I didn't know what you were after."

Schickel said, "We really need a complete list of everybody in the church. The cult. If you give me your list, I'll get out there, talk to people I know, off the record. See who has younger kids."

"I can do that, too," Brown said. "I've got relatives out there; they'll know a few."

"Just looking for a crack in the wall," Virgil said.

Brown shook his head. "I hope you're right about this thing. That we're not doing something awful to them. You hang a child-abuse sign on them, they'll be talking about this all over the country. And these people have been around for a long time. Good farmers, most of them. Never a problem with the law, outside of some drunk driving, and like that. Came over together from the Old Country, just like my great-grandparents. Their name was Braun, B-R-A-U-N, got changed to Brown during the First World War. Good people."

They all sat, thinking about that for a few seconds, then Virgil said to Coakley, "We better get going to Spooner's." To the others: "And you guys . . . a crack in the wall. All we need is a crack we can wiggle through."

15

Virgil, Coakley, Schickel, and a deputy named Marcia Wright, who'd been trained in crime-scene work, went in a three-truck caravan to Spooner's apartment in Jackson, where they were met by two Jackson police officers and Spooner's landlord. The Jackson cops looked at the search warrant, and the landlord, a fat man with a waxed mustache, gave them a key. He wanted to come in and look around, but they shooed him away. One of the Jackson cops left, but the other had been designated to hang around, as an observer.

Virgil went straight to Spooner's computer, an old iMac G4, which sat on a small wooden desk in the second bedroom. A narrow single bed was pushed against the wall opposite the desk, a white coverlet looking yellowed and a bit dusty—a guest-room bed with not many guests, Virgil thought.

While he was looking at it, a call came in from St. Paul. A technician named Marty Lopez said, "We got your match. The hair you sent us matches the saliva on the victim's penis."

Virgil told Coakley, who was working through the main bedroom. "That confirms what she just told us," she said. "Kind of a letdown."

"Yeah. Well, what the hell."

Wright was searching the kitchen—women most often hid things in the kitchen or the bedroom, men in the garage or the basement. Schickel, who claimed no special search skills, took the least likely place, the basement, more to eliminate it than in expectation of finding anything.

The Jackson cop watched for a couple minutes, then offered to go for coffee and doughnuts.

Virgil was stymied by the computer: It wanted a password, and he tried a few possibilities, built around Spooner's name. Nothing worked. He began pulling drawers out on the desk, found a miscellaneous accumulation of pencils, ChapSticks, Scotch tape, a stapler, old glasses, pushpins, and other similar office stuff in one; index cards, return-address labels, envelopes, and checks for a Wells Fargo bank account, in a second.

Coakley came out of the main bedroom carrying a plastic file box filled with photos. "I don't think there'll be much here—it all looks like stuff from a Wal-Mart processing machine." She sat on the guest bed and pulled out a handful of photographs.

"Have to look," Virgil said.

"What about the computer?"

"Locked out. We'll have to send it to the guys up in the Cities."

He went back to the desk. The file drawer held a dozen files, with appliance warranties, paycheck stubs, bank statements, and other routine household account paper; a bottom drawer was full of what must've been a couple of years of paid bills; and the other bottom drawer had some computer cables, a box of carpet casters for a business chair, a couple of screwdrivers, a tape measure.

Nothing.

"Anything?" he asked Coakley.

"Pictures of Jim Crocker, back when they were married. Some pictures that look like they might have been taken at church services—you know, outside in farmyards. Might be able to use them to figure out who's in the church."

"In other words . . ."

"Nothing good."

THE SECOND BEDROOM was spare, with an old chest of drawers that looked like it might have come from a Goodwill store, and when Virgil pulled out the drawers, found it stacked with worn blankets and sheets, and, in the bottom drawer, with what looked like old winter clothing. He pawed through it, came up empty. The bedroom closet also had what looked like older, no-longer-used clothing. He was checking the pockets when he noticed the typing tray on the desk—it was tucked under the top ledge, and he simply hadn't seen it. When he stepped over and pulled it out, he found a white index card, like those found in the desk, with a list of what looked like code words:

WF—69bugsy
Van—1bugsy1
Amazon—69bugsy
Email—69Bugsy
Visa—2bugsy2

He sat down, typed "bugsy" into the sign-on prompt, and got kicked back; typed in "69Bugsy," and he was in.

"Here we go," he said.

Coakley came over and stood behind him as he called up Spooner's mail. There were 458 incoming, and 366 outgoing e-mails, going back to 1997, with forty or fifty of each from the past year. "She doesn't use it much," Virgil said.

Coakley stroked the back of his neck, just once, with her fingertips, and said, "Get in the browser, see what she looks at."

The old machine used an early version of Safari, but it was familiar enough. He popped up the history, just as he had with Bob Tripp's, and found that Spooner, unlike Tripp, spent her time on cooking, gardening, and gun sites, and not very often, at that.

Virgil said, "Not much . . . I'm going back to the e-mail."

He started with the most recent letters. The few of interest involved the church, and simply listed meeting locations, a month at a time. The meetings seemed to rotate through about a dozen homes—maybe used because they were the largest ones, Virgil thought. There must have been seventy or eighty people at the meeting they'd spied on, and not many farms would have the space.

Coakley said, "Here's something."

Virgil turned and she handed him a photograph. Three men, two of them bare-chested, the other wearing a T-shirt, standing on a lakeshore beach in swimsuits. "The man on the left is Jake Flood," she said.

"Yeah?"

"Look at his stomach."

Virgil looked at Flood's stomach, and could make out an arm of a tattoo, rising out of Flood's bathing suit.

"Yeah, that's it—but we knew that," Virgil said. "And we don't need Flood to be Liberty—we need evidence that Rouse is Liberty, so we can crack that house."

Virgil went back to the e-mail, found nothing useful, checked the e-mail trash, and found a half dozen e-mails. Began opening them.

OPENED ONE and found: "The whole thing is crazy. We're going to meet at Flood's."

> NEXT: "We're good with Jake. Can you be with Jim if we need to?"
>
> A REPLY: "Okay, but I don't like it."
>
> NEXT: "You're in it, too."
>
> A REPLY: "I am not in it. I had nothing to do with it."
>
> NEXT, a couple of days later: "Jim's clear. We're okay."

Virgil said, "Look at this."

Coakley stepped back over, read the messages. Virgil

tapped the dates. "This is the day and a few days after Kelly Baker was killed. That's what they're talking about here."

She turned it over in her mind, then shook her head. "It's a detail, and a good prosecutor could turn it into something, but I don't know if it stands up on its own."

"It might not, but she intended to delete these things—she just didn't realize that after you delete something, you have to empty the trash. So now we've got them. I'll ship the computer north, leave a receipt to tell her what happened with it, and then, soon—day after tomorrow—tell her we've got her. Offer her a deal: Give us Rouse. If we can just get in there. . . ."

"But there's not enough here."

"The question is not whether there's enough, it's what she remembers about it. That, along with the whole deal on being with Crocker when he died. If we agree not to file charges on Crocker, and limit the time she could serve on whatever comes out of our investigation . . . We can tell her that she can either talk, or go down with the rest of them, no second chance."

Coakley said, "Okay, it's there if we need it. But if you're right about everything, that she killed Crocker and knew about Baker, was involved in some kind of conspiracy to cover it up, there's gonna be an enormous stink if she walks. We could be giving immunity to one of the major players."

"So we keep looking," Virgil said.

Wright finished with the kitchen and came to the bedroom doorway and said she'd found nothing of serious interest, except four hundred and twenty dollars in a plastic cup hidden under the flour in a flour crock; and Shickel came up empty in the basement.

"Nothing down there but a washer, dryer, and water heater, and a lot of dust and old junk. Looks like she only goes down to do the wash." He went to help Wright in the living room, while Virgil continued working through the computer, and Coakley, finished with the photos, went back to the master bedroom.

Virgil opened a primitive version of iPhoto and found none. He stuck his head in the hallway: "Anybody found a camera?"

Coakley: "There's an Instamatic in here, but there's nothing in it."

"Doesn't she have a junk room anywhere?"

"Bunch of cupboards in the mudroom off the kitchen, there was an old Polaroid in there, looked like it hadn't been used in years," Wright said.

"No digital?"

Nobody had seen a digital camera. Nobody had seen any guns, either. "I'm starting to think that she cleaned the place up, just in case," Virgil told Coakley. "We ought to take a look at her car."

The car was included in the search warrant as a matter of course. Coakley called back to her office, got Greg Dunn to check around the parking lot for Spooner's car. "Get Stupek to open it up, go through it, get back to me.

We'd be interested in paper, photographs, cameras, guns, whatever."

Virgil said, quietly to Coakley, when they were alone, "You know what? We didn't take Dennis's advice seriously enough—you know, that we hit Spooner with a search warrant. She's implicated Flood and Crocker in the Baker case: Let's hit Flood with a search warrant. If we could separate Alma Flood from her daughters for a while, get somebody with Social Services with the kids, see what the kids have to say . . ."

"Then they'd know what we're looking at, and if it didn't pan out, we'd be screwed," Coakley said. "I hate to give up that edge. The word would spread with these people in an instant—cell phones. They'll destroy every bit of physical evidence that might be around. If they warn Rouse, do you think those pictures will still be in the closet?"

Virgil scratched his forehead, thinking. "Let's get the computer and everything else, like the photo of Flood, locked up in your office, or up at the BCA. We don't arrest Spooner . . . we let her slide."

"That might be up to Harris Toms, depending on what he sees in her story," Coakley said.

"Talk to him. No big rush. Ask him to let it slide for a few days," Virgil said. "Spread the word that I've gone back to Mankato on another case. I'll stop by the café and mention it there."

"And in real life, you actually . . ."

"I'm going to track down this Birdy woman and see what she has to say," Virgil said.

"I looked, but I couldn't find her."

"I've got somebody who can, unless she's completely changed her name. . . . I've just been negligent in getting her started. I'll call her right now."

He got Sandy on the phone and explained the problem.

"You don't know whether she's alive or dead, or where she might have run to?"

"No, but she's a Midwestern farm woman who was on her own, with some cash. I don't know how much, but as I understand it, her husband was reasonably affluent, and she cleaned out his accounts. So, where do Midwestern farm women run to? Florida? California? Arizona? Or maybe someplace else in the Midwest?"

"Does she have any relatives she might be in touch with?"

"Sandy, it's like this," Virgil said. "I don't know anything about her, except her name, and I can't ask, because that would tip off people that we're looking for her."

"Interesting," she said. "If she's on her own, she probably had to get a job, so she should be in Social Security records."

"And in state employment records, and probably DMV records, possibly insurance records . . . The way people talked, her husband doesn't know where she went, so she probably never served him with divorce papers."

Coakley, in the background, said, "She's not in the NCIC, I looked." Virgil passed that on, and Sandy said, "Unless she's gone completely underground—changed her name, got a fake Social Security number, and so on, or is dead, or is on the street, this shouldn't be too hard. I'll get back to you in a bit."

"I'll be on my cell," Virgil said.

VIRGIL LOADED Spooner's computer into his truck, leaving behind a receipt. When he went back in the apartment, Coakley was on the phone with Dunn, the deputy who was searching Spooner's car. Schickel was listening in. When she got off, she said to Virgil, "Nothing in the car at all."

"We know she had a gun, because I saw it," Virgil said. "She cleaned the house out before she came in, and stuck stuff away somewhere."

"How do we find it?" Coakley asked.

Virgil shrugged. "We don't. She's not a dumb woman. Could be in a safe-deposit box in some small bank fifty miles from here—or in a friend's basement. No way to tell."

Schickel said, "You saw her gun?"

"Yeah, she was carrying one in her pocket."

"Come here and look at this."

Virgil followed him into the front room and showed him a small pocket roughly sewn to the side of a couch. The couch was set diagonally from a wall, with the pocket against the wall, where it couldn't be seen.

"Couldn't figure out what the hell it is. You think it could be, like, a holster?"

Virgil got down on the rug, pulled the pocket open

with a finger, and sniffed it, leaned back and said, "Smells like Hoppe's to me." Hoppe's was the most popular brand of gun solvent and lubricant, with a distinct, oily-acid odor.

He moved aside, and Schickel sniffed it. "Yeah. So why would she have a gun pocket sewn to the side of her couch, for gosh sakes?"

"Maybe she's scared, or a gun nut," Virgil said. "We can ask her, but it won't get us anywhere. She thought this out."

"But the computer . . ."

"She didn't understand the computer, and screwed up," Virgil said.

THEY DIDN'T FIND anything else immediately, and Virgil and Coakley headed back to Homestead in Virgil's truck, leaving Schickel and Wright to finish. "If we knew more about the church members in detail, we might be able pick out some weak ones. Maybe that's the way to go: slow down, find the weak ones," Coakley said.

"I'd have to leave that to you," Virgil said. "I just can't pick up and move down here and devote my life to it: I'm doing three or four cases at a time, as it is."

She thought that over, then said, "Cold out here."

Virgil looked across the barren landscape and said, "Amazing the change between fall and winter. From harvest time to January. In September it looks like you could feed the world with one hand tied behind your back; in January, even the buildings look starved."

Somewhere along the way, they agreed that Virgil should sneak her in the back of the Holiday Inn, so she wouldn't have to go through the lobby. They did that, and wound up in bed again, more intense this time, and less happy: the cloud of the case hanging over them.

"Some way," she said, "we'll be able to get into the Rouses' place. The question is, will they know we're coming, and get rid of the photographs and whatever else they have. I mean, Virgil, it's right there, the whole case, and we can't touch it. It's driving me crazy."

They were propped up on the extra pillows, snuggled together, when Virgil's phone rang. He picked it up, looked at the incoming number on the display, and said, "Sandy. Maybe she found Birdy."

He clicked on the phone and asked, without preamble, "You find her?"

"No, but I didn't find her in a pretty interesting way," she said. "When she ran away, she just disappeared. I can't find a single sign of her. Social Security stopped—they still have her farm address as her address—driver's license expired, no new driver's license anywhere I can find. Anywhere in the U.S. No income tax returns, U.S. or state. Her husband divorced her six years ago for abandonment, and she never responded to the court in any way, and she probably had some alimony coming if she'd wanted it. She's so gone that I suspect she's dead. That one of your suspects down there killed her and buried her out in a field somewhere."

"Ah, man," Virgil said. "What all did you check?"

Sandy took a minute to lay it out, and then said, "I ran

the whole search again under her maiden name, Lucy McCain—Birdy was just a nickname, Olms was her married name—and that came up dry, too. Lots of Lucy McCains, but she isn't one of them, as far as I can tell."

"Wait a minute," Virgil said. "Her maiden name was McCain?"

"That's right."

"Do you know where she was from originally? I mean, was it down here in Warren County?"

"Nope. She was from Sleepy Eye."

"Sleepy Eye. Does she have any family there?" Virgil asked.

"Parents, both alive, Ed and Ruth, brothers Robert and William, twin sister Louise."

"Louise McCain?"

"Louise Gordon, now. Married Ronald Gordon, divorced three years ago. She works at Charles Winston, Auctioneers."

"Still in Sleepy Eye?"

"Yes. You want the address?"

VIRGIL TOOK DOWN addresses, then hung up and put his arm around Coakley's back, cupped her right breast in his right hand, and twiddled her nipple while he thought about it. "What?" she asked.

"Birdy dropped off the face of the earth. Our researcher could find Hitler, if he was still alive, and she got nothing on Birdy. Her name was Lucy McCain, by the way. Not a German name, and she's not from Warren

County. She was born in Sleepy Eye, and still has a twin sister living there."

"If they were close . . ."

"That's what I'm thinking," Virgil said. "If anybody would know where she is, it'd be her sister, or maybe her folks. Or maybe all of them. I better run up there."

"What about Spooner?"

"Think about her. Threaten her. Tell her we know there's something else going on, and she'll get no mercy if she doesn't talk to us about everything. Tell her we're taking her down for murder, we'll put her on the stand, we'll make her perjure herself, and send her to prison for that, when we finally break it."

"In other words, rain all over her," Coakley said.

"Exactly. I don't think it'll work, but if things start to crumble, she might want to get out in front of it." He gave her nipple a final twiddle and said, "I'm outa here."

SLEEPY EYE WAS roughly seventy miles straight north, a little more than an hour on the two-lane state highways. Night was falling by the time he drove into town, past the implement dealer and the car dealer and a Lutheran church where his father once substituted for a sick pastor, taking a right on Burnside, then slowing, looking for house numbers.

Louise Gordon lived in a brown-and-white bungalow with a covered porch and a one-car garage down the back. Both the living room window and the back, kitchen window showed lights; he pulled into the driveway, killed the engine, and walked up the porch, which had been cleared of snow, and knocked and rang the doorbell.

Gordon was a slightly heavy, middle-sized woman of perhaps thirty-five, with curly reddish-brown hair. She came to the door holding a half-eaten raw carrot, peeked at him through the glass, opened the inner door, the storm door, just a crack, and said, "Hello?"

Virgil held up his ID. "I'm an agent with the Bureau of Criminal Apprehension. If you're Louise Gordon, I'd like to speak to you about your sister, Lucy. Birdy."

"Lucy," she said, and, "Pardon me, but you don't look much like a police officer."

"Well, mmm, you could check with my office. . . ."

"What if I called the police here?" She said it in a challenging way, to see if he'd run.

"Good idea," Virgil said. "Go call them, I'll wait in my truck."

She nodded, pulled the door shut, and Virgil went and sat in his truck. Five or six minutes later, a Chevy Tahoe parked across the end of the driveway, and a man in civilian clothes hopped out. Virgil climbed out of his truck, and the man came up and said, "Charlie Lane . . . you're with the state?"

Virgil gave him his ID. "I'm Virgil Flowers with the BCA. I need to talk to Miz Gordon about her sister."

"Hey, Virgil. I've heard of you." He tipped the ID into the light from Virgil's open truck door, looked at Virgil's face, then passed the ID back. "Come on, I'll introduce you."

LOUISE GORDON DENIED knowing where her sister was, but she denied it with a relish that said she was lying. "When she disappeared, we were all shocked, but I said, 'That's Lucy. If she's run away, there's a good reason for it.'"

"What was the reason?" Virgil asked. "Her husband?"

"Of course it was her husband; what else would it be? Lucy and I are the first women in our family to be divorced. Ever. With me, it was because I got tired of putting up with my husband's laziness. With Lucy, it was worse. Rollo beat her. And worse than that."

"Rollo?"

"Roland. Her husband."

"What's worse than getting beaten? Did he sexually mistreat her?"

A moment of hesitation, then, "That's what I understand, yes."

They were sitting in Gordon's living room and Virgil leaned forward and said, "Miz Gordon—I spend a lot of time interviewing people, and I know when they're lying to me. You're lying to me when you say you don't know where she is, or how to get in touch. I need to talk to her, and we're not fooling around. I don't want to have to threaten you."

"Wouldn't make any difference if you did," she said.

"It might, if you knew what the threats were. But I will tell you—and I don't want you talking about this to anyone—we believe that her husband was part of a cult, or a sect, or whatever you'd call it, that sexually victimizes its own children. Its own daughters. We think Lucy, Birdy, can help us with this. We think she could provide testimony that would get us inside the houses of some of these people, to get them away from their children, and their children to a safe place, where we could find out what was going on. If you resist, in my opinion you're as bad as the people doing these things. You're making it possible for them to continue."

"I don't know anything about any children," she said, but she was defensive, her eyes searching for a way out.

"You may not, but Lucy might," Virgil said. "Has she ever told you explicitly what she . . . encountered . . . with her husband?"

"A bit. He wanted to . . . he wanted to do some wife-swapping, is what it sounded like. Or maybe she went along with that, and it was something worse."

"How, worse?"

"I don't know. We didn't talk about details," Gordon said.

"How long were they married?"

"Fifteen months. Not long. But, do you want to know why she didn't just come home? Why she hid?"

"Yes. I do want to know that."

Gordon said, "Because she was afraid Rollo might kill her. He beat her, and said that if she tried to run, he'd strangle her and bury her behind the barn. He told her that other women had gotten what they deserved, and she believed him."

Virgil said nothing for a minute, then, "I gotta talk to her. We're already looking at four dead people."

Gordon said, "I'll call her. You go away, and I'll call her, and I'll call you back tomorrow morning, and tell her what you've told me. Then, I'll let her decide."

"You better tell her that it's not a matter for her to decide—it's a matter of whether we track her down and put her in jail, and you along with her," Virgil said, rolling out the threats. "If they're doing what we think they're doing, she's acting as an accomplice by not telling us what she knows about criminal behavior, and you are an accomplice because you're hiding her. Make sure she knows that, Miz Gordon. Make sure she knows what the stakes are."

AFTER VIRGIL LEFT, Gordon thought about it and realized that if she called from her house, or with her cell phone, the police could check the phone calls and trace them to Lucy. So she got her book, a novel by Diana Gabaldon, and tried to read it for twenty minutes, and finally put it down with the sense that she was ruining the story for herself. Couldn't stop thinking about Flowers; she hadn't liked the man at all, she decided. He had long hair, like some kind of reformed hippie, and spoke to her without kindness.

Still, if he was telling the truth about the children . . .

She made herself watch TV for another twenty minutes, an animal show about meerkats, finally couldn't stand it, got up, put on her parka, went out to the garage, backed her Honda into the street, and turned toward

Gina Becker's house. Gina Becker was an old friend, and a night owl: It was eight o'clock, and she'd still be up. As she turned into the street, she watched her rearview mirror for headlights, but there was nothing there. Paranoia, she thought, and went on across town.

VIRGIL HAD BEEN WAITING on the street behind Gordon's house. When the car's headlights came on, shining through the side windows of the garage, he watched through an intervening hedge as Gordon backed out of her driveway and headed west. He followed her, no lights, moving slowly, on the parallel streets, until he ran out of street, and then cut over behind her, three blocks back, saw her turn, then hurried on, went across the street where she'd turned, saw her two blocks down. Did a U-turn, and went after her.

As was the case in Homestead, the trip was limited by the small size of the town. Four or five minutes after she left home, she stopped in front of another house, got out of the truck. Virgil was parked on the side of the road, a block away, watching, as she rang the doorbell, then apparently was invited inside.

The question he had was simple enough: Was this Lucy's house? Had she simply come home, and lived anonymously? He thought probably not; it would have been too easy for her husband to check up on that.

Most likely, Gordon had decided that she didn't want to use her home phone or her cell.

He sat and watched, and Gordon stayed at the second house for twenty minutes, then emerged, again looked both ways, searching for him, got in her car, did a U-turn, and came back past him.

She turned back toward her own home, and Virgil started the truck, drove down to the house she'd visited, marked it in his mind, then went after her. He didn't catch up until she was almost home: He watched her pull into her garage, then, satisfied, went back to the house she'd visited, got the street name and number.

Rather than go back to Homestead, he drove twenty-five minutes to a Holiday Inn at New Ulm, a place he'd stayed several times, and called Davenport at home.

"I need somebody to track a phone call for me. It was made between eight-twelve and eight-thirty. . . . I don't have the name, but I've got an address."

Davenport took the information down and said, "You want it tonight? That could be a hassle."

"Tomorrow morning would be fine," Virgil said. "I'm gonna bag out in New Ulm for the night."

"Running from the law, huh?"

"Not necessarily the case—"

"Oh, bullshit, I know all about Lee Coakley," Davenport said. "I actually spent a little time with her years ago, right after I got on with the BCA."

"You can't be serious," Virgil said.

"Of course I'm not serious, you fuckin' moron. I've never seen the woman in my life," Davenport said. "I'll call you in the morning with that phone number."

"Hey, Lucas . . ."

"Yeah."

"You got me."

They both laughed, and Virgil went to bed and thought about God and girl children, and why God would let happen what was happening. And he thought about Lee Coakley a little.

16

Early the next morning, Spooner drove over to Einstadt's house and caught him at breakfast. "They say they're going to investigate further, but they're not going to charge me at this time," she told him. "They came over and searched my house, and took my computer, but I'd cleaned the place out and cleaned the computer out, so there's nothing to find. We're okay."

Einstadt was gnawing through a six-inch stack of buttermilk pancakes and bacon, soaked in a crimson-colored berry syrup that looked like blood. He chewed with his mouth half open, while he thought about it, then said, "What'd the state guy tell you? Flowers?"

"I didn't see him after the morning. And he didn't tell me anything," Spooner said.

"His truck wasn't at the Holiday overnight," Einstadt said.

"You're watching him? What for?" she asked.

"My boys check around every once in a while, just to see where he is, and who he's talking to. He spent the afternoon talking to Coakley, if that's what they were doing."

"What if they weren't talking?" Spooner asked. "What if they were in there fucking like bunnies? So what? They're adults, and they're allowed. But you're sneaking around watching them, they're gonna catch you at it, and that won't be good. It's time to lie low, Emmett. That's all we can do."

"Shooting Jim is what you call lying low?" he asked.

"If I hadn't shot him, they'd have strung you up by now, and not by your neck," she said. "You owe me, and everybody in the Spirit owes me. Jim was a loose cannon, and he was going to take us all with him."

Einstadt scowled and said, "We're not stupid, Kathleen. We're already doing it. Lying low. There won't be any spirit pools for a few weeks. Everything will stay private and quiet."

"That's all I wanted to know," she said, pushing herself to her feet. "I will still be taking the Fischl brothers to school. I'm sure they won't mind."

Einstadt held up a finger. "About this Flowers guy. He's stirring things up. Junior had an idea about that."

"Oh, God help me," Spooner said. "If that boy were any dumber, he'd have to be watered twice a week."

"Shut up. He's a good boy. Listen to this: What if Flowers walked into a holdup at Loren's?" Einstadt peered at her. "What if he got a tip from one of his pals down at the Yellow Dog that Loren knew something, and he goes over there and walks right into a holdup and gets his ass shot dead?"

"Are you . . . you mean, by me? A fake holdup?"

"Well, since you're the one with all the experience. Loren would say it was a couple of bikers in an old Chevy, and they took off, and that's all he knows."

Spooner sat down again, clenched her hands on the table, leaned forward. "I'll say this as serious as I can, Emmett. When I turned myself in to Coakley, she called Flowers. He came down and they both asked questions, and they both knew everything that was going on. And there were two other cops listening in, and they all knew it, too. This isn't one guy figuring everything out, like in a movie. They all know what's going on. You'd have to kill the whole sheriff's department to wipe out what Flowers knows. And if Flowers gets shot, they'll be all over us, like red ants. *Just don't do anything.* We're okay right now. Stop watching them. Don't do *anything.*"

Einstadt had finished all but a half pancake. He picked it up by its edge, sopped up all the loose syrup and bacon grease, rolled it, and stuffed it in his mouth, chewed for a while, then said, "It really ain't what Flowers knows. It's what he can figure out. He's not some country cop. So, okay, for now—you got good points. But the situation could change."

VIRGIL GOT UP a little later than he had been, took his cell phone into the bathroom. Davenport called, of course, just as he'd finished smearing shaving cream over his face. He wiped half of it off, answered, and Davenport said, "The call went to a Lenore Mackey in Omaha."

Virgil got his notebook and wrote down the information that Davenport had, and said, “Lucy McCain, Lenore Mackey. That’s her. I’m going to Omaha. You want to call the Nebraska guys and tell them I’m coming?”

“I can do that,” Davenport said. “Drive safely.”

Virgil called Coakley and told her where he was going, packed up, and headed out. There was really no efficient way to get from New Ulm to Omaha. He went cross-country, over a web of state highways, until he got to I-29 outside Sioux City, Iowa, and then south, the time marked more by the music than by the terrain, which was all the same, country houses and snow, bare trees and rolling prairie; and Billy Joe Shaver, “Georgia on a Fast Train”; “The Devil Made Me Do It the First Time (The Second Time I Done It on My Own)”; James McMurtry, “Choctaw Bingo”; Don Williams, “Tulsa Time.” Like that, until he crossed the Missouri River bridge north of Council Bluffs and rolled down into Omaha.

In addition to singing along, he spoke to a Lieutenant Joe Murphy from the Nebraska Patrol’s investigative division, who told him how to get to Lenore Mackey’s house, which was northwest of Omaha’s downtown area. They agreed to meet at a pizza place off Saddle Creek Road, a half mile from Mackey’s.

MURPHY WAS a chunky, black-haired, crew-cut guy with a skeptical cast to his face, maybe a bit annoyed to be on escort duty for a guy from Minnesota. They were sitting in a booth waiting for a pepperoni and sausage, and

Murphy said, "So if she tells you to go away, you turn around and drive five hours back."

"If I can talk to her for two minutes, I can probably get her to talk for half an hour," Virgil said. "I didn't want to call ahead, because I was afraid that she'd go on vacation somewhere."

Murphy looked at his watch. "I cruised by her place and didn't see anybody around. She might be working."

"So, I sit," Virgil said. "You could go on and do whatever you're doing. I could give you a ring when she shows up."

"Ah, the boss told me to stick with you. He's pals with your boss up in St. Paul. So, we both sit—if she's not there."

SHE WASN'T.

Her house was an uninflected, rectangular white rambler with a one-car garage at the west end. They knocked on her door, without much hope—the afternoon was moving on, and there wasn't a light anywhere in the house. No answer. On the other hand, there was a single letter in the mailbox, a bill, which meant that the mail hadn't been turned off, and had been picked up recently.

They found a spot down the block and sat in Virgil's truck, engine running, listening to the radio. Murphy liked Billy Joel and Paul Simon, which seemed Omaha-like, to Virgil, and was all right with him, for a while, anyway. Virgil outlined the problem in Homestead, and they talked awhile about their careers, and sports. Murphy's father worked for an Omaha insurance company, and he'd lived in Maryland when he was in school, and had been a lacrosse player.

Virgil wasn't too interested in lacrosse, which sounded to him like French hockey, but Murphy corrected him, told him how Native Americans invented it, and then went on an extended riff about the game. Virgil had played football, basketball, and baseball in high school, and enjoyed team sports, and when Murphy finally shut up, he said, "Well, I sort of wish we'd had that in Marshall. Sounds like a good game."

He said that for diplomatic reasons, since it still sounded like French hockey, and he didn't even particularly like real hockey.

They were in the car for an hour and a half before Mackey showed up. She rolled up her driveway, got out, manually lifted the door on the garage, and drove inside. A minute later, lights started coming on in the house.

"How do you want to do this?" Murphy asked.

"Straight. Get your ID out. I'll knock on the door, introduce myself, introduce you, get a foot in the door. Just let me talk . . ."

LENORE MACKEY OPENED the door, a wrinkle in her forehead—Louise Gordon's identical twin sister, still identical after thirty-five years or so. Virgil held up his ID and said, "Miz Mackey—Lenore, Lucy—I'm Virgil

Flowers from the Minnesota Bureau of Criminal Apprehension, and this is Lieutenant Joe Murphy of the Nebraska State Patrol. We need to talk to you about a series of murders in Homestead, Minnesota, involving the World of Spirit."

She said, "Oh, shit."

But they got in the door, and on her couch, and she said, "I hope you tracked me through my sister, and not somebody in the church."

"Yes, we did—we checked a phone call your sister made," Virgil said. "We really had no choice. You dropped off the face of the earth, and we seriously need to talk with you."

"What have they done?"

Virgil outlined the series of murders, then said, "We think the murders are essentially solved. We think Crocker and Flood were present when Baker was killed, and we think Flood was killed by Bobby Tripp because of that. Then Tripp and Crocker were killed to contain the information. We're pretty sure that Miz Spooner murdered Crocker, but we're not sure we can prove it—she has a story that's about as likely as ours."

"I remember her, a little. She was around, though I didn't know her well," Mackey said. "I couldn't tell you anything about her, though."

"We don't want to talk about that—we've got that figured out," Virgil said. "What happens from here is more or less up to the prosecutors. What we're more interested in is the church. The World of Spirit."

"Why?" she asked, but she knew.

"Because of the sex," Virgil said.

"Oh, boy . . ."

"I don't want to influence your story, so just tell us what you know about it."

She looked at the two men and colored a bit, then said, "It's embarrassing."

"This has pretty much gone past embarrassing," Virgil said. "There are four dead, including a young girl."

She nodded, and said, "I was twenty-six when I met Roland. I worked for a few years after I got out of high school, at the HyVee, but I could see that wasn't going anywhere, so I went to school up in Mankato, studying business systems. That's where I met Roland. . . ."

She said that she never felt that she was pretty; that Roland had wooed her, and said she was. She never particularly wanted to marry a farmer, but Roland seemed nice enough. "Basically, I thought he might be my last chance, if I didn't want to wind up being an old maid somewhere. Which I probably will, now. In Omaha."

They married, moved to a farmstead down the highway from his parents' farm, and worked for Roland's parents, as well as some land he leased from a real estate company in Minneapolis. Everything went fine, she said, for about six months.

"We had these friends, the Bosches, and the Waldts. Dick and Mary, Dick and Sandy. We'd go out with them, to the movies, or whatever, two or three times a week, sometimes. They had taco night at this bar, and we'd go there. Anyway, after about six months, Roland asked me what I thought about Dick Bosche, you know, whether I liked him. . . ."

The conversation widened. She liked him, but how much did she like him? After a couple of weeks, the question arose, would she be interested in sleeping with Dick Bosche? Dick had mentioned that he found her really powerfully attractive, and Roland thought Mary looked pretty good, and Mary was willing. . . .

"So, we tried it. I have to say, Dick was more interesting than Roland, when it came to sex," Mackey said. "I wasn't that experienced, and he . . . liked to do things. Anyway, we went like this for a few weeks, trading off."

Then the question came up, wouldn't it be fun for the friends to get together. Like, all in the same place. They tried that.

"Then, they all said, wouldn't it be fun to bring in Dick and Sandy. By this time, I was really shaky about the whole thing. It was fun, but in sort of a sick-making way. I'd lie awake and think about it, and afterwards, when it was done . . ."

She shook her head.

"We don't really need all the details," Virgil said, trying to be kind. "How did it end up? Were you all together? All six of you?"

"Yes. Eventually. And the guys wanted, you know, to do things together, so there'd be like two of them with one of us women, or two women with one of the guys, and they wanted us women to do things with each other so they could watch. . . ."

"How long did this go on?" Virgil asked.

"A year and a half. We got married in May, and then about the time it started snowing, we first got with Dick and Mary, and then, a few weeks later, Dick and Sandy. And that went on for a year. Then, they told me about the church. How the World of Spirit involved a merger of the spirit and the flesh between people . . . and I started figuring out that they had this whole group of people and that they passed each other around and they wanted to pass me around. To a lot of people. All the time."

"That's when you left?"

"I didn't leave right away. I argued about it, and Roland got really crazy, and he started slapping me. I mean, hard. I finally decided, this was no good, and I told him I was going to leave. He said if I left, the church would kill me, because I knew what they were doing, and the World of Law would wreck the church if they knew about it. I told him that I wouldn't tell anybody, but then Emmett Einstadt came over—he's like the big guru—and told me that once I was in, I couldn't get out. And I was in. After that, I had the feeling that they were watching me, all the time."

"And . . ."

She said, "So I got passed around for a while."

"If it was against your will, it was rape," Virgil said.

"Right. Then I'd have to go to court and say, yes, I'd voluntarily slept with twenty different men, sometimes two at a time, sometimes with five or six or ten people watching us, and with women, but this one time, it was rape."

"That's a tough one," Virgil agreed. "So you ran away."

She smiled, then. "I took Roland's tax money—money he put aside to pay his taxes. He never really looked at the account, except at tax time. I cleaned it out, called my sister, told her I was going to run away. And I did. I got Roland to drive me to the doctor, which always took forever, went out the back door, got in the car with Louise, who was waiting, and we were gone. They came looking for me, they kept coming back on Louise, but she never told. . . . In fact, she told them that she thought somebody might have killed me. They went away after that."

"How'd you get your name?"

"A dead girl. From Sleepy Eye. We were good friends with her mother, we told her what was happening, not all of it, and she gave us her driver's license and Social Security card. I came here to Omaha and got a job in business systems . . . like, being a secretary."

Virgil asked, "Did you know a man named Rouse?"

"Karl Rouse? Oh, yeah. I got passed to him."

"Can you tell us anything about Rouse specifically? Did you have involuntary sex with him?"

"I couldn't really say that."

"What was the youngest person you were involved with?" Virgil asked.

The wrinkle came back to her forehead. "Why? I mean, we were all about the same age. Some of the guys were a little older. . . ."

"We believe that some of the people involved in the

World of Spirit are very young. Children. Did you see any of that?"

She hesitated, then said, "No, I didn't. But I never went to the Wednesday night services. You weren't allowed to go there until you were sanctified. I was close to being pulled in, but I never went all the way."

"Do you think there might have been kids?"

"On Wednesday nights. When we were doing one of those group things, the guys would talk. And sometimes, they talked about the women they'd been with, and I got the impression that some of them might have been younger. I never knew exactly what they were talking about, if it was seventeen or thirteen, but they were . . . new to sex. And these guys were breaking them in. They'd talk about that, breaking them in. Same with young boys. The women would break them in."

"You don't know specifically how young?"

"No. I never actually saw any of them. They were pretty secretive."

Virgil looked at Murphy, who shrugged. No help. Back to Mackey. "Would you like to go back to your real name?"

"Not if that would help them find me. I really was pretty scared. I still am."

Virgil explained the problem: that they *knew* that children were being abused, but that the system was so guarded that there was no way to get enough information to get a search warrant. "We need to find a way to break into the circle. Once we're inside, we've got tools we can use to break out everybody."

She was shaking her head. "They won't talk about each other. If they get caught, they'll just take it. You'll put some of them away, but they'll never talk about each other."

"We've got to do something," Virgil said.

"I can't," she said. "I've got a decent life going here. I've got a boyfriend. If he found out . . . I'm sorry."

They talked to her for a half hour more, but she wouldn't budge.

Out on the steps, Murphy said, "Sorry about that. What're you going to do?"

"I'm going to drive five hours back to Minnesota and think about it."

HE WAS BACK in Homestead at 10:30. At ten, rolling east on I-90, he called Coakley. "We need to talk. Things didn't work out real well in Omaha."

"But that was Birdy?"

"Yeah, but she's not going to be much help. She doesn't know for sure about any young people. Listen, I don't want to talk on the cell phone about this."

"I'll see you in a half hour at the Holiday—in the bar."

"In the bar."

"Half hour."

Hmm, Virgil thought, something might have happened. As it turned out, something had, just not what he thought.

COAKLEY LEANED AWAY from him in the booth and said, "I was in the Yellow Dog and Bill asked, 'How's Virgil?' He . . . sorta knows. Not for sure."

"So what?"

"I'd rather he didn't," she said. "So, I want people to see me walking out of here, without you, and you going down to your room by yourself."

"It's really cold and lonesome," he said.

"Now, don't worry, Virgil. I'm going to drive home, and I'm going to take my oldest boy's car, and I'll be back," Coakley said. "Now, there's some old friends of mine, sitting up at the end, and I'm going to get up and leave, and stop and talk to them about the case, and you can go by and say, 'See you tomorrow,' and leave. Like, really cool-like."

"I don't think that'll work," Virgil said. "The town's too small."

"It might not totally work, but it'll confuse them," she said.

SHE WAS BACK in an hour, satisfied that everybody was confused. "I told my son that we were working a surveillance," she said, as she pulled her sweater over her head and shook out her hair. "So. Tell me about Omaha."

He told her, and she said, "Too bad. So we stay local."

"Looks like."

"You know what we could have done? We could have mailed one of those pictures of Rouse to ourselves. An anonymous tip. Then we raid the place—"

"That would involve some heavy-duty lying in court," Virgil said. "I'm up for an occasional breaking-and-entering, but serious perjury . . ."

She nodded. "Good. I agree."

"Just checking?"

"Ah, God, I don't know," she said. "Ever since I started thinking about it, I've had all kinds of ideas, most of them bad. But I can't stop thinking. It's like a disease."

Virgil was sitting on the bed, and he reached over and caught her by the belt, pulled her close, and began unbuckling it, and she scratched his scalp with her fingernails, and said, "Schickel and Brown were all over the west end of the county today, but they didn't get much. I'm sure the rumors are starting to spread, though."

Virgil dropped her jeans to her ankles, and she stepped out of them, and he stroked her thighs with his fingertips. "I do have one idea. But it's probably crazier than anything you've thought of."

"Tell me about it," she said. "Later."

LATER, HE SAID, "Birdy has been gone for eight or nine years. The World of Spirit people threatened her, but they've got no idea of where she might be."

Coakley sat up and said, "Virgil, you can't tell them."

"No, I don't want to do that. For one thing, she's in Nebraska, and we don't have the resources there to cover her. But. She has a twin sister here in Minnesota, and the twin looks exactly like her, and sounds like her."

"Virgil, jeez . . ."

"I'd tell her about it," Virgil said. "Go up there and explain what we're trying to do. Maybe Birdy can't get involved, but maybe her sister would be willing to. We put her in a house where we can give her good cover, get a phone. She calls Roland Olms, says, 'Virgil Flowers was here and he's investigating a murder of some kind. Kelly Baker. He says if I don't talk about the church, they're going to indict me, too, as an accessory. What should I do? I'm really scared.' Then we cover her, and see who shows up."

"She'll tell them where she's at?"

"No—but they'll have her phone number," Virgil said. "We'll make sure she's in a reverse directory, that they can look her up."

"That sounds complicated."

"If we can talk her into it, it'd only take a couple days to set up," Virgil said. "We've got a house where we stash witnesses, up in Burnsville; it's empty right now. We could do it."

"Let's try to think of something better than that," she said. "I mean, I think it's unlikely that she'd even go along with it."

VIRGIL GOT UP in the morning, still a little worn from the long drive the day before, and headed in to the Yellow Dog. Coakley was already there, eating pancakes, and Jacoby came over with a menu and asked, "Anything new?"

"Nah. I'm thinking about heading out," Virgil said. "Short stack of blueberry pancakes, Diet Coke."

"So she's gonna get away with it?"

"We don't know that, Bill," Coakley said, her voice crisp. "We don't actually know that she did anything."

"Well, Jesus, that just isn't right," Jacoby said. He wandered off to talk with the cook.

Virgil asked Coakley, "Did you think about it?"

"Not much," she said. "My brains were banged too loose."

"Nasty expression," Virgil said. "Nasty."

"I heard it from you," she said.

"But women aren't supposed to use it," Virgil said.

"Pig," she said. "Anyway, it seems to me to be too crazy. We should be able to figure out things here."

"That Loewe guy," Virgil said. "We got him scared. He's been stewing for a while—let's go back. Right after breakfast. Let on that we know more than we do, see if he'll cave."

"That's a plan," she said. "We should take Schickel with us, to add to the pressure."

They finished breakfast and Virgil followed her over to the sheriff's office, where they picked up Schickel, who rode with Coakley, Virgil leading in his own truck. When they got to Loewe's place, they knocked for a while, but got no answer.

No sign of a truck: Virgil looked in the garage and found it empty.

"That's better'n if it'd been here," Coakley said. "Then I'd have to worry that he was dead in there."

"Probably just went downtown for something," Schickel said. "We could go talk to his folks, see when he's coming back."

Virgil tracked around to the front porch, nine inches deep in snow, and peered in the front windows. Through the glass, he could see five or six pieces of furniture bagged up with plastic sheeting; he could see just a corner of the kitchen counter, and it was completely bare.

Schickel and Coakley had walked along the driveway so they could see him on the porch, and when Virgil said, "Uh-oh," Coakley called, "What?"

"I think he's gone. It looks like he mothballed the house."

"Oh, boy. He can't . . . Well, I guess he can."

"I'm gonna try to look in another window," Virgil said. He tramped around the house, but the windows were too high. He looked in the garage, found an old wooden stepladder, put it against the kitchen window, and looked through the open blades of the venetian blind. The kitchen was empty—the dinette table cleaned and wrapped in transparent plastic. Schickel had walked away from the house, and walked back and said, "No heat coming out of the chimney."

"Let's go talk to his folks," Coakley said.

"You go ahead and do that," Virgil said. "I'm going to get my camera and take some shots through the window."

"What for?" Schickel asked.

Virgil didn't want to tell the truth—*to get you out of the way while I break in*—so he said, "Just documenting it. That he ran. Maybe . . . I doubt it, but it might help get a search warrant."

Schickel shrugged, and Coakley said, "We'll give you a call when we get out."

Virgil walked around to her door, as Schickel was getting in the other side, and said, "Rouse."

She nodded.

Coakley backed in a circle and headed out. Virgil got his Nikon from the truck, just in case, recovered the butter knife from under the front seat, and went to work on the kitchen door. In one minute, he decided that the knife wouldn't work; the lock was too new, and the door too tight.

He checked for a key above the door frame, found nothing, checked the adjacent window frame, came up empty, went back to the garage, looked for a key hanging from a nail on one of the exposed studs, found nothing there, and then knocked it off the top of the door frame.

The key worked fine, and he was in. He walked through in thirty seconds: Loewe was gone, no doubt about it. No note, nothing to look at, although there was a room full of cardboard boxes, packed with dishes and other household stuff, covered with a sheet of plastic. Nothing perishable.

The refrigerator and stove were unplugged, the microwave was missing, the water was turned off.

Virgil let himself out, put the key back, and walked around to the front porch, with the Nikon, and took a few shots.

When he was done, he sat in the truck, waiting, and

daydreamed possible ways to get at the photos at the Rouses' place. Had to get them. Had to get just the smallest edge, just enough to get in there.

Maybe lie.

COAKLEY CALLED and said, "His folks say he decided to take off for the Cities, check out some job possibilities. They don't know exactly where he's staying, and they don't know when he'll be back."

"Is that the truth?"

"I don't think so. His mother had that 'I've got a secret' look on her face. She was messing with us. Gene thinks so, too."

"You want to come up to Sleepy Eye with me?"

"I don't think so. I'm going to look for Loewe. Give me a call when you get there, though. . . . I'm still skeptical about the whole idea."

"It's what we've got," Virgil said. "I'm gonna give it a shot."

On the way north again, Virgil thought about the idea of using Louise Gordon as bait in a trap: and thought better of the idea of putting her in a BCA witness-protection house. The problem was, the house was in Burnsville, a Twin Cities suburb that was simply too large. They needed a small town, like Sleepy Eye, he thought, so they could spot whoever came in after her.

That could be handled, he thought: Minnesota had no shortage of small towns, where strangers would be picked up in a minute.

Sleepy Eye had thirty-five hundred residents, more or less, the usual clutter of small businesses, including two cafés. Virgil had eaten at Doreen's once before. He stopped at Gordon's house, knocked, found it empty, because she was at work, and went down to Doreen's.

The place was going through the afternoon slump, and there were only two other customers in the place, a couple of older men huddled at one end of the counter, arguing about medical care. Virgil ordered a hamburger and fries, and when they came, showed the waitress his ID and asked, "You know where Louise Gordon works? I just went by her house and there was nobody home."

"What's going on with Louise?" she asked.

"Nothing, really. I was talking to her night before last, about a person she knew—actually, her sister—and I need to talk to her again. I forgot to ask her where she works."

The woman took another look at his ID, then said, "She's down at Phillips'. The Ace Hardware. She's not in trouble, or nothing?"

"Not at all. I just need to check in with her," Virgil said. And, "You guys got any berry pie?"

"Five kinds—cherry, blueberry, raspberry, strawberry, and mixed berry."

"Put a piece of raspberry on there, too."

"Warmed up?"

"Yeah, go ahead."

"Ice cream?"

"Might as well," Virgil said. "Long as there's no calories in there."

She snorted: the laugh of a woman who'd heard the line six hundred times, and was being polite. "Lucy. That's her name. Louise's sister. Twin sister."

"Nice lady, too," Virgil said.

LOUISE WAS SORTING nuts and bolts into metal bins at the back of the somnambulant hardware store. When Virgil walked in, he could hear two men's voices, working in a small-engine repair shop, then the *tink-tink* of metal on metal, and when he turned the corner, Louise spotted him, frowned, and asked, "How'd you do that? Find my call?"

"Lucy called you? Lenore? Birdy?"

"As soon as you left," Louise said. "She knew you must've figured it out from my call. I don't call her in three months, and then I do, and you show up the next day."

Virgil bobbed his head and said, "Well, she's right. I followed you down to your friend's house and had the outgoing calls checked the next morning."

"I watched to see if anybody was following me," she said.

"I was over on the street behind your house, so I could see when you got in the garage. I stayed on parallel streets as much as I could, and then, way back."

"Tricky," she said. She looked at a bunch of nuts in

her hand, selected one, and threw it in a bin. "So what do you want now?"

"I want to tell you a story, and then see if you could help me out."

"Why should I help you out?"

Virgil said, "Because you're a good person? Because it'd be a lot more exciting than sorting nuts?"

She looked at the nuts in her hand and said, "Let's go get a cup of coffee."

They wound up back at Doreen's, sitting in a booth, and Virgil made his pitch, starting with a couple of questions, spoken quietly. "How much do you know about Lucy's love life? When she was married to Roland?"

"Enough," she said. "I know about the swapping and so on. And you said that they might be abusing children now."

"Not just now . . . for a long time. Generations." He told her about Kelly Baker and the evidence of multiple partners, and sadism. He told her about Bobby Tripp, and his murder of Jake Flood.

"I'm not a prude. I've been married and divorced a lot, and I like women a lot—but that's not what we're talking about here," Virgil said. "And this isn't some phonied-up sex ring where there're a bunch of wannabe therapists manipulating the kids. . . . This is hard stuff, with hard evidence. And it may have been going on for a long time. Maybe a hundred years. Their grandparents might have brought it over from Germany with them, a long time ago."

"So exactly what do you want me to do?" she asked.

"Lucy won't help, because she doesn't want to have to go to court and testify about her sex life," Virgil said. He didn't mention that Birdy was scared to death. "But: You look exactly like her, and you sound like her, even now."

"We were always pretty identical. Nobody could tell us apart," she said.

"And they haven't seen her for years. Now. If we put you in a small town a hundred miles from here, if we can get them to bite, if we can get them to threaten you, we can hit them with search warrants. If we can just get inside a couple of their houses, if we can just get the kids by themselves, we can make our case."

"What if they shoot me?"

Virgil grinned and said, "That'd certainly make the case for us."

Her eyebrows went up, and he quickly added, "No, no, no. You'd be covered twenty-four hours a day. That's why I want to stage it in a small town. Have you ever heard of Hayfield?"

"No. It's in Minnesota?"

"Yeah, it's up north of Austin. I got involved in a missing-kid case up there. People thought a kid had been kidnapped, but he hadn't been—he'd drowned, actually. I mean, a tragedy. But I know a lot of people in town from the investigation. The thing is, we could put you in a house there, and talk to the neighbors, and when anybody unfamiliar went by, we'd get an instant alert. I mean, the town's half as big as Sleepy Eye. Maybe less than half."

"How long would it take?"

"If they didn't bite in a few days, they wouldn't," Virgil said. "You could just come back here, and be done with it."

"Would I get paid?" she asked.

"Sure, we could fix something up. Not a lot, but something."

"The thing is, work is really slow right now," she said. "Dave would be happy to see me take a couple of weeks off."

Virgil said, "So. We got a deal?"

"Better'n sorting nuts," she said. "Or bolts. I'll do it."

They talked about it awhile longer, and then Virgil walked her back to the Ace Hardware. "I'll get back to you—but it'll be in the next couple of days. Soon. I've got to run over to Hayfield and set up a house, get some guys to work it with me. Then we'll go for it."

VIRGIL CALLED COAKLEY: "She'll do it. I've got to call my boss, get his okay, and then I'm going to run over to Hayfield and see if I can find a house. I know an old guy up there who I think will help us out."

"Loewe is in the wind," Coakley said. "He sold his truck yesterday up in the Cities, got cash for it. Went right to the bank with the buyer. I called his bank here, and he took everything but five dollars. That's confidential, by the way. I got that on a friendship basis."

"I think we let him go, for now," Virgil said. "If we said anything publicly . . ."

"That's what I think. You're coming back tonight?"

"I think so. I'll see what happens in Hayfield," he said. "If we're going to do this, we want to do it quick. I keep worrying that somebody will tell them about the young-sex angle, and those pictures go up in smoke."

"So we hurry," she said. "We hurry."

17

Virgil headed for Hayfield, and got on the phone with Davenport to tell him what he wanted to do.

"I worry about bringing in a civilian," Davenport said. "What if they walk through the door and pop her?"

"This isn't about bringing in a civilian—it's about bringing in the only person who could do the job, Birdy's twin," Virgil said. "I'll put her in a vest, but I don't think they'll go right to guns. They'll want to know what she said to me before they do that. I need a couple of guys, though. Del, Shrake, Jenkins, you, I don't care, but at least two."

"I can't do it, but I'll get you two. Do you have a house in mind?"

"Yeah, an old guy named Clay Holley, and some people in his neighborhood. I got to know them pretty good, and I think they'll go for it."

"When are you going to make the call?" Davenport asked.

"Tomorrow, or the day after, if Holley goes along," Virgil said.

"All right, I'll see who I can shake free. Stay in touch. And, Virgil . . . you're sure about this sex thing?"

"I'm sure."

"If you're so sure, why can't you just file on it, get a search warrant?" Davenport asked.

Virgil said, "That's a sensitive issue."

After a moment of silence, Davenport said, "I've had a few issues myself. Good luck with that."

CLAYTON HOLLEY WAS eighty-nine years old and lived in the perfect house—perfect for a minimum-wage farm woman who'd fled her husband. The house was old and very small, white clapboard, two bedrooms, a narrow living room, a kitchen a little larger than the house deserved, a damp basement that smelled of mildew, rusting tools, sour drains, and clothes-dryer exhaust, along with the slightly musty alcoholic odor from five or six barrels of Concord grape and rhubarb wine that Holley usually had cooking in the basement.

Holley came to the front door when Virgil knocked, adjusted his glasses as he looked through the storm door window, then smiled and said in a frog's croaking voice, "That effin' Flowers, as I live and die." He pushed the storm door open. "Come on in. What the hell are you doing here?"

Virgil kicked the snow off his boots and tracked into

the living room, and Holley clicked off what looked like a new television and pointed Virgil at one of two purple corduroy La-Z-Boys.

Virgil sat, and said, "You gettin' any?"

Holley scratched his crotch and said, "Matter of fact—"

"Okay, I don't want to hear about it," Virgil said. "How old is she?"

"A nice, crisp sixty-four," Holley said. "She has an orgasm, the neighbors run for the tornado cellars."

"Jesus, Clay, she's a child. You've got kids older than she is," Virgil said.

"Yup. Two of them, anyway," Holley said. "Why are we talking about my sex life? It's not all that interesting."

"I was hoping you were shacked up with somebody so you could go away for a couple days," Virgil said. "I want to borrow your house. And maybe a few of your friends."

Holley studied him for a moment, then chuckled. "This is gonna be good, isn't it?"

HOLLEY LISTENED to the story and said, "Marie lives two houses down, so I could stay there—I stay over every once in a while anyway, when I'm too fucked-out to walk back to the house. I'll tell you what, that Viagra stuff can be the curse of old age."

"Man, I *really* don't want to hear about it," Virgil said.

"Anyway, we definitely could set up a surveillance system. We've got the Johnsons down on the one corner, and the Johnsons down on the other corner—they're not related—and the Pells, and the Schooners . . . they're all retired, they've all got cell phones. I can call them up right now, we can meet over at Marie's. She's got the biggest house. These folks'll all go for it."

"So you're ready to say 'yes'?"

"Hell, yes. Goddamn interesting thing you got going here, Virgil," Holley said. "I'll call up the TV and give 'em an interview when you bust everybody. Be a hero."

"You're welcome to do that—I can even give you a name or two," Virgil said. "All right. Call your friends. Let's see if we can do it tomorrow."

IT ALL WENT BETTER than Virgil had any right to hope, he told Coakley later that evening, when he got back to Homestead.

"His girlfriend slapped together a batch of oatmeal cookies, and we got all of these old folks there, having a party, and told them what we wanted to do, and they were all for it," Virgil said. They were back in bed, covers up to their chins. "I called Gordon, and she's up for it. I'll go up there tomorrow, pick her up, truck her ass over to Hayfield. Davenport got me Shrake and Jenkins, a couple of thugs, perfect for this, and they're coming down tomorrow. We'll make the call tomorrow, noon or early afternoon. That'll give Roland time to talk to other people, get organized, and get up there."

"I think we're putting a lot of weight on the idea that they'll be able to trace the call," Coakley said.

"Got to," Virgil said. "They wouldn't take any other kind of hook. They've got to work for it. They've all got computers, and it won't take a genius to work the reverse directory. Clay's in there, C. Holley. They'll find it."

"What if they don't come?" Coakley asked.

"Well, I'm gonna put a bug in their ear," Virgil said. "I'm gonna go talk to Alma Flood tomorrow, sometime when this weird guy isn't there—the chicken plucker."

"Wally Rooney."

"Yeah. I'm going to let it slip that we've got information coming, and see if I can squeeze anything out of her. Talk the Bible to her for a while. There's something going on with her; I don't know what. But—I'm gonna let her know that we've got a source, and that we're closing in on them. That'll give them a push."

"Can't talk about child sex to her," Coakley said. "Not yet."

"Not yet. But I can talk about Kelly Baker, and how she was abused. I can wonder if more church members might have been involved. Leave the impression that I'm ignorant, but learning, and that we have this source—"

"What do I do?"

"If we snap the trap on these guys tomorrow evening or the next day, you gotta be ready to get a warrant and hit Rouse," Virgil said. "Rouse is the key. There're a lot of photos—that'll bring down the whole thing. So we snap the trap, if we get one inch of info, from anybody we get, about Rouse, I call you, and you go with all the guys you can get."

"Say I believe you when you say they'll track her

down. But what if the people who show up aren't the people you know? But she should know? And she goes to the door, and she doesn't know who Roland is—"

"She knows Roland," Virgil said. "She saw him a lot, when Lucy was first married. And she can refuse to let him in . . . unless he's the only one who shows. But I see what you mean."

"Best shot would be to take Dennis and Gene with you. They might be able to pick out who they are."

"Let's talk to them," Virgil said. "Too late tonight, but first thing in the morning. Damn, this is going to be interesting."

Her hand slipped down his thigh, and groped, and found him, and she sighed and said, "I'm gonna miss you, Virgil."

"Yeah? How much?"

THE NEXT DAY was a rush. Instead of picking up Gordon, which would have been a two-hour detour, he called her and she agreed to drive to Hayfield on her own. She was excited.

"This is a *lot* better than sorting nuts. I bought a new pair of shoes. I just, uh . . . I don't know why I did that."

Virgil said, "Take it easy, drive carefully. We don't need you winding up in a ditch."

Dennis Brown, the police chief, and Schickel agreed to go, and would drive over together. Virgil told them to take binoculars and be prepared to stay late, and maybe overnight. "We'll pick up a motel tab, if you have to stay over. If they don't come by the second day, they won't be coming."

Virgil was out of the motel at eight o'clock, heading west on I-90, to the Flood place. When he pulled in, one of the girls, dressed in work clothes, came out of the barn and took a look at him; went back in the barn and, a few seconds later, came back out with her sister, who was carrying a basket containing a half dozen eggs.

"Whatcha want?" Edna asked.

"I need to talk to your mother again," Virgil said. "Is Mr. Rooney around?"

"He's run into town. He'll be back in an hour," Helen said. "Whatcha want him for?"

"I don't," Virgil said. "Just wondering if he was around."

The two of them, standing side by side in the snow-covered yard, looked like a black-and-white photo from the 1930s, a couple of orphan girls in a coal town in West Virginia, or out on the prairie in a sod house, or something, drab, colorless clothes, too-fair skin, and pale eyes. And they carried with them the general sense of solemnity he often saw in old photos. Edna said, "Well, Mother's inside. She's been a little off-center, ever since the last time you were here. Maybe got a bug. But we'll go tell her you're here."

AND ALMA FLOOD looked like one of the old photos, too, Virgil thought, when the girls took him up to the front room. She was sitting in the same chair, dressed in a long black skirt and a gray shirt with a darker gray cardigan sweater, buttoned almost to the top. The pocket of the sweater showed some wads of toilet tissue; a reading light shone over her shoulder, and she had one finger inserted in her Bible, toward the very end.

"What is it this time?" she asked.

"I wanted to talk to you," Virgil said, taking a chair without asking. "I've been trying to settle the whole Kelly Baker murder in my mind. I'm pretty sure I know what happened. I believe your husband and Jim Crocker were involved in a sexual relationship with her, and were present when she died, and that the Tripp boy found out about it. That set him off, and his arrest set off Crocker, and Crocker was killed to keep him quiet."

"Impossible to prove all that," she said. "Everybody's dead."

"But proving it, if we could do it, would still be interesting, because there might have been a third man involved, or even more," Virgil said. "Which brings up the whole question of the World of Spirit. All of these people were members, including Kelly and her parents. So the question comes up, was this a church thing? I mean, a regular church thing, allowed and supervised by the church? How many people were involved?"

"It's not the church," she said. "It can't be the church." But she was stressed, and, Virgil thought, maybe lying.

"It would be hard to believe," Virgil said. He nodded at her Bible. "Anyone who takes the Bible seriously, who believes that we'll go on to another world, couldn't be involved in this kind of thing. Child abuse, murder. But we know about the problems that the Catholic Church has had. . . . There will be, Miz Flood, hell to pay. Literally. You read in your Good Book where John the Revelator says, when he talks about the City that has no need of the Sun, because it has the Light of the Lord. He says, 'There shall in no wise enter into it anything unclean, or he that maketh an abomination and a lie: but only they that are written in the Lamb's book of life.' Will the people in the church enter that City?"

She sat as if stricken, didn't say a word, but fixed him with an eye like a dead bird's, not even blinking.

One of the girls said, "Mom? Are you okay?"

"'They repented not of their murders, nor of their sorceries, nor of their fornication, nor of their thefts,'" Virgil said, leaning forward, pounding it in. "And then there's the part that says, 'And I saw, and behold, a pale horse: and he that sat upon him, his name was Death, and Hades followed with him.'"

No response. One of the girls said, "I think you should go now."

Virgil stood and said to Alma Flood, "I've got a source who knows about the church. I spoke to her yesterday, and it's possible that the sins of the church will come back to haunt all of you. Save yourself and your daughters, Miz Flood. Help me out, if you can."

Finally, she moved, to shake her head. "You go on now," she said. "Go on out of here."

Virgil turned away, and she said, "Maybe."

"What?"

"Maybe something will happen. Maybe the pale horse

is already here." She held up her hand and looked at it in the light of her reading lamp, and said, "You go on. But I will talk to you one more time. Not now."

THE TWO GIRLS came as far as the side door.

Edna said, "Rooney wouldn't like to see you here. He says you have a bad effect on our minds."

Virgil said, "I'd like to hear you speak your minds, what you two really think. What you talk about at night, between the two of you. You're old enough to have your own thoughts. Then we could decide whether I'm bad for you, or Rooney is."

Neither one said anything, and Virgil walked away, turning once to see them standing on the porch, watching him. Helen's lips were moving; she was speaking to Edna without looking at her, tracking Virgil instead; or maybe it was a prayer. Virgil was thoroughly creeped out, not only by Alma Flood and the two girls, but by himself.

There was, he thought, something fundamentally crooked about using the Bible to crack a Bible-believer, and that feeling of being stained by his own actions, if that's what he felt, reached so far back into his childhood that he'd never escape it.

He looked back at the house, snarled, "Fuck it," over his shoulder, and headed down the drive.

SOMETHING LIKE two hours over to Hayfield, but he made it in a bit more than an hour and a half, by driving way too fast. As Virgil pulled in to the curb in front of Holley's place, a brown Cadillac sedan came around the corner and pulled up behind him. Jenkins and Shrake, the BCA's muscle, got out of Shrake's Cadillac, and Shrake said, "Yet another case he can't handle on his own."

Virgil asked, "You guys bring your guns?"

Jenkins said, "Oh, shit, I knew we forgot something." He was carrying a canvas bag and he lifted it and said, "Radios."

Shrake was looking at the house and said, "Are we all going to fit in there?"

"Probably not. Probably only me. I'll be in a bedroom closet, and one more guy, down the basement," Virgil said. "The other guy will be next door, and when the talk stops, you'll come out to the side door. If we need you, you're five steps away."

"Couldn't hear—"

"I'll be able to," Virgil said, "and I'll yell."

LOUISE GORDON, Dennis Brown, and Schickel were sitting in Holley's living room, watching television, with a couple of sacks of Doritos and brown bottles of root beer. Gordon got up when Virgil knocked and came in, and said, "Are we going to do it?"

"Sure, we're good," Virgil said, smiling at her. He introduced Shrake and Jenkins to the others, and asked Gordon, "You study your lines?"

"Yes, I did. But Clayton said they sounded stilted—he used to be in a little theater."

"I was pretty good, too," Holley said. "I once played the Nazi in *The Sound of Music*. That was sort of the high point of my career."

"We don't want a play," Virgil began, but Schickel interrupted.

"You want an improv," Schickel said. "So we've been practicing, like we're talking on the telephone with her. We got it going."

"All right," Virgil said. "I'll bite. Let's say I'm Roland. . . ."

They went through the phone call, and Virgil stopped it a few times and went off in different directions, and she always brought him back, sounding appropriately flustered and, at times, frightened.

"Okay, I'm impressed," Virgil said. She was a natural bullshitter. "Let's make the call."

"What if he's not home?" Gordon asked.

"Then we make the call later," Virgil said. "Keep making it until he answers. We know he's around the farm, because Sheriff Coakley has seen him."

They made the call and he wasn't home.

THEY SPENT the next half hour going around to the neighbors, and talking about where to leave the cars, and deciding who would be doing what; fifteen minutes into the half hour, Gordon called again, and got no answer. At the end of the half hour, as they were all getting back to Holley's, she made a third call and suddenly lit up, and asked, in a hushed voice, "Roland? . . . This is Lucy. Lucy."

They couldn't hear the other end of the conversation, but they could hear the pitch.

Gordon: "I'm a little scared here. I don't know how they tracked me down, but this state agent said if I protect you, then I'm an accomplice. I haven't even been there in forever, and he says that makes no difference. He wants me to testify against you, against the Spirit and Emmett and all them. . . . No, I'm not going to tell you where I'm at. What I'm going to do is, I'm going to get a suitcase and tomorrow morning I'm going to Florida or California or Hawaii or someplace and let you clean up your own messes. . . . I don't want to hear about any money, you sonofabitch; you passed me around like I was a side of beef, you owed me that money and more. . . . But you . . . I don't care, I'm just telling you. They're coming and you better hide out, because this Flowers guy is going to put you all in prison. . . . I didn't tell him anything, I told him I didn't have anything to tell, but he knows I was lying. Now I'm going, I'm on my way, and I've said what I was going to say, and I only got one more thing to say to you, which is, go fuck yourself."

And she slammed the old-fashioned phone back on the receiver and looked around, a thin veil of sweat on her forehead and upper lip. "How'd I do?"

Shrake launched himself out of his chair and said, "Goddamn! That was so amazing, you *oughta* be in the theater."

"Awful good," Virgil said. He was beaming, and he beamed on. "Awful good. Okay, folks, the fire is lit. They couldn't get here in less than a couple hours and probably not less than four or five. I say we order up some pizza and beer, see if we can get a decent movie. . . . Clay's got a Blu-ray."

"Party on," Jenkins said. "Goddamn, I like this kind of detectin'. You detect good, Flowers."

THEY GOT the pizza and beer and soda and a Bruce Willis *Die Hard* movie about a computer genius; and Holley got a couple of the cooperating neighbors over, and it was a little like an old-fashioned Christmas.

While that was going on, Virgil took Shrake and Jenkins in the back bedroom and they sat on a bed with a bowl of chips and Virgil said, "If they come, and if they say or do something that we can pop them for, we're going to go straight at them. Read them their rights, but roll right through that, threats, whatever it takes. If they ask for an attorney, we'll tell them that we're taking them up to Ramsey County, and they'll get an attorney there. We ask no more questions, but we talk among ourselves, you know . . ."

"We know . . ."

"Right at the beginning, even before reading the rights, we break them apart. We've got two bedrooms, the kitchen and living room, the car, however many there are, we isolate them. I'll come and talk to each of them, in turn. I'm looking for one good solid piece of information—"

"What?" Jenkins asked.

"I don't know, but I'll know it when I hear it," Virgil

said. "I'm looking for something I can use in a search warrant. If I get it, I'm going to take off, and you'll be on your own for moving these people up north. I haven't talked to the sheriff here, but we could probably get a car if we needed it."

"We can work that out," Jenkins said.

"I know it's all sort of ramshackle, but I'm in a big hurry, and this is what I've got," Virgil said.

Two hours went by, and they moved the cars around the block, scattering them. Jenkins and Virgil stayed in the house with Gordon, while Dennis Brown went to the house on one side of Holley's, Shrake and Schickel to the house on the other side, and Holley went down to his girlfriend's place. Everybody would be watching the street, linked with cell phones and radios.

Gordon started cleaning up after the party, and Jenkins set up a half dozen wireless microphones, with recording equipment under the bed. Virgil, Jenkins, and Shrake would have headphones to monitor the talk, although Shrake's wouldn't work until he was just outside the house.

And they waited, watching TV.

They asked one question, two hundred times. "Do you think they looked up the phone number?"

Virgil found it hard to believe that they'd be too stupid to do that; that somebody wouldn't do it.

"Our big problem is gonna be if they come hat in hand, are polite, say their piece, and leave," Virgil said. "Even if there are some little threats buried in there . . . you know, 'We'd sure be unhappy, Miz Lucy, to hear you were telling lies about us.' If they go that way, we've got nothing."

They got past three hours, and past four hours, but they didn't get past five hours.

18

They came in a crew-cab pickup, three of them. The first word came from an elderly couple who lived at the end of the block, an excited woman on her cell to Virgil: "Big pickup, not from town, turning the corner like they're lost, looking at house numbers."

Virgil clocked his radio. "Incoming," he said.

"We got them," Dennis Brown said. "The guy in the driver's seat is Emmett Einstadt Junior. They call him 'Junior.' There are two more, I think, but I can't see who they are. Could be one in the back—that'd make four."

The big Chevy crew cab stopped in front of Holley's house, and a minute later three men climbed out, awkwardly, a little stiff from the ride, and regrouped on the sidewalk.

Jenkins hurried across the house and down the stairs into the basement, while Virgil crouched in the front bedroom, looking out through a hole in a venetian blind. Gordon stood behind him, in the doorway, twisting her hands nervously. They had wrapped a woman's bullet-proof vest around her, and covered it with a thick quilted housecoat. She still looked a little porky, but with her round face and fleshy hands, not unconvincing.

A radio beeped, and Virgil said, "Yeah?"

"The guy with the black watch cap is Roland Olms, and the third guy—"

"Wally Rooney," Virgil said. Outside, Rooney had pulled off his baseball cap to scrub at his hair, and then replaced it. "Excellent."

He turned and repeated the information to Gordon, and she repeated it, "Cowboy hat is Junior, the other guy is Wally Rooney, and I know Roland. . . ."

She was almost hyperventilating, and Virgil grinned at her and said, "Take it easy. This isn't as hard as it looks, and it's gonna be interesting. They didn't bring their shooter with them, so I don't think we have to worry about that. You just get out there and argue with them."

"They brought this Rooney man you told me about—do you want me to tell them that you think he's messing with Flood's daughters?"

"Keep it in mind, and if it comes up, mention it. Don't force anything," Virgil said. "Okay, they're coming up the walk. When the doorbell rings—"

"Count to five."

"Jenkins is right at the bottom of the basement stairs. I'll be right here. . . . Leave the bedroom door open." He was looking out through the blind. "Okay, they're on the porch. Here we go."

He put the radio to his face and said, "Shrake, as soon as they're inside, and talking, I'll double-click, and you get up by the side door."

"Got that," Shrake said.

The doorbell rang, and Virgil stepped over to the bedroom closet and said, "Break a leg," and stepped inside and plugged in the radio earpiece and turned off the speaker. Gordon was headed toward the door and he said into the radio, "Showtime."

GORDON PULLED the inside door open and looked through the storm door. Roland Olms was there, and she looked at him and said, aloud, "Oh, no. Go away."

Olms pulled at the storm door handle, got it open, and said, "We need to talk to you, Birdy."

"I said everything I was going to say. What if the police are watching? Go away, go away," Gordon said.

Olms was just under six feet tall, and thick through the chest. He stepped directly at her and said, at the same time, "We can't do that. We need to talk," and his momentum pushed her back without touching her. She backed into the living room, and Junior Einstadt followed, with Rooney right behind. He pushed the inner door shut with a solid *thunk*, and they were all standing in a circle.

Roland Olms asked, "You been here the whole time?" and, "You spend all my money?"

"If this Flowers gets on to you, you won't need any money," Gordon said. "He says you all killed some girl and left her body in a cemetery. Some underage girl, and he's like death on that. He says somebody beat her with a whip, and more than once, more than the time she was killed. He says she was gang-raped—"

"Wasn't no rape," Einstadt said. "She was glad to get it any way she could."

"You were there?" Gordon asked, and her hand went to her mouth.

"Didn't say that," Einstadt said. "But it wasn't no rape. She was friendly, and she liked it. She'd get in a pool, and she could get seven or eight of us in one night. More the merrier."

Rooney said, uneasily, "That's not something we ought to talk about."

"Why not?" Einstadt said. "Old Birdy here was the same way, hot to get it on."

"Was not," Gordon said. "That's why I ran away, you sonofabitch."

They were still standing and she began backing away from them.

Olms said, "I oughta take my money's worth right now."

Rooney said, "Shut up, Roll. We're not here to fuck around." He looked at Gordon. "What all did Flowers ask you? We want to know all of it."

"He said that this dead girl got raped by a bunch of you," Gordon said. "He said that you were all church members, and he wanted to know if the church, you know, made little girls do it."

"He mention anybody?" Rooney asked. Gordon's

mouth flapped for a moment, as she tried to decide whether to mention Rouse, and it looked to the three men as though she was trying to avoid saying something, and Rooney pressed: "Did he mention me?"

"Well . . . he sorta wanted to know about you and the Flood girls. The girls were just little bitty kids before, I couldn't even remember them, hardly."

"Sonofabuck," Rooney said to Einstadt. "He knows."

Gordon said, "He was asking about some other people . . . the Bakers, a boy named Loewe. I think he was that little queer back then—"

"Didn't know you knew him," Olms said.

"I knew who he was; some of the women thought he was queer . . . and Flowers is telling me all these things. Rouse? Rouse's daughter, riding around with people? Does that mean anything?"

"Ah, shit," Einstadt said. "Who's talking to him?"

"I think he's talked to a lot of neighbors."

"If he's asking about the Rouses, we got a problem," Olms said. "Greta Rouse has been serviced by everybody in the Spirit. If they get hold of them—"

"We gotta get back," Rooney said. "We need a meeting tonight. With everybody. We gotta call Emmett, right now."

Einstadt looked at Gordon for a moment, then said, "We got a friend who's going to stay with you overnight. Just to make sure you don't go talking to cops until we can have our meeting."

"You're not staying here," Gordon said. She had pulled enough out of the three men that she expected Virgil to burst into the living room. She wanted to look back toward the open bedroom door, but didn't.

"We're not. But you remember Kathleen Spooner?" Einstadt asked. "She'll be here in a few minutes. She's gonna stay with you. We don't have time to fuck around, Birdy. So we'll bring Kathleen in, and tomorrow morning, we'll have figured out what we're gonna do, and she'll be gone."

"I'm not—"

"We're not asking," Olms snapped. "We're telling you." And he reached out and slapped her hard, and she staggered and almost fell: still did not look at the bedroom door, although she was now murderously angry, and it showed. Olms smiled at her. "You remember that, don't you?"

"Fuck you," she hissed, but she moved away from him, her shoulders hunched, one hand up to deflect another slap.

Einstadt went to the door and waved at the truck, and Gordon wondered where Virgil was.

VIRGIL, in the closet, clicked the radio a couple of times, which meant, "Wait." Gordon had gotten more out of the men than he could have hoped for. But with Spooner—he wanted Spooner, too.

SPOONER CAME across the porch steps and inside. "What?"

"It's worse than we thought," Rooney said. "We need

to call a general meeting and get back. You've got to babysit."

Spooner showed her teeth to Gordon. "I can do that. We'll get along fine."

"I don't want you here," Gordon said.

"Tough shit," Spooner said.

Einstadt said to Spooner, "You know what we talked about. The Flowers guy is all over her."

Spooner nodded and said, "Okay."

"We're going," Rooney said, and they tramped out, and as he went through the door, Olms turned and said, "You never were any good."

THEY WERE GONE, Einstadt pulling the door shut behind him, and still no Virgil.

Gordon faced Spooner and said, "I don't want you here. And to tell you the truth, when those men are gone, I'm going to throw you out of here. You might as well go peacefully . . . you're just making me madder and madder."

Spooner said, "We're just going to sit down and relax for a while."

"No, we're not. I'm telling you—"

Gordon took a step forward and Spooner lifted a hand out of her jacket pocket and showed her a gun, a compact .45. She said, "You're not telling me anything."

Gordon said, "She's got a gun. She's got a gun."

Spooner, confused, asked, "Who're you talking to?"

From the front bedroom door, Virgil said, "Me. I'm

aiming a pistol at your head, Miz Spooner. If you even start to move the gun, I'm going to kill you."

From the kitchen door, Jenkins said, "And if he misses, I won't."

Spooner stood stricken for a minute, then realized, and said, "Oh, my God."

"It's all done," Virgil said. "Stoop down, lay the gun on the floor, and then we need to talk. You've still got a chance."

She put the gun on the floor and stood up, and Virgil and Jenkins moved her to a wall and patted her down, and Jenkins put the cuffs on. Spooner said to Gordon, "Birdy, how could you—"

"Eh, not Birdy," Gordon said, with a smile. "You can refer to me as Louise."

Virgil put his arm around Gordon's shoulder and gave her a squeeze. "You were so good."

Jenkins said, "You were so good you made me laugh."

Shrake came in the side door and asked, "Are we taking them on the highway?"

"We gotta figure that out," Virgil said.

Shrake said to Gordon, "You can work with me anytime. That was prime rib."

Gordon was pleased and flustered, and said, "I missed my calling. I should have been a cop."

BROWN AND SCHICKEL came in, and then Holley and his girlfriend, and the BCA agents moved Spooner to a bedroom, sat her on a bed, and read her rights, and then

Virgil said, "If you want an attorney, we won't say another word to you until you have one. That's because by the time you get an attorney, everything will have broken open, and you'll have nothing to give us. At this point, I think a jury will listen to those tapes and understand that you were here to kill Birdy—Louise—and they'll convict you of killing Crocker. So if you want a little break, we can tell the prosecutor that you were cooperative, or that you weren't. I have three yes-or-no questions, that's all. Do you understand?"

"I want an attorney," she said.

Virgil said to Shrake, "Move her up to Ramsey County. Murder one, conspiracy to commit murder, conspiracy to commit child abuse, false imprisonment, no bail. Get her a public defender."

Shrake nodded. "Okay. You headed back to Homestead?"

"Yeah." To Jenkins: "You better come with me. We may need the help. We'll be rounding up a lot of people."

"What were the questions?" Spooner asked.

Virgil looked at her, then called to Schickel and Brown, "Could you guys come in here for a minute?"

They came in, and Virgil said, "She asked for an attorney, and we signed off on her. Now she wants to know what my questions were going to be. We want you to witness this: We're offering to take her to Ramsey County jail and get her a public defender. No pressure. I'm going to ask her the questions, and if she answers, you're witnessing that she's answering voluntarily. Okay?"

They nodded, and Brown asked her, "You want to know the questions?"

"I'm not saying I'll answer them," she said.

Virgil asked, "To your knowledge, does Wally Rooney have a sexual relationship with the daughters of Jacob Flood? Edna and Helen?"

She looked away from them, then shook her head and said, "Yes. I think so."

"The daughter of Karl and Greta Rouse. To your knowledge, does she have sexual relationships with the men of the World of Spirit?"

Again, the sour twisting away, the head shake, and, "Yes."

"To your knowledge, do the Bakers, Kelly Baker's parents, know who was with their daughter when she was killed?"

She looked down at the floor now, shook her head a last time, and said, "Yes. But she wasn't murdered, she died. Maybe . . . too much excitement."

Virgil wanted to punch her, but instead, said to Shrake, "Take her," and to the others, "Let's go, guys."

VIRGIL WENT out the door, feeling a cop-like elation: He had them. But even as he went, he thought, *Should I be happy that I was right, and that children are being abused?* So he said that to Jenkins: "I got this rush, you know, being right about this. Being right about kids getting abused."

"That's not why you got the rush," Jenkins said. "You got the rush because we're going to stop it."

"That's right," Virgil said. "I like your reconceptualization."

"I'm really good at that," Jenkins said. "Let me get some stuff out of Shrake's trunk."

What he got out of Shrake's trunk were a bulletproof vest and two M16s with low-light Red-Dot scopes and ten thirty-round magazines. "I brought one for you, if you want it," he said.

"Might be a little overgunned," Virgil said.

Jenkins said, "I've never been overgunned. I *have* been under-gunned. After that happened, I reconceptualized."

THEY HEADED SOUTH down Highway 56 for I-90; Brown and Schickel would be five minutes behind, Brown saying that he needed to hit the can and then stop in town for a couple of bottles of Pepsi. "All Clay has is Cokes, and I can't stand that shit," he said.

Jenkins drove while Virgil worked his cell phone. He called Coakley and told her about it: described the scene, and what they'd gotten on tape.

"It's everything we need. The thing is, those three guys are headed your way, and they're probably on the phone themselves. They know we're looking at kids, so we gotta nail down the Rouse place right now. *Right now.* Get your guys, and get out there."

"We're going now, four of us. The warrant's ready, I

talked to the judge, clued him in; he'll sign it as soon as you say, 'go.'"

"Go."

JENKINS DROVE TOO FAST, better than eighty-five: They came over a hill, and a car coming toward them popped up its light bar, and Jenkins said, "Ah, shit, it's the cops."

He braked and moved to the side, and a highway patrol car passed them and swung through a U-turn. Virgil reached over and clicked on his own flashers, front and back, and when the cop stopped behind them, Jenkins started to get out and the patrolman yelled, "Stay in the car, sir."

Virgil was done with Coakley, clicked off, and clicked through on his speed dial to the duty officer at the BCA: "We might want to borrow a highway patrolman for a heavy-duty issue in Homestead," he said. "I'll get you the guy's name in a minute. Can you make the connection?"

"Give me the name," the duty officer said.

The patrolman shined a flashlight in the back window of the truck, saw the two naked M16s on the floor, and Jenkins stuck his hand out the window with his ID and said, "BCA. We're on an emergency run to Homestead."

The cop eased up and took the ID, and Virgil said, "We're calling the patrol headquarters right now. We may need to take you with us."

Now the cop came to the window. "What do you mean, take me with you? I was going home for dinner."

"That may have to wait," Virgil said. "We're on our way to Homestead, and we're gonna need some help."

"Ah, for cripes sakes, what are you guys up to? Driving near ninety miles per in a fifty-five . . . Are you that fuckin' Flowers?"

Virgil said, "That's me. And hey, give Jenkins a ticket if you want. You can write it up on the way, would be better—but you'll be getting a call."

He got the cop's name, Andersson, with two *s*'s, called it in, and Andersson, who walked back to his own car, got a call, talked for a moment, then walked back. "Well, I guess I'm going with you. If we're going fast—"

At that moment, Brown and Schickel came screaming over the hill, at ninety per. The driver saw their lights and as Andersson shouted, "Holy shit," they swerved to the side of the road a hundred yards ahead. "More of us," Virgil called to him. "Take the lead. We'll be right behind. We're in a hurry. Go. Go."

WHEN THEY WERE back on the road, Jenkins said, "Thanks a lot, asshole. You think he's really going to give me a ticket?"

"Depends on how bad he wanted to get home for dinner," Virgil said. "We'll keep him occupied, maybe he'll forget. But nah . . . he wouldn't do that."

"Had a mean voice," Jenkins said.

Virgil got himself patched through to the highway patrol car and asked Andersson to call in to patrol headquarters and see if they could get more patrolmen to rendezvous at the Warren County sheriff's office.

"What the hell is going on?" Andersson asked.

"We're busting the biggest child sex ring in the history of the state," Virgil said. "You're gonna be a highway patrol folk hero."

Jenkins started to laugh, and Andersson, maybe pissed, but maybe not, took them up close to a hundred and held them there, and they flashed through the night, heading south and then west.

19

Virgil said, "Go," and Coakley put down the phone and called the judge: "I'm bringing the search warrant over right now."

"So it's true. I hoped it wasn't," he said.

"It's true. I'll see you in fifteen minutes."

The judge's house was five minutes away, but she took five minutes to call in the patrol deputies. Three were already off-duty, two were working, in their cars, and Schickel was with Virgil. Not that much to work with, if there were a hundred families involved in the World of Spirit. Brown had loaned her two city officers, and she called them, and then called the sheriffs of Martin and Jackson counties, with whom Warren County had co-op agreements, to tell them that extra jail space might be needed.

Beau Harrison, from Martin, asked, "What the hell you up to over there? Border Patrol stuff?"

"Worse than that, Beau," Coakley said. "I'll tell you about it if we need the space. We don't know how this will work out yet."

THE JUDGE WAS SITTING in his kitchen, drinking orange juice and talking to his wife, while his wife played a game of Scrabble solitaire. Coakley knocked on the door, said, "Good evening, John," when the judge answered, and "Hi, Doris," to his wife, and gave the judge the papers. He looked them over, said, "Bless me—I hope you don't find any of this stuff. I wouldn't want to have a trial like this in my court. Murder, yes. Child sexual abuse, take it somewhere else . . . I don't believe I know Mr. Rouse, though."

He scrawled his name on the warrant and handed it back to her, and Coakley said, "I know what you mean. I just, uh . . . I know what you mean."

The judge patted her on the back and sent her on the way.

VIRGIL CALLED as she was on her way back to the office. "We're coming fast, but I doubt we'll catch up with Einstadt and Rooney and Olms. They had more than a half hour start on us, and we got slowed down by a highway patrol guy, so . . . they're coming in. We've been talking about it and can't decide whether we should try to intercept them, or let them go and see what they stir up. They're going to have some kind of a meeting out there. What do you think?"

"We've got them, right?" Coakley asked.

"Yeah, we've got them."

"So if they go and talk to a bunch of people, and decide to do something, then we'll maybe have all of them for conspiracy," Coakley said." If we pick them up, that might even warn the others." She whipped her car into the courthouse parking lot.

"Your call," Virgil said. "But you should put somebody out on the highway, there, watching for them. They'll be coming right down I-90, probably in the next forty-five minutes or so. Have somebody spot them, trail them to where they're going."

"All right. I've got a couple guys coming in right now, in their private cars. I'll get them out on the highway. . . . We'll need a description of the truck and a tag number."

"We got those," Virgil said.

Coakley, still in her car, jotted the information in a notebook and said, "I've got the warrant in my hand. We're heading out to Rouse's in ten minutes. Listen, if this happens the way we think, we're going to need more people here to talk to kids than we've got. What do you think?"

Virgil said, "Goddamnit, that's what happens when you slap something together. I'll call Davenport, tell him we need to borrow people from the state, and maybe Hennepin and Ramsey counties. Get them started."

"Do that. I reserved some extra jail space. . . . Man, I hope we're not fucking up, here. But you say we got 'em."

"Yeah, we got 'em. Some of them, anyway. So good luck. And hey, Coakley, watch your ass, huh? When you hit Rouse, these guys'll know that the shit is about to start raining down on them."

"I'll do that—with my ass."

She was getting cranked: She called her oldest son, told him that she wouldn't be home that night. "You guys take care of yourselves. I love you all. Okay?"

"Are you on a . . . date?" her son asked.

She half-laughed and said, "No. I'm on a bust. The biggest one ever. I'll tell you all about it in the morning, and it'll be in the papers. All the papers."

BACK AT the sheriff's office, the two on-duty patrol officers, one male and one female, were waiting in the hall outside her office. She said, "We got an emergency," and unlocked her door, and another patrol officer, the second woman, who'd been off-duty, came through the outer door and called, "What's up?"

The next half hour was like walking through waist-deep glue. She and Virgil had agreed to keep the details of the case secret, but now people had to know: She briefed the deputies, figured out who'd be on the highway and who'd be going on the raid at the Rouse place. The other two off-duty deputies drifted in, and one of the two city cops, the other having gone to Des Moines for reasons unknown, and she had to bring them up to date. She needed three cops, at least, in two cars, to cover the truck coming back from Hayfield; she wanted no less than a one-to-one ratio on those.

She needed to leave one at the office, to handle incoming arrests, which left her with two, in addition to herself, to cover the Rouse warrant. Virgil would be coming with at least five more people—he'd picked up a second highway patrolman along the way.

When she'd worked through it, one eye on the clock, nearly a half hour had passed.

"We've got to move—Einstadt and the others will be coming through anytime. Rob, Don, Sherry, you get out to the overpass. Do *not* let them get by you. Go. And talk to me. Talk to me all the time."

To the others, Greg Dunn and Bob Hart, she said, "Let's go. Separate cars. It's possible that they'll have gone to this meeting. If not, we arrest them, and isolate their daughter, instantly. Okay? And we never leave them alone."

SHE FELT LONESOME on the way out. She was one of the few female sheriffs in the country, and that was a burden; people watched her. Now she was way out on a limb, and Virgil, God bless him, would do what he could to help her, but if this whole thing turned out to be a mistake, she was done.

Done after a month in office . . .

On the other hand, if it was what it looked like . . . she was going to be a movie star. And she would like that, she admitted to herself. She would take her movie stardom, take a picture of it, and stick it straight up her ex-husband's ass. . . .

She was thinking about being a movie star and almost missed the off-ramp; as it was, she went up it at eighty miles an hour and had to stand on the brakes not to miss the turn at the top.

She called Virgil. "Where are you?"

"Twenty minutes out of Homestead. Coming fast."

"I just came off I-90 turning toward the Rouses'. I'll be there in five minutes. . . ." She summarized the rest of the disposition of forces, and Virgil said, "If they're meeting at the Rouses', don't go busting in with just the three of you. I'm thirty minutes away from you."

Her radio burped and she said, "Hold on," and picked up the radio: "Yes?"

Sherry, the deputy with the group waiting for the Einstadt truck, said, "They just blew past us. Rob and Don are trailing me, I'm about to pass them, just to check the tag. I'll get off at Einstadt's exit but turn the other way. Rob and Don are staying back. Okay, I'm coming up. Yup, the tag is right. It's them. I'm going by, and can't see in the window. . . ."

"That's great, guys. Stick with them. And talk to me. Talk to me." To Virgil, she said, "We've got Einstadt tagged. We're watching him."

"We're coming—we're coming."

She led her short caravan down the country roads to the Rouse place and looked up the hill, and saw a light in the house. Only one, and from a distance, it looked like one of the houses in the romance novels she used to read when she was in high school, one of the novels with a young woman fleeing down a hill looking back at a house with a single lit window.

She shivered, and turned up the drive.

INSIDE THE HOUSE, Kristy Rouse was on the Internet, looking at her forbidden Facebook page, which she held under a fake name. She talked about sex a little, on the page, pretending that she was older than she was, and had gotten quite a few friends, a couple of whom had offered to drive out to Minnesota to meet her.

She wasn't that dumb.

When the headlights swept through the room, she quickly killed the browser history, then started running through a list of bookmarked religious pages, Bible pages, and homework pages, opening and closing them, so that there'd be a history on the machine, though she was not sure her parents even knew about the feature.

She'd done four pages when she realized that there were several cars coming up the hill, and she ran to the window and looked out: In the headlights of the second one, she could see the leader, and the leader had a roof rack with police lights on top.

She looked at the computer, then the phone, and went for the phone as she continued to run through pages. Her mother came up on her cell, asking impatiently, "Kristy, what is it? We're really busy—"

"I think a whole bunch of police are here," Kristy said. "Three cars. They're coming up the hill right now."

"Oh, God, oh no . . . Kristy, listen to me. Listen to me. They may ask you questions. . . . Ask for a lawyer. Right away, ask for a lawyer. . . . Don't tell them anything about anything. Just don't talk. Some of the men are coming to get you. They're coming."

There was a loud knock at the door and Kristy said, "They're here."

"Listen to me, Kristy—"

Another knock, and her mother said, "Do you understand what I'm saying, Kristy? You're a big girl—"

"I think they're knocking the door down," Kristy said, her voice cool. She felt cool.

"Don't say anything to them. The men are coming," her mother said.

She put the phone down. She knew what they were afraid of. A lot of photographs, taken by her father. Of people doing things to each other. Of people doing things to her. She smiled, and went to answer the door.

DUNN REACHED past Coakley and gave the door a solid *thwack-thwack-thwack* with his fist, hitting it hard enough to shake it, and then said, "Want us to kick it?"

Coakley saw a shadow moving toward them and said, "I think somebody's coming. Off to the side, guys," and she took her pistol out of her holster and held it by her side, the only time in her life she'd ever drawn it in the line of duty. Dunn and Hart were doing the same, and then the shadow hardened, and the door's lock rattled, and the door opened and a girl looked out. "Yes?"

"Are you Kristy?" Coakley asked.

"Yup. My parents aren't here," Kristy said.

"We have a search warrant for your house. We're going to have to come in."

"Well, then I guess you better," Kristy said.

"Are you alone?"

"Yup. They all went to a meeting at Emmett Einstadt's."

Coakley looked at Dunn and tipped her head, and he nodded and went back outside. He'd call the cars trailing the Einstadt truck. Coakley said to Kristy, "Well, let's go in, and I'll explain this all to you."

THEY WENT UP the short flight of stairs, Kristy leading them to the kitchen, where she pulled out a chair and pointed Coakley and Hart at the others, and Coakley took one and asked, "How old are you?"

"Fifteen. Last month."

"Okay, we're here because we've heard—we've had people tell us—that the World of Spirit church has involved adults having sex with younger people, like yourself, and like Kelly Baker. We're here to search your house to see if we can find evidence of that."

"I thought somebody might come someday, especially after Kelly died," Kristy said. She turned and looked at Dunn, who'd come back in, and who nodded at Coakley. She continued: "I don't know exactly what happened to her, but I heard people talking for a while, then they hushed it all up. She was providing service to three or four of the men, and she suffocated, is what the rumor is. Jacob Flood had a great big cock and he left it in her throat too long and something happened and she couldn't start breathing again when he took it out. He was like that. He was a jerk like that. He liked to see girls choke on it."

Coakley looked at Dunn and Hart, whose mouths were hanging open, and Hart said, "Oh, Jesus."

Coakley said, "Your father is a photographer. Did he ever take any pictures of anybody doing these things?"

"Sure," she said. "There's boxes and boxes of them up in a secret cubbyhole in their bedroom. Father likes to look at them to get excited, before we service him."

"Who's . . . we?" Dunn asked.

"Mom and me. Or one or the other of us. And sometimes other women. And he gets more excited if there are other men there, and everybody is servicing everybody."

"Could you show me the boxes?" Coakley asked.

"Sure. My mother would have a heart attack if she knew I was showing it all to you," Kristy said.

"Why are you?" Coakley asked.

"Because you're going to save me, and take me away from it, and then I'm going to get psychological help and try to lead a normal life, although that might not be possible anymore," Kristy said. "If it is, I'd like to go to L.A."

Hart asked, "Where did you hear about psychological help?"

"Facebook," she said. "I've read all about it. I don't think I'm insane yet. Some girls are insane, we think. I think my mother is insane. We talk about it sometimes, the ones on Facebook. Our parents don't know about Facebook."

"Okay," Coakley said, exhaling. "Could you show me the boxes?"

On the way up the stairs, Dunn said, "This is awful. This is the most awful thing I've ever heard. And Crocker knew about it. I wonder if he took the job to watch us?"

"Dunno," Coakley said.

Hart asked Kristy, "Why do you want to go to L.A? I mean, just to get away from . . . *them*?"

"Oh, no. It's just that it's so dark and cold here," Kristy said. "I'd like to go where it's warmer. Miami would be okay. Basically, it's just the weather."

She went on up the next flight, and Dunn murmured to Coakley, "That's the most insane thing she's said yet. The weather's the problem."

They fished a box out of the closet—the top box was the current one, Kristy said, and Coakley knew it was the one that Virgil had opened. Coakley sat on the bed and started looking through the pictures. Kristy would point to one in which she was prominent, with both men and boys. In one, she was having sex with a boy who didn't look more than twelve, while a group of people watched with parental pride, the children's faces turned toward the camera. The boy, Kristy said, "had come into his manhood," and was being shown how it worked. "After me, the older women would take him, and get him taught."

"So it wasn't just men with girls."

"No, it was the women with the boys, too. Pretty much, all of us with all of us. It's always been that way, since we came from the Old Country."

Dunn was pulling more boxes out of the hidden cubbyhole, five in all, with photos going back at least a full generation, the earliest ones showing men in military uniforms, apparently after World War II.

"Grandfather took pictures, too," Kristy said.

"All right," Coakley said. She turned to the two men and said, "Start turning the place over. Kristy, you come downstairs and sit with me. I want the names of all the people in these photographs."

She remembered Virgil and called him: "We arrived at the Rouse place," she said formally, "and Kristy Rouse informed us of the presence of several boxes of photographs hidden in her parents' closet, which show a wide variety of sexuality between adults and children."

Virgil said, "Great. Schickel has been talking to your guys, the ones tagging Einstadt, and they say that there are a hundred cars at the Einstadts', and there are people all over the place. Lots of cars coming and going. Our guys are a little stressed. If there's nothing going on with you, I'm going to send Schickel and Brown, and the two highway patrol guys, to keep an eye on things until we start down the bust list."

"Good. We're here all by ourselves. I've got two people tearing up the house while I talk to Kristy. But everything is right here. All the photos."

"I'll be there in fifteen minutes," Virgil said. "I'm peeling off these other guys right now."

"Fifteen," Coakley said. And, "Virgil, however bad you think this is—it's worse."

COAKLEY CARRIED the first box of photos down the stairs, and she and Kristy sat at the kitchen table and started going through the photos—many were Polaroids, but more were recent digital-printed shots—Kristy giving her names as they went, Coakley writing them in her notebook.

Five minutes in, Kristy told her that there were lots more that her father had never printed, that were on the computer. They went into what had been a first-floor bedroom, now converted to a workroom.

A wide-screen iMac sat in the middle of a worktable, and Kristy brought it up and went to a Lightroom program and rolled out the Lightroom database as pages of thumbnail photos. Not all the photos were sexual, but hundreds of them were: In the library module, Kristy tapped an "All photographs" number: There were 8,421 photos in the collection.

Coakley was sitting, transfixed, at the desk, when headlights swept up the hill, and she said, "Virgil. He's gonna be freaked out."

Dunn went to look and came back and said, "I don't think it's Virgil. There's a whole line of cars coming in." He went to the stairway and shouted, "Bob. Bob, get down here."

Hart came running down the stairs, and they all went to the side entrance, and Dunn, looking out the window, said, "They've got guns, some guys are running around to the front," and Coakley snapped at Hart, "Watch the front door. Don't let anybody in."

Hart pulled his gun, his eyes wide and his Adam's apple bobbing in what might have been fear, and Coakley heard glass breaking at the front, and heard Hart shout, "Stay out of here—stay out of here. We're the police—"

BANG!

A gunshot, right there, in the front room, and Coakley ran that way and saw a man's arm smashing through the glass of the front door, and Hart lying on the floor with a huge wound in his neck, looking very dead, and Coakley, without thinking, gun already in her hand, fired two fast shots through the door window and heard a man scream. . . .

A half dozen shots poured through the door, straight in, going over Hart's supine body, and she fired twice more through the wall and heard men yelling, Kristy screaming, lying on the kitchen linoleum with her hands over her ears, and then came another shot, close by, and Dunn was screaming something at her, and she looked that way and saw him crouching by the side door, wild-eyed, gun in his hand, and he fired twice and looked back at her and shouted something, which she didn't pick up, and then more shots came ripping through the house, shots from high-powered hunting rifles, the way they went through, spraying plaster and wood splinters.

Dunn scrambled across the floor to where she was now lying, with Kristy, and he said, "We've got to get upstairs. We've got to get higher. If we can get up the stairs to the bathroom, we can get in that old tub and have a close shot at anybody who comes up the stairs. . . . Where's Bob?"

"Bob's dead," she blurted. He looked at her, uncertain, then scrambled past and looked in the front room, then crawled back and said, "We gotta run for it." He grabbed Kristy and pulled the girl's hands down, and said, "Kristy, we've got to run up the stairs—"

Coakley shouted, "Wait, wait," and she slid across the kitchen and grabbed the box of photographs and crawled back, her gun rapping on the floor like a horseshoe. A bullet smashed through a wall a foot in front of her face, spraying her with plaster, and she spat and kept going. The house was being torn apart by gunfire, and they all half-crawled, half-ran across the kitchen floor and around the corner and up the stairs, and Dunn pointed down the hall and said, "You guys get in the tub. Lee, you gotta keep the stairway clear. If anybody comes up the stairs, you gotta keep it clear. You understand? You gotta kill 'em."

"Yeah. Where are you going?"

"Up by the side window. Most of them are in the side yard; I'm gonna try to knock a couple of them down, then I'll be back here right on top of you."

"I'll call Virgil," Coakley shouted after him as he ran down the hall. "He's gotta be close."

VIRGIL CAME UP and Coakley shouted at him, and he said, "Stop yelling, I can't understand," and she reined herself in and said, "We're in the Rouse house. There're guys outside with guns, lots of them. They're shooting the place to pieces. There are some of them inside now. We're upstairs in the bathtub. . . . Bob Hart is dead. . . ."

Kristy was lying under her, weeping, and a rifle bullet, coming at a shallow angle, upward, clanged off the side of the tub, and they both screamed, and Virgil said, "Hold on, five minutes . . . five minutes. Listen for your phone."

Three shots from the front, Dunn, followed by a volley through the front wall, and Dunn crawled into the hallway and shouted, "How much ammo you got?" and Coakley shouted, "The clip in the gun and one more."

"Be careful with it," Dunn shouted, and a slug crashed through a wall above his head and he put a hand over his head and pressed himself to the floor. A man poked his head around the corner of the stairs and saw Dunn on the floor and twisted toward him, with a shotgun, and before he could fire, Coakley shot him in the back and then in the head, and Dunn screamed, "Jesus, Jesus, Jesus . . ." and looked down the hall at her, and at the long gun that the man had dropped. He scrambled down the hall and grabbed it, and rolled over and checked the safety, then did another peek down the stairs. All Coakley could see was the dead man's hand, and Dunn pushed it down the stairs and called, "Good," and at that moment, a gunshot came through the floor and hit him in the foot and he screamed, and came flailing down the hall toward Coakley, and dropped beside the bathtub and groaned, "I'm hit . . ."

"Get behind the back of the tub. Nothing's coming from the back but there's been some from the front," Coakley told him.

Dunn obeyed, leaving a trail of blood, and Coakley pulled a bath towel off a shower stall hanger. "You got a knife? We got to get some pressure on the wound."

She looked over the edge of the tub, and Dunn's face was bright red and sweating, contorted with pain, but he was controlled, the captured shotgun aimed down the hall, and he dug a switchblade out of his pocket and flicked it open. Coakley used it to cut a long strip out of the towel and said, "Wrap it tight as you can . . ."

She could hear men shouting down the stairs, but couldn't hear what they were saying. She said to Dunn, "Wrap that, give me the shotgun," and she slipped out of the tub, took the shotgun, the safety was showing red, and she padded as quietly as she could down the hall. The shooting had slowed, but gunshots were still coming through, blowing plaster and wood, and she did a quick peek at the stairway, saw nobody but the dead man. She stepped across the stairway quickly, went in the first bedroom, did a peek at the window, saw nobody in the yard, checked the stairway again, and slugs started ripping methodically down the hallway, straight up, coming through the floor.

She went to the window in the second bedroom, did a peek, saw a man, or part of a man, squatting by the corner of the shed across the side yard. She didn't hesitate, but fired two fast shotgun shots through the glass, then dashed back down the hallway.

Whoever was down below was still firing through the floor. He was the most dangerous one, she thought; the bathtub had nearly been penetrated by the glancing shot, and if he shot up straight through the bottom of the tub, he'd kill both Kristy and her; but as she watched the shots coming through, she realized that the shots were so vertical—coming up through the floor and into the ceiling—that he must be right under them. She waited for the next shot, fifteen feet away, ran back to it, and emptied the pistol magazine through the floor.

She heard no screaming, but wanted to believe that she'd at least scared the shit out of him.

Back in the bathroom, she reloaded and said, to Kristy, as her cell phone rang, "We're doing fine, honey. We'll be okay."

She answered the phone, and Virgil was there: "There are too many of them, we can't come straight in. There are a dozen shooters around the place. . . . We're coming across the field in the back. If you see people coming in the back, don't fire at us."

"Hurry," she said. "We've only got a minute or two before they get us. You gotta hurry, Virgil."

"We're running in," he said. "We're running."

20

Virgil had sent the two highway patrolmen and the two local cops on their way north to watch the meeting at Einstadt's, and turned south off the highway to go on down to the Rouse place.

"This goes to about eleven on the weird-shit-o-meter," Jenkins said. He'd pushed his seat all the way back and had one foot up on the dash. "I gotta admit, Virgil, this country makes me a little uncomfortable. I'm not really that much of a country guy. I'll take an alley."

Virgil asked, "What happened to that bag of Cheetos?"

"Ah, I think they're right behind your elbow. Let me see . . ." Jenkins fished the bag out, held it while Virgil took a handful of Cheetos, getting sticky orange cheese goop all over his fingers.

Virgil said, between chews, "As far as your weird-shit-o-meter goes . . . give me one of those little hand wipes, will you? . . . it would be very hard to find anything a lot weirder than that case you and Shrake had out in Lake Elmo. The mummy."

Jenkins considered for a moment, put a finger in his ear to wiggle out an itch, then said, "Yeah, well. All right, that was probably a nine."

"Nine, my ass," Virgil said. "You're giving child abuse an eleven—" His phone rang, and he one-handed it out of the equipment bin. "And you're saying the mummy was only a nine? Lots of child abuse around. How many mummies have you run into?"

He put the phone to his ear, and Coakley was shouting at him, and when she slowed down enough to make herself understood, Virgil said, "Hold on, five minutes. Five minutes. Listen for your phone," and she was gone.

They'd been ambling along on the back highway, and Virgil floored it and said, "Get the fuckin' rifles loaded up, man. They've got some kind of lynch mob out there, shooting the place up. There're a lot of guys, they've already got a dead cop. . . ."

"Told you it was weird out here." Jenkins unsnapped his safety belt as they rocketed along the road and pulled up one of the rifles and slapped a magazine in it and jacked a shell into the chamber, put the rifle beside his leg, picked up the other one, did the same, then struggled into his vest and dragged Virgil's vest out of the back. They went through a long sweeping curve and he asked, "What're we doing? Are we going straight in?"

"I don't think so. She said there were a lot of them. And they're all farm guys and they'll have hunting rifles."

"These vests won't stop a .30-06," Jenkins said.

"Gotta try," Virgil said. "They might blow up hollow point, I don't know."

"Lift your arm up." Virgil lifted his arm, and Jenkins said, "I'm putting four mags in your pocket. We got five apiece, thirty rounds each."

"There they are," Virgil said. The house, bathed in car headlights, looked like a white lighthouse, sitting on a hill on the prairie. Virgil reached under the dash and threw a switch that killed his lights: The switch was normally used on surveillance operations, so a person being followed wouldn't see a car pulling away from a curb.

The sudden darkness didn't quite blind them—he could see the dark ribbon of road between the snow-mounded shoulders on either side, but he had to slow down. The last half-mile took a full minute, and he hoped it wasn't too long; at the end of it, he took an even narrower lane that ran off the main road, parallel to the side of the Rouse place, and stopped.

They piled out, and Virgil pulled on his vest and put his coat back on, made sure the extra mags were safely snapped inside his pocket, took out his phone, and called Coakley.

"THERE ARE too many of them, we can't come straight in," he said. "There are a dozen shooters around the place. . . . We're coming across the field in the back. If you see people coming in the back, don't fire at us."

"Hurry," she said. "We've only got a minute or two before they get us. You gotta hurry, Virgil."

"We're running in," he said, as he and Jenkins crossed

the ditch to the first fence, snow up to their shins. "We're running."

"Oh, my God, listen to that," Jenkins said. "It's a war. They're shooting the place to pieces."

And it sounded like a war, like a battle, a spaced *boom-boom-boom* of heavier rifles, with a quicker *crack-crack-crack* of a semiauto, probably a .223 like their own. The field they were crossing was probably forty acres, a sixteenth of a square mile, some 440 yards across. It had been plowed in the fall, and the running was tough over the invisible, snow-covered, hard-as-rock furrows.

"Easy," Virgil said, when Jenkins nearly went down. "You don't need a broken leg."

They were both breathing hard, running in heavy coats, vests, and boots. Jenkins said, "Listen, when we come up, I think, I dunno, it looks like they've got the place surrounded, but most of them are in the front. They're probably trying to make sure that nobody can get out."

"Look, there's somebody inside, I think, on the ground floor. See, in the window . . . Coakley said they were upstairs. . . ."

"I say we hit them in the back, clear that out, get our people out a back door or a window . . . however—"

Virgil, gasping for air: "Okay. She said some of them are inside the house. When we clear the back, I'll call her again, make sure they're still upstairs, and then we both fire full mags right through the house . . . blow them out of there, pin them down, really chop the place up, scare the shit out of the, the ones who survive. . . . Watch for my burst."

"Good, good. Slow down, slow down now, we're making too much noise. . . . I'm going to move off to the right . . . watch for my bursts."

They'd come at a back corner of the house, on the woodlot side, and the firing was continuing, which meant that maybe somebody was still alive inside. A hundred yards out, Jenkins dissolved in the dark, and Virgil closed in, to come up on the corner of the house, where he could see both the back and one side. He moved into the trees, stumbled over a downed wire fence, and then crept fifty yards through the trees, stalking now, slow hunting, aware that time was passing, listening to the shots pounding the house.

At the end of the woodlot, he saw a sudden flash off to his left, saw a shape, heard the metallic clatter of a shell being ejected and another being loaded, in a bolt-action rifle, and waited for another flash, moving toward it. He could see a lump, wasn't sure that it was a man, saw another flash, decided it was, and shot the man in the back. The man half stood, then pitched forward. Virgil moved up and found a body, an indistinct gray mass, trembling and kicking, as the brain died.

Got on his phone, called Coakley: She came up and said, "Hurry."

"Everybody still upstairs?"

"Yes, but I think . . . we can smell smoke . . . I think they're gonna try to burn us out."

"Stay there for a minute, stay on the phone, we're about to hose the place down."

He looked to his left, then moved that way, slowly, slowly . . . saw another lump moving and with no alternative, called, "Jenkins?"

In reply: "Yes. We clear that way?"

"We're clear to the corner," Virgil said.

"There were two guys here," Jenkins said. "They're gone."

"Let's clear out the bottom floor. Find a tree and get down. Are you ready?"

"Go ahead, I'll follow."

Virgil got half behind a thick tree, clicked his rifle over to full auto, stood and aimed at windowsill level and lashed out with a full-auto burst, blowing the whole magazine through the house, playing it across the clapboard siding, which shuddered with the impact. As the burst ended, Jenkins opened fire, the muzzle flashes suppressed but still visible, a stuttering flash that flickered across the snow.

Virgil had just slapped the second mag into the rifle when he saw movement to his right, turned and lashed at it, couldn't tell if he'd hit it.

Jenkins shouted, "Going around right, get them out of the house."

"If I have to go in, I'll go in the back door," Virgil called back. "Keep up the pressure." He got on the phone, and Coakley was there. "Can you make it down to the bottom floor, to the back door?"

She said, "Dunn's hurt; he's hit in the foot. He's bleeding pretty bad. He can't walk."

There was another long stuttering burst, Jenkins working around to the right. Virgil said, "I'm coming through the back door. I'll be there in a minute or two. Don't shoot me."

"There's a fire—"

"I'm coming."

First he moved down to his right, where he'd seen the movement. Didn't see more. Moved slowly up, still didn't see anything. Had he imagined it? Possible. Had to make a decision, and made it.

SCARED OUT OF HIS MIND, Virgil ran down the tree line, banging through the underbrush and ricocheting off the smaller trees that he couldn't see coming, until he was even with the back door, and then dropped on the ground, silent, listening for reaction. Somebody was shooting one of the semiautos, but most of the other guns were silent, and then there was a *BOOM-BOOM* on the far side, a shotgun, and he feared for Jenkins, but then got an answering burst. Jenkins wasn't dead yet; other than that, there were no guarantees.

A truck backed wildly down the driveway, and another followed it, and men were screaming. He was directly at the back of the house now, couldn't see anybody in either direction—heard another short burst from Jenkins, now firing down the far side of the house—and dashed across the open space to the back door.

He kicked it once, as hard as he'd ever kicked a door in his life, felt it sag, kicked it a second time and the lock and latch blew open, and he was inside, at the bottom of a four-step set of stairs. He climbed the stairs, leading with the muzzle of the M16, did a quick peek, saw that he was coming into the back of the kitchen. The kitchen floor was smeared with blood. Light from heavy flames, and a boiling black smoke, poured from the living room beyond.

There were no more bullets going through the house. He heard another burst from Jenkins's rifle, and thought that the farmers around the place were probably more worried about being attacked by a guy with a machine gun than continuing their attack.

Whatever.

He looked both ways, and dashed across the kitchen. The living room had apparently been splashed with gasoline, and the fire was large and growing quickly, the furniture fully involved. He could see a body stretched in the flames, already badly burned, unrecognizable. Nothing to do about that. He turned up the stairs, shouting, "Virgil, Virgil," turned the corner at the landing, saw a dead man lying on the stairs. He hopped over him, shouted, "Virgil," turned the corner at the top and saw Coakley standing in the open bathroom doorway.

He went that way, saw Dunn sitting behind the bathtub, and a young girl inside it. He shouted, "Come on," and Dunn said, "My foot's gone," and Virgil said, "Push yourself up the wall."

He handed the rifle to Coakley, who was holding the

cardboard photo box, said, "Give the box to the kid. C'mon, you lead."

Virgil half squatted, told Dunn to drape himself over his shoulders, got one arm between the other man's legs, and lifted him in a fireman's carry.

They went down the hall, Coakley leading with the rifle muzzle, the girl following, and then the girl darted into a side room, and Coakley screamed at her, and she came back out, carrying a coat. Virgil and Dunn last; Dunn probably weighed two hundred pounds, but wasn't so much heavy as awkward.

Nobody on the stairs, the fire growing wilder, and down they went, into the kitchen, to the top of the stairs by the back door, and Coakley said, "Oh, shit," and turned and gave the rifle to Virgil and said, "I'll be right back. Ten seconds."

"Where the hell . . ."

But she was gone, and a minute later, over the sounds of shouting outside, and the sounds of cars, and more gunfire, there was a sudden crash of glass, and then Coakley was back, took the rifle and they were out and Virgil was shouting, "Right into the trees, right into the trees."

He ran as best he could, with Dunn on his shoulders, and when they got into the tree line, they stopped, crouching behind the thick-trunked box elders, and Virgil put Dunn down. Dunn groaned as he did it, and then said, "Man, thanks. Thank you."

Virgil took the gun from Coakley and said, "You guys stay here. There's another guy with me, he'll be coming round the back of the house, probably, don't shoot him. His name is Jenkins."

"Where're you going?" Coakley asked.

"I'm going to shoot some more people," he said.

HE DIDN'T. There'd probably been a dozen of them, or even twenty, but they'd taken casualties and had finally broken, running for it, piling into their trucks and cars as Jenkins gave them a send-off. One truck was nose-down in the driveway ditch, with its headlights still burning. There were two bodies on the ground in front of the house.

And it was silent, finally, and then somebody moaned. Virgil, moving slow again, walked down the side of a shed and found a man on the ground, his face and neck a mass of blood; he'd been hit in the face with a shotgun, Virgil thought, and if he didn't die, he'd be blind.

The man had been firing a hunting rifle into the house, and the rifle lay on the ground next to him. Virgil kicked it away, and the man heard him and tried to say something, but was so badly hurt that he mostly swallowed blood: But he might have said, "Help me."

Virgil got down behind a tractor wheel on an old John Deere parked next to the shed, and called, loud as he could, "Jenkins!"

A moment later, "Here."

"You okay?"

"Okay. I'll meet you back where we started."

VIRGIL MOVED SLOWLY to the back of the house. He got to Coakley, Dunn, and the girl just before Jenkins came in. Virgil was on the phone, calling the highway patrol guys and the local cops off the watch at the Einstadt meeting, and warning them about men with guns.

"We need you here, but stay clear of any big bunch of cars—they may be coming your way. We've got one dead cop and one wounded. We're gonna need a fast run into town. . . . We need a fire truck. . . ."

"We're coming."

Coakley asked, "Are we clear?"

"I think so," Jenkins said. "There may be some wounded who still want to fight. Gotta be careful."

"Bob's dead," Coakley said. "Ah, God, what am I gonna tell Jenny? Ah, God . . ."

Virgil ignored that and asked Dunn, "How bad's the bleeding?"

"I tied a couple strips of towel around it." He groaned. "They're soaked, but I don't think I'll die from it. My foot's a mess. . . . I can feel the bones moving around. Man, it hurts. It really hurts."

"You warm?" Virgil asked.

"Huh? Yeah, warm enough."

The fire was really blowing up now, had climbed the stairs as though it were a chimney and was spreading into the second floor. Coakley stood up and said, "I've got to run around to the other side. Right now. Somebody needs to cover me."

She started moving and Virgil said, "I'll take it," and followed as she dashed around the back of the house, and then down the far side. Virgil kept the rifle up, now on its third magazine, looking for movement. Heavy black smoke was boiling out of the house now, and glass was beginning to break, and Virgil could smell burning meat.

Two bodies, at least. Could have been Coakley and Dunn and the girl, as well.

Coakley went to the side of the house, knelt, then stood, staggering a little, carrying a computer. She got back to Virgil and said, "I threw it out the window. Eight thousand pictures. I couldn't let it burn. I hope the hard drive's okay."

Jenkins said, "Our guys are coming in," and Virgil looked out of the woodlot down the road and saw a car coming fast, light bar on the roof, and, at right angles to it, on another road, another car with a light bar. The highway patrolmen. The first car pulled into the driveway and Virgil's phone rang. "Everything clear?"

"I don't know. We've got at least two wounded, one of us and one of them. I don't think anybody's holding out to ambush us, but take it easy. Wait for your other guy, check the truck across the road, and we'll start clearing out the buildings here. Watch your gun, careful not to shoot each other—"

"Okay. Every ambulance in three counties is on the way. It looks like a fuckin' war, man."

"It *was* a fuckin' war," Virgil said, and clicked off.

He said to Jenkins, "Let's clear the outbuildings, and the trucks."

Four trucks were sitting empty in front of the house and along the sides, all pocked with bullet holes. Jenkins said, "I was doing everything I could to scare the shit out of them, get them running. Nothing scares a shitkicker like somebody shooting up his truck."

Virgil might have laughed but Jenkins sounded so intent that he didn't; instead he said, "Let's clear them."

They went off together, using Coakley's flashlight, cleared the first, small shed, a repair shop smelling of gasoline; and in the second, large shed, which was full of farm machinery, they moved the light around and a man's voice said, "Don't kill me."

"Come out of there," Virgil said. He came out with his hands over his head, a tall, rawboned man maybe twenty years old, with long hair, in a camo jacket. In the dark, and in the military jacket, he looked like a surrendering German in old World War II books that Virgil had seen.

"Move out into the light," Virgil said. And, "I can't fool around here. If you do anything quick, I'm gonna shoot you. Get down on the ground, flat on your face."

The man got down, and Jenkins came up and cuffed him, and then patted him down. The man said, "They left me. Ran like chickens."

"Don't worry," Virgil said. "You're gonna have a lot of time to talk to them about it."

THEY CLEARED the trucks, found another wounded man, an older man, face wet with pain-sweat, going into shock, shot through both legs. He said, "Help me," and they threw his gun into the snow and then hastily cut strips of cloth out of the back of his coat and put pressure pads on the leg wounds.

They cuffed him to the steering wheel when they were done, and moved on, but found nobody else. Virgil said, "Jesus, Jenkins, you went through here like Mad Dog McGurk."

"I was feeling uncharitable," Jenkins said. "And hell, I didn't even see most of these guys. Once they got in the trucks, I just started unloading on the vehicles, to mark them."

Another car came steaming down the highway and up the drive: Brown and Schickel.

Virgil met them at the top of the hill: The house was now fully aflame, and he could feel the heat on his back, and water from melting snow was starting to run down the driveway.

"We need to get Dunn to the hospital like right now: Can you take him?"

Brown took him, and five minutes later the first of the ambulances arrived. They put the blind man in first, and then the man shot through the legs. The second ambulance arrived, and the highway patrol cops loaded a man from the ditched truck; he'd been hit in the back. One of the ambulance people said he thought that one of the men lying in front of the house was still alive. But maybe not.

They took him.

More cops started coming in, everybody from Warren, Martin, and Jackson counties, cars parking up and down the road, searchlights and flashlights looking behind trees, following tracks out across the fields.

Coakley said to Virgil, "We need to get Kristy to town while she can still talk. We need a batch of warrants, and we need to get all these cops in there. We can leave three or four out here to watch the place until morning, but there's not much left. . . ."

"You do it," Virgil said. "You're the sheriff. I just want to sit down for a couple of minutes."

So she did it, and he sat, looking at the shambles.

Jenkins said, at one point, "Fifteen."

Virgil asked, "What?" and, "Oh, yeah." The weird-shit-o-meter.

Jenkins asked, "How you doing?"

"Sorta freaked, 'cause you know what? I feel pretty fuckin' good, like I could do it again," Virgil said. "Man: What a fuckin' rush."

Jenkins grinned at him in the firelight and said, "Shhh. We don't tell anybody that."

21

Coakley was good at organization, and the shoot-out—with one of their own among the dead—galvanized what Virgil thought of as a "community reaction" among the arriving cops. He'd seen it often enough in small towns, usually after a tornado, where there wasn't the infrastructure to deal with a major emergency, and so everybody pitched in simply because there wasn't anybody else to do it.

Warren County was twice the area of all of New York City, and Coakley had twelve deputies to cover all but the city of Homestead, and had to have at least one patrolman on, seven days a week, twenty-four hours a day. She also had two sergeants and an investigator, two part-time deputies, and fifteen corrections officers; plus twenty or so officers from adjoining counties.

She rounded up all of them, matched cops who knew the county with those who didn't, and sent a dozen teams to round up families whose children had been identified by Kristy in the photos from the closet. The rest she sent into the sheriff's department in Homestead, where they'd meet in a courtroom and produce warrants for the next day, while the corrections officers would be processing those arrested into the jail. The other four would remain at the Rouse place overnight, guarding the scene.

Kristy was sent to the sheriff's department with a county child welfare worker, who was told to give her a bed in a jail cell, with the door unlocked. They wanted her secure, but not frightened.

Two fire trucks had arrived from the local volunteer fire department, plus two more from the Homestead fire department, but they were doing nothing except to make sure that the fire went nowhere, because there wasn't anything to be done. The house was mostly down, and letting the rest of it burn, at least until the standing walls and overhead beams were down, was considered the safest solution, even though there were bodies inside.

Virgil and Jenkins were standing with the firemen, close enough to get the warmth of the house fire without toasting themselves, and Coakley came up and said, "We're going. We need to get your computer guy down here tonight. Did you get a chance . . . ?"

"They're coming, and they've got an iMac just like the one you saved," Virgil said. "If the hard drive works, we should be able to look at it in three or four hours."

"I wish I hadn't had to throw it out the window, but I had to be able to use the gun. Anyway . . ." She trailed off, her eyes moving left, past Virgil's ear, and she said, "What the heck is that?"

Far off in the distance, a golden-white light flared on

the horizon, out of place, too large and too bright for something as distant as it must be. Virgil said, "It's another house."

The firemen were looking at it, and one of them said, "We better get over there . . . maybe it's just a barn." They began organizing to leave, yelling at each other, loading up. One would be left behind, the other three were backing out.

"I've got a really bad feeling about that," Virgil said. "Let's go see who it is."

VIRGIL AND JENKINS led the way out, Coakley and Schickel following, all of them behind the lead fire truck, because the truck driver seemed to know where he was going; the fire was southeast of the Rouse farm, and they took a zigzag route over the irregular road grid. A mile out, the fire resolved itself into two separate blazes, a house and a separate shed, but not the barn.

A half mile out, Coakley called and said, "It's the Becker farm. They're another WOS family."

The fire truck went straight up the low slope off the road to the burning house. The rest of the caravan pulled into a semicircle behind it, but as was the case with the Rouse fire, there was nothing much to do: Both the house and the smaller shed were fully involved. The galvanized roof on the shed had already caved as the support beams burned, and the interior of the house was collapsing.

Virgil and Jenkins got with Coakley, and Virgil asked, "What do you think?"

"I don't know what to think," she said. "It doesn't seem like it could be a coincidence."

Virgil sniffed at the heat coming off the fire, turned to the other two, and asked, "Do you smell it?"

"What?"

"There's somebody in there—I can smell the body burning."

The blood drained from Coakley's face. "Are they suiciding? Are they killing themselves? Is it like Waco?"

"Ah, man," Virgil said. "I didn't mean that . . . I didn't think—"

A cop came hustling up and said, "There's another one. Another fire. You can see it on the horizon from the other side of the house."

They followed behind him, and he pointed: another spark, far south. A fireman came over and said, "Can you smell the body?"

They said yes, and the fireman added, "There's a truck in that shed. It looks like they built a pyre around it, stacked it with lumber and firewood, and soaked it in gasoline and oil. It's so goddamn hot it's melting the car."

The thought came to Virgil and he blurted it out: "They're destroying evidence. If the body in this house was a dead man, one of the men killed back at Rouse's place, and we find nothing here but some teeth and wrist bones . . . if the car melts, if they tore out any bullet holes . . ."

"But why?" Coakley asked.

"No conviction. No evidence even for an insurance company lawsuit," he said.

"I can't believe that," she said. "Where's Becker's wife and kids? Are they outside, or inside?"

"I bet we find them," Virgil said. "I bet they're at friends' houses. I bet we find no more dead men, and we find no injured men. But I bet some men will be gone, disappear, and they'll tell us they deserted their wives, or something, and those will be the wounded ones. The dead ones, the ones in these houses . . . I don't know. I wouldn't be surprised if they said we did it."

FOUR HOUSES BURNED, and in all four of them, trucks were burned with the houses. Whether there'd be discoverable bullet holes in them couldn't be determined until daylight, when the fires died.

VIRGIL, COAKLEY, and Jenkins got back to the sheriff's department at two o'clock in the morning and found a chaotic scene of shouting men and women, children being separated from their families, some of them crying and screaming for help from their handcuffed parents.

A woman saw Coakley walk through the courthouse doors and began screaming, "Devil, devil, devil . . ." and other women took it up. Coakley kept walking.

The parents were being processed into the jail, while the children were sequestered in the two courtrooms on the second floor of the courthouse, under the supervision of child welfare workers from Warren and Jackson counties.

Schickel had come in earlier than Virgil and Coakley, and he walked over and said, "We've got fourteen families, thirty-one adults and forty-two children and teenagers. We've got no space. We're going to have to start parceling them out."

"Where's Kristy?"

"We couldn't keep her in the jail, and we didn't want to put her with the other kids, so she's down in the communications center. We got her some pizza and a Pepsi, and she seems okay," Schickel said.

"Good," Coakley said. "Stay on top of all that. I've got to go get Jenny Hart out of bed."

"I think she already knows. Larry Cortt heard about it, asked me, I confirmed, and since they were pretty close, he went over there," Schickel said. "I know you think you should have done it, but the word was going all over the place, and I thought it was better that she heard it from a friend than having a neighbor banging on her door with a rumor."

Coakley patted him on the shoulder. "Thanks, Gene. You did good. I better get over there."

Schickel said, "Dunn's heel is gone; he's gong to need a lot of rehab, but they say he'll keep his foot."

A mustachioed cop came over and said to Coakley, "I brought four of the kids in. They were pretty freaked and I was talking to them. . . . These kids are messed up. It's not just old guys with the young girls; they're doing the young boys, too, some of them. Everybody's doing everybody."

"You know which boys? You get their names?" Virgil asked.

"I got them, but I'll tell you what—their folks told them that it was all right, it's what Jesus wanted. Honest to God, I got so mad I couldn't spit. If we wanted to do the right thing, we'd take these people outside and shoot 'em."

Coakley said, "I know what you mean, Buddy, but keep your voice down, okay?" And she said to Virgil: "That's why Loewe was scared—if he was involved with boys."

"He may have been one of the boys himself," Virgil said. "Probably was."

Coakley said, "I'm going."

VIRGIL WENT THROUGH to the jail and found that while the men were being processed into cells, the women were being handcuffed to chairs brought down from the County Commission chambers. No space for them all.

Back in the sheriff's office, he took the box of photographs from the Rouse place into Coakley's office, threw them on a table, and began sorting them. Some showed only clothed people, and they went into a pile; some showed nude people, or sexually engaged adults, and they went into another pile. Others showed adults with children, or partners who might be children, and they went into a third pile.

When he was done, he counted them: 436 photographs.

Then he took the third pile, sat down, and began to scan them. Ten minutes in, he found a shot that showed a nude girl, probably thirteen or fourteen, and a nude man, both on their feet, as though they were chatting; the foot of a bed was off to one side, and the photo was poorly framed, as though Rouse had taken it surreptitiously. From the background, Emmett Einstadt peered at the two nude people.

That was good enough, he thought. And he said aloud, into the space, "I got you, you old sonofabitch."

He went slowly through the others, found one more with Einstadt, and a dozen more with Kristy Rouse and various men.

He thought about Rouse: She was, as she'd so insanely said earlier, undoubtedly damaged. He wondered how much more damage testimony and trials would do, and whether they'd be worth the damage. Whether it'd be possible to confine the damage to a few kids . . . if it would be possible to find those children who'd been most widely abused, and use only their testimony, while letting the other children slide away.

He wondered if they'd be allowed to slide away: He wondered if the media would let them.

Coakley came in, shut the door, and he stepped over to her, pressed her against the wall, kissed her, asked, "Are you okay?"

"No, I'm not." She held on to his shoulders and said, "I'm really screwed up."

"It's not going to get better," he said. He took her arm, guided her to her desk chair, and pushed the two photos with Einstadt across her desk. "I'm gonna go get him."

"Right now?"

"We've got enough work here for two weeks, but Einstadt was a leader in the church, and I want him. I want him before he has a chance to run," Virgil said. "I think we should go as soon as we can round up enough cops."

She got on her phone, dialed, said, "Step in here a minute, will you?" hung up, and asked, "What else?"

"I'm not sure you understand how big a deal this is going to be. . . ."

A woman deputy stuck her head in the door and said, "You rang?"

"We need at least ten guys for a fast run out into the countryside, to snatch a guy. We need vests, and volunteers."

"I'll volunteer," the woman said.

"Okay, so nine more. Get them lined up," Coakley said.

The woman left, and Coakley turned back to Virgil. "You were saying, I didn't know how big a deal this is going to be . . . ?"

"This is going to be a huge media event," Virgil said. "You've got to be ready for it—it'll be all over the place by tomorrow noon, and there'll be a lot of television, radio, newspapers, you name it. You'll have to have a couple of press conferences tomorrow, as things develop. You probably ought to try to get a little sleep before that happens. You need a fresh uniform. I'd suggest that we get the BCA media guy down here to talk to you, tell you how it's going to work. Or I could do it, but a pro might be better. . . . It's gonna be crazier than this." He nodded back toward the jail.

"What else?" she asked. She was taking notes on a steno pad.

"I've got to talk to my people up in the Cities, get some of them started down here. You'll need professionals taking statements, sorting everything out. You're going to need lots of legal advice—probably get a team down from the attorney general's office. You'll need some extra public defenders—you've got to get the regional public defender down here right now, have him call in some backups," Virgil said. "We need more people to take care of the kids; we need to get the state child welfare people moving. . . . We need to feed all these people, we need to give them access to bathrooms."

"What else?"

"Most of all, you have to be out front on this," he said. "You're the guy. You need a coherent statement of what happened, an outline of the events that led to the arrests. You should turn this whole area over to whoever you trust to do it, and start pulling together your statement. You'll have one chance: If you're good, smooth, crisp, knowledgeable, modest, all of that—no humor, no humor in this, we've got a dead cop—you'll be okay forever. The first impression is the key thing."

"That's a lot to do, if I'm chasing Einstadt all over the countryside," she said.

"You shouldn't do that," Virgil said. "You've got to be the organizer now. You're the boss. I'll get these guys after Einstadt, you get things sorted here."

She thought about it for a minute, then nodded. "You're right: That's the way to do it. I'll get our people lined up, and I'll get to the rest of it. Can you get the BCA people started?"

"I'll do all the state stuff. I'll call my boss up in the Cities, get him going. Get him jerking people out of bed—he's got the clout."

"Do it," she said, and stood up. "I'll have my people ready to roll in fifteen."

VIRGIL WOKE UP an unhappy Lucas Davenport, who groaned into the phone, "This better be good."

Virgil said, "I've got one dead cop and one badly wounded cop and an unknown number of dead perpetrators, but at least five, and four wounded perpetrators and probably some wounded we haven't found yet. I have thirty-one adults under arrest for mass child abuse, both heterosexual and homosexual; I've got four houses burned to the ground. I've got maybe fifty or seventy-five more perpetrators running loose, with probably more than a hundred children, and God only knows where they've gone. I've got four hundred and thirty-six photographs documenting abuse so gross that you can't imagine it; and maybe eight thousand more in a computer. So if it's not too much fucking trouble, I'm asking you to drag your ass out of bed and do some actual fucking work."

"Okay," Davenport said. "What do you need?"

Virgil told him, and then went out where a bunch of cops were milling around with combat gear, and Coakley was talking loud, and a cop was leading three weeping children through the crowd.

Coakley stopped talking and turned to look at him and said, "You ready, cowboy?"

"Saddle up," Virgil said to the crowd. "We're going."

22

Fifty people were milling around in the parking lot, cars coming and going, lights flashing over the back of the courthouse; it looked like the half hour after a small-town carnival. Schickel climbed into Virgil's truck, because he knew where the old man's house was, a mile up the road and around a couple of corners from the Flood place.

Virgil waited in the street until the other cops were lined up and ready to go, and then led the way out of town to I-90. "This is gonna be something I'll tell my grandkids when they grow up," Schickel said. "There's never been anything like this." He turned to look at the line of cop cars and trucks coming behind him. "We got a *posse*."

Virgil didn't have much to say about that, because he was thinking about the man he'd shot in the back at the Rouse farm. He'd killed a man once before, and that had shaken him. He'd been in a couple of shoot-outs, and once had shot a woman in the foot. This was different:

What was bothering him this time wasn't so much the killing, but the way he'd done it without thinking.

Not that he'd been wrong, but that he'd internalized the problems of shooting and killing to the point where they'd become automatic, and there was something essentially wrong with that, he thought. Or maybe he felt bad because he wasn't feeling worse. . . .

Schickel was going on, and finally wound up with some kind of question, and Virgil shook his head and said, "I'm sorry, I'm a little distracted."

"I am, myself," Schickel said. "We've been up too long. I was wondering, are you planning to go straight in, all of us? We could get ambushed going up his driveway."

"Have to see what the situation is. I don't think they'll take us on, after what happened at the Rouse place."

"I wasn't too clear on that. Lee was in the bathtub with the Rouse girl . . . ?"

Virgil told him about it, and how he and Jenkins had cleared the house out with the M16s, and about the temporary high he'd felt after the fight, and the low that came on as the night continued. "You didn't have any choice with what you did, Virgil," Schickel said. "Any one shot could have killed Lee and the girl both. And the guy you shot, I mean, if you hadn't done that, if you'd fired past him or something, just sure as anything, he'da shot one of yours as he was getting away."

They rode along for a while, then Schickel said, "About feeling high after the fight . . . Sometimes I wonder if the people up in this country don't just like war. Kind of like the southerners. My old man was in World War Two, he signed up when he was seventeen. He'd tell all these stories about it, how tough it was, but when you boiled it all down, I think it was probably the best time of his life. He *liked* it, that's the only word I can come up with, for the way he acted. Same with a lot of his buddies. They'd get in the Legion Hall and the VFW and they talked about it forever, and when they died, they got sent off by a honor guard."

"Doesn't mean they *liked* it," Virgil said. "It was big and important, but that's not the same thing. My old man talks about Vietnam all the time, but he didn't like it."

"Well, sometime when you're not doing anything, think about the difference between liking something and sitting around and talking about it all the time. You might come to the conclusion that there isn't much difference. . . . I knew one guy in my life—my godfather, in fact—who was a submariner in the war, out in the Pacific. He *never* talked about it. Somebody'd be talking about the war, and he'd walk away. He couldn't stand talking about it. That's somebody who didn't like it. That's somebody who hated it."

Virgil grinned into the dim light coming off the dash: "Are you saying I got some kind of gene that likes killing people?"

"Not exactly. But sort of over in that direction," Schickel said.

"You gotta quit smoking that shit, man."

"Yeah, I know. It makes my teeth all yellow."

THEY WERE FLASHING along the interstate, a long rosary of cars linked by their headlights, then up an exit and down to the right, out on the grid of farm-to-market roads, straight north, straight west, straight north again, another jog to the west, and then Schickel said, "That's it, off to the left."

He got on the radio, called the other cars. They were coming in from a long way out, and anybody at Einstadt's would see them coming and would know who they were.

"What do you think?" Schickel asked, when he got off the radio.

"I don't see much," Virgil said. "There's a light in the bottom floor."

"Could be full of people."

"Don't see any trucks."

But as he said it, taillights flared near the house, and then disappeared—the truck they'd been on had either driven into a barn or behind it. A yard light off to one side showed no more trucks, and Virgil said, "Fuck it," and turned up the drive and stepped on the accelerator. They were bouncing hard enough, in and out of frozen snow ruts, that they'd make a hard target for a sniper, and as they came up the rise to the house, Virgil saw the truck taillights out ahead of them.

"They're cutting cross-country, whoever it is," Schickel said, and he got on his radio again, sending some of the following cop cars on parallel roads, in an effort to get out in front of the runaway.

Virgil pulled up into the yard, and then through it, back toward the barn, couldn't pick out any tracks in the snow. A board fence loomed in front of them, and across it, he could see the taillights bouncing away from them. He braked to a stop. "How the hell did he get out there?"

Schickel said, "Maybe went behind one of the sheds? Or through them? Maybe went through the barn and pulled the door shut? He won't get too far, though, I don't think. He can't outrun the guys on the roads."

"If he gets down to I-90, he'll fade into the traffic."

"Well, we're not gonna catch him, Virgil, not us personally. I do think some of the boys will get him."

Virgil nodded and said, "Shoot. I wanted to put my own hands on him." And, a few seconds later, as the distant taillights suddenly disappeared behind an invisible hill, or into an invisible creek bed, "Let's look at the house."

FOUR COP CARS were in the farmyard or in the driveway. Cops were arrayed on the far side of the cars, with rifles pointed at the house. Virgil backed up until he was across from the side door, watching for any movement from what would be the kitchen and living room windows. There was light in the windows, though not much, and Schickel said, "Doesn't look right."

Virgil put the truck in park, but left the engine running, and slipped out, ready to move fast at the first sign of any movement; but the night was as quiet as a butterfly, and cold.

Schickel had gotten out of the far side of the truck and was pointing a rifle at the upstairs windows. He asked, "What do you think?"

"Gonna go knock on the door," Virgil said.

He walked across the yard, the hair on his neck prickling, got to the door, and banged on it, loud. Nothing. He pulled open the storm door and tried the doorknob on the interior door. It turned, and he pushed it open.

And smelled the gasoline.

"We got gasoline," he shouted back at Schickel.

Another cop yelled at him, "Get out of there, Virgil."

Virgil sniffed at it: heavy, but not overwhelming. "I'm gonna take a quick peek," he shouted.

"Careful . . ."

He stepped inside, up the short flight of stairs, the gasoline odor heavier now. A light was flickering from where the dining room must be. A door creaked behind him, and he turned and saw Schickel standing there. He turned back to the kitchen, took a long breath, and walked quickly across the linoleum floor and looked into the dining room.

The dining table had been pushed against the wall, and a dead man lay on an old threadbare Persian carpet. He was faceup, with his hands by his sides; the rug and the room had been soaked in gasoline, a half dozen votive candles sat around the dead man, on the rug. It looked like the candles had been cut down, for none was more than a half-inch thick.

"Goddamn," Schickel breathed. "Gotta get out of here, Virgil. It's a time bomb."

"Do you know that guy?" The gasoline odor was burned into his nose and the back of his throat.

Schickel said, "It's Junior Einstadt, the old man's son. He must have been down at Rouse's."

Virgil studied the scene for another few seconds, then said, "No way to move him. If we touch that rug, some of that flame could come down off a candle, it'd blow."

"Let's get out of here," Schickel said.

"Walk careful," Virgil said, and the two of them tiptoed away.

Outside again, Schickel called for a fire truck, and Virgil got the other cars backed away from the house. Then they sat and watched, one minute, three minutes, and Virgil said, "Maybe we could have gotten him out."

Schickel was on the radio and he said, "They can see the truck but he's half a mile ahead of them and he's down at 90. He's gonna make it to the highway."

"Not much traffic this time of the night. Morning. Whatever it is," Virgil said.

"But what there is, is mostly farmers in pickup trucks," Schickel said. "But where're they going to run to? We'll get him, it's just a matter of time."

And the house blew. First there was a brighter light, then immediately a *whoosh*, when the gas went all at once; they watched the fire climb through the house, and Virgil said, "One more place tonight, Gene. Let's see what's happening at the Floods'."

JENKINS HAD RIDDEN along in the caravan with another cop, and Virgil got him and the other cop to follow as they went down the road to the Flood place.

As with the Einstadt house, there were lights: They drove up the driveway and found a pickup sitting next to the side door. They stopped, and Virgil said, "Run it," and Jenkins got out of his truck and pointed his M16 at the house.

Schickel was talking to the comm center about the truck's tags, and the name came back thirty seconds later.

"It's Emmett Einstadt's truck," Schickel said. "You lucked out. You got the old man after all."

Jenkins shouted, "We got movement."

The side door was opening, and a few seconds later, a young girl called, "Don't shoot me."

Virgil called, "Take it easy, everybody." And, "Is that you, Edna?"

"Is that you, Virgil Flowers?"

Virgil called back, "Yes. It's me. Are you okay?"

"I'm okay. My mom wants you to come in. Only you. If anybody else comes in . . . she's got a gun."

"What about your grandpa?" Virgil called.

"He's here, sitting in his chair. Rooney's here, too."

Virgil looked at Schickel, and shrugged. "Give me the radio," he said.

"You're really going in?"

"Yeah." He called back to Edna, "I'll be there in just a minute. I've got to get my men spaced around. I'll be right there."

He climbed back in the truck, with Schickel's radio,

got a roll of duct tape out of his console, and taped the broadcast button down. "I'll leave the radio on, much as I can. You guys listen close; I don't know how much you hear. If you hear a shot, come in and get me."

He stepped away from his truck and Jenkins called, "You got your gun?"

That made him smile, and he called back, "Yeah, this time."

And he called to Edna, "I'm coming in, honey."

23

Virgil didn't know what to expect when he went in, but he went in behind the muzzle of his pistol. At the top of the entry stairs, he saw Edna looking at him from the doorway to the living room. She was dressed from head to foot in a dress that was either dark blue or dark gray, and fell in one line from her neck. She said, "There's nobody to shoot."

Virgil said, "Why don't you come around behind me?"

She shook her head and said, "No, we're all in here," and she stepped away into the living room. Virgil expected something weird, in keeping with the rest of the night. Instead of following, he edged backward across the kitchen to the mudroom, made sure there was nobody there, who'd be behind him.

Edna came to the doorway again and watched him as he crossed the kitchen—somebody had been frying chicken, but a while ago, without cleaning up, and he could smell the cold grease. He paused at the dining room door, then stepped through: It was empty, but another arch at the end of the dining room led into the living room. With a last glance at the girl in the doorway, he stepped into the dining room, and she said, to somebody he couldn't see, "He's coming. He's checking the dining room."

A woman's voice—Alma Flood's, Virgil thought—said, "Pull that other chair around for him." He moved forward slowly, got to the arch, did a quick peek into the living room, then moved into it, still behind the muzzle of his gun.

The room was lit by two lamps and a television that had been muted; it had been tuned to either a religious channel or a history channel, because the show involved a tour of Jerusalem.

Virgil was somewhat behind Alma Flood, who was sitting in her platform rocker, facing Wally Rooney and Emmett Einstadt, who sat in two recliners, which had been dragged around to face her. Both men were leaning back with their feet up. The two girls, Edna and Helen, sat to one side, on dining room chairs. And an empty chair sat next to them.

FLOOD WAS LOOKING at Einstadt and Rooney, but when she heard Virgil's boots on the floor, she glanced at him and said, "Put the gun down, Virgil. Take a seat."

"I really don't have a lot of time for conversation—" Virgil began.

Einstadt snapped, "Sit down, goddamnit, she's got a shotgun pointed at me."

Alma was left-handed, Virgil noted, which explained why he hadn't seen the long gun. She had the butt braced against the back of the chair, under her arm, with her trigger hand by her side, her other hand on the forestock. Not a pump; the gun was a Remington semiauto twelve-gauge. The muzzle was about six feet from Einstadt's belly. That also explained why the men were sitting the way they were. With their feet up, higher than their hips, they couldn't move quickly. If Alma really wanted to shoot them, she could.

Virgil asked, "What's going on?"

"Sit down," Alma Flood said.

"I don't want to shoot you, Miz Flood," Virgil said. "There's been enough shooting tonight."

"Maybe and maybe not," she said. "But I've got this trigger about half pulled, and if you move that gun toward me, I'll pull it the rest of the way. You'll be killing two Einstadts with one shot."

"Sit down, please, sit down," Rooney whined. Rooney was sweating hard, though the room was cool.

Virgil sat. He kept the gun in his hand, resting on his right leg, and put the radio down between his legs, with the microphone up, and hoped that Schickel and Jenkins and the others could hear it. "What happened here?" he asked.

"From what I hear, you know most of it," Alma said. "We're talking about that."

"We're having a trial," Helen said. "Because of Rooney, mostly, but then maybe for Grandfather, too."

"What'd Rooney do?"

The shotgun barrel swung to Rooney, the muzzle moving a short four or five inches, not nearly enough time for Virgil to do anything even if he'd been prepared. Alma said, "In the World of Spirit, nothing too serious. He took his women, just like the rules say he can. That being me, and then the girls. But as I understand it, under most laws, and maybe even normal Bible laws, we were raped."

"If you didn't consent, then it's rape. If he had sexual relations with the girls, it's rape whether or not they consented, because they're too young to give consent," Virgil said.

"I was taught it was the right thing, from the time I was a boy," Rooney said, a pleading note in his voice.

Edna said, "We were begging you not to."

"We was always taught girls need to be broke in," Rooney said. "It's not my fault we was always taught that."

Virgil said to Alma, "Let the law take care of this. If you shoot him, you're going to go to prison. After what you've been through, that hardly seems right."

"What do you think I've been in, for forty-three years?" Alma asked.

Helen said to Virgil, "He took me upstairs and he was so ready, he was like a bull; he pulled all my clothes off and he ripped my blouse, not on the seam, but right across the fabric so I can't fix it, and it'll always have a rip in it."

She was fingering her dress; Virgil said, "That's not such a big deal anymore, even if it was—"

"We're only allowed two dresses," Edna said. "More than that would be vanity."

Alma said, "What'd he do after he pushed you on the bed?"

"He made me suck on him and then he serviced me, and then he made Edna suck on him and he serviced her, and then he made both of us suck on him, and then he went into me the dirty way."

Alma said, "Tell Mr. Flowers how often he did that."

"Almost every day. He'd hit me, slap me, really hard. . . ." The girl's voice was rising, as though she were reliving it.

Virgil jumped in and said, "Miz Flood, maybe you shouldn't be putting the girls through this. They need treatment."

"I think they do, and I'm sure they'll get it, that you'll see to it if I can't," Alma said. "But that's not the question here. The question is Rooney. Now, I'm an old crow, and these men don't like me as much as they used to, and I won't tell you what Rooney did to me, but I'll tell you that he had to work harder to get himself excited than he did with the fresh ones. Didn't you, Wally?"

"I'm sorry, I'm sorry if you didn't like it. I thought you liked it," Rooney said.

Alma got angry. "Don't you go saying that. Don't you go saying that I liked it. I told you I didn't like it, I screamed at you that I didn't like it, and the last time, there was blood, and how in the hell can somebody be bleeding like that, how can you think they're having a good time?"

"Jake used to do it; I seen him," Rooney said.

"That's all you got to say? Jake used to do it? I'll tell you, Wally, if Jake was here, he'd be sitting right next to you, all three of you like birds on a wire."

"Don't shoot me, Alma. Please don't shoot me. I never meant you any harm," Rooney said.

The muzzle of the gun never moved, but Alma said to her father, "What do you have to say for him?"

Emmett Einstadt said, "Women are supposed to serve men. That's why God put them on Earth. Rooney might not be the best we got, but he tries hard enough. You'da got used to him if you'd gave him some time."

She shook her head and said, "I don't believe I would have. I started out liking Jake, and ended up hating him; I started out hating Rooney. How you could ever give us to him, I'll never understand. How many times did we say no?"

"I didn't even know that you said no," Rooney said. "I'm sorry for what you think I've done. I didn't mean any harm by it. But that's just nature taking its way."

Virgil said, "Miz Flood, from what they've said, we can take both of them in, and I think I can promise you that they'll be sent to the state prison forever. When word of this gets out, when a judge and jury hears about this, I mean, they'll be out of your life. Just as clean as if you killed them; but at least you won't have to pay for killing them."

"I'm not exactly getting an eye for an eye, though, am I?" she asked.

Virgil's cell phone rang. They all jumped, and a smile might have flickered over Alma Flood's face. She said, "Well, answer it. Or the ringing will drive us crazy."

Virgil fished the cell phone out of his pocket with his free hand, and said, "Yeah?"

"This is Gene. We can hear you. Jenkins is in that tree in the front yard, looking through the front window. He says he's got a shot at her, but there's two panes of glass between them and he can't guarantee that nobody else would get hurt. He said you and the two girls are in his background. He thinks he can probably miss them, but maybe not. He wants you to say yes or no."

Virgil said, "No, not yet. Definitely no. I really don't think that would be appropriate at all. I could probably get that done myself; but, I'm really busy here, so I'll talk to you later. Okay? Yeah, she's fine, they're all fine. Listen, I gotta go. I'll call you later."

He clicked off and put the phone back in his pocket.

"That was ridiculous," Alma Flood said.

"Yes, it was," Virgil said. "Miz Flood, I'll tell you what . . ."

She shook her head and said, "Let me finish something here. Girls. What do you think about Wally? Guilty, or not guilty?"

"Don't do that to the girls," Virgil said.

Alma asked, "You know what they say about girls out

here, Mr. Flowers? They say, 'Old enough to bleed, old enough to butcher.' And that's what they do." She turned to her older daughter and said, "Edna, what do you say?"

"Guilty," the girl said.

Helen nodded, her face solemn, and she said, "Me, too. Guilty."

"Alma . . ." Rooney said.

Alma said, "I vote guilty as charged," and she pulled the trigger.

THE BLAST in the small living room was deafening, and Virgil rocked back away from the flash, almost tipped off his chair, and by the time he recovered, the shotgun was pointing at Einstadt and Alma shouted at Virgil, "Don't. Don't move that gun."

Rooney had been knocked back when the blast hit him in the upper chest, throat, and face, but the recliner chair was tipped back so far that he didn't slump forward; instead, he sat in the chair and bubbled to death, the last breath squeezed out of his lungs as a bloody foam.

Virgil's phone rang again and he opened it and said, "I'm okay. Miz Flood just shot and killed Wally Rooney. Everybody sit tight, we're talking."

Helen said from her chair, about Rooney, "He looks awful."

"That's because your mother just shot him in the face," Einstadt said. "Look at that. That's what she's threatening to do to your grandpa. Shoot him just like a sick horse."

Edna said, "I like him better this way."

"He was sick. He was sick in the head," Alma said. "He needed to be put down, just like you'd do with a sick dog. A dog that's got rabies."

"You've got rabies," Einstadt said. "Killing an old friend."

"It's time to talk about you, Father," Alma said. She looked over at Virgil. "I want to be fair, and since you're the law around here, and you want to do everything proper, I appoint you the defense attorney. You can say what you want in his defense, and I will listen to every word. How's that for fair?"

"Hell, he wants me dead," Einstadt said. He wiggled in his chair, and the shotgun muzzle, which had been an inch off line, came up.

VIRGIL WAS LOOKING at Rooney, at the mess that used to be Rooney before Rooney left the building. He thought that he might do a tap dance, stalling for time, because the longer they sat looking at the dead man, the more oppressive the body would become. So he asked, looking at Alma, and then at Einstadt, "How did this happen? How did you get here? I can understand, a hundred years ago, it might be all right to marry off young girls, but even then, *this* wasn't all right. What happened?"

Alma said, "The church got taken over by perverts, including my own father. And grandfather. I don't think it was like that before then."

Einstadt said, "No TV."

Virgil: "What?"

"Sex was what they had before electricity out here until after World War Two. So every night was dark, or lit by lanterns, and there just wasn't a hell of a lot to do. Hard to read. They were poor, didn't have much in the way of musical instruments. In the wintertime, you just couldn't get anywhere, and everybody in the church was really close. . . . I don't know when it started, but it might have gone right back to the beginning, in Germany. Exchanging wives and some of the wives were young, like you said. Thirteen. Boys were men when they were fourteen, and set to work. Hell, some famous rock-and-roll star married a thirteen-year-old girl back in the sixties, because it was done even then, wasn't no hundred years ago. . . ."

"But how did that fit with the idea of a church?" Virgil asked.

"You can read the Bible any way you want, and they did," Alma said.

"No, no, no," Einstadt said impatiently. "It's all there, what they did, the patriarchs, and it went unpunished, because it wasn't wrong. Look at Lot. It's beautiful. The World of Law says it's all right to go to Iraq and kill a hundred thousand people, but it's wrong to have sex with people close to you? Does that sound even a little bit reasonable? What we did was all right—"

"What you did was probably the most fucked-up crime in the history of the state of Minnesota," Virgil said. "Pardon the language. And to tell the truth, I'm not all that happy with the war in Iraq, but there are arguments for and against it, greater evil versus lesser evil, and unless you're a simpleminded moron, you can't make the kind of comparison you just did."

"We didn't live in your World of Law," Einstadt said. "We lived in the World of Spirit, and it was better. It is better, and it'll be better again. We'll make some changes—"

"You won't be making any changes; you're going to be in prison," Virgil said.

"It's a religion," Einstadt said. "You're going to persecute us because of our religion?"

"Damn straight," Virgil said.

ALMA HAD BEEN STARING at her father, and now she turned to look at Virgil, her dark eyes glittering in the light from the muted television. She said, "Not everybody in the church were involved. Some pulled back, and some left the church entirely and moved away, so it's not all the church. It's people in the church."

Virgil said, "But if people *knew* what was going on, even if they didn't take part, then they're to blame, too. You have to go to the law."

"We went to the Spirit," Einstadt said. "The Spirit says there's nothing wrong with a proper sexual attachment between—"

"We're not talking about sex," Virgil said. "There's nothing wrong with sex, but this isn't about sex. This is about slavery. The children don't have a proper choice. They can't say no. We've got photographs taken by Karl

Rouse, hundreds of them, and they don't show sex: They show humiliation, bondage, slavery, desperate children being used by old men for their own enjoyment. I honest-to-God want to get you into a proper court, but I don't understand how human beings could do what you people did. You're monsters in this day and age; throwbacks to the days of slavery, and the slaves were your own children. I'm disgusted just looking at you."

"Disgusted by physical love—"

"Bullshit," Virgil said. "I talked to one of the victims—Karl Rouse's daughter. The language she uses isn't love language, it's language right out of a porno film. I'm a cop, I've seen some of everything, and she shocked the hell out of me. And she doesn't even know—"

Alma said to her father, picking up on Virgil: "You remember what you did the first time you took me up to the bedroom? You remember Mother down crying in the kitchen, and you hit her? How many times did you hit her, Father? She had blood in her mouth, and then you took me up to the bedroom. You remember what you made me do? I didn't even understand. I didn't know what happened. One day I get my monthlies, and as soon as they stop, you stopped being my father and started to be the man who came to rape me every week."

"It wasn't like that," Einstadt said. "You liked it. You remember taking my hand? You remember—"

"I was hoping you wouldn't hurt me."

Virgil said, "Whoa. Alma, I've heard enough here. You've got to let me have him. Believe me."

"So you can put this all out in a trial? So we can all talk about it? You think I want to get up there and talk about it? I don't. That's why we're having this *here* trial."

She said to the girls: "And he did the same to you. Did you take his hand?"

The two girls shook their heads, and the older one, Edna, said, "I don't remember so much when Father took me up, or Grandfather took me up, as when they took Helen up. I thought that all the awful things were coming to her now. I thought even that my night dreams would go away, because Helen would have them instead. I thought maybe they wouldn't service me anymore. I prayed to the Lord Jesus that they wouldn't come anymore, that they'd only service Helen."

Helen said, "I got the night dreams from you, but not about Father and Grandfather. I had night dreams about Mr. Mueller, after you told me about going in the pool. But I was hoping that I wouldn't have to go in the pool. Mr. Mueller would look at me during Spirit worship. I know what he was thinking. . . . At least I didn't go in the pool."

Alma said to Virgil, "After World of Spirit, some girls were taken in a pool to be serviced by the men who wanted to service them."

"Is that what happened to Kelly Baker?" Virgil asked. "A pool?"

"No. That was . . . something different. Some of the girls went a little crazy, and they *asked* for it. Kathleen Spooner—what have you done with Kathleen Spooner?"

"She's in custody. We ran a trap for her, and some

of the other men," Virgil said. "They went up to talk to Birdy and gave themselves away. We were recording everything. They left Kathleen behind to kill Birdy. Kathleen's . . . agreed to help us."

Einstadt said, "She's made a deal? She's the devil's own daughter, Kathleen is. She's worse than anyone here. She killed Jim Crocker—"

"We knew that," Virgil said.

"And she would have killed anyone else who got close to her, if you gave her the chance. She had guns and she always wanted to use them."

"Good for her," Alma said. "She kept the worst of you away from her."

Virgil: "What happened to Kelly Baker?"

Alma said, "She was like Kathleen Spooner—I got sidetracked there. Kathleen liked being serviced. So did Kelly. And she liked other things: We heard that she had whip marks on her legs. Father might know more details, but as I understand it, my dead brother, Junior, my husband, Jacob, Jim Crocker, and John Baker took her out to the Baker barn and had their own little pool. She choked on Jacob's thing and they couldn't get her to breathe again. They knew what would happen with the World of Law, so they took her car to town, and put her in the cemetery."

"They washed her body before they did that," Virgil said. "Was that some kind of religious death thing?"

Alma said, "They were talking about this DNA thing. They say they live outside the World of Law, but they know all about it. You think we got one hundred years of this thing, if Father is right, without keeping an eye on the World of Law?"

"Was Jim Crocker in on that? Keeping an eye on the law."

"Of course he was," Alma said. "He wasn't any regular church member—you wouldn't see him praying—but he was sure there when it came time to service the girls."

"Your dead brother, Junior. Is he the one who was laid out in your father's house?"

"He was. He was shot," Alma said. "Everybody who was shot and killed was laid out, and the houses burned, because somebody said that the fires would get so hot that nobody could prove they was shot, and so the World of Law couldn't take the farms away. The houses weren't worth so much; it's the land that's worth a lot."

Helen said, "I'm glad Junior's dead."

Edna: "So am I. I'd service him, but he was just mean. Mean, and he never washed."

Virgil asked the girls: "How many men were you involved with . . . over the years?"

The younger one said, "I was only with family, because I wasn't in the pool yet."

The older one said, "I don't know. Most of the men who were still in our part of the church. How many is that?"

Alma said, "Many."

ALMA SAID, "We're getting close to a verdict, seems to me. Mr. Flowers, you've been asking questions, but you haven't been putting up a defense." She said it as "dee-fence."

Virgil said, "Miz Flood, I'll tell you the honest-to-God truth, and that's that I don't care much about what happens to your father. I came out here to arrest him, and put him in jail for the rest of his natural life. And while I don't believe in hell, I understand that you folks do, and I suspect that if there is, he's going to be burning there forever after. So, from my point of view, your father's taken care of. He might as well be dead.

"But if you kill him, *you're* going to have to pay. If you—"

"I already killed Wally; I'm going to have to pay for that, anyway," she said. "What are they going to do, make me pay twice?"

"It goes beyond that," Virgil said. "You're not only threatening to kill him, you're dragging your daughters into it, by making them vote. And you think it's not going to hurt them, growing up without parents, after everything that they've been through? Killing Wally, you're going to have to pay for—but given what was going on, I've got to believe that a judge will let you out pretty quick. Plead temporary insanity—"

"It's not temporary," she said.

"Plead insanity. I think you'd get off, and given some time, you'd get out to see your children. Maybe even some grandchildren, someday. Edna and Helen will be taken care of by the state, and given treatment, and maybe, there's a possibility that everything will work out for them. So the thing we've got to think about here, is not your father, but what happens to you and the girls."

"I don't care much what happens to me," Edna said. "The World of Spirit is coming to an end, and I don't know if I can live in the World of Law."

"You'll fit right in," Virgil lied. "You'll be amazed. You're young enough that in a few years, with treatment, this life will be like a bad dream."

Alma said, "Pretty smart. Taking that path, I mean. Saying it's not about Father, it's about us. You're a smart fella, Mr. Flowers."

"I got more, if you want it," Virgil said. "You've been reading the Bible, I know, the New Testament and the Old Testament, and they both have a lot to say about killing, and it's not good. If you hope . . . if you have a soul, killing won't do it any good."

"Do I have a soul?" Alma asked.

"I believe you do," Virgil said.

"Of course you do," Einstadt said. "Maybe you think what happened here was wrong, I can see you believing that. But you do have a soul, Alma. It may be a pitiful thing, covered with bloodstains from poor Rooney here, but it's still alive; it can still be saved. You can't shoot your own father."

"Sure I can," she said. "I just pull the trigger."

"Don't do it," Virgil said.

ALMA SAID to Edna: "So what do you have to say? Guilty or not guilty?"

The young girl looked straight at her grandfather and said, "It's not only what you made us do to you, all the men want that; it's what you made us do to each other, after Helen got old enough. And that wasn't Spirit. That was you wanting it to be like pictures on the Internet. That was not right and you should burn in hell for that."

"I'm your grandfather," Einstadt said. "You remember the toys you got for Christmas? Where did those come from? You remember when we built the swings?"

"This is pathetic," Alma said. "Edna, say what you think."

"Oh, he's guilty," she said. "But I leave it up to you, Mother. Mr. Flowers might be right. It might hurt us more than it hurts Grandfather."

"Listen to your daughter, Miz Flood," Virgil said. "She's a smart one."

Alma said to Helen, "What do you think?"

Helen looked at her grandfather and said, "You hurt me really bad. I think you liked hurting me, after that first time, when you found out how much it hurt. I think you're a rotten old man who never thought of anything but himself."

"You never told me any of this," Einstadt said. "Why didn't you tell me? I thought—"

"You thought we liked it?" Alma said.

"I don't know." He looked away.

Helen said, "But I think the same as Edna—that Mr. Flowers might be right. I think I would like to get to live with you, Mother, after all this is done, and maybe the World of Law will let you get away with Rooney, because of what he did, but I don't know if they'll let you shoot two. Two seems like a lot more than one."

"Guilty or not?"

"He's guilty. We all know he's guilty. I don't even know why we have to have a trial. But should we shoot him? I don't know about that. Maybe we should listen to Mr. Flowers."

ALMA SAID to Virgil, "You made an impression on the girls, anyway. But you haven't said one word in Father's defense. You want to say that word now?"

Virgil shook his head. "Miz Flood, I think just like Edna. He is guilty, I believe, but let the law take care of it for you."

Alma said, "I'm a child of the World of Spirit, Mr. Flowers, and I don't pay too much attention to the World of Law. My father was right about that: The World of Law is crazy. We see it on the television, and we know how crazy it is—people go around killing other people, and nothing happens to them; people stealing money so big that you could buy all the farms in this whole country for the money they steal, and nothing happens. That's crazy. I don't give two bits for your World of Law."

"Miz Flood—"

"Don't 'Miz Flood' me, Mr. Flowers. Either say your defense, or give up."

"I don't have a defense," he said. "But don't do this to yourself."

Einstadt said, "For God's sakes, Alma, don't be crazy. Put up the gun and let's go with Flowers."

As she turned back to Einstadt, Virgil, who'd had his feet flat on the floor, slowly pulled them back, got his toes cocked: Given a half-second distraction, he might be able to knock the shotgun sideways. Most people thought of shotguns as being infallible at short distances, as though the shot goes out in a wide screen. In fact, at the distance that separated Alma and her father, the spread would only be a couple of inches across, or maybe three or four at the most. If he could knock it just a bit sideways . . .

He said, "Miz Flood . . . I do have one more thing to say. . . ."

She off-paced him again. As Virgil was getting ready to fling himself at her, leaning forward, cocked, ready, she said, "Father. I always wanted to do this."

And she pulled the trigger, with the same tremendous blast as the one that killed Rooney, and Virgil flung himself from the chair and knocked the shotgun sideways, and then wrestled it away from her.

Too late for Einstadt: The shot had hit him in the stomach and lower chest, and though he was still alive, he wouldn't be for long, with a hole that you could put a fist into.

Einstadt was trying to speak, but couldn't, and Virgil yelled at the radio, "Get somebody in here, I've got the gun," and at that instant, Jenkins burst in, and then stopped. "Holy shit."

Alma leaned forward, putting her face in front of her father's clouding eyes, and said, "You're on your way to hell, Father. Maybe I'll see you there sometime. I hope not, but maybe I will. In the meantime, I hope you burn like a sausage on a griddle."

Einstadt might have heard some of it—his eyes flicked with the words—but he didn't hear the griddle part, because at some point between "on your way to hell" and "sausage," he died.

JENKINS SAID to Virgil, "We recorded it. Some of it was a little dim." He picked up the taped radio and pulled the tape off, clicked it, and said, "Gene, keep most of the people out of here. We've got a crime scene."

Schickel came back: "Copy that."

Jenkins said to Alma, "Miz Flood, I'm sorry for your troubles. I truly am. And I gotta tell you, I would have pulled the trigger. If you want to call me up in court, I'll tell them that. I think you did the right thing."

She looked up at him and said, "So you don't agree with Mr. Flowers, that it was about us? Me and the girls?"

"I have a different view of it," Jenkins said. "If you'd seen that old sonofabitch living in prison, getting three meals a day and hanging out with his pals, you would have wondered where the justice was. Well, you know where it is now." He put out a hand to her. "Come on along. I'll take you and the girls into town."

24

Virgil lay between Coakley's long legs, with his head on her tummy, and she lazily scratched his scalp with her nails, and she said, "I keep thinking, one more day and it'll be back to normal."

Virgil said, "Yeah."

"Oh, I know," she said. "I had four more media interviews today, but I'm going to give them up. I'll do *People*, but I'll be damned if I'm going on *National Outrage*, or whatever it is."

"Good decision," Virgil said. He found his sex life tended to be enhanced if he let her ramble for a while; in the meantime, he observed, she had the most consistently clean belly button he'd ever encountered.

"The attorney general's office is complaining about our record-keeping," Coakley said. "Their lead attorney got really snarky about the evidence stream, and I said, 'We had seven dead and nine wounded people and a hundred abused kids and nobody knows how many more from the past, and you're worried that I didn't use the right paper clips?' She's like twenty-nine."

"Paper clips?" Virgil asked. He was now re-contemplating her laser job, and wondering why it had resulted in a pubic trapezoid (a four-sided polygon having exactly one pair of parallel sides, the parallel sides being referred to as the bases, or, in Coakley's case, the top and bottom, and being composed of short reddish-blond hair; the sum of the angles being 360 degrees).

"Of course, the paper clips aren't important now, but a year from now they might be, when all the trials get going," Coakley said. "I've told the commission that I need to hire a couple of retired attorneys to come in and do the paperwork. The AG's office will handle all the actual victim interviews, the regional public defender will take all the defense stuff, so what I need to do is organize the arrest-level records. Starting now. Forget the interviews."

"Sounds right." The question being, Virgil thought, Why a trapezoid? Why not a regular triangle, say, or a rhombus? Or something baroque, with curves?

"But then," Coakley asked, "how do you say no to the *Today* show?"

"Dunno," Virgil muttered.

"You know what? I'm the one who put the M16 on the wall behind the desk. I had John do it, right before the interview," she said. "I didn't want any of this 'Housewife-sheriff makes big fuss.' That reporter from the *Times* kept wanting to talk about baking bread and raising children as a single working mother. I kept telling her, 'Hey,

I'm the sheriff. I carry a gun. I shoot at people.' And she was like, 'Do you grow your own rosemary?' I think it was the first time she'd ever been out of New York City. I wanted to apologize for not making artisanal goat cheese in my spare time."

Virgil said, "Mmm, artisanal goat cheese."

That made her laugh, and she scratched again, which Virgil thought was pretty erotic. She said, "You know what I like about you, Virgil?"

"Whazat?"

"You really listen to me. So many guys don't really listen to women."

A WEEK HAD GONE BY since the chaos of the shoot-outs, the first arrests, the fires, the sequestering of children from World of Spirit families. The church situation was more complicated than Virgil had known it to be—there were World of Spirit families that did not participate in the church's sexual activities, and those families usually met for services separate from the branch of the church led by the late Emmett Einstadt. Those families had known of the child abuse, though, and so were not entirely out of the woods.

The commissioner of Public Safety, Rose Marie Roux, and Virgil's boss, Lucas Davenport, had come down the next day, and Roux had offered priority service with the BCA labs on any evidence collected during the follow-up. Teams were going through the burned houses, based on the report from Virgil and Schickel on the immolation of Junior Einstadt. Only a few bone fragments were found, and only one, a piece of jawbone, had anything that looked like a bullet hole. The whole question of proving the dead men's participation in the assault on the Rouse place was up in the air.

The governor, sounding as though he'd had one too many manhattans, called Virgil late one night and asked, "Is it possible for you to stay out of trouble for one year in a row? I mean, the whole goddamned state's embarrassed by this. It's almost like we're Massachusetts or something."

"Well, hell, Governor, if you can't spin it better than that—"

"I can spin it better than that—this proves our system works, that we're ever-vigilant when it comes to child welfare, et cetera. Hey—are you pimping me?"

"Maybe," Virgil said.

"Huh. Well played, Virgil. Come see me when you get back. I got a new pair of Tres Outlaws cowboy boots you should see."

THE AG'S OFFICE had looked at the investigatory chain that led from the first tip about Karl Rouse taking lots of Polaroids, to Kathleen Spooner's confirmation of child abuse by the Rouses, through the search warrant, and had given that chain its stamp of approval. A continuing stream of information from Kristy Rouse had included the identification of all the participants in child sex in the photos, and including background watchers of the sexual activities, had eventually led to the arrest or charging of most of the members of the church.

Twelve families had simply vanished. They were being sought. Twenty-two adult males had also fled, leaving their families behind. Several of the families and individual males were known to have crossed into Canada. Kristy Rouse told AG interviewers that some World of Spirit families had moved to Canada years ago and started a colony there, but she didn't know exactly where. Alma Flood confirmed it, but also said she didn't know exactly where, but she thought Alberta.

Canadian authorities were inquiring after them, but since Alberta was considerably bigger than France, and full of rapidly growing industries with tens of thousands of outsiders, progress could be slow.

Assets had been frozen. The World of Spirit members had been on the land for a long time, and had generally prospered. Most of their farms covered a square mile or more, often had small or no mortgages, and the land was worth $4,000 an acre. The average net value of more than two million dollars each brought defense attorneys flocking to Homestead, and a general strategy was beginning to emerge: blame the males.

They were generally toast anyway, the thinking went, and if the wives and children could blame the husbands, they might stay out of prison and hold on to the land, less the cost of their legal defense, of course.

Virgil ran into Tom Parker, the attorney he'd spoken to his first day in town, and his associate, Laurie, whose last name Virgil never discovered. Parker said, "I'm gonna get you made an honorary member of the Warren County Bar Association. I mean, holy cow, Virgil. If we don't get run over by all these outsiders, we've got ten years' work for every guy in town."

"That wasn't an essential part of my plan," Virgil said.

"Oh, hell, I know that—but this is always what happens, isn't it?" Parker said, in good cheer. "In a book, everybody walks away from the dead bodies, but in real life, there's always more trouble after the fight than before. You can tear down a house in a day, but cleanup takes a week."

Laurie said, "I've spoken to Alma Flood, and she's going to sign me up to do her defense. I admire that little talk you gave, about sex and slavery, before she shot those men. I expect I'll ask you to repeat it to a jury, if it gets that far. And Mr. Jenkins, of course; we will be talking with him."

"I'll look forward to it. It'll give me another chance to eat at the Yellow Dog," Virgil said.

FLOOD WAS UNDERGOING psychiatric examination. Virgil doubted that she'd be convicted of anything, unless Laurie was a fool, but it would be some time before Flood was free; years, maybe.

Flood's daughters, Edna and Helen, were primary sources of information about the World of Spirit, as was Kristy Rouse. Rouse's father had vanished, but her mother had been arrested and jailed. The Rouses' computer, which Coakley had thrown out the window of the burning house, was damaged, but the FBI computer lab had recovered the contents of the hard drive, including all eight-thousand-plus photos.

THE CHILDREN had been sequestered, interviewed, and counseled by a battalion of lawyers, psychologists, and social workers. Some were phlegmatic and silent; others were gushers of information, accusations, and horror stories. Incest had been routine, as had rape. One peculiarity that had been winkled out by a reporter from the *Los Angeles Times*: They almost all tested close to the top in academic achievement for their equivalent grade levels. That finding started a minor pie fight among the state educational establishment, which eventually ended in an agreement that other Minnesota children would get equal educations if educator salaries were higher.

THE MEDIA ATTENTION had been intense. There were no rooms in I-90 motels between Blue Earth, to the east, and Worthington in the west. Virgil had succeeded in staying out of sight, but Coakley had shown an interesting ability to deal with the media, and Virgil had heard talk of a reality TV show called *Law Woman*.

"The way I see it," he told Coakley, as he lay between her legs, "you do two years of *Law Woman* at a million dollars per year, before it gets canceled because nobody's watching it, but you'll have made about what you could expect to get for, what? Twenty-five years of working in Homestead?"

"No way that'd happen," she said, although she seemed interested in the idea. "There are women sheriffs of a lot bigger counties than this. The TV people would want something where you got a shooting every week."

"But those women are bureaucrats, not heroines," Virgil said. "You're a heroine. You saved a little girl from a lynch mob."

"You and Jenkins saved *me* from a lynch mob."

"But we weren't inside the Alamo with the girl child and the box of evidence, and you were. Gunfights in the hallway, fire creeping up the stairs," Virgil said. "Remember, we're talking about a TV show."

THEY HAD no idea where Harvey Loewe had gone. He'd simply disappeared. Testimony from WOS kids said that Harvey had abused several of the younger boys, and had been thoroughly abused himself when he was a teenager.

Virgil couldn't figure out the equities of that, and had trouble working out the exact definition of justice for so many other WOS members. Some of the women had turned out to be as vicious as their husbands, but some had actually seemed to be more captive than anything else. If somebody had been hammered into submission since childhood, could you really blame them for not sneaking out and running for the law?

Birdy Olms had run because she had already been in

the World of Law. Kathleen Spooner hadn't run when she could have. Prosecutors were reviewing Spooner's file, and the general thinking was that she'd be charged with murder, along with a list of other, sex-related crimes.

Two other female members of the WOS had suggested that they hadn't run from their husbands because they believed they would be murdered by Spooner. They'd heard rumors of other members drifting from the church and suddenly disappearing. Virgil tended to believe them; tended to believe that Spooner might be the rare female serial killer.

KELLY BAKER'S PARENTS were both arrested and jailed, and both were found in the Rouse photo collection, in sexual contact with children. If enough evidence could be found that they had known what had happened to their daughter, and had covered it up, they would both be charged with murder. But since they were both headed for lifetime prison terms, and Minnesota did not have capital punishment, a murder charge was basically moot.

The John Baker family, from Iowa, was among those that disappeared into Canada. Iowa investigators found that he'd taken a large equity loan on his home earlier in the winter, had kept it in cash in the bank, and had cleaned it out starting on the day that Virgil and Bill Clinton had visited them. Based on information from Alma Flood and other cooperating church members, a murder warrant was issued for both Baker and his wife, in Kelly Baker's death. There were indications that Baker had been growing marijuana out in an otherwise useless low spot in one of his fields; none of the church members seemed to know about that.

AND FINALLY, Bob Tripp was spun out of the story as a kind of folk hero, taking out a major bad guy, in revenge for what was done to his friend Kelly Baker. Tripp's parents had been on several national television shows, talking about his athletic accomplishments, and the sense of fair play earned on Homestead's athletic fields. Virgil hadn't decided what to think about that, either—Tripp might have been better going to the sheriff with his story about Kelly Baker . . . but what if he'd innocently talked to Jim Crocker, and had been killed for what he knew? The World of Spirit might have continued untouched. . . .

He never did work it out, but that didn't bother him too much, because he believed that a lot of the things that happened in the world couldn't be adequately or logically settled. Bob Tripp was like a modern-day John Brown, written small: a murderer in a good cause.

VIRGIL AND COAKLEY had been conferring fairly often, and most of the town of Homestead knew it. Bill Jacoby, owner of the Yellow Dog, made a couple of cryptic references to relationships and midlife sex, and Virgil realized he was probing for evidence. He gave him none; but neither did Jacoby quit probing.

As for the relationship itself, Virgil could see it lasting

awhile . . . but not forever. Coakley was a hell of a woman, but was looking for a little more stability than Virgil could offer. In the meantime, the conferences continued.

"WHAT DOES 'The Virgins' mean?" she asked one night, sitting on the edge of the bed.

"It's a band," Virgil said.

"You look . . . odd. You know, walking around in a 'Virgins' T-shirt and your penis sticking straight out from under it. It's like 'Virgins' is some kind of caption."

"Hmm. Yes, it is sticking straight out. Maybe sniffing out an opportunity."

"Well, what the heck better does it have to do, on a cold winter night in Minnesota?" Coakley asked. "Come over here, Virgil."

And now a special excerpt
from the next Virgil Flowers novel
by John Sandford . . .

SHOCK WAVE

Available in hardcover from G. P. Putnam's Sons!

From the boardroom windows, high atop the Pye Pinnacle, you could see almost nothing for a very long way. A white farmhouse, surrounded by a scattering of metal sheds, huddled in a fir-tree windbreak a half mile out and thirty degrees to the right. Another farmhouse, with a red barn, sat three-quarters of a mile away and thirty degrees to the left. Straight north it was corn, beans, and alfalfa, and after that, more corn, beans, and alfalfa.

Somebody once claimed to have spotted a cow, but that had never been confirmed: The top floor was so high that the board members rarely even saw birds, though every September, a couple dozen turkey vultures, at the far northern limit of their range, would gather above Pye Plaza and circle through the thermals rising off the concrete and glass.

There were rumors that the vultures so pissed off Willard Pye that he would go up to the roof, hide in a blind disguised as an air-conditioner vent, and try to blast them out of the sky with a twelve-gauge shotgun.

Angela (Jelly) Brown, Pye's executive assistant, didn't believe that rumor, though she admitted to her husband it *sounded* like something Pye would do. She knew he hated the buzzards, and the saucer-sized buzzard droppings that spotted the emerald-green glass of the Pinnacle.

But that was in the autumn.

On a sunny Wednesday morning in the middle of May, Jelly Brown got to the boardroom early, pulled the drapes to let the light in, and opened four small vent windows for the fresh air. That done, she went around the board table, and at each chair laid out three yellow #2 pencils, all finely sharpened and equipped with unused rubber erasers; a yellow legal pad; and a water glass on a PyeMart coaster. She checked the circuit breakers at the end of the table, to make sure that the laptop plug-ins were live.

As she did that, Sally Humboldt from Food Services brought in a tray covered with cookies, bagels, and jelly doughnuts; two tanks of hot coffee, one each of regular and decaf; a pitcher of orange juice and one of cranberry juice.

The first board members began trickling in at 8:45. Instead of going to the boardroom, they stopped at the hospitality suite, where they could get something a little stronger than coffee and orange juice: V-8 Bloody Marys were a favorite, and Screwdrivers—both excellent sources of vodka. The meeting itself would start around 9:30.

Jelly Brown had checked the consumables before the board members arrived. She'd put an extra bottle of Reyka in the hospitality suite, because the heavy drinkers from Texas and California were scheduled to show up.

A few minutes after nine o'clock, she went back to the boardroom to close the windows and turn on the air-conditioning. Sally Humboldt had come back with a tray of miniature pumpkin pies, each with a little pig-tailed squirt of whipped cream and a birthday candle. They always had pie at a Pye board meeting, but these were special: Willard Pye would be seventy in three days, and the board members, who'd all grown either rich or richer because of Pye's entrepreneurial magic, would sing a hardy "Happy Birthday."

Jelly Brown had closed the last window when she noticed that somebody had switched chairs. Pye was a man of less than average height, dealing with men and even a couple of women on the tall side, so he liked his chair six inches higher than standard, even if his feet dangled a bit.

She said, *Oh, shit*, to herself. Almost a bad mistake. Pye would have been mightily pissed if he'd had to trade chairs with somebody—no graceful way to do that. She then made a much worse mistake: She pulled his chair out from the spot at the corner of the table and started dragging it around to the head of the table.

The bomb was in a cardboard box on the bottom shelf

of a credenza on the side wall opposite the windows. When it detonated, Jelly Brown had just pulled the chair out away from the table, and that put her right next to the credenza. She never felt the explosion: never felt the blizzard of steel and wooden splinters that tore her body to pieces.

Sally Humboldt was bent over a serving table, at the far end of the room. Between her and the bomb were several heavy chairs, the four-inch-thick tabletop, and the four-foot-wide leg at the end of the table. All those barriers protected her from the blast wave that killed Jelly Brown and blew out the windows.

The blast did flatten her, and broken glass rained on her stunned, upturned face. She didn't actually hear the bomb go off—had no sense of that—and remembered Pye screaming orders, but she really wasn't herself until she woke up in the hospital in Grand Rapids, and found her face and upper body wrapped in bandages.

The bandages covered her eyes, so she couldn't see anything, and she couldn't hear anything except the drone of words, and a persistent, loud, high-pitched ringing. For a moment she thought she might be dead and buried, except that she found she could move her hands, and when she did, she felt the bandages.

And she blurted, "God help me, where am I? Am I blind?"

There were some wordlike noises, but she couldn't make out the individual words, and then, after a confusing few seconds, somebody took a bandage pad off her left eye. She could see okay, with that eye, anyway, and found herself looking at a nurse, and then what she assumed was a doctor.

The doctor spoke to her, and she said, "I can't hear," and he nodded, and held up a finger, meaning, "One moment," and then he came back with a yellow legal pad and a wide-tipped marker and wrote in oversized block letters: YOU WERE INJURED IN AN EXPLOSION. DO YOU UNDERSTAND?

She said, "Yes, I do."

He held up a finger again, and wrote: YOU HAVE TEMPORARILY LOST YOUR HEARING BECAUSE OF THE BLAST. Another page: YOU HAVE MANY LITTLE CUTS FROM GLASS FRAGMENTS. Turned the page: YOUR OTHER EYELID IS BADLY CUT, BUT NOT THE EYE ITSELF. Another page: YOUR VISION SHOULD BE FINE. Another: YOU ALSO SUFFERED A MINOR CONCUSSION AND PERHAPS OTHER IMPACT INJURIES. Finally: YOUR VITAL SIGNS ARE EXCELLENT.

"What time is it?" she asked. The light in the room looked odd.

FIVE O'CLOCK. YOU'VE BEEN COMING AND GOING FOR ALMOST EIGHT HOURS. THAT'S THE CONCUSSION.

There was some more back and forth, and finally she asked, "Was it a gas leak?"

The doctor wrote: THE POLICE BELIEVE IT WAS A BOMB. THEY WANT TO TALK TO YOU AS SOON AS YOU ARE ABLE.

"What about Jelly? She was in the room with me."

The doctor, his expression grim, wrote: I'M SORRY. SHE WASN'T AS LUCKY AS YOU.

More or less the same thing happened all over again, three weeks later and 450 miles to the west, in Butternut Falls, Minnesota. Gilbert Kingsley, the construction superintendent, and Mike Sullivan, a civil engineer, arrived early Monday morning at the construction trailer at a new PyeMart site just inside the Butternut Falls city limits.

Kingsley, unfortunately for him, had the key, and walked up the metal steps to the trailer door, while Sullivan yawned into the back of his hand three steps below. Kingsley turned and said, "If we can get the grade . . ."

He was rudely interrupted by the bomb. Parts of the top half of Kingsley's body were blown right back over Sullivan's head, while the lower half, and what was left of the top, plastered itself to Sullivan and knocked him flat.

Sullivan sat up, then rolled onto his hands and knees, and then pushed up to his knees, and scraped blood and flesh from his eyes. He saw a man running toward him from the crew's parking area, and off to his left, a round thing that he realized had Kingsley's face on it, and he started retching, and turned and saw more people running . . .

He couldn't hear a thing, and never again could hear very well.

But like Sally Humboldt, he was alive to tell the tale.

The ATF—its full name, seldom used, was the Bureau of Alcohol, Tobacco, Firearms and Explosives—instantly got involved. An ATF supervisor in Washington called the Minnesota Bureau of Criminal Apprehension and asked for a local liaison in Butternut Falls.

The request got booted around, and at an afternoon meeting at BCA headquarters in St. Paul, Lucas Davenport, a senior agent, said, "Let's send that fuckin' Flowers up there. He hasn't done anything for us lately."

"He's off today," somebody said.

Davenport said, "So what?"

Virgil Flowers was sitting on a bale of hay on a jacked-up snowmobile trailer behind Bob's Bad Boy Barbeque & Bar in North Mankato, Minnesota, watching four Minnesota farm girls duke it out in the semifinals of the 5B's Third International Beach Volleyball Tournament.

The contestants were not the skinny, sun-blasted beach-blanket-bingo chicks who played in places like Venice Beach, or down below the bluffs at Laguna and La Jolla. Not at all. These women were white as paper in January, six-three and six-four, and ran close to two hundred pounds each, in their plus-sized bikinis. They'd spent the early parts of their lives carrying heifers around barnyards, and jumping up and down from haylofts; they could get up in the *air.*

Well, somewhat.

And when they spiked the ball, the ball didn't just amble across the net like a balloon; the ball *shrieked.* And the guys watching, with their beers, didn't call out sissy stuff like, *Good one!* or *No way!* They moaned: *Whoa, doggy!* and *Let that ball live. Have mercy!*

Of course, they were mostly dead drunk.

Sitting there in the mixed odors of sawdust and wet sand, sweaty female flesh and beer, Virgil thought the world felt perfect. If it needed anything at all, nose-wise, it'd be a whiff of two-stroke oil-and-gas mixture from a twenty-five-horse outboard. That'd be heaven.

Johnson Johnson, sitting on the next bale over, leaned toward Virgil, his forehead damp with beer sweat, and said, "I'm going for it. She wants me."

"She *does* want you," Virgil agreed. They both looked at one of the bigger women on the sand; she'd been sneaking glances at Johnson. "But you're gonna be helpless putty in her hands, man. Whatever she wants to do, you're gonna have to do, or she'll pull your arms off."

"I'll take the chance of that," Johnson said. "I can handle it." He was a dark-complected man, heavily muscled, like a guy who moved timber around—which he did. Johnson ran a custom sawmill in the hardwood hills of southeast Minnesota. He'd taken his T-shirt off so the girls could see his tattoos: A screaming eagle on one arm, its mouth open, carrying a ribbon that said not *E Pluribus Unum*, but *Bite Me*; and on the other arm, an outboard motor schematic, with the man's name, *Johnson Johnson*, proudly scrawled on its cowling.

"Personally, I'd say your chances of handling it are slim and none, and slim is outa town," Virgil said. "She's gonna eat you alive. But, you got no choice. The honor of the Johnsons is at stake. The *honor* of the Johnsons."

Virgil was thinner, taller, and fairer, with blond surfer-boy hair curling down over his ears and falling onto the back of his neck. He was wearing aviator sunglasses, a pink Freelance Whales T-shirt, faded jeans and sandals.

They were just coming up to game point when his cell phone rang, playing the opening bars of Nouvelle Vague's "Ever Fallen in Love." He took the phone out of his pocket, looked at it, and carefully slipped it back in his pocket. It stopped after four bars, then started again a minute later.

"Work?" Johnson asked.

"Looks like," Virgil said.

"But you're off."

"That's true," Virgil said. "Hang on here, while I go lock the thing in the truck."

Johnson tipped the beer bottle toward him: "Good thinkin'," he said. And, "Man, that's a lotta woman, right there."

The woman hit the volleyball with a smack that sounded like a short-track race-car collision, and Virgil flinched. "Be right back," he said.

As he walked down the side road to his truck, carefully stepping around the patches of sandburs, he was tempted to call Davenport. That would have been the right thing to do, he thought. But the day was hot, and the women, too, and the beer was cold and the world smelled so damn good on a great summer day . . . And he was off.

The fact was, the only reason that Davenport would call was that somebody had gotten his or her ass murdered somewhere. Virgil was already late getting there—

he was always the last to know—so another few hours wouldn't make any difference. The powers that be in St. Paul would want him to go anyway, because it'd look good.

He popped the door on the truck, dropped the phone on the front seat, locked the door and went back to the 5B.

Virgil was based in Mankato, Minnesota, two hours southwest of St. Paul, depending on road conditions and the thickness of the highway patrol. He routinely covered the southern part of the state. On nonroutine cases, he'd be picked up by Davenport's team, and moved to wherever Davenport thought he should go.

A couple of hours after Davenport first called, Virgil left Johnson at the 5B, romancing the volleyball player. Their attachment was such that Virgil would not be required to drive Johnson back to his truck, so he headed home, across the river into Mankato.

Once on the road, he picked up his phone and pushed the Call button, and two seconds later, was talking to Davenport.

"We got a bomb early this morning," Davenport said. "One killed, one injured, in Butternut Falls. We need you to get up there."

"What's the deal?"

Davenport told him about the explosion and the casualties, and said that the ATF would be on the scene now, or shortly.

"I'll be on my way in an hour," Virgil said. "Wasn't there another PyeMart bomb, killed somebody in Michigan a couple weeks back?"

"Yeah. Killed one, injured one. If it'd gone off twenty minutes later, it would have taken out the board of directors along with Pye himself," Davenport said. "This guy is serious, whoever he is."

"But if he started in Michigan, he could be a traveler. Unless we've got fingerprints or DNA . . ."

"We've got two things on that," Davenport said. "The first thing is, the explosives are tagged by the manufacturer. The ATF has already identified the tags in the Michigan bomb as Pelex, which is TNT mixed with some other stuff, and is mostly used in quarries. In April, somebody cracked a quarry shed up by Cold Spring—that's about an hour northeast of Butternut Falls—and two boxes of Pelex were taken. Other than the theft in Cold Spring, the ATF doesn't have any other reports of Pelex theft in the last couple of years. So, the bomber's probably local."

"Okay," Virgil said. "What's the other thing?"

"Butternut is having a civil war over the PyeMart. People are saying the mayor and city council were bought, and the DNR is being sued by a trout-fishing group that says some trout stream is going to be hurt by the runoff. Lot of angry stuff going on. Over-the-top stuff. Threats."

"There's runoff going into the Butternut? Man, that's not just a crime, that's a mortal sin," Virgil said.

"Whatever," Davenport said. "In any case, the DNR okayed their environmental impact statement. I guess they're already building the store."

"What else?"

"That's all I got," Davenport said. "Interesting case, though. I didn't want to take you away from your sheriff . . ."

"Ah, she's out in L.A., being a consultant," Virgil said. "Having dinner with producers. Guys with suits like yours."

"Sounds like the bloom has gone off the rose," Davenport said.

"Maybe," Virgil conceded.

"I can hear your heart breaking from here," Davenport said. "Have a good time in Butternut."

Virgil lived in a small white house in Mankato, two bedrooms, one-and-a-half baths, not far from the state university. He traveled a lot, and so was almost always ready to go. He told the old lady who lived next door that he'd be leaving again, asked her to keep an eye on the place, and gave her a six-pack of Leinies for her trouble. He packed a week's clothes into his travel bag, mostly T-shirts and jeans, put a cased shotgun on the floor of his 4Runner, along with a couple boxes of shells, and stuck his pistol in a custom gun safe under the passenger seat, along with two spare magazines and a box of 9-millimeter shells.

A quick Google check showed that Butternut Falls was two hours away. He printed out a map of the town, and while it was printing, turned the air-conditioning off, checked the doors to make sure they were locked, and turned on the alarm system. On the way out, he thought, with his last look, that the house looked lonely; too quiet, with dust motes floating in the sunlight over the kitchen sink. Nothing to disturb them. He needed . . . What? A wife? Kids? More insurance policies? Maybe a dog?

When the truck was loaded and the house secure, Virgil pulled out of the driveway into the street, reversed, and backed up in front of his boat, which had been parked on the other side of the driveway. His fishing gear was already aboard. But then, it was always aboard. After a quick look at the tires, he hitched up the trailer, folded up the trailer jack, and took off.

He got fifty feet, pulled over, jogged back to the garage, opened a locker, took out a pile of fly-fishing gear, including a vest, chest waders, rod case and tackle box, and carried them back to the truck.

Better to have a fly rod, and not need it, than to need a fly rod and not have it. He climbed back in the truck, and took off again.

Packing up and getting out of town took an hour, just as he told Davenport it would. The sun was still high in the sky, and he'd be in Butternut well before sundown, he thought. The longest day of the year was just around the corner, and those days, in Minnesota, were long.

And he thought a little about the sheriff out in L.A., Lee Coakley. She was still warm enough on the telephone, but she'd been infected by show business. She'd gone out as a consultant on a made-for-TV movie, based on one of her cases, and had been asked to consult on another. And then another. Women cops were hot in the movies and on TV, and there was work to be had. Her kids liked it out there, the whole surfer thing. Just yesterday, she'd had lunch in Malibu . . .

Once you'd seen Malibu, would you come back to Minnesota? To the Butternut Falls of the world? To Butternut cops?

"Ah, poop," Virgil said out loud, his heart cracked, if not yet broken.